From The Windswept Silence of Masada
to the Wild, Sensual Decadence
of Rome...
Ernest K. Gann's...

THE TRIUMPH

"*THE TRIUMPH* IS A MAGIC CARPET RIDE
INTO HISTORY...."

—*Tulsa Daily World*

"ERNEST K. GANN HAS A KNACK FOR
WRITING TENSE, EXCITING HISTORICAL
NOVELS...IN *THE TRIUMPH*, HE HAS
WRITTEN A WORTHY SUCCESSOR TO *THE
ANTAGONISTS*."

—*Milwaukee Sentinel*

"A GRAND CLIMAX, CARRIED OFF WITH
CONSIDERABLE SKILL...PULSATING STO-
RYTELLING..."

Kirkus Reviews

"THE REAL PLEASURE OF *THE
TRIUMPH* IS THE EFFORTLESS RICHNESS
OF ITS DETAILS....COMPELLING...A FINE
NOVEL."

—*Washington Times*

"IMAGINATIVE ROMANCE SPICED WITH
SEX; POLITICAL INTRIGUE MIXED WITH VI-
OLENCE AND ACCURATE DETAILS OF THE
PERIOD...DEVOTEES OF POPULAR HIS-
TORICAL FICTION WILL FIND AMPLE SATIS-
FACTION IN *THE TRIUMPH*."

—*Seattle Times*

Books by Ernest K. Gann

The Antagonists
Band of Brothers
Fate Is the Hunter
The High and the Mighty
The Company of Eagles
Soldier of Fortune
Song of the Sirens
The Triumph

Published by POCKET BOOKS

ERNEST K. GANN

THE TRIUMPH

PUBLISHED BY POCKET BOOKS NEW YORK

POCKET BOOKS, a division of Simon & Schuster, Inc.
1230 Avenue of the Americas, New York, N.Y. 10020

Copyright © 1986 by Ernest K. Gann
Cover artwork copyright © 1987 Roger Kastel

Library of Congress Catalog Card Number: 85-26211

ISBN: 0-671-64549-8

First Pocket Books printing October 1987

10 9 8 7 6 5 4 3 2 1

POCKET and colophon are registered trademarks
of Simon & Schuster, Inc.

Printed in the U.S.A.

FOR THE READER'S INTEREST

Vespasian became Emperor in A.D. 70.

Masada fell in A.D. 73 or 74 (date in dispute).

Vespasian died in A.D. June of 79.

Titus succeeded his father in A.D. 79 at age thirty-eight.

Mount Vesuvius exploded in August of A.D. 79
and continued erupting through A.D. 80.

Titus ruled only until A.D. 81. (The actual cause of his
death is disputed.)

General Flavius Silva Nonius Bassus was made *consul
ordinarius* in A.D. 81. It is possible he was subject
to *damnatio memoriae*, since his name was removed
from a monument in Judea presumably before his
death (date unknown).

Domitian succeeded Titus and ruled until A.D. 96.*

---

*No fewer than ten men of consular rank were put to death on various
petty charges by Domitian. General Flavius Silva was not on the list.*

S.P.Q.R.

Anno Domini 73
During the fourth year of Vespasian

Though I speak with the tongues of men and angels, and have not love, I am become as sounding brass or tinkling cymbal. And though I have the gift of preaching, and understand all mysteries, and have all knowledge; and though I have all faith so that I can move mountains; if I have not love I am nothing. . . .

—*From Paul's essay on love*

I

For in those days when skies and earth were new,
men came from oaks or dust and parentless, they
chose different lives from ones we frame.

—Juvenal

ONE

M OST SECRET
From Titus—Praetorian Prefect

To Flavius Silva—Commanding Tenth Legion Frentensis Judea

We must prepare even now for the day when we shall see a momentous and most difficult transition in state affairs. Because of the demands upon him as Emperor, the great Vespasian is aging with undue rapidity. My brother lusts for the throne and waits only upon our father's death. Another civil war may result unless the most urgent measures are taken to guarantee the internal Roman peace our Emperor worked so hard to achieve. We must begin soon.

We need a man popular with the Legions—one who can rally their force to our protection.

Therefore, when you are finished with the Jews at Masada, hold yourself ready for a return to Rome via Africa. The propitious time may be a year, even two years from now. While the date may be uncertain, the future need is not. It will be of the utmost importance that the Legions stationed in Africa and elsewhere must be alerted to my brother's illegitimate ambitions, and their loyalty assured.

Meanwhile, in the spirit of our longtime friendship, I congratulate you on your appointment to the governorship of Judea.

THE TRIUMPH

The great mountain rose out of the Palestinian desert like a storm-beaten ship run up on the shore and left to bake forever in the sun. The mountain rose beside the Sea of Asphaltum, or the Dead Sea as some called it, and beyond the sea to the eastward rose the bronze corrugated mountains of Moab. The nearest settlement some thirty miles to the north was the frontier town of Qumran. No one visited this barren region unless it was absolutely necessary.

The great mountain was called Masada. King Herod had once built a refuge from the sun and his enemies on the swollen knuckle of rock which was the northern end. Cleopatra knew of the mountain and coveted it. She tried to persuade Marc Antony to give it to her along with other Judean toys. Unforeseen and tragic events prevented his fulfilling that desire.

Long afterward, when the mountain appeared to rise even higher from yet another of its long sleeps, it so undulated and shimmered in the heat that it appeared to be a living thing. Buzzards and ravens caught the thermals rising from its flat summit and circled expectantly, for this was where the last Jews who still dared to defy the might of Rome had gathered with their families. The Romans, anxious victors over the whole of Judea, knew this pocket of resistance could not be tolerated in a land they had supposedly conquered.

Only the majestic conceit of Rome would have allowed sane men to suppose defenders atop the mountain might be approached and slain, for Masada rose almost straight upward around its entire perimeter, and the Jews were better supplied with water and food than their adversaries below. Moreover, Eleazar ben Yair, a man as remarkable as the mountain itself, was their leader. Yet there were no limitations on Roman imagination and enterprise.

The desert echoed with anguished cries as the Romans employed their whips on ten thousand captive Jews to build an enormous ramp against the western face of the mountain. The Romans engineered it in such a way that it would accommodate their battering rams and assault towers. The sun blazed down on these labors for months until the ramp was completed. More than twenty Romans died from wounds inflicted by bolts and arrows sent down from aloft, while hundreds of captive Jews on the ramp perished from beatings and exhaustion. In contrast, the Jews who defended the fortress lived comparatively well until it became woefully obvious that the might of Rome would not be denied.

Not even the most impregnable rock in the world could withstand the thundering energy that flowed from Rome to the outermost regions of the world. For those who served with the Roman Legions, total confidence was their shield and vanity their flower. They believed utterly in the authority of steel.

At last, one star-strewn night, an eerie quiet fell upon the desert and the contrast was such that the tranquillity became a noise in itself. Gone were the outraged squeaks and groans of the heavy Roman war machines. The babble of the thousands of Jews laboring beneath the Roman whips subsided until by midnight only an occasional sound of human voices broke the stillness. The great stone and gravel ramp that would carry the Romans to the walls of Masada was completed. The relative quiet signaled to the Jewish defenders that their ultimate hour was near, and the Romans accepted it as the smell of the victory they had so long anticipated.

No one in the Roman Tenth Legion foresaw the disturbing spectacle they would witness just after dawn. Lest the rising sun blind their eyes, the Romans had chosen first light as the time for their attack and, indeed, all went as planned. As they approached without opposition and broke over the western rampart of Masada, they were still unopposed; they could not account for such a phenomenon until they caught their breaths and looked about. Then, gradually, a few of the legionaries began to understand.

General Flavius Silva stood on the summit of Masada and studied the gore around him. He saw that the dust atop the mountain was soaked with the blood of the Jews who had first slain their families and then cut their own throats, and he knew their incredible act had cheated him of true victory. Silva had lived with death and soldiering since his days as a young tribune, but he found himself appalled by the specter scattered everywhere about him. Surely the Jews were a strange people, yet they were of a totally different mettle than the German barbarians along the Danube or the hirsute savages who inhabited the hills and fens of Britain. The Jews understood the power of the mind. If they knew nothing now,

Silva thought, they must have savored the thought of his inevitable disappointment during their last hours.

He made his way slowly through the prostrate bodies, which were already bloating in the morning sun. They were huddled in rows, frying in the dirt, and already covered with flies. Silva walked as if he were in a dream, pausing occasionally to prod at a body with his foot to test the certainty of death. He found the silence on the mountain eerie. It was broken only by the occasional clink of metal from his exploring legionaries and the steady humming of the flies.

As Silva regarded the bundles of men, women, and children, often in their last embrace, his dejection became nearly overwhelming. He squinted at the spectacle with his one good blue eye; the other had been nearly blinded by a Gaul who had mistaken Silva's rather spare frame for an easy kill. Since the Gaul's knife had severed his left upper orbicularis muscle, the eyelid drooped and a deep scar extended from his eye to his chin. He was otherwise a handsome man, although now gaunt from so long a time in the desert, and his manner denoted the middle aristocracy of his birth. Like so many Romans of culture, he had an easy and gracious style, the confident result of his key heritage in the greatest and most successful empire the world had ever known. His petty wants had been satisfied ever since birth, and as he matured he had become accustomed to the automatic provision of his grander needs whether it was necessary to voice them or not. Although he was not of the ruling Flavian family, he was very near to them and had proven his worth and loyalty in countless engagements abroad. As a soldier, absolute obedience to orders was without question. As a Roman citizen, he was at ease amid all levels of Roman society, and he was privy to the desires and frustrations of Roman nobility. He had been advised that he might go far in the government should he give up soldiering, but now in his thirty-eighth year he sensed that it was too late.

Flavius Silva had often thought that if his beloved wife, Livia, had lived longer he might have surrendered to city life, but her loss left nothing for a widower to enjoy in Rome except licentiousness, which soon palled, and the pursuit of money, which was not at all to his taste. A pox on Rome. It was the playground of homosexuals and every greedy merchant in the world. The mighty were totally engrossed in their own affairs, whether they involved the seizing of additional power or the fondling of voluptuous curvatures beneath a silken gown. This perpetual indulgence of those in his class with all manner of erotica was not to Silva's liking, for in his experience there was little true trust to be found among its devotees.

No, Silva thought as he glanced up at the brilliant blue sky. Miserable as it was here, the famous Tenth Legion was his home until that distant day when he could retire to the house he was causing to be built in Praeneste. The legionaries could be trusted; they knew precisely where they stood and what was required of them at all times. It was not only steel but their camaraderie that ruled the civilized world, and Flavius Silva, who had spent all but his earliest years in service with the Legions, was renowned as a good soldier.

Silva watched his troops moving about with an unnatural lassitude. They were disappointed in the lack of targets for their swords and the apparent nonexistence of loot. They had been cremating under the desert sun for months. For various reasons twenty-nine of their comrades had been lost since their arrival in the desert, and now they had survived to find only a stinking abbatoir. There was no satisfaction in thrusting a blade into a dead Jew.

Silva knew that his officers were going to spend the rest of the day answering questions.

He wandered northward along the flat top of Masada until he came to the structures which had long ago been King Herod's palace. Geminus, the centurion who commanded his personal guard, was herding an old woman and four terrified children up the steps of what had once been a lovely pavilion. A fifth child, considerably older than the others, was being dragged along by two legionaries. He seemed not in the least afraid of his captors and kicked and screamed invectives at them. A blow across his mouth silenced him momentarily.

"These are your prisoners?" Silva asked.

"There are no more. These were hiding in a small cistern the next level down."

Silva passed his hand across his forehead. He wondered if he was losing his mind. Was this all he had to show for the enormous efforts expended by the whole Tenth Legion after so many months?

Since his Hebrew was inadequate, Silva spoke to the children in Greek, but they appeared indifferent, if indeed they understood. He spoke to Geminus wearily. "I'm going to leave this place."

Silva thought that he would certainly vomit if he lingered, and he wondered why anyone who had seen so many battlefields should now be shocked. Perhaps it was the grisly visions of man and wife and child slaughtered and lying together that represented the destruction of something he had always held so dear—the love of a wife, which had been lost to him, and the siring of a son, which had never been his good fortune.

He told Geminus to take the children to the Nabatean camp followers and place them with the best families he could find. He would provide a hundred shekels from his personal purse for their care. "When you take them through what's up above," he said, "cover their eyes until they are well out of the place. If they see what is on top, they will never see anything else for the rest of their lives."

"Did you see their leader up there?" Geminus asked.

"Yes. That face is unmistakable."

"I think I'll piss on him."

"You do, and I'll have you whipped. Eleazar ben Yair was a very brave man."

Just as Silva turned away, the older boy, still twisting between two legionaries, bit one on the hand. The legionary grunted with pain and dealt the boy a hard blow to the side of his head.

Silva regarded the boy thoughtfully. "He has daring," he said. "He's inflicted more combat wounds this day than all the rest of his tribe."

Silva climbed back to the fortress level of Masada and made his way through the fractured barriers that had fallen to his rams. He sucked gratefully at the dry desert air when he came to the top of the great ramp and had left the stench of the dead behind him. As he started down the ramp, his breastplate, adorned with the head of Medusa flanked by two rearing horses, combined with his sweat to irritate the back of his neck and the skin beneath his arms. Even the rattle of his *phalerae*, the circular discs representing his awards for bravery and several campaigns, annoyed him almost beyond tolerance. He could not understand his abnormally ill temper except that what should have been a significant victory was not his. What should have marked the very end of all resistance in Judea had dissolved without a whimper, leaving the famous Tenth Legion in the role of a burial detail. Indeed, Vespasian and all other Romans could barely be blamed for their skepticism if he reported there had simply been a mass suicide. Some nine hundred, one of his staff had calculated.

Silva longed to reach his camp, which was established at the very base of Masada. There were six other camps placed strategically around the mountain, and the whole of the great rock was surrounded by a circumvallation connecting units of the Tenth Legion. His own tent would be relatively cool. Once there, he would throw off his armor, and Sheva, the Alexandrian Jewess who had been his mistress almost since the siege began, would soothe him with cool water. She might be persuaded to massage his bad leg, the result of a Tracian javelin that had found its target during his service as a young tribune. The wound had left him a permanent limp and a sporadic pain that seemed to intensify in the desert heat.

Now he tried to think of Sheva as the one tender element in all of Judea. She had become his sole refuge, for all else in this wretched land was scorching heat, frustration, hard living, and death. A soldier, he thought, should be required to leave the scene of combat immediately, whether victorious or defeated, for the aftermath of battle was utterly devoid of nobility. Too long . . . too long, Silva thought unhappily. He had been on the Palestinian battlefield since before the fall of Jerusalem.

Halfway down the ramp he paused, hoping to relieve the pain in his bad leg. He looked up at the dazzling sky and was suddenly compelled to whisper the name of his former adversary, "Eleazar ben Yair! You cunning Jew! You have tricked me!" After a moment he added, " . . . and for what good?"

Even before he actually passed through the curtained entrance to his tent, Silva sensed something was wrong. As he hesitated long enough to wipe sweat from his face, he sensed that Sheva's peculiar aura—a factor in which he had come to believe devoutly—was absent. It was an atmosphere, a strangely seductive Oriental odor combined with a mystifying presence that seemed to radiate from her wherever she might be. There had even been times when he could close his eyes and experiment with anticipating the moment of her entrance to his tent. And usually he had been right.

Silva removed his helmet and shook his head in an attempt to drive away a sense of foreboding. Was it because of what he had seen on the mountain? He wiped the sweat from his face and questioned whether it was his worn and torn body that sometimes made him feel fifty rather than thirty-eight, or was it his constant awareness that Sheva was only twenty? How many times he had reminded himself that he had been fighting before she was born. Now, as always, the notion made him uneasy.

He looked about for Epos, the tongueless Numidian who served as his personal servant. He had always greeted his return with a smile, but now? Had the rascal taken off for the mountain to see the sights? He entered the tent and blinked at the gloom because even his good eye was still half-blind from the sun. Then he saw Sheva sprawled on the couch, her arms spread across her breasts, his ceremonial dagger clutched in one hand. Blood had gushed from the cut arteries in her wrists and had cascaded along her bare arms to form a pool between her legs. Her eyes were wide open and staring directly at him.

He groaned and rushed to her. He took her limp body in his arms and sobbed her name endlessly. Her blood smeared his breastplate and his hands and face as he kissed her, and he murmured all the little endearments they had known together. He tried as best as he could to convince himself he was having a nightmare. "Why?" he kept whispering, "why?"

When he realized that he knew why Sheva had chosen to end her young life, his despair multiplied beyond endurance. She knew the fate of the Jews on Masada was hopeless, and she must have known how they had planned to defeat the very man who had been her lover. She could not allow herself to survive.

Suddenly, he lost sight of the body in his arms and saw nothing but blood. It was everywhere, in his eyes, in his heart, and smeared across his brain. Rivers of blood ran down his body.

He raised his bloody hands upward and cried out with all the strength in his lungs—and yet he could make no sound. He turned away from the couch, then rushed out of the tent and stood before the entrance, looking up at the forge-hot mountain in the sun. He shook his fists at it, raving incomprehensible oaths at its promontories, cursing the mountain and the Jews who had held it for so long. Then suddenly, exhausted from his tirade, he crumpled to his knees in the hot sand and retched violently. Moments later, Epos, his Numidian, appeared and dragged him into the tent.

The collapse of Silva's legendary poise shocked both officers and men of the Tenth Legion. They had grudgingly accepted Silva's falling in love with a Jewess—after all, he was a general and privileged. Titus, the emperor designate, had done the same with a woman known as Berenice. But grieving so over an Alexandrian whore? Their normally serene general was making a donkey of himself.

Searching for some comforting explanation, those of Silva's staff who were closest to him argued that he was irresistibly compelled to emulate his ancestor, Marc Antony, who had been so captivated by another Alexandrian, Cleopatra, that he had deserted his troops in Mesopotamia to go off on a lust-filled holiday in Egypt. If Cleopatra had a thousand ways to flatter a man, as Plato claimed, then Silva's Jewess had been of the same magic tongue. It was even rumored that Silva had almost abandoned the siege of Masada for her.

Word of General Silva's embarrassing behavior went no further than camp boundaries. The Tenth Legion was like a five-thousand-member family. Scandals, mistakes, fraternal squabbles, even military disasters, were their own affair, and outsiders were admonished to mind their own business.

Prior to every engagement, Silva had always addressed his troops as "my brothers in blood." Now, to their astonishment, he grieved over the corpse of the Jewess and lost himself in buckets of wine. He issued nearly hysterical and often confusing orders. A rabbi was to be fetched from the Nabatean camp followers to officiate at his woman's cremation.

Geminus found a rabbi called Kittius, a cringing fellow who was certain that he was about to be crucified unless he did exactly as he was told—hence he did not attempt to explain that cremation was not the custom of the Jews.

"I want the best!" Silva yelled at him. "I want it to be as if she were your queen!"

As the fire consumed her, the rabbi muttered a litany of phrases that were meaningless to Silva, but he was satisfied that things had been done right. The next day he ordered the five survivors of Masada to be brought to his tent. He stared at them in silence for a long time, rubbing at his good eye as if to improve the focus. His head was so heavy with wine that he had forgotten why he had sent for them. They stood squirming in silence until he remembered.

"You there," he said, pointing an unsteady finger at the oldest boy. "How many years do you have?"

Kittius translated and said, "He has twelve years."

The boy spoke out and the rabbi translated again. "He says he is the son of Eleazar ben Yair, the leader of the Jews, and you . . ."—the rabbi hesitated—"you are a great and kind man."

Geminus, who spoke some Hebrew, interrupted: "That's not what he said at all, Sire. He said you stink like camel shit."

Silva frowned and then suddenly burst into laughter. "By the gods, the lad has spirit! I want him sent to Alexandria, not as a captive, but as a student. Maybe someday he might even become an example for his wretched people."

Once they had departed, Silva bade his Numidian to open the special amphora he had brought with him all the way from Praeneste. It was filled with the exquisite Falernum wine made from grapes of his own vineyard that he had hauled across the sea and desert in anticipation of an appropriate occasion when his nose and tongue might delight in its rediscovery. His idea had been to celebrate the fall of Masada surrounded by his officers, with Sheva acting as hostess. He had planned the usual toasts, *"Beni Miri . . . Bene Voris,"* then a rousing series of toasts to the mountain of Masada itself, bottoms up one after the other in the old style, according to the number of letters in the name. But there would be no skeleton on display, as was the occasional custom of parties in Rome. There would be no *"Vivamus, Dum Licet Esse Bene,"* for there was not a soldier in the field who needed reminding that he had better drink and be merry while he was still alive.

Silva had also intended to announce that the Tenth Legion Frentensis would soon be leaving this hostile and desolate place for Caesarea, where the cool sea air would restore both spirit and body. Even more exciting for himself, he had planned to announce that as soon as his duties permitted, which would of course depend upon the whims of the Emperor Vespasian, he would take Sheva with him to Praeneste. There he would bury his sword forever, and devote the rest of his days to the simple life of a farmer. The fact that he knew nothing whatever of farming did not deter him; he would learn. He had persuaded himself that the local *plebs* would be more than pleased to share their knowledge with a man who had fought so long and honorably for Rome.

His dreams of Praeneste had made life in the desert more tolerable. He had visualized Sheva fussing with flowers in the peristyle of the house. He had seen himself in the atrium, surrounded by distinguished visitors who had journeyed the twenty-one miles from Rome to enjoy his hospitality. He saw them all admiring the extensive view down into the valley— and if it was a clear day, all the way to the horizon, where the Mare Tuscam met the land at Anzio. The fact that because of the idiocy of Mamilianus, the architect, and the cupidity of Proculus, the contractor, the house was still unfinished after four years did not disturb Silva's dreams. The mere contemplation of the house restored his spirits, and he admitted, laughing, that it had become an obsession with him.

Now his dreams were as dead as the Jews on top of Masada. He sat for hours in the battered ebony chair which had furnished his tent in Germany, Britain, and Gaul, as well as in this accursed desert, and he sipped slowly at the Falernum, feeling it take over his senses and dull his grief a little more with each cup.

Silva was drunk for the six days it took before the Tenth Legion departed Masada. His officers, faced with a commander incapable of speech, much less in any mood to issue logical orders, reached silent agreement. Dispatches describing the victory at Masada in glowing terms were sent off to Rome, the bodies of the Jews were heaped in piles and set afire, the fortress and Herod's old palace were swept clean of the disappointing loot, and a maniple of legionaries was left to bemoan their fate as custodians of the mountain. The anger and frustrations of the Tenth, created by even a few hours' delay in the scorching sun, were soothed with promises of bountiful fornication once Caesarea was reached, and hints of a possible donation by either Vespasian or his son, Titus, *imperator designatus*.

When it became obvious that Silva was becoming an acute problem and in danger of falling if he were required to mount his horse, a litter was built for him, and word passed throughout the ranks that he was ill. Relief teams of legionaries were assigned to carry him out of the desert and toward the sea, where, the Legion's Greek doctors were instructed to say, Silva would soon recover from his mysterious ailment. Care was taken that Silva should not want for wine during the long march. Epos, his Numidian, had suffered the loss of his tongue because he had known too much about the intimate life of his previous owner. Now, on the second day of the retreat, he managed to convey to Fabatus, the Legion's supply tribune, that the amphora of Falernum was empty. Eventually Fabatus found a jug of vile Jewish wine among the Nabatean camp followers. It was placed in Silva's litter, and such was his distress and state of consciousness that no complaints were heard. Nor was there any other indication that Silva might resume active command of the Tenth. Occasionally the litter would be set down while Silva staggered behind the nearest bush or rock for defecation (he suffered from dysentery like all the legionaries), and at night when his tent had been pitched he was sometimes heard singing softly to himself.

The war had been cruel to the once-handsome city of Caesarea. Most of the original residents had been slaughtered and their homes and businesses set afire until there was little remaining except charred ruins. Yet there seemed to be some substance to the prediction of the Legion's Greek doctors who had been obliged to lie so eloquently. None of them had any faith in the restorative powers of the sea on Silva's affliction, and the priests who were also assigned to the Legion were equally dubious. They had duly sacrificed a chicken on Silva's behalf and inspected the liver for firmness and blood. They found it leached and tough: nevertheless the augurs declared that it favored Silva's early recovery. In so doing, they managed to calm everyone's principal concern; for incredible as it might seem, in a Legion so renowned as the Tenth, the morale of the common soldiers was deeply affected by their general's disappearance. They did not want to be led by a sick man—even toward the sea.

Early on in the march, Geminus and Larcus Liberalis, the intelligence tribune, considered the situation dangerous. Never had they heard so much grim muttering among the troops, whose mood became fouler with every mile of their progress. When they came in sight of Engedi, simmering and bubbling in the sun, and turned away from it toward Caesarea and the sea, a near-mutiny broke out, involving twenty members of the second cohort. As a consequence of such disgraceful behavior, two legionaries were chosen at random from the unit, and since there was no wood for the customary crucifixion, their own centurion was ordered to slit their throats. He was afterward demoted to the ranks, and the bodies of the victims were left lying in the sun. The buzzards arrived before the column moved on.

The ignominious retreat of the once-proud Tenth from Masada remained a secret only because the officers were anxious not to be identified with such a shameful series of events, and the majority of the soldiers were so invigorated to escape the desert that they eventually forgot their ordeal in the wine and makeshift brothels of Caesarea. As for their general, they confounded their officers' fears by turning sympathetic toward him. They reasoned that his Jewish whore was responsible for his derangement. They did not believe the story that he was too ill to ride his horse. In spite of the officers' lies, the men knew that Silva was on a monumental drunk.

Silva was Silva, after all, the best general most of them had ever known, and it had been his name they had shouted in triumph. He had been a proven leader in countless skirmishes and battles throughout much of the Empire, and he was still young enough to understand the needs of his troops. They sensed that he would provide for them as he was able, and they even understood the strict discipline he maintained throughout the Legion. Fear was the lot of a soldier, and they knew, or thought they knew, that when they had finally served their twenty-odd years, Silva or his like would see that they received what pay they had deposited in the regimental bank. Perhaps they might also be lucky enough to be granted a bit of land to call their own.

As they marched into what was left of Caesarea, the legionaries' combative instincts warned them that the Jews surrounding them were only temporarily subdued. They would have agreed with the cynics in Rome who whispered that the elaborate celebrations and minting of coinage commemorating the conquest of Judea were premature. Who was to say what Jews would do? At Jotapata, when the battle was going badly for them, their General Joseph ben Matthias had displayed his singular wisdom by surrendering himself to the Legion—exactly the opposite behavior to those on Masada. The general was now living comfortably in Rome and had taken the name Flavius Josephus in gratitude for his deliverance.

Now, with any luck, the Tenth could look forward to a long spell of peaceful garrison duty. Hail Silva! The man was mad, but in the cool air of the seashore, he would recover, as would everyone else in the Legion.

TWO

NEARLY TWO YEARS had passed since General Flavius Silva, legate of Judea, twice awarded the golden crown medal as well as the equally rare *corona muralis*, had been carried like a sack of meal into the house that had been commandeered for him. The house belonged to an exporting merchant of some wealth who had chosen a site overlooking the sea, yet far enough from the harbor of Caesarea to escape its busy traffic, which had multiplied significantly since peace had at last seemed genuine.

When he finally sobered, Silva found he was pleased with the house. The architecture was sufficiently Oriental to suit the climate, and there was almost always a leisurely sea breeze whispering along the promontory upon which the house stood. Since it faced west, Silva took pleasure in standing on the terrace and watching the sun set into the Mare Internum. As the months passed he became more and more addicted to the often spectacular display, and all of his appointments were scheduled so they would not interfere with his precious hour of contemplation. He was not at all sure why he so enjoyed this little time except that it represented a total escape from the noisy rebuilding of Caesarea and the countless troubles of the Jews throughout the land. It was his private time, and he guarded it ever more zealously as the balance of his day became more and more crowded with the overall recovery of Judea.

Silva was very particular concerning who, if anyone, would

17

be allowed to join him in viewing the last of the day. Geminus bored him with his endless recital of regimental problems. Silva thought the man was as straightforward and faithful as a well-conformed horse but hopelessly insensitive and utterly devoid of imagination. He had once made the mistake of commenting on a sunset, "As far as I'm concerned, Sire, it's just marking the end of another day, but not the end of my troubles. The sun is not going to tell us what to do with young Arvianus, who has taken to confiscating dates from the Jews in the name of Vespasian and shipping them back to Rome for the glory of his own purse—"

Silva cut him short. "Don't you see the clouds laced around the sun, Geminus? Don't you see enough beauty there to satisfy an artist for months? Are you blind, man? Look at that emerald in the upper sky and that rose lower down. Look how it's all reflected in the sea. For the love of the gods, Geminus, how can you watch such a grand show and clutter your mind with the faults of a mere tribune like Arvianus? I know his family. He comes of good stock and when he's had a bit more seasoning he will learn not to kill the golden goose."

"I was only thinking of my duty, Sire."

"Experiment. Try to let your military mind wander around a bit and see the rest of the world. It may surprise you."

"No doubt, Sire," Geminus said, uncomprehending. "No doubt."

Other guests invited to the view from the terrace were rare. Silva could not bring himself to explore even the possibility of a further liaison with one or more of the available Jewish women, even if one of sufficient class and sophistication could be found.

Now that peace had been achieved, Silva sometimes found himself restless almost beyond measure. Perhaps the Greek doctors had been correct in their prediction that once by the sea their general would return to his normal vigor and disdain abuse of the grape. Now, even his limp seemed less obvious and his good eye sparkled with the wit and intelligence that had always blessed him. Yet there were times when it seemed he could reach out and touch the loneliness that hung about him like a pall, almost as if it were a dangling part of his physique. Even strangers noticed and remarked on his air of detachment. However interested and patient he might be in the supplication of a person who complained that Silva's legionaries were practicing extortion, or another who wanted a raise in pay for the Jews contracted to repair the wharves, he always seemed to be waiting for someone. Whether that individual was Roman, Jew, Egyptian, or Greek was anyone's guess, but the atmosphere of anticipation was always present. During one of his monthly dinners for his officers, he had shocked them by laughing as he said, "I'm not always sure what I'm doing here, but as long as Rome doesn't know either, I suppose the job will last indefinitely."

There was no question that Silva was proving a superb legate while governing one of the most cantankerous regions in the Empire. He was managing to keep the Jews as reasonably quiet and content as could be expected. They regarded him as a man to be trusted as far as any Roman could be, and the country about was beginning to prosper. Some of the ravages of the long war were being erased, and new provisions were made for the housing and affairs of the Jews and other inhabitants of Judea. As the countryside prospered, so did the shipping; Rome was now a steady customer for the fruits of Palestine, and there was already a promising trade with ports in Africa, Macedonia, and Cilicia. Apparently, the urge to rebellion had subsided in the Jews, or at least it was not manifest in the daily affairs of the province. There were even times, Silva thought, when he wondered if he was worth the thousand sesterces a week salary for his services as *legati Caesaris* in addition to his honorarium as general of the Tenth. While it was his privilege to impose local taxes toward his own profit, he had refrained from doing so. He had enough for his immediate needs, and were it not for the continual bleeding of his purse by the house in Praeneste, he would be as fat and fancy financially as any high Roman official. Although Rome had been somewhat vexed by the amount of time Silva had taken to conquer Masada, Vespasian had directed that his fasces should be decorated with a wreath of laurel, and he had been designated a patrician.

Silva knew such honors should have been more than enough for any thirty-eight-year-old soldier; yet he could not seem to conquer his sense of discontent. He recognized that a part of his trouble was his relative isolation from the atmosphere and events of Rome. A man who was too long away from the capital of the world was soon as forgotten as an exile. He became a name only, a ghost more difficult to remember as time went by. Opportunities for advancement rarely reached out to the colonies, and in some locations the official assigned either went so native he could no longer be considered a true Roman—or he went crazy. Now, after so many years of violent service, Silva found himself bewildered with tranquillity. Here there was none of the excitement a Roman commander might find in Gaul, Britain, or Germany. There were no audacious chieftains like Vindex here, or even a Civilis; there were no outrageously vicious women like Boudicca, who chopped up a legion and then went on to Londinium and Verulamium, where she slew more than fifty thousand Romans and their allies. There was no civilizing to do here as there always was among the barbarians of Upper and Lower Germany, and there was nothing to compare with the insolent hostility of the Marcomanni or Quadi tribes. The Jews were already civilized, and often their protestations had an alarming ring of the truth.

The crux of the matter, Silva gradually realized, was not only his boredom with Geminus and the company of his other officers, but with his own life as well. At least at Masada he had been party to endless conversations with Rubrius Gallus, his engineering officer. Ah, those had been stimulating sessions, admittedly somewhat curtailed when Sheva was brought to share his tent. Then that accursed Jewish arrow had flown from the top of Masada and struck Gallus directly in his mouth. It had pierced his neck, and there went the end of a priceless friendship. It was Gallus who had been responsible for building the great ramp. It was Gallus who could turn out the calculations necessary for the construction of siege machinery or whatever the Legion required. And it was Gallus alone who could express himself most eloquently on art and literature. He had been older, a friend of the elder Pliny; he was well read of Lucan, Epicurus, Epictetus, and he knew the satires of Menippus the Syrian. He was both a Stoic and a Cynic, a sensualist and a hard soldier. The arrow that had entered between his teeth had silenced forever the impeccable Latin of a Roman who spoke with the clarity of Seneca.

All gone now and what was left? A young-old soldier wandering alone around a veritable palace, whistling sometimes to himself as an antidote to drunkenness—someone had said that it was impossible to whistle with the same lips and wind that had passed too much wine—and staring alone at the stars, the moon, or whatever display was offered by the nocturnal heavens.

Who knew the slavery of loneliness better than Flavius Silva? He was sick of it. There were times when it became like an invisible whip, lashing out and stinging his brain ceaselessly. There had been times when the demons who were the sole company of the lonely were indefatigable in their insistence that their subject never be allowed the leisure of random thinking. The best pronouncements of all philosophers were never the product of company, merry or otherwise, but were born in a gloomy nest of solitude where ordinary men rarely ventured.

While soaking in the battered bronze tub he had carried with him on all his campaigns, Silva brooded over the lack of what he considered a proper bath in the house. Despite the many Semitic luxuries the merchant-owner had provided, he had not anticipated that his house would one day shelter a Roman. So the old tub with its feet of ornamental rams' heads would have to do, Silva thought, at least until he was relieved of command or skilled artisans could be imported from Rome to accomplish extensive remodeling. The expense involved would be considerable, and certainly a man who was already pouring his fortune into an unseen house far away had no business correcting the mistakes of a fatheaded landlord.

Silva found his immediate repose was not altogether unpleasant here in the old tub because he had had it installed amid the foliage of the peristyle. From this vantage it was possible to survey the open sky, which this afternoon was a stunning azure, and he could contemplate a bubbling fountain nicely fringed with exotic flowers. Employing a clever arrangement of fluid hydraulics, the fountain cascaded water continuously, and the gurgling became extraordinarily soothing in this land where liquid was so precious. The fountain was proof again, Silva thought, that the Jews were a most resourceful people, since it used the same water supply over and over again. Such simplicity of approach was something Rome would never understand.

When necessary, Silva had been known to conduct hearings from the comfort of his tub, and official visitors were astonished to discover the naked body of the grand general taking his ease in so Roman a fashion. He did not care what his visitors thought. If his peace were to be destroyed, then they could take him as they found him; if the glory of Rome could not survive occasional informality, then it stood upon legs even more wobbly than his own.

Now, when he was told that a courier had arrived from Rome with an urgent message, Silva ordered the man to be brought before him.

At last, he thought, there would be news from Titus concerning his proposed African expedition. Rumors of Vespasian's declining health had even reached Judea, and it was no longer a secret anywhere in the Empire that Titus' brother, Domitian, intended to succeed their father.

Silva remembered the man well. When they had all tutored together as children, Domitian was always the sullen one. While the other children were full of laughter, mischief, and bounce, Domitian would be brooding in some corner. Now, Silva recalled that he was fat and toadlike, and given to masturbating regardless of where he might be or who surrounded him.

Very well! The Third Augusta and Ninth Hispana Legions were in Africa, and he knew their commanders well. The Third Cyrenaica and the Twenty-second Deiotariana were both in Egypt, and he thought it reasonable to expect a welcome if he spoke in the name of the much-admired Titus. He would prepare for departure this very night and be on his way by dawn of the second day. And then there would be Rome!

He was still engaged in planning details when the courier approached the end of the bathtub. He proved to be a huge, slack-jawed man with deep-set, watery eyes and a dirty stubble of beard. Silva thought to reprimand him for his appearance and then realized the man was very weary.

The courier became momentarily tongue-tied at the sight of the procurator of Judea in so casual a pose. He started to relate his credentials and then had trouble swallowing.

Silva thought it ironic that he knew what the courier had to say, yet the man himself seemed confused. "Come, come, man. Say your say and be gone. If I must mix business with hot water, then be brief."

22

The courier frowned unhappily at Epos, who was massaging Silva's neck with fragrant oil.

"Sire," the courier said, "you . . ." He glanced at Epos again and managed to say, "Sire, . . . my message must be given to you in total secrecy. I must request that your servant leave us alone."

"Yes, yes. I know. I've had a previous communication on the matter. But no fear about Epos here. He has been at my side in peace and war for ten years . . . and besides, he has no tongue. Show him, Epos."

Epos opened his mouth in a mischievous grin and exposed the scarlet stump of his tongue. He wagged the stump at the courier.

"Speak up, man," Silva said. "Both the water and my patience are chilling."

"You must make immediate preparations, Sire. Within two days . . . perhaps three at the most, your guests will arrive . . . and of course they must stay here. I have come far and with all speed . . ."

"You're talking in riddles. I've not invited any guests."

"These hardly need inviting, if I may say so, General. Domitillia and her party will be eight . . . not including servants. They will naturally expect all the amenities. There will be merely thirty of the Praetorian Guard, and they may be billeted as you please."

Silva remained silent for a long time. He regarded the sky, pursed his lips, and shook his head in wonder. Domitillia! The Emperor's daughter? He remembered her as a little girl, knock-kneed, rambunctious, and given to outrageous profanity she had acquired from some mysterious source.

He told Epos to go easier with the rubbing, since he had just received very distressing news. He raised the brow of his good eye, and his voice took on a sour note when he addressed the courier.

"By Domitillia I assume you mean the Emperor's daughter? And if that be true, then how am I to provide with such short notice? What's the matter with the people in Rome? Do they think I can snap my fingers and create a paradise? I must warn you that there are not *any* amenities in Judea, for Domitillia or anyone else . . . as witness this ancient tub. Rome doesn't see fit to provide its frontiers with comforts of any sort, possibly in fear that we who man such posts will become as soft as they are. Can you tell me what in the name of all the gods Vespasian is thinking . . . sending his daughter way out here? Don't Roman children go to school any longer?"

"Domitillia may hardly be thought of as a child, Sire."

Silva stared at the surface of the tub water a moment and reflected on the Flavian family. Vespasian was no ordinary emperor in the manner of such scoundrels as Nero, Caligula, and Tiberius. He had never been one to stand on imperial protocol, since he was still a simple soldier at heart, come to his exalted station because he had brought an end to the civil strife created by two other generals, Galba and Vitellius. Their lust for power had nearly destroyed the empirical prize they sought. And the Legions had wanted a man they could trust on the throne.

Vespasian's incredibly rapid ascent from a mere military career had not changed him in the slightest. He affected no airs, he was determined to balance the budget, and he had inaugurated countless frugal measures, even taxing the public toilets, all in his efforts to keep his government from the customary extravagances. He had brought Rome up from its knees until now it had regained its noble posture, and he was showing more respect for the Senate than had been prevalent since the days of the Republic.

"I assume," Silva said coldly, "that the party is coming by sea and bringing their own commissary and supplies? We haven't much here, we do not live the good life, but we survive. They'll have to understand that Judea is barely recovered from the wars. There's no Nile here, and this is no Egypt or Numidia. We're occupying a harsh land and its people have a long history of discomforts. Domitillia and her party must realize that there is even some danger, since we haven't been able to eliminate every potential assassin. The Jews are given to murder . . . and they're very capable at it. One stroke of a knife in a crowd or a bolt fired from a hidden window and you have another dead Roman. I don't like accepting the responsibility for their safety and will so advise the Emperor by tomorrow's post."

"Perhaps I may ease your concern," the courier said, smiling. "The party is bringing the Emperor's donative to the Tenth Legion for their meritorious service in Judea. The total amount will be one-half million denarii, a sum I should think would make your troops very happy."

Silva caught his breath, and for the first time since the courier's appearance, he sat absolutely still in the tub. Yes, yes, of course, he thought. Now the pattern was emerging, for Vespasian had made no secret that he intended to found a dynasty. Now the substance of Titus' most secret message sent months ago made sense. Soon after taking the throne, Vespasian had declared his elder son, Titus, as imperator designatus, his successor, and he had indicated that Domitian, his younger son, would be the next in line. It was quite logical then that he should cover all risks by appointing his daughter to some sort of official duty—in this case the delivery of an imperial bounty—that would not only display her in a favorable light, but make the Tenth his willing slave for the rest of his time. It was otherwise inconceivable that a man so thrifty as Vespasian would be so generous.

"Very well," Silva said in almost a whisper. "I'll see that in spite of our limited resources some kind of a welcome is prepared. We will do everything possible to make Domitillia and her party comfortable. Who are they to be?"

Now, relieved at Silva's resigned manner, the courier became almost haughty. "There will be Egnatius Emilius Camillus, the captain of her Praetorians; Rufus Valerius Pedanius, the senator; Gallus Appius Septicius, doing double duty as keeper of the treasury and master of protocol; and Julius Fabius Scribonia, who—"

"Stop! Stop!" Silva was mindful of the wearisome confusion surrounding Roman names. Since ancient times Romans had been divided into various clans known as *gentes*, and those of the same family were known as *gentiles*. To distinguish individuals of the same blood, most Romans had three or even four names which, in the passing of centuries, multiplied the jumble. Silva smiled bitterly at the mouthful which identified himself, Flavius Silva Nonius Bassus. Now, who but himself would trouble to recall that? He said, "I can hardly remember my own name sometimes, much less that mulch of syllables. But I recognize one . . . Scribonia. If I have the right Scribonia, what is he doing in such company?"

"It is not my place to comment, Sire."

"Well, by the gods, you'd better tell me, if you want a place to sleep yourself! I don't like spies in my camp, particularly those from my own country." Julius Scribonia, Silva knew, was one of the *frumentarii*, the quasi-police intelligence unit that kept the Emperor informed on the moods and doings of Rome. They were dangerous and despicable people, in Silva's opinion, and were as likely to inform on the innocent as the guilty if it advantaged them. Vespasian himself had sometimes castigated the breed, yet he was obliged to keep them on active status as a protection for his life. As with all Roman Emperors, both good and bad, the specter of assassination was an inherent part of the office.

After the courier had left him, Silva sat long in his tub, his thoughts alternating between what he could do to provide for and entertain such a number of eminent guests, and memories of his early youth playing with Titus, Domitillia, and sometimes—when he was not in a pout—with Domitian. The brothers were not always happy to have their much-younger sister around. Still, Domitillia had been a persistent little brat and would sometimes appear in the middle of their games as if she had sprouted from the earth.

He reviewed the accommodations of his house. At least his solitude would be temporarily relieved. Domitillia would take his bedroom, of course, because it was by far the most spacious and looked almost directly down at the sea. How little-girl monsters did progress if they happened to have the right father! The rest, including that wily fellow, Scribonia, would just have to make do in the series of cubicles around the perimeter of the atrium. They would all dine together, a function from which he planned to absent himself as often as possible. He would arrange that duty would call in one form or another to take him away from the prolonged ceremony so characteristic of a Roman civilian meal. Those who had no need to labor—and they were a great many—were given to lying around on their couches endlessly, chewing on the latest gossip and the most inane menus their host and his chef could conceive. No soldier could afford to lounge for hours and pick at such delicacies as Lucrine oysters or peacocks. The Roman soldier ate to keep up his strength, which he needed very badly when marching twenty miles in five hours, carrying sixty pounds of equipment. He was not only a fighting man, but a beast of burden, and he considered himself lucky if he could maintain a constant ration of grains and water mixed with vinegar to wash it down.

Just after the sun had passed the zenith on the second day following the arrival of the courier, Silva spied a huge lateen sail on the horizon. He pointed it out to Geminus, who said that he could also see it, which was not entirely factual since his eyesight was faulty except at very close range. It was his custom to agree with others who saw things in the distance, be it an enemy horde or a single horseman, and thus avoid any chance that he might be considered unfit for duty. Geminus was not aware that the whole of the Tenth Legion knew of his myopia and excused it, because they knew someone would always be nearby to identify friend from foe.

Silva chuckled softly to himself and could not resist a moment's teasing. "Do you make out the color of the sail?" he asked.

Geminus hesitated then answered, "Why, red, I believe . . . or is it striped?"

A safe response, Silva thought. Most of the sails in the Mediterranean were red because they were dipped in oxblood to discourage rot, and those not red were striped.

"It's bound to be the ship with our guests," Silva said. "Is everything in readiness?"

"The first cohort is already posted along the wharf. The second is standing by to line the street all the way up to this house. Fabatus has found two cows somewhere—I didn't inquire too closely—and they'll be slaughtered this afternoon."

"Spare one for later eating. I'm not going to sacrifice the last available cows in Palestine for a scruffy bunch of Roman politicians."

"We have about twenty sheep, or I should say goats, again thanks to Fabatus. There is ample grain for bread and a handful of chickens some Jew failed to hide from our dear supply officer. He also managed some grapes, cherries, and some measly-looking oranges." Geminus growled on, reciting his statistics in a deliberate monotone as if, Silva thought, he were shifting the beads on an abacus. What a pity that the one man in Judea whose friendship he most valued should be such a dull fellow.

"Fabatus says that if you will authorize considerable expense, he'll be able to find enough herbs and spices to make things look better."

"I will not."

There was such a tone of finality in Silva's voice that Geminus did not respond at once. Finally, he said, "Why are you so antagonistic toward these people, Flavius? You don't really know them."

"I know Scribonia. I can smell him from here."

"What harm can he do? They'll be gone in a few days."

"The *frumentarii* are never gone. They're worse than Judean nits, gnawing away until they get to the bare bone. Then they say to the Emperor, 'Look what we found! This son of a bitch is disloyal!' They go right down to the marrow while they prove your grandmother was a Persian and therefore you must be traitorous. So they recommend that the Emperor remove your head before you bite. They keep fertilizing the fears of the Emperor with that kind of manure and add a little lime as they go along. With all our other problems here, we don't need that kind of trouble."

"You do know Domitillia?"

"Only as a little hoyden. As I recall, she was more the lion's cub than the kitten. She used to hit Domitian regularly with anything handy and saw to it that he got the blame for any mischief they might have been up to. She was an absolutely awful little brat."

"How did she get along with Titus?"

Silva smiled because he was enjoying his memories of more carefree days. "She adored Titus. Doesn't everyone to this day? She trailed around after him like a street urchin waiting for the drop of a coin. Once when he was taking a nap, she bit him in the leg because she thought that would show greater affection than a kiss."

"How did Titus react to that?"

"After he quit screaming and she stopped bawling, he took her in his arms and forgave her. When I last saw them they were well along the road to incest . . . but if you tell anyone I said that, you may expect to see my head dripping from a spear before a month has passed."

What little wind there had been expired during the afternoon, and it was nearly evening before the three banks of long oars brought the trireme to harbor. Silva stood waiting patiently on the wharf, oblivious of the crowds milling around behind the line of legionaries. Some inexplicable, magic word had been passed around Caesarea and, just as he had feared, everyone in the area was aware that a very important personage was about to arrive. The whole town, it seemed, had gathered in the vicinity of the wharf. There was no reliable prediction of their mood; while it was doubtful they would display any open hostility toward Domitillia, a few rascals might start throwing things and trigger a mass reaction. It was all very well for Rome to announce that Judea was conquered, since all organized resistance had been stopped, but resentment of their betters was still a powerful emotion among the Jews. It seemed that no amount of punishment would discourage those who could not appreciate the benefits of Roman rule.

Only the week before, Silva recalled, he had been obliged to crucify four young Jews who had promised a maniple of his legionaries opportunities for exotic fornication if they would leave their camp and follow them to a nearby wadi. Two foolish legionaries swallowed the bait and paid with their lives. They were reported missing at next morning's roll call, and their bodies were soon discovered; their throats had been slit after their penises had been removed.

On Silva's personal orders retaliation had been swift and efficient. By late morning four young Caesareans were hanging upside down from crosses erected in front of the synagogue. Whether those Jews selected were actually guilty of the crime was immaterial. They resembled those who had murdered the legionaries, and that was enough.

Now Silva hoped there would be no additional incidents, because maintaining discipline over a breed of people who simply had no conception of discipline might be difficult under the inquiring eyes of Scribonia and the rest of Domitillia's fancy party. Never having fought the Jews, they would not understand how obstinate they could be . . . or how very dangerous.

Silva was wearing his *toga picta* for the occasion, and as if to demonstrate how peace had indeed come to Judea, he had decided against wearing any armor. Now, surprised at the number of people who obviously considered it their business to greet the great trireme, he wondered if he had made a foolish decision. He was utterly vulnerable to a knife, bolt, or arrow, and somewhere in that rabble there was probably one Jew who had been waiting for such carelessness. Then it would be farewell to Flavius Silva Nonius Bassus, procurator of Judea, soldier who was so stupid as to let his guard down for a few hours.

Geminus had not been so foolish. There he stood, massive and unblinking as a monument in full armor, the last of the sun glistening on his helmet. One great hairy hand was resting on the jeweled handle of his broadsword, a treasured souvenir he had taken from the body of a German chieftain. The sword was Geminus' only treasure; by his own word he cared for nothing else on earth except that special blade and the welfare of his Legion. A priest of Mars, Silva thought, a true soldier without all the complications attending upon an inquisitive mind.

As the sailors of the trireme jumped to the wharf and secured their lines, Silva knew a moment of almost overwhelming homesickness. This very ship had come from Ostia, the port of Rome. Her captain and sailing crew were Romans like himself; they must know the Campus Martius, Mons Aventinus, the Capitolium, and perhaps even the theater of Marcellus. They came from the heart of the world, the lush, entrancing, maddening fountain from which flowed enormous energy to an empire so vast that few could comprehend its limits.

For a moment the trireme became the symbol of everything lost to his life. Livia, his wife . . . gone forever. Sheva . . . destroyed by her own hand. And now what was left to him? The spoils of Judea, a good portion of which should have been his, had proven very disappointing. His desire for recognition had been soothed by his appointment as legate, but in this colony it was a dubious honor. It was difficult to accomplish something with almost nothing, and the chances of his returning home in the near future now rested on a contest between two brothers, over which he had no control. Perhaps I shall die here in this wretched land, he thought; perhaps I will never see the finished house in Praeneste, hear the rumble of the Roman streets, taste another oyster, or know the satisfactions to be found in an unlimited supply of Falernum. As I stand here, he thought, I exist in genteel exile, a man put away until the next time Rome needs someone to defend what it has . . . or acquire more than it has.

Once the trireme was alongside the wharf, Silva nodded his head slightly and the trumpeters of the Legion who were assembled behind him lifted their shoulder-borne instruments to their lips and blared the ceremonial salute. When they had finished, Silva walked to the trireme, adjusting his pace to the dignity of the moment.

The crowd hushed in anticipation and then he saw her. She was nearly hidden by six tall Praetorians who surrounded her, all clad in full armor. She was standing just outside the door to the deckhouse, which covered the entire poop of the vessel, and she was wearing a gown of royal purple, which was her family right. For a moment Silva wondered if he had mistaken the diminutive figure he saw for the Domitillia he had known so long ago. Perhaps she had brought some court females to keep her company, in which event new problems abounded. Then she turned and he recognized the way she tilted her head inquiringly; the gesture was unmistakable, so individual to Domitillia that he remembered it after so many years. There had always been a rebellious note to that gesture, an expression of total confidence she had employed long before her father became Emperor.

Their eyes met and Silva halted. He saw her lips twist in a mischievous smile and knew instantly that she recognized him. She raised one hand and fluttered it at him, a birdlike, somehow patronizing movement that he might have resented had he not seen the amusement in her dark eyes. He knew she was saying to him, "You may be the supreme commander here, but I am Domitillia and will do exactly as I please."

She continued to hold his total attention as she moved to the ship's gangway with the Praetorians hovering protectively about her.

Instead of being annoyed or disappointed as he had feared, Silva found that he was both proud and stunned by Domitillia's beauty. Her graceful progress toward him was as fine a representation of Roman confidence as he had ever seen— power without the trappings of pomposity. He saw a whole culture exhibited in her, a refined and visible elite all contained in one very small female. He thought Vespasian had indeed shown perception in sending his representative via a mere trireme rather than in some mighty warship. This modest display said Rome had nothing to fear, domination was where it should be, and those few who had arrived were visiting in the cause of the colonial welfare. Certainly it was inconceivable that such a doll-like individual could offer the slightest threat. The Jews would see and discuss this simple arrival endlessly, just as they discussed everything that happened. Soon word would spread throughout Judea that the bloody years were already history, that Rome was not a monster to be taunted, but a benign force dedicated to their own good. For an instant Silva allowed himself to envision what might have been—half a dozen naval vessels escorting a grand quinquereme with drums pounding to set the beat of a thousand oarsmen; a cohort or more of the Praetorian Guard, horns proclaiming the sequence of each event; and a crowd of bureaucrats, senatorial officers, and court hangers-on, all bound to make their presence known and in their ignorance of the local situation just as certain to make trouble. This, he decided, was as it should be.

He extended his right hand to Domitillia and she took it in her own. He felt the softness of her flesh and thought it had been an eternity since he touched anything so soothing.

"Welcome," he said, "welcome to a peaceful Judea. On behalf of the Tenth Legion Frentensis I assure you of our loyalty to the Flavian house."

Silva found his speech halting, his words stumbling over each other and very nearly out of control. The formal little address he had rehearsed had somehow evaporated into the setting sun. His thoughts were a jumble of what he really wanted to say: "By the gods, you are a delicious-looking little imp. What has become of the scrawny, pugnacious Domitillia I knew so long ago? Your eyes . . . that mouth, the mellow amber of your skin . . . and most of all, the way you are standing there as if all the world is yours, which, of course, in a way it is . . ."

Domitillia squeezed his hand and said, "Flavius Silva, companion of my childhood. You're as handsome as ever."

"I'm in ruins," Silva said and thought that it was not his various wounds that had inspired such a silly statement, but the shattering effect Domitillia was having on him. He glanced at the dignitaries who were standing to form a half circle around them and sensed that they were feeling ignored. He saw Julius Scribonia closing in as rapidly as possible. His foxlike eyes were disapproving.

"Don't be so abused, Flavius," Domitillia was saying, "you look very fit. I bring you greetings from the Emperor and from my brother, Titus. They both treasure your friendship and depend on the loyalty of you and your Legion."

"We are privileged," Silva answered with a slight bow of his head. He realized that he longed to be alone with Domitillia, and he wondered why, in the name of the gods, they had to go through all this blather.

"I hope you had an easy voyage," he added, but Domitillia had already turned to introduce her company. She began as she should with Rufus Pedanius, the senator; followed by Egnatius Camillus, the commander of her Praetorian Guard. Julius Scribonia was next. He smiled condescendingly and said, "I am delighted to see you again, General. Please accept my belated and most humble congratulations on your appointment as governor."

Humble, my ass, Silva thought. If there had ever been any true humility in the person of Julius Scribonia, it had long since evaporated. To Silva the man resembled a poised hawk looking for a kill, and his beaked nose between his vigilant eyes only completed the image. Silva could not remember when he had last seen Scribonia; probably it had been in Macedonia, where he had arrived to investigate rumors of mass desertion from the Fourth Legion. As a result of his meddling, what had amounted to the disaffection of a handful of auxiliaries became a major rebellion, and the Fourth Legion was disbanded in disgrace and declared *damnatio memoriae*. It had never been reorganized and any man who had served with the Fourth was marked forever. In contrast, Scribonia had done very well for himself, having chosen his time when the upstart Vitellius had temporarily usurped the throne. The new Emperor had been so terrified of trouble in the Legions that he would believe anything the *frumentarii* chose to tell him. Thus, he had elevated Scribonia to one of the higher offices in the organization, and it was easy enough to suppose that his ambitions had not stopped there. At the first opportunity Silva resolved to ask Domitillia why she had allowed such a conniving rascal to join her party.

Domitillia introduced Gallus Septicius, her master of protocol, and said that he was a very important man, indeed, and Silva would do well to see to his comfort. "Gallus is in charge of the donative to your Legion," she said, then laughed, "and you know how Father is about money."

Gallus Septicius was a thin, balding man with a hand so frail that Silva released it quickly lest he break the bones. Although Septicius' smile revealed two rows of bad teeth and he gave the impression of general ill health, his eyes became alight with his pleasure of the moment, and Silva found a special warmth in his manner. His toga was overlarge for his frame and fell like a small waterfall from his shoulders, yet he had a quiet dignity that seemed lacking in the others. Vespasian, whose notorious caution with wealth was the result of his relatively humble origins, would never entrust a half million denarii to any ordinary human being.

"I am honored to meet such a distinguished general," Septicius said.

"The honor is mine. We'll do the best we can to make your stay in this primitive land as comfortable as possible."

"I'll need a place of safekeeping for the donative," Septicius said. "It will require at least three days to make the distribution."

Silva called Geminus to his side and told him to see that everything was done to the satisfaction of their guest. Then he smiled at Domitillia and nodded at the litter, which stood waiting just inside the line of legionaries. It was the only litter in all of Judea, the same one that had transported him away from Masada. He found the sight of it displeasing now, but at least Geminus or someone on his staff had the taste to dress it up a bit with flowers and muslin curtains, rather than the half-cured hides that had been his lot. He hoped the stink of himself during the distressing journey had also been removed.

Domitillia glanced at the litter and said, "Are you suggesting I ride in that?"

"It's a steep climb to the house and you must be tired from your voyage."

"I'm frothing with energy and restless as an alley cat after so long on that ship. I intend to walk for as long as I have your arm." She slipped her hand beneath his elbow and glanced down at Silva's sandals. They were ornamented with small lions' heads and the lacing thongs passed through their open mouths. "What precious footgear, dear Flavius. I do believe you've worn those just for me."

"I wouldn't care to try campaigning in them."

"I'm touched. Let's put them one in front of the other." She pulled him around until he had no choice but to escort her down the street that led upward from the wharf. Domitillia glanced at the crowd standing solemnly behind the ranks of legionaries. "Where are the women? I see only men. Don't you have any women in Judea?"

"The Jews take a different attitude toward their women. They prefer them to stay at home."

"And you approve?"

"I find it best to let them live according to their own customs."

"Really? Then do I gather you're like so many soldiers and believe women are only needed for stimulating your gonads."

Silva saw in her eyes that she was amused, and he decided to accept her teasing. "Of course. They also come in handy as beasts of burden."

She halted, then reached up and slapped the palms of her hands gently against his cheeks. "Flavius Silva, you ironhead! I've always loved you!"

Silva glanced at the escort behind them. If they saw anything odd in her behavior, they were managing to conceal it. A pity, he thought, that the Jews who had witnessed the little show had not been able to watch Domitillia in her girlhood. Perhaps they would have now looked less bewildered. To them, he knew such conduct from the Emperor's daughter must be incomprehensible. They would have been even more shocked if they had understood what she had said. At least, Silva decided, the gossip in their dwellings tonight would be more imaginative than usual.

THREE

IT WAS LONG past the usual hour of Silva's evening meal before Domitillia and her party had bathed as best they could, sorted out their individual belongings, and experimented with the makeshift furniture available. Silva was appalled at the amount of their baggage; it took their slaves and additional help from the legionaries until very late before all their paraphernalia had been brought from the ship and distributed to each sleeping room. Since it was a standard of Roman architecture to provide only cell-like sleeping rooms in even the finest of houses, Silva thought that the Jew who had built this place must have agreed with the Roman theory that there was no use wasting space on a prone person.

Silva's personal cook was an enlisted legionary as the necessities of campaigning demanded, but his heart was with the Tenth and not his stove. His name was Rubrius and he was classed as an *immune* along with the medical orderlies, farriers, surveyors, glassfitters, helmet makers, and other specialists within the unit. They were all excused from the ordinary legionary's heavy work and were treated with corresponding respect by their comrades.

Rubrius was beside himself with the excitement of cooking for such an august assembly. Silva was certain that if they were lucky enough to avoid a total culinary disaster, everyone's patience would still be tried to the utmost before the meal was finished. Hoping to assuage the temper of his guests, Silva had ordered his wine to be served as if the supply was unending. Most of it had been stored in leather bags to facilitate shipping from Ostia and for later traveling with the Legion. Thus it bore a tartness that was only partly removed when decanted into earthen jugs. Such army-issue wine, Silva thought, was without name because it was ashamed of any identity. The legionaries usually mixed it with water and sometimes bits of fruit to make it less offensive to the tongue.

There were no beautiful boys to serve the wine here, an omission Silva was sure would displease Scribonia, whose well-known homosexual preferences were easily accepted by Roman society.

As if to emphasize the Spartan quality of the evening, the wine goblets were identical to those used by the local peasantry. There were no musicians; Silva had considered calling upon one of his young tribunes who had not a bad voice, but unfortunately his repertoire consisted only of the most forlorn ditties Silva had ever heard, and he thought such renditions might lead the repast into a general depression. As for entertainers, it would not help matters to requisition those few local Jews who made any pretense of levity. Their most energetic dance seemed to be a gentle and somewhat preoccupied shuffle with never a hint of erotica. Better they not see how poorly their masters fared, anyway.

Thus Silva was almost entirely dependent on the wine to make this first night a success, and he was pleasantly surprised at how genial the party became. Septicius proved to be particularly adroit at luring Scribonia into making an ass of himself. The conversation cantered along and sometimes galloped through the usual rhetoric of Roman gossip before it would hang to one subject for a while as if the eloquence of the speakers was caught in a net. Silva had been gone from Rome for so long that he found most of the conversation puzzling.

As he allowed the general conversation to drift past him, he noticed that Domitillia continued to watch him with a smile he found totally beguiling. It was impossible for him to avoid meeting her eyes, which were so full of inquiry and invitation. She was, he thought, positively stunning in the lamplight, but her beauty was not alone responsible for his devotion. He knew a far more powerful influence was at work, and he found himself helpless to reject it. By all the gods, he thought, all have mercy on me because I'm falling in love with the Emperor's daughter, who is also the wife of one of the richest men in the Empire. Hold on tight to your better sense, soldier, or you will lose more than your job!

He was relieved when he realized that Domitillia understood his boredom with the others. "You're not with us, Flavius," she said. "Do I guess the reason is our provincialism? Believe me, I'm fed up with it. The same old drivel has been chewed upon and regurgitated for the entire week of our voyage. It never stopped even when they were throwing up."

Pedanius the senator, who was given to belly laughs, wiped the perspiration from his chops and said that unless the likes of Cicero could be revived, the level of Roman meal conversation was bound to be unexciting.

Septicius took exception. "That's not true. The most beautiful poetry, as witness Homer, the finest writings, as witness Seneca, were products of relatively peaceful environments. We're all either Stoics or Epicureans, and personally I prefer the latter." He glanced quickly at Scribonia and inquired, "Or might that be considered a dangerous thought, dear Julius?"

Scribonia pushed his beak nose deeply into his goblet and his black eyes darted rapidly back and forth along the rim. He seemed content to let the challenge pass for a moment, then at last he bared his white teeth in what might have suggested a smile and said to Septicius, "There are countless letters and essays written by those in history who have chosen to swim upstream. May I remind you that most have been written from exile?"

"Are you suggesting that the recent expulsion of certain philosophers from Rome is of benefit to the Empire?"

Silva was astonished at Septicius' daring and wondered if there was not much more being said behind these few words than he understood. Among the more thoughtful and influential Romans a certain Musonius Rufus had become the sole survivor after Vespasian decided to be rid of all philosophers. Rufus was a consistent champion of Stoicism, or the "right conduct." Among other dictates, he demanded that men follow the same moral code as they imposed on their women, and insisted that sexual relations were solely for the marriage and procreation of more Romans. While Vespasian had kept Rufus around as if to endorse the Stoic philosophy, it was common knowledge that he had not dismissed his own concubines.

Silva saw that Domitillia was signaling to him. She took on a doleful look and made a circular motion with one finger near the side of her head. He interpreted the gesture as saying that Septicius might be a bit crazy. Then she yawned and covered her mouth in such a way that only Silva was aware of it. He found the sense of intimacy altogether delightful, and he faked a yawn in response. Silva became so lost in the warmth he saw in Domitillia's eyes, he was hardly aware that the general conversation had not subsided since their provocative sharing of the moment.

As his attention drifted back to the others, Senator Pedanius was proclaiming his regret that Cicero was not still mortal instead of immortal, and he offered his defense of Murena against Cato's prosecution as an example of genius personified. Had he not won over both the crowd and the judges with his amusing banter? Who but the dullest of Stoics would compare Demosthenes with such a man?

Septicius countered with the argument that the oratory of Demosthenes had not been charged with a yearning for personal distinction. "On the contrary," he insisted, "Demosthenes always conducted himself with exquisite grace and majesty of mind."

Silva's attention was captured briefly by Scribonia, who smirked knowingly and said, "Demosthenes was a crook. Everyone knew that he took bribes from the King of Persia, and the gods alone know how many others contributed to his greed. No one mourned his exile."

Septicius pointed his bony finger at Scribonia accusingly and said, "Ah! but Demosthenes had the courage to keep his poison close at hand and finally use it, which is more than can be said for Cicero."

"Cicero was murdered."

"That's beside the point. He became a miserable old man, cringing and hiding from death when it would soon be natural anyway. He fell from oratorical splendor into a swamp of confusion!" Septicius turned to glance at Silva, but there was no malice in his eyes when he added, "That senile old man advocated replacing the toga with the sword, and the diplomacy of speech with the sound of military trumpets."

Silva had returned to watching Domitillia. For a change, her black eyes were still. She was obviously bored with her dinner companions. Silva assured himself that their conversation was out of his depth. Suddenly, Domitillia caught his eye and winked. By my oath, he thought, here is one wonderful minx of a woman!

" . . . you may be sure, dear Septicius," Scribonia was saying quite out of context with what had gone before, "that whatever the Emperor decides to do is ultimately for the good of the Empire."

"Here! Here!" said Camillus, who seemed to be having trouble focusing his eyes. Silva remembered he had never seen a Praetorian who could hold his drink, and this one was proving to be no exception. He was a big, beautiful, dumb animal with the brain of a sparrow.

Pedanius belly-laughed and said that those who would suck a dry grape could expect to suffer from puckered lips.

Watching him, Silva decided that the senator was very pleased with himself, and he thought that if all members of the Senate were of the same feather-brained variety, then Vespasian had made the right decision in almost ignoring them.

At the last minute Fabatus, the Legion's supply officer, had found a dove coot and provided Silva's kitchen with thirty pair of birds. Now they were delivered to the makeshift dining area in the atrium by Domitillia's servants, and the once-plump little birds were proof that anxiety in the kitchen can bungle the menu. For the doves were overdone to the point of cremation and had shrunken to the size of wrens. The sausages that followed were underdone and swimming in tepid grease. Only the bread was fit to eat, but by the time it arrived Silva saw that his guests were so full of wine they cared little whether they ate or not. It takes a drunkard, he thought, to understand a drunkard; the sudden ugly images of his own behavior when he had been too much with the grape now revolted him.

Domitillia alone seemed to have limited herself. As the seemingly endless evening continued, Silva found it increasingly difficult to avoid staring at her. He saw that she had Vespasian's determined jaw and regular features, but she was not cut out of stone as her father so often appeared to be. There was a timeless softness about her features, a lush, molded beauty made all the more pronounced by the way she carried it. Best of all, here was no Narcissus ever-conscious of her beauty. Here was a young woman who had joined Pedanius in honest belly laughs. Silva thought that a female who could so abandon herself to merriment could be trusted.

He knew now that his compelling interest in her was becoming far more than the dutiful regard of a mere general for the daughter of his commander in chief. There had been too many exchanges of eye-understanding between them; they had managed to say so much without uttering a word. When Septicius was baiting Scribonia, it was very obvious that they shared the same appreciation for his sly insults. Somehow, he must get her off alone. He must discover if the promise he saw in her eyes was real.

Now he apologized. "Tomorrow night we'll have beef, which even my cook can manage, and the next night— weather and the god of the Jews permitting—we'll have fish. I only hope my cook can make a sauce to please you."

He knew she was teasing when she said, "Dear Flavius, how can you imagine I would be satisfied without stuffed capons and pastry pigs? You must do something about your commissary."

"If you'll speak to your father and have me assigned to a more civilized country, then maybe I can indulge myself occasionally. This is the fare of your legionary officers . . . when they are very, very lucky."

He saw her eyes narrow momentarily when she asked, "Would you really want to be transferred out of the Tenth Legion?"

"No. It's my only family."

"You have Flavian blood in you . . . somewhere. Have you ever tried to find out how we're related?"

"I remember being told we were third or fourth cousins."

They fell to exploring what they knew of their common bloodline and were surprised at how little they knew. Soon Silva realized that the rest of the party had become bored with trying to eavesdrop on their ancestral guessing game and had turned to a debate concerning the recent death of Varus Alfemus, the chieftain of the obstreperous and admittedly courageous Batavian tribe, and what his demise would mean to the Legions stationed in Germany.

Silva had always been puzzled by the interest of civilians in obscure military matters of which they usually knew very little. Now he was amused to find that the preoccupation of the others with such distant events had nearly isolated him with Domitillia. He asked her if she would like a stroll on the terrace. If their departure was noticed, the others remained discreetly indifferent. Even Scribonia, who appeared to be the most sober of the lot, pretended to be unaware of their leaving.

They stood in the starlight looking down at the dead black sea, and for a moment it was so tranquil that Silva could hear his own breathing. Domitillia took his hand. You old fool, he thought, you are falling in love again.

Domitillia sighed and said, "It's so beautiful here. The air . . . it's so different from home . . . so soft . . . so? . . . quite licentious."

"I'll breathe it quite differently now. Strange how fast we can change an impression. Before you came I thought Judea had a rancid odor, and I blamed the stench on the speeches of various prophets who infest the region."

"Christianii?"

"Yes. They're harmless soothsayers, but in some ways the same as the Jews. They're always seeking ways to challenge us."

"What do you do when that happens?"

"Give them one day to repent, and if they refuse, we have little choice."

"What's your alternative?"

Silva thought he detected an ever so slight chill in her voice, but she made no attempt to release his arm. "Why are you so interested?" he asked.

"Father told me to learn all I can."

"We put most of them at hard labor until they change their attitude."

"What about the others?"

"They die."

"You mean they are killed?"

"What difference does it make? We can't let them roam around at their own will."

"Why not?"

"You're as full of questions as when you were a little girl.

Because they stir up trouble and they incite the Jews to making even more."

They stood in silence again and he sensed that he had said too much. He wondered if Domitillia was one of those Romans who seemed quite incapable of realizing that the Empire had not been built on sweet meditation and certainly could not be maintained without an occasional application of the whip. A rule without discipline could not survive. The Legions were the mortar of the Empire, and if there were any comparable power in the world the situation could be considered precarious; for all of the Legions were influenced by the attitude of their individual generals. The Legions were stretched from farthest Britain to Assyria and Armenia in the east, Lusitania and Mauretania in the west, and Ethiopia in the south. Local crises were perpetual and once allowed to fester could easily explode beyond the ability of the Legions to control. Gaul had been at peace for nearly a century before Vindex and Civilis led a revolt that probably would have succeeded if the people had not preferred ease and security to freedom. In Britain the so-called Brigantes had been persuaded by anti-Romans to rebel, and it had taken Cerialis, who had just put down another rebellion on the Rhine, to teach the tribes of Britain a stern lesson.

Silva knew several officers serving with the three Legions presently occupying Britain, and he was thankful that his own assignment to Judea at least included soft nights like this one. His brief experience in Britain as a very young tribune had convinced him that neither sun nor warmth was rarely to be known in that inconsistent land. Did Domitillia believe that the Brigantes or the Chatti tribe in western Germany could be held in check with a soft hand? When he had served in the north with the Twenty-first Legion Repax, he had reluctantly concluded that the tribes of all those regions were savages with the hearts of hyenas. Once Rome showed the slightest sign of weakness, they would rush to the feast.

Silva resolved to change the subject. In a momentary escape from his euphoria, he reminded himself that what he said to Domitillia might be passed on to her father and possibly be misinterpreted.

Silva was also acutely aware that Domitillia had still not released his hand. If anything, her grip seemed firmer, and he wondered why she was showing such a strong attachment. Or was he the one who was misinterpreting? He looked down at her face so softly outlined in the starlight and took a deep breath. "What's the perfume you're wearing? Marvelous."

"Titus brought it to me from Dalmatia. He claimed it had magic powers, but you know what a tease he can be."

"The scent is influencing my better judgment."

"It arouses you? How exciting! I've been saving it for a victim like you."

"I've nearly forgotten what it's like to be this close to a woman. I'm resisting a powerful urge to take you in my arms." The words had leapt impulsively from his lips. Flavius, he thought, your head will soon grace a spear.

He saw that she was looking up at him, but there was not enough light to reveal her expression. She took one of his hands and placed it on her breast. "Why are you resisting, Flavius? We're not exactly strangers."

"I . . . I was thinking of your husband."

"I'm not." She moved to him until her whole body was pressed against his.

"But—?"

"Hush!" she whispered as she placed her fingers to his lips. "I've waited a long time for this. My marriage was arranged and my husband is a total bore. You may rape me any time you please."

"Are you just playing with me?"

She took his hand and pressed it gently against her pelvis. She moved his hand slowly up and down. "When you were still a boy, sometimes you'd let me play with your toys. Well . . . now it's my turn."

Silva hesitated, then embraced her. He lowered his mouth to hers and felt her hands slide upward to the back of his head. He sent his tongue flickering along her lips and then full into her mouth. He surrendered himself totally; never, not with Livia, not with Sheva, had he been so instantly and deeply aroused. As if by mutual agreement they began to undulate slowly, the rhythm of their movement increasing as time passed. They whispered hurried little thoughts. "I don't understand this—"

"I knew it must happen the instant I saw you again—"

"I've been so long alone . . ."

They began breathing together, their mouths locked in passion. Silva's hand sought the nipples of her breasts, then slipped down to feel the moist warmth of her again. She reached to fondle him, but almost at once they broke apart. They heard a shuffling of sandals on the terrace steps and turned to see Julius Scribonia approaching.

Domitillia was the first to regain her calm. Her voice took on unnatural force as she said, " . . . and that, dear General, should fill you in on the protocol for tomorrow."

"I appreciate your advice," Silva had time to say before Scribonia halted. Even in the darkness Silva sensed that he was smiling and wondered how much he had actually seen.

"It's such a lovely evening, I thought to take a stroll," Scribonia said.

"At the end of the terrace you'll find steps," Silva responded as casually as he could manage. "The steps lead down to the beach."

"I don't suppose you'd care to join me? The stars are lonely."

"Not just now," Domitillia said almost too quickly.

"Of course not . . . under the circumstances . . ." Scribonia hesitated, then bowed slightly and moved on.

Domitillia emitted a long sigh. "That man," she said, "is everywhere. He is going to drive me insane."

"Why did you bring him along?"

"It was not my choice. Domitian arranged it. And now, since he's ruined a beautiful moment, I should clear your thoughts. My marriage to Marcus Clemens two long years ago was one of convenience. It pleased a great many people."

"I know the man. I cannot applaud. It's not like you to do anything just to please other people." Silva told himself that he had no right to be angry, but he could not restrain himself. "How can a woman like you marry a man like Marcus Clemens? It's such a waste."

"Domitian wanted it and my father wanted it."

"What about Titus? What does he think of it?"

"You know Titus is the most easily agreeable man in the world. He just said I should marry whom I wanted. I was twenty-four and still a spinster. In Rome that's worse than having leprosy."

"If a mere general is caught making love to the married

daughter of an Emperor, it could be worse. I doubt if our friend Scribonia just wanted to give himself an astronomy lesson."

Domitillia remained silent for a long time, and he wished he had been less sarcastic. "I'm sorry," he said simply. "I just don't trust that man. I've lived so long by the code of the army that I become unreasonable when I'm reminded that there's another way of life. The best soldier is celibate . . . he's married to his unit."

She reached out her hand and brushed it gently along his cheek. "Poor Flavius," she said, "you've become what I've always hoped you would be. You never knew that when I was only ten or eleven I was madly in love with you? You were so tall and dignified . . . so friendly when both of my brothers were angry with me. Do you remember the night of the thunderstorm? Bolts of lightning were flashing all around Rome and the thunder terrified me. I spied you standing on the hill with Titus and Domitian watching the display, and after an awful explosion and a blinding flash I ran screaming to you. While my brothers laughed and said the gods were angry with me, and Domitian said the lightning would make me blind by morning, you reached out and picked me up and held me tightly until I quit sobbing. I'll never forget that, Flavius. I still think of it as one of the high moments of my life. . . . You were protection and understanding and trusted authority all at once, and so my love for you knew no bounds."

"You were trembling like a little bird. It started to rain and we both got soaking wet before we found shelter in the Basilica Julia."

"You touched my eyes and promised on your oath that I would see perfectly well in the morning. You also said the lightning was my friend and a reflection of my beauty . . ."

"Shameless of me. What a romantic. As I recall, it was right after that the lightning struck a house up on the Quirinalis and set it on fire."

"I didn't care. For the first time in my life someone had suggested that I might not be an ugly duckling. I was warmed and felt marvelous. No matter what happened from then on, I knew I would always love you for those words."

"I wonder what was on my mind . . ."

"You were probably lascivious and didn't know it. Soon

after that you went away to Germany and I bawled again
. . . for awhile. Now it seems to me I was bawling about one
thing or another most of my younger days. Once in a while I'd
hear some word of my faraway soldier boy and I'd go into
another fit of tears. So tonight there is a good excuse for
falling into your arms. It was like recapturing something I
thought was lost forever."

"I'm afraid your soldier is far from being what he was.
When I look at the wreckage in a mirror, I realize that the
Empire is very hard on carcasses. In the Legion we say that if
you manage to live long enough, your medals will outweigh
what's left of your body."

She reached for his hand again, but this time he knew there
would be no embrace. A wave of hoarse laughter drifted down
from the dining area of the house, and she looked quickly over
her shoulder as if she sensed the arrival of an unknown enemy.
"Dear one of my childhood," she began, "the time will soon
come when I shall need you to pick me up in your arms again.
If I'm betraying my husband in asking for your help, then so
be it. The time is still to come, but we must prepare for it
now. It will be the very few people like yourself who can save
us all from calamity. You're aware that my husband is very
friendly with Domitian?"

"I haven't seen either man in several years, but my memory
tells me they are two of a kind."

"They drink a great deal together. When my husband is
drunk he always tells me more than he should. I know who is
to be trusted in the Praetorians and who might turn on Titus
when he becomes Emperor. Father is failing fast. We imported
two of the greatest doctors from Athens. They decided that the
cause of Father's deterioration is syphilis. They were afraid to
tell him the truth and so they said it was malaria, even though
they treated him with mercury according to Celsus. At one
point Domitian decided to call in a healer who recommended
treatment with lizard offal and boy's dung. Titus called the
man a quack and threatened him with a beating of the bastinado if he failed to leave Rome immediately. Nothing seems to
help. No one except the family knows how sick he is, and the
public must not know until the very last. Father has already
turned over most of his duties to Titus. He told me that when I
returned I might find him already on the throne."

47

Silva fought down an almost overwhelming sense of abandonment. Vespasian had been like a father to him, his solid rock in a world that often seemed to have gone mad. It had been Vespasian, the soldier's soldier, who had first marked him for advancement. Vespasian had taken him from the rank of *primus pilus* and had seen to it that he served under the best commanders, and that his term as a young tribune was spent on the most active frontiers, rather than rotting in some tranquil eastern province, or worse, becoming lost at some staff job in Rome itself. Most legionaries agreed that long ago Vespasian had deserved to join the gods. "If the old man goes?" he asked softly. "I've always thought he was indestructible."

"Father said he knew your friendship with Titus would eventually do enormous good for the Empire. But you must understand what kind of a man Domitian is. He has resented his brother and me since he was a child. He has been scheming with my husband and intends to kill Titus. Even now, he and his friends are making preparations for the day when the throne will be his."

"And Scribonia is one of his crowd?"

"I'm not sure. He could be."

"Titus must have heard about this. No one can keep a secret very long in Rome."

"Only if you're as clever as Domitian. He went directly to Titus and told him that there was a plot against his life and warned him to guard himself well."

"What did Titus do about it?"

"Nothing. He just laughed as he always does and said that anyone who was near the throne or on it could expect at least one attempt on his life a week . . . and probably more if he was worth anything."

"What do you want me to do?"

"The Greek physicians said Father may survive for as long as a year. Domitian is afraid to move until he is gone. Before I sailed from Ostia, Titus took me aside and asked that I tell you the time has come. As soon as I have departed, you are to activate his most secret message."

"You may depend on me, but I can't stop Domitian by myself."

"You can if you'll bring the African Legions to our side."

She reached out for him and he held her close to him for as

long as he dared. At last, she eased away and covered his hands with kisses. "Now," she said, "before those tongue-waggers realize how long we've been gone, we'd best go back to them."

"Will I see you again . . . alone?" Silva became uneasy before she replied. Somehow he must learn to control his tongue even when his desire was so powerful.

"Yes," she replied. "Be aware that Domitian will have your life if he learns what you're doing. A man who is brave enough to attempt what Titus has asked will risk seeing the stars from my room."

II

"Nothing is left, nothing for future times,
to add to the full catalogue of crimes."

—Juvenal

FOUR

NOW, AS IF to emphasize the profound peace that had at last come to the Empire, the man most responsible for this unusual situation was a man of the sword. Vespasian's ability as a soldier was unquestioned, although his qualifications as an Emperor were subject to complaint and ridicule by the sophists and were viewed with trepidation by the Senate. After all, the man could hardly be considered an aristocrat; his father had been a common soldier and his grandfather a petty bureaucrat. Even his spoken words revealed him, for he pronounced his *b*'s like *v*'s, his *w*'s like *b*'s, and he was given to abandoning his final Latin consonants in the manner of the Gauls. No one had ever heard of the Flavian family before Vespasian emerged and took the world in his powerful hands. There were whispered suggestions that he still ate most simply, that his personal habits were those of a peasant, and that his open intentions to found a dynasty through the succession of his sons, Titus and Domitian, meant a reversion to the abuses and privileges propitiated by the former emperors of the Julio-Claudian house. Augustus had brought the Senate to his way of thinking by at least going through the motions and ceremonious consultations with individual members, but apparently Vespasian believed the approval of the senators was not worth the bother. They could agree or disagree; Titus would succeed him regardless of their opinions.

Some of the resentment against such imperious action was modified by Titus' personal charm, which had become renowned wherever in the Empire he had been. Vespasian had seen to it that even the coinage identified Titus as the *imperator designatus*. He was reasonably content that his son would maintain his programs for more effective government.

After the wretched descendants of the Emperor Augustus, with their posturing and pretense of divine appointments, nearly any ordered government was tolerable by comparison. There had been the suspicious and hostile Tiberius lurking like some terrible monster in a variety of elegant caves. Then came Caligula with his degenerate license and contemptuous disregard of public welfare. His successor was the secretive and wise Claudius, who never had an open chance to employ his talents to notable effect because he was himself the victim of powerful and malicious relatives. That collection of miscreants had been followed by Nero, the most profligate and self-centered of them all, who had left only token contributions to the Empire. Finally, in quick succession, had come Otho, Galba, and Vitellius, all of a military nature and all given to cruelty and reckless ambitions. By the time Vespasian was persuaded to take the throne through the enthusiasm and force of the Legions, the blood of the old and honorable Roman families had been diluted until outspoken individuals were rare, and newcomers, accustomed to tyranny, were willing to endorse anything that might promise them substance and a reasonable degree of tranquility.

Now, on this gray and chilling afternoon, Vespasian was trying with all his will to appear as hearty and formidable a man as he had once been. With his head tilted upward and his powerful chin pointing almost defiantly at the low cloud cover, he had come to view progress on his favorite project, the building of a gigantic coliseum capable of accommodating fifty thousand people. The site he had chosen had been a lake in the garden of Nero's Golden House and was an easy walk from the Palatine Hill. With the exception of the pyramids, nothing so grand had ever been constructed before. For three years the streets of the surrounding area had reverberated with the rumble of wagons bringing travertine stone to the site. No one complained. The Romans were by nature a noisy people much given to the sound of their own voices in oratory and happiest when in the midst of auditory pandemonium. Noise was an essential element of Roman city life; the shoutings of tradesmen, the yelling of roisterers, and even yelps of those in the hands of hair pluckers were considered vital contributions to human affairs. The city was uncomfortable with so much as an approximation of silence; even in the middle of the night, when the metropolitan activity lessened enough to identify separate sounds, the slosh of human waste being thrown from windows in the apartmentized neighborhoods and the squeals and cryings of the prostitutes became reassuring. The city Roman knew that the night would bring another dawn, that he would have fresh cause for complaint of his sleeplessness, and that at first light Rome would still be there, as it always had been.

Vespasian was surrounded by a mixed assembly of architects, contractors, and several senators who had made bold to endorse such an extravagant project. Because the enormous cost of building the Coliseum had been anything but popular, Vespasian had always countered with the observation that he had to keep the poor working. To that intent he had deliberately forbidden the employment of various labor-saving machines.

Also about the Emperor now was a small corps of the *frumentarii* in various concealments, including that of stone mason and surveyor. His much more visible guardians were a half century of Praetorians in full armor. Vespasian himself wore his red military cloak pulled high around his throat against the weather. They stood in the very center of the amphitheater, many of them remarking on the frigid wind for this time of year, the softer of them trying to utter sentences of admiration for what they beheld while enduring spasms of shivering.

Clodius Levilla, the principal architect, held a sketch before Vespasian and, pointing at the open sky to the southwest, indicated where the seating of the imperial party would be. "Then opposite your station, Sire, will be a podium large enough to accommodate the pulvinars of the Vestal Virgins. There will also be room in that area for important dignitaries."

"Make sure you provide comfortable seating for foreign envoys. Our relations abroad are extremely important."

Later Levilla described the various subterranean elements beneath the amphitheater. "We should be able to cage approximately one hundred wild animals down there," he said, "and there will also be a waiting area for about fifty gladiators and any other performers required."

"See there is some provision for refreshment. Water for the beasts and wine for the men. They'll fight better."

Levilla displayed a drawing of the enormous cloth roof that would shelter the spectators from both sun and rain.

Vespasian studied the drawing a moment, then stared at the rim of the structure and pursed his lips. "That's quite some expanse of rag. What are we going to do if there's a high wind?"

"We thought to employ sailors from the fleet. They're experts at rigging."

"I've always mistrusted experts."

"We'll require about a hundred sailors each time the canopy is deployed."

"By all the gods! That's expensive. Can't you do it with fifty?"

"No, Sire. And we'd like to petition for them now."

"We'll just raise the price of admission. You can have the sailors unless the navy needs them for war."

Levilla bowed slightly. "Thanks to you, Sire . . . a most unlikely event."

Vespasian's attention had already drifted, as seemed to be a habit these days. There was so much on his mind that he was content if he could just keep track of any matter until it was resolved one way or the other. There was this haunting sense of mortality, the steady march of age that came along on all fours as if to ambush a man. The normal curse of forgetfulness was acceptable and even sometimes amusing, but the ever-increasing weariness was nearly impossible to defy.

Vespasian wondered if these twilight days of his life were responsible for his recent fretting like an old woman; the very same picky-picky immersion in detail that he had found irritating in some army officers during the days when they should have been thinking only of how Rome could be restored after the strife of civil war. Now it was just as objectionable to himself. Of course, if it was what the gods ordained . . .

Clodius Levilla waxed ever more enthusiastic about the heights of the supporting walls encircling the amphitheater and the millions of feet of stone still to be hauled. "Two hundred wagons per day, Sire . . . four hundred oxen . . .

fifty thousand wagons in total, because only a third will be bringing rock . . . a third waiting to unload . . . and a third on their way back to the quarries. It's very hard on the Via Tiburtina. I keep a crew of a thousand just filling the potholes . . ."

Vespasian only half heard what Levilla was saying; he was thinking of Domitian, who was hardly more than a youth when he addressed the Senate during the most confusing times of the civil war. How had he managed to sire such an obstreperous son? Compared to Titus, he was a voluble burden that made life miserable for everyone around him. But then there was no comparison with Titus—anywhere. When the Coliseum was completed, the arch commemorating Titus' victory in Judea would be visible from it. A good and proper combination. The spoils and souvenirs of the Jews were displayed in temples and many other structures throughout Rome, thanks to Titus. They were a constant reminder of Roman purpose and determination.

There was no question about Titus' capabilities for the throne, Vespasian assured himself. Possibly he would make a far better Emperor than this ailing old man . . . *if* he rid himself of that dreadful woman he had brought from Judea and had made his mistress. Berenice must go. No man could sit soundly on the throne with a Jewess in his bed.

Levilla was still apologizing for the chilly weather when Vespasian left him to his task. "You can build a mighty structure like this, but there is nothing whatever you can do about the temperature," he said. "If you're not already aware of your true importance, then be sure the gods will remind you."

It was Vespasian's intention to cross the Via Tiburtina on foot, passing through the heavy traffic as must any other Roman citizen. The centurion of the Praetorians objected, saying he had not enough men to guarantee full protection unless he was allowed to stop the traffic.

"You will do no such thing," Vespasian said, insisting with such severity as he could muster. "You'll back up the wagons for miles and throw the whole convoy into confusion. We're not going to pay laborers to sit on their asses and wait while I cross a road!"

So saying, the first citizen of the Roman Empire set off through the dust and noise of the continuous parade, dodging the wagons and teams until he emerged almost alone on the opposite side. His intention had been to continue uphill along the Via Sacra until he could turn left to an even steeper avenue and mount the Palatine Hill.

He had not walked a hundred paces before he knew that he must accept the inevitable. He had suddenly become so weary! He announced that there was a stone in his sandal which had caused a blister, and perhaps it would be wise to send for a sedan chair. A Praetorian was dispatched at once to fulfill the need. While waiting, Vespasian carried on a deliberately sprightly conversation with those near him. They must carry the word, he thought, that their Emperor was in high spirits and suffered only a blister. They must let Rome know that their old war-horse was as sound as ever and had many more years to come.

Vespasian had been a widower so long he had nearly forgotten what the mother of his children had looked like. Yet there had been moments when he was lying in the darkness with one of his concubines that the vision of his wife had returned and instantly made him impotent. There were other occasions when her image flashed before him, as it was now reflected in the faces of Titus and Domitian. They were lounging on two benches flanking his own, picking at the simple meal they had been specifically invited to share. Titus had his mother's strong Roman nose and a tendency toward fat that had also been a curse of his mother's. Perhaps a jovial attitude toward all the world might have been responsible for that; certainly in later life he would be carrying too much weight. He had a look of power in his face that contrasted strangely with his rather delicate complexion. He was fair-haired and already balding, but all else went usually unnoticed when his hazel eyes sparked with amusement and his sensuous mouth parted in an almost irresistible smile.

Some found it strange that Titus could be so easygoing and forgiving on all personal matters, yet unmercifully severe in war or to any challenge against what he believed was established authority. There were now rumors that since Titus' appointment to the command of the Praetorians he had used at least some of those palace troops to hunt down and kill people who were reported as antagonistic toward him. Reported?

Who did the reporting, Vespasian asked himself. There were always so many rumors about anyone close to the throne that it was almost impossible to separate lie from fact.

Vespasian scratched at his bald head. There again, he thought, was this nit-picking at minor details. Titus was a totally reliable young man with a rather narrow view of his duties. Left alone he would do very well at whatever task came to hand, for he was a perfectionist in all things. His toga was always immaculate, his hair trimmed, and his beard freshly plucked. Indeed he was a lively portrait of what a Roman leader should be, and with some slight adjustments in his personal life (namely, Berenice), he was bound to bring honor to the nation.

Now, watching them as they ate, Vespasian was impressed with the contrast between his sons. While Titus was fair, Domitian was dark. The strength and solidity in Titus' face was exchanged for puffiness in Domitian. Despite his younger age his nose was already laced with red and purple veins and his eyes were weak. He suffered perpetual digestive problems that made him prone to frequent belchings and fartings. While Titus sipped at his wine, Domitian kept a slave busy bringing him more. Domitian's appearance often bordered on the scruffy after he had spent a few nights in what he called "celebration." Celebration of what? When asked, Domitian had always replied, "The existence of Rome, of course. Can you imagine what the world would be like without us?"

There were those, Vespasian knew, who could imagine that the world might be much better off without the Flavians, particularly without Domitian, whom the *frumetarii* claimed put on disguises and hosted very rambunctious affairs at the better whorehouses. Why couldn't these boys keep their cocks where they belonged? Vespasian tried to smile at his unspoken question. Envy, he thought wistfully, was not the most pleasant of masculine emotions!

Domitian had a sullen streak, which Titus lacked. There was no telling what might set him off, but sometimes he would disappear from view for days, and only the *frumentarii* knew where he was hiding. From what? Had he been hurt by some unintended slight and was simply licking his wounds, or had he been up to some clandestine mischief?

At least, Vespasian thought, Domitian also had a most winning smile when he chose to display it, and much of his mother's logic of thought. Further to his credit was his ability to quickly analyze any situation military or civil, and his perception of how to solve the most complicated problems approached the magical. There was no way to be sure of Domitian. He was a puzzling son and therefore to be treated with care.

Vespasian had deliberately neglected to invite his son-in-law, Marcus Clemens, to this little supper party, because these days he preferred to be alone with his blood sons. Despite his marriage to Domitillia, Clemens was not a Flavian, and this evening there were delicate family matters to discuss.

Three charcoal braziers warmed the air about each bench, for it was still bitterly cold. The elevation of the Palatine Hill caught the wind much stronger than in the Forum or other protected areas of the city. The wind swept through the palace, which had been only partially restored since the great fire. Both sons sympathized with their father for his relatively open exposure to the elements. Titus lived on Mons Aventinus and Domitian on the Collis Viminalis, both of which were hills; but the great fire had not reached their houses and so none of the protective greenery had been lost.

"I fear for your health in this place," Titus said to his father. "By my oath, it's like being in Britain."

Vespasian managed a chuckle. "What's happened to you two? Has Rome made you so soft you can't stand a little breeze? Are you shivering ninnies going to rule the Empire from your *caldariums?* Maybe I should start a war and send you both to the frontier."

Titus joined his laughter and said, "Even a good soldier can't serve his country well if he is down with the ague."

Vespasian watched his sons in silence. He sought for signs of the animosity that he knew existed between them, but he could find nothing obvious. They are being very careful around the old man, he thought; they don't want to make me nervous.

"At least I have something to warm your hearts," he said. "A courier came today with a letter from your dear sister. Listen."

Vespasian unrolled a scroll and read,

To my Revered father, greetings, et cetera. We arrived in Caesarea after a voyage of six days, quite slow according to our captain. Our old friend Flavius Silva met me with all the poop-de-do fitting to the occasion. Distribution of the donative began this morning, and I assure you the soldiers of the Tenth Legion are quite ready to deify you.

I shall not like leaving this lovely weather (why do so many of our colonies enjoy a better climate than our own?), but once this distribution is completed, I suppose there is no real excuse for my staying.

I am impressed with Flavius Silva, and we have had some delightful hours reviewing memories of our ever so much younger days together. But I am also worried about him. Once you penetrate beneath his official poise, you discover a truly melancholy man. Perhaps he has been in Judea too long?

Vespasian paused and turned to Titus. "How long has Silva been in Judea?"

"I'm not sure. He was at Jerusalem with me and, of course, he took Masada. Nasty business. By my oath . . . now that I think about it, I suppose he's been out there all of five years . . ." Titus added thoughtfully, "Where has the time gone?"

"My son, I try to solve that riddle at the end of every day. Have we got anything closer to home for Silva? Too much foreign service can twist a man . . . sometimes so radically that the Roman in him disappears. "

Domitian said, "Flavius has been back to Rome twice. He's building a house in Praeneste and returns for a look at the progress now and then."

"May I ask how you know so much about the movements of your old playmate?"

Domitian mumbled some reply into his cup and Vespasian was displeased. "Take that cup off your face and speak up!" he said harshly.

Domitian obeyed. He spoke in his most formal Latin, and Vespasian thought it was as if he were being addressed by a stranger. "For your protection, Sire, as well as for my brother's and my own safety, I find it expedient to keep informed."

"I'm under the impression the *frumentarii* are handling that sort of thing very well. Are you employing additional informers?"

Domitian shrugged his shoulders and massaged the large wen on his right cheek. He made no answer. It was as if he had not heard his father.

Vespasian was vexed. Why had Domitian been such a pain in the ass ever since he was a little boy? He warned himself to abandon the subject. It was not worth the risk of falling out with his younger son.

"Father, with your permission," Titus said, "I'll find something for Flavius. He was a good comrade in battle and I think he deserves all the rewards we can give him."

Vespasian wanted to say that Silva's well-being was apparently in good hands, but restrained himself lest he betray a confidence. "Do as you think best," he said. He was surprised that he had really lost the essence of the subject, if only because the very end of Domitillia's letter had been so distracting.

Father, my beloved father, I place my eager heart in your tender hands. I go on my knees to beg your understanding and can only hope that my filial devotion to your every cause and whim is stronger than Roman social tradition . . . I am in love, dear precious father.

You hasten to ask what of Marcus Clemens, the husband you approved for me? If that great heart of yours which has wrought such miracles for Rome will spare one beat for your always-troublesome little daughter, I will know the greatest happiness of my life. Perhaps then you might raise your little finger and bring two Romans together. I assure you we already think of you as a god. The man I do love is Flavius Silva.

Vespasian was dismayed at how easily he had let himself suggest that Flavius Silva might have spent too long a time abroad. Domitillia had not expressed an instant of regret for the feelings of Marcus Clemens . . . that is, providing he had any feelings. No wonder the true Emperor of the imperial house was a feisty young woman whose mother had chosen to call her Domitillia under the strange impression that she was, even at age one day, indomitable.

I have lived too long, Vespasian thought. The world is shifting beneath my very feet, and the old and reliable ideas are being discarded regardless of what I may say.

Vespasian remembered that his first reaction on reading the letter had been to have Silva beheaded as soon as a sword could find his neck. Domitillia would be exiled to some uncomfortable island until she came to her senses. That was the old way and the proper way, and Roman society would understand. Honor, integrity, and love of country. Those were the values to cherish, not illicit affairs with a woman whose marriage vows should still be echoing in her ears. But now? What to do with a woman and her lover when one of her brothers was a known voluptuary for girls barely sprouting pubic hair and boys not yet eligible to wear the toga virilis? And her other brother? Titus had proven his contempt for society by bringing his Jewish mistress to Rome.

Because he had little appetite these days, Vespasian took only token nibbles of the roast lamb that had been set before them. He had passed the word to his kitchens countless times that the food served on the Palatine was far too much in quantity for the whole imperial family and their most distant relatives to eat, but the cooks and the stewards had always contrived to detour around his objections. So be it. *Their* most distant relatives dined in style on the leftovers and thought their Emperor not such an old skinflint after all. There were a million tributaries to the imperial river and there was no unbearable extravagance as long as the flow could be controlled. It was like the matter of Domitillia and Flavius Silva; on reflection it seemed best to keep news of their perilous liaison to himself. Perhaps it would blow away.

Vespasian's thoughts drifted to another problem for which, he hoped, there might be a more rational solution. Rome had just experienced near panic, because bad weather at sea had long delayed the importation of grain from Egypt. At last the winds had abated enough to allow cargo vessels entry to the port of Ostia, but the ugly grain riots of Rome must never again be repeated.

Vespasian took a small sip of his wine. He must keep his

wits about him, for it was a rare occasion when he could gather both sons to his home at the same time.

"What can we do about the grain situation?" he asked. "Another long spell of bad weather and the people will be hungry again. Need I remind you that hungry people do not make good citizens?"

Titus was quick to respond. "If you'll forgive me, Father, I believe the fault may lie with us. We, the government, have too much control of the economy, and grain is only one victim of our lead-footed bureaucracy. We own the fisheries, the salt-works, the mines . . . most of our natural resources . . . not to mention the sources of most of our grain in Africa. This monopoly makes for sluggish administration. Our bureaucrats grow fatter because they're secure, and they prosper by the rule of never making a voluntary decision for fear of making the wrong one."

Vespasian saw that Domitian was shaking his head in disap-proval. "The government has to be in charge," he argued. "Otherwise, what are you going to do about the unemployed? Take away our construction projects, for example, and you'll see some very nasty riots. Ask any Praetorian if he thinks they can control a Rome that's really aroused. People become very difficult to handle when they have nothing to lose."

Titus said, "I think we should give the shipowner some sort of a bounty for making the voyage from Egypt regardless of weather. That would ease his fear of losing his ship."

"He's already guaranteed loss and still he won't sail," Ves-pasian countered. "Even now they're exempted from paying property tax. How far can we go?"

"I think the more encouragement we give to freedmen the more efficient things will be. Make sure they have a good chance at profit, let the aediles look the other way on some tax matters . . . and let the merchant make his own choice on how many slaves he needs and how he feeds them."

"Maybe," Domitian said sourly, "the reason the ships won't sail in bad weather has nothing to do with the bureaucracy or the owners. Maybe the crews just don't want to drown."

Vespasian grumbled and said, "We're the richest people in the world, so I can't understand why we have so much trouble getting enough to eat."

"I would suggest," Domitian offered, "that we make more

effort to feed ourselves. There's enough farmland on the Peninsula to provide us with all the grain we'll ever need. All we have to do is grow it. But our farmers are lazy and they need a good prodding."

"What do you know about farming?" Vespasian asked with a definite chill in his voice. "Do you think you just stand in the middle of a field and say, 'Produce!' It's not quite so simple. There is a reason why our farmers are so reluctant to grow grain, and I charge you to find out why."

"Very well, Sire. Do I have your permission to kick a few of the lazier farmers in the ass and thereby guarantee some results?"

"If I hear of you or any one of our staff so much as touching one of our farmers or insulting him in any fashion, you'll be sent to duty in Britain for a long time. Do you hear me?"

"Perfectly, Father."

"Now to other matters. I am considering the idea of the state paying our teachers. I'm not sure how the Senate will react to such a proposal and don't really care what they think. The hearing on that scoundrel Priscus and his revolting activities in Africa is scheduled for next week. I'm hoping our Senators will be so preoccupied with all the hot air Tacitus and young Pliny will be mouthing, they'll let the teachers pay mandate slide through. They will probably do some debating on what a subsidy will do to the teachers' value as educators . . . that sort of thing. Some will say they will teach only what the state wants taught. . . . What are your thoughts?"

Domitian said, "It's a waste of money and potentially dangerous. Those who want an education ought to pay for it." His elbow slipped off the couch arm and he spilled wine on himself. The slave who stood behind him jumped to wipe it away as he continued, "It would be like all the other state charity offerings. There is no end to them. Soon after the teachers find themselves on the state payroll, they'll start fighting among themselves, saying one is worth more than the other. Next, they'll be demanding free admission to the theaters and the games. Those who teach in rhetoric school will be asking for as much salary as a centurion."

There were times, Vespasian considered, when his younger son displayed a cynical attitude more suitable to a much older man. A pity his intelligence was not better disciplined. Never mind, he was going ahead with the project anyway.

Titus was laughing as he said, "I never thought I'd see my father subsidizing a training ground for homosexuals! Can you imagine our dear teachers in a paradise where they're guaranteed pay while they play with all the little boys in their classes? Especially those who are teaching Greek."

Vespasian held his temper. It was inconceivable that Titus would mock him. "I would prefer a man smell of the earth than of perfume," he said acidly, "and I wonder if you're in any position to question the morals of others?"

There, it was out, Vespasian thought. He felt the lamb sour in his throat. Now he must declare himself and put an end to his timidity toward his favorite son.

"What do you mean by that, Father? It's obvious I have displeased you."

"Berenice," Vespasian said as calmly as he could manage.

"What has she to do with this discussion?"

"A great deal. You must be rid of her."

"Surely, you're jesting, Sire."

"Indeed I'm not! Send her off before any more time passes. I will remind you of your duty."

"Duty? I thought that my record in various campaigns should be reminder enough for anyone . . . including yourself, Sire."

"No one discounts your record except yourself. You disgrace it and the very arch of your triumph frowns on your behavior. How do you think the people of Rome feel about the conqueror of Judea taking a Jewish mistress—and worse, having the unmitigated nerve to bring her to live with him here in the capital?"

"There are many Jews in Rome."

"That's beside the point! You are the emperor designate. You have insulted the Roman families who lost relatives in Judea. You've spit on their memory of their fathers and sons. The only way you will be forgiven is to throw the Jewess out immediately. Then, in time, the citizens may forget."

There followed such a long silence that Domitian could be heard gulping at his wine.

"I refuse, Father." Titus spoke softly but firmly. His words so shocked Vespasian that it was moments before he could regain his composure.

"Listen to me," Vespasian said at last. "You're not only challenging your father, but the Emperor of the Roman Empire. You will do as I say, just as any soldier will obey his commander in chief . . . that is, unless you wish to be treated as a mutineer. My time is growing very short. Soon I will retire to Reate and die. I do not wish to leave this world, listening to the house of Flavius being criticized and ridiculed. Upon my death the Senate will jump like jackals at every opportunity to discredit our family and thereby bring authority back to themselves. You will rid yourself of the Jewess tomorrow, or I shall reconsider the choice of my successor!"

"Bravo," Domitian whispered so softly he could not be heard even in the heavy silence that followed.

Later, when they had left him, Vespasian called for a bowl and vomited into it. When his nostrils had ceased stinging, he was able to wonder at the natures of his progeny. One daughter an adultress? Who knew what the wagging tongues in the Senate would do with that? One son a shameless voluptuary with a fast developing overinterest in the grape. An eldest son throwing away his brilliance and marvelous abilities on a Jewish whore when the rotten odor of her people still offended the Roman nose.

Vespasian rubbed at his haggard eyes. What to do? Unless he changed his mind, Titus could only be considered a mutineer. Since he was still in the army the punishment for such conduct was an immediate beheading. But, of course, he knew his father would never give such an order. Put him in chains? He already was, with the Jewess forging the links.

He sighed heavily and thought that his task was too great for one man. The old system of appointing several consuls to the Senate who could handle many of the governmental matters had much to recommend it, but finding the right man for the post—individuals who would not try to undermine the throne—was almost impossible these days. No one really wanted to accept responsibility, which was another word for blame, unless they were paid an outrageous reward.

In fact, he thought, the whole of Rome had gone so mad for money and the comforts it bought that it was extremely difficult to get anything done. The price of slaves had gone out of all reason, an ironic result of no wars. Instead, fighting men of all races were flocking to the capital in search of rumored wealth. The city was a beehive of activity with the streets and narrow alleys crammed with Armenians, Jews, Spaniards, Africans, Greeks, Assyrians, Macedonians, Egyptians, and Arabians.

As a consequence, the native Romans were trying to protect their employment with trade corporations. Whether they be shoemakers, potters, masons, blacksmiths, or flute players, they were each united according to their trade, and they set a price on even the semiskilled endeavors. *They* set the time when they would commence work and when they would cease, not the customer or the builder or even the state. They had become such a powerful political force that several senators were indebted to their support and were thus rendered incapable of honest voting on many matters.

Vespasian found himself reviewing the whole senatorial system and concluded, as he had many times before, that it was awkward and cumbersome. When too many people were involved in making decisions, perspective became lost in the contest of personalities. So the chances of a decision being the right one were not very high. The senators, impressed with themselves in their black buckskins and silver crescents on their sandals, were too quick to shout their *"Omnes! . . . Omnes!"* in approval of propositions placed before them by skillful orators.

Now, as the burden of Vespasian's troubled family disturbed his peace of mind, he could recall two laws voted by the Senate which he considered little short of ridiculous. Here was Rome starving for grain periodically, and yet senators who could best afford to invest in ships were not allowed to own one with cargo space for more than three hundred amphorae. Why? Because the senator might make too much profit if he owned any vessel large enough to be of any value. Meanwhile, the population could go hungry while the Senate debated a thousand alternatives.

There was also the law that forbade any enemy delegate to enter through the walls of Rome. How then to negotiate an end to hostilities without placing yourself outside the walls and at the mercy of the enemy? The same law extended even to Roman generals if they were in active command of a unit.

If Flavius Silva wanted to address the Senate on any serious matters concerning his governorship of Judea, then the whole Senate would have to be transported outside the walls and assembled in some place like the Temple of Bellona.

Vespasian snorted in frustration. Sometimes, he thought, that ancient Etruscan, Tarquin the Proud, knew how to accomplish things. He would never have tolerated the opposition of a Senate, or the laws they made. *Lex Regia!*

Vespasian walked slowly to the room he had chosen for his sleeping quarters. It was a small windowless room, barren of furniture except for a single chair and a bed. His thought at the time he had become Emperor was to keep his habits as simple as possible—he would be the soldier's soldier come to town with a job to do and nothing more. Here was this very weary old man stumbling toward the bed with the weight of the world on his head. Meanwhile, the family of the Flavians was wallowing in their perquisites as if born to the purple.

Vespasian removed his toga and jerkin. The bending effort required to remove his sandals caused him to groan with deep pain. My back, he thought, is going to fly apart some day and scatter all over Rome like hailstones. It was discouraging to think that because of his back, which the doctors said had nothing to do with his main disease, he could never risk mounting a horse again. So much for the glory of an Emperor.

On the morrow, he thought, it might be expedient to make a sacrifice to Apollo. Perhaps such a signal of devotion might ease this pain . . . at least it could do no harm.

As he lowered himself to his bed he called to the centurion who stood constant guard at his door. "Send her to me," he ordered.

Moments later, Rosanus, his favorite concubine, appeared out of the shadows. As she had done for months now, she began to rub Vespasian's back and soothe him with soft words.

FIVE

IT WAS TO be a day of unusual activity for Flavius Silva. He was up with the sun, rehearsing the speech he would make to his Legion and planning the later part of the day's program in such a way that he might enjoy the maximum time alone with Domitillia. The week of her stay had gone much too swiftly, and he dreaded the time when he would be obliged to see her off to another life. Their mutual infatuation had exploded with such rapidity and force that he still could not believe it had actually happened. He tried not to think about how long it might be before they could be together again.

The routine business of paying out Vespasian's donative had been accomplished. His legionaries had stood in the hot sun for the better part of four days while Gallus Septicius, his onion skin more transparent than ever, sat under an awning and supervised the payment of a fortune in brass sesterces. Septicius' slaves fanned the air about their frail owner in an attempt to keep him comfortable while he spoke briefly with each recipient. For awhile, Silva had listened as Septicius' gentle voice contrasted with the gruff responses of the legionaries.

Since even standing in the same place with Julius Scribonia annoyed him, Silva soon departed with the excuse that there were other matters pressing for his attention. Scribonia was a dangerous nuisance, Silva thought. He had managed to insert himself into every event since the ship docked. There was no escaping his ubiquitous presence. If he was actually spying rather than just making sure he would not be ignored, then why did he seem to focus on Domitillia and himself? Was his curiosity just habit—an indulgence of the breed—or was he serving some distant master? And if so, why?

Silva hoped he was being overly suspicious and uneasy, but he resolved to be wary. Julius Scribonia was like a peacock with the best in him always on parade. But most certainly there was another side to him.

The more intelligent legionaries grumbled that the coins issued them were devoid of gold content, which was true; but most accepted the bonus without question and promptly changed their sesterces for shekels to spend locally. As a consequence, the resident money changers and the harlots did a thriving business in the streets of Caesarea.

Gallus Septicius tried to make sure that every legionary knew where the money was coming from, but as Silva had warned him, he had soon discovered that the Legion was not made up exclusively of fine young and patriotic Romans; at least half were foreigners from distant colonies and understood only a minimum of Latin. Silva had explained that without recruitment from the colonies the entire Roman Army would be but a token force.

The payment was complicated by the differences in rank and seniority within the Legion and the consulting of the records to make sure that each man was who he said he was. This was a duty to which Julius Scribonia had appointed himself, and Silva watched unhappily as his questioning caused frequent delays in the movement of the line. His contemptuous manner often created an atmosphere of hostility among the lower ranks—too often, Silva thought. At the annual pay of 225 denarii, with deductions for clothing, food, and arms, his legionaries were hardly overpaid, and they did not appreciate Scribonia's final inquiries as to their eligibility.

While it was not an absolute mandate that Roman generals speak to their troops on a regular basis, it was a long-established custom to which Silva was obedient. He disliked making speeches and considered himself quite inept with words, but he did the best he could before and after battles, and on occasions deserving of special recognition, such as the launching of new campaigns or the Emperor's birthday. Since this was only the second distribution of a donative in Silva's experience, he considered it worthy of at least some acknowledgment on his part. He also was anxious that Domitillia's mission become an outstanding success in the eyes of Rome. Vespasian might be a man of simple tastes, but he was still an army general and a stickler for military protocol. He would expect the local commander to address the troops in his behalf; Silva was quite certain he would be displeased if the ceremony was neglected. Thus, in the first warmth of the sun he paced his terrace and spoke haltingly to the air about him.

"Soldiers of the Tenth Legion . . . comrades in arms! To you who fought at Jerusalem and went on to Masada with us . . . I bring you greetings from our glorious Emperor who has seen to your reward in a most handsome fashion. I ask you to give a hearty cheer to his daughter, Domitillia, who is seated on my right . . ."

Was it necessary to say, "on my right"? If the carpenters had done their job, there would now be a small platform built in the center of the Legion's camp, and most certainly Domitillia would be the only woman present. So why point out the obvious? How about a cheer for the rest of her party . . . Scribonia? . . . Camillus? . . . Pedanius? By the gods, *no!* Gallus Septicius perhaps, but then the noses of the others would be out of shape unless they were cheered, but why wear out good legionary throats for such people?

So? Now on with the mumbo jumbo. "In commemoration of your courage and devotion to the keeping of peace and order within this far corner of the Empire, the Emperor has confirmed my own opinion that . . . the Tenth is the finest Legion in the Roman Army . . . and I want you to know that I consider it a great honor to be your commander. While many of your comrades died gallantly at Jerusalem, those of you who were at Masada know that what we had to endure there in the way of scorching heat, all manner of insects and reptiles . . . added to the savage excursions of the Jews themselves . . ."

No, he thought, pausing for breath. That was a considerable exaggeration. There had indeed been unbearable heat and there had been insects if not many reptiles. Like a living monster the desert heat had influenced the daily life of every man while they built the great ramp that had enabled the deployment of the rams against the walls of Masada. The ramp had taken a terrible toll including, alas, that superb engineer and companion of his lonely nights, Rubrius Gallus. It had been dear Gallus in whom he had confided his passion and vexation with Sheva, and had he not been struck in the mouth by a bolt fired from Masada, it would have been Gallus who would have comforted him when she had taken her life.

Now, he thought, dear Gallus, how I long for your sage counsel concerning another woman who has taken command of my life!

As for savage attacks? Despite the loss of that splendid Roman, engineer Gallus, the single lucky shot could hardly be classed as an attack.

"Very well," he said softly, then raised his voice: "You who were with us at Masada know that it was rotten duty, which you served without complaint . . ."

Nonsense. There had been several times when mutiny seemed possible and when it was actually attempted, or so he had been told. He had been bouncing around in a litter stone-drunk when there had been trouble during the retreat from Masada . . . hardly a heroic portrait. Still, it was the way of the military to at least pretend that everything always went according to plan.

"Soldiers of Rome! It is men like yourselves who have brought peace to the world . . ." Silva became aware of soft applause floating down to him from a window of the house. He looked up to see Domitillia watching him. She smiled and clapped her hands softly again.

"Bravo," she said, laughing. "Very impressive."

"What are you doing up at this hour? Go back to sleep."

"And miss this show? Never."

Silva saw that her eyes were filled with merriment. He thought that there was nothing so winning as a good-natured woman in the early morning. And nothing so aggravating as one who was not.

"I was never taught oratory and I really dislike it," Silva said apologetically. "So I have to rehearse . . ."

"You might wish to say something about Father's deep appreciation of their loyalty . . ."

"I've already said that."

"Let them hear it again. How about a summation of the future?"

"Even if he stays alive, a soldier doesn't have much of a future."

"Make one up. And relax, beloved General. By tomorrow they'll have forgotten what you said anyway."

A slow smile crept across Silva's mouth. "Are you telling me not to take myself too seriously?"

"Yes. The gods will favor a soldier who knows how to laugh at himself. Especially if he's a general. No one else dares."

Silva walked toward her until he stood directly beneath the window. He regretted that she was too high for him to reach out and touch her hand, but the sense of being present at her awakening pleased him. He spread his arms and said, "You have a saucy tongue, but your face does grace the beauty of this morning."

"You've had too much sun and it has addled your eyes. Unlike your soldiers I'll remember what you just said. Fancy words, General. If only they could echo down through the next five thousand mornings I'd feel like an immortal. It takes a reckless man to spout such eyewash at sunup. Where have you been all my life?"

"I was about to ask you the same."

"You did. Last night after your third cup of wine. You've already forgotten my answer. So it is with most ordinary men, but I was naive enough to hope that you might be different."

Silva tried desperately to remember the answer she had made to his question, but now he found that he could not even remember the question. Curse the effect of wine on the memory—especially when trying to recall a conversation with a female! They must lock each word said to them in a solid bronze casket and open it only when needed.

Suddenly her answer came to him—at least in part. "You said I lived too much in the past."

"Is that all you remember?"

"No. You made some kind of a riddle. You asked why our relationship was like the stars. You said it had no past or future . . . because it had always been there."

"That's reasonably accurate. I hope you keep that thought in mind."

"I'd rather be told that you're staying another week . . ."

He saw there was no point in finishing his sentence. Domitillia had blown him a quick kiss and disappeared from the window. He sighed, irritated with himself and with Domitillia. He knew that he was behaving like a young lover lost in his first devotion, and he told himself that, also like a young fool, he was risking a separation of his head from his body if he continued to pursue Domitillia. No matter how many times he had warned himself that she was royalty as well as a wife, he could not seem to stay away from her. Even the arguments that she might simply be amusing herself with a brief affair in a faraway land, or that she was just ensuring his aid in thwarting Domitian's plans against her other brother had little effect on his desire. It was puzzling because she seemed to care so little for the consequences if they were discovered. Perhaps she thought her political activities would be screened by a romantic attachment? After all, what did one do in a socially desolate place like Judea? As a woman with a very high-ranking husband and the most powerful man in the world for a father, it was unlikely she would have to pay much for an indiscretion as long as she kept her dallying from becoming a public exhibition. But for Flavius Silva, a mere soldier whose continued usefulness to Rome might be in doubt, the punishment could be very hard. Certainly he would lose command of the Tenth, as well as his governorship. And if sufficiently aggravated, Vespasian, who was an unforgiving man, might insist on his head.

Silva shrugged his shoulders as if to shake off the gloom that had so suddenly crept upon him. At least, he thought, no one yet knew of their liaison, and for this last remaining day and night of the royal visit, they must be cautious.

Silva had often marveled at the way the packet of priests who were attached to each legion always managed to make themselves appear so essential. Their industry in their own behalf was astounding, and only when they had finished their interminable ceremonies could matters proceed with any dispatch. Was the wife of Vulcan unfaithful to him? Ask the priests. Was Neptune hostile to the Romans? Ask the priests. Was Mars, who was called Quirinus when in a peaceable mood, pleased with a prospective plan for a battle, or was he going to pout because the liver of a sacrificed chicken (or a woodpecker, if one could be captured) proved to be mealy?

Ask the priests—or more likely, they would tell you. Their presumption of attention and authority had always annoyed Silva, particularly since there was nothing he could do about it.

The high priests in Rome were a different sort and were chosen from among the most honorable patricians. The Pontifex Maximus who ruled all Roman religion was officially accountable to the Roman people, but since the decline of the Republic and the time of the Emperors formality had often been circumvented. The Pontifex M. and his college of priests regulated the Roman year and the public calendar. They proclaimed the religious days and festivals. In certain cases the Pontifex M. had the power of life and death, and only an unwise man would cross him. Most emperors arranged to have themselves appointed Pontifex Maximus.

The augurs were appointed by the college of priests, and while some remained in Rome many were sent to serve with the Legions. They forecast the future of most military endeavors by tokens observed in five sources: the heavens, thunder and lightning, the singing of birds, and a variety of uncommon accidents. The birds gave omens by singing; the raven, crow, owl, eagle, and vulture were favored. Reading his military history, Silva had been made aware that in the First Punic War, P. Claudius had disregarded the ominous prophecy of his priests when they found that the chickens they kept for ceremonial purposes would not eat. Claudius had ordered the disobedient chickens thrown into the sea and declared, "If they won't eat, let them drink." Afterward he engaged the enemy and lost his entire fleet.

There were all manner of prognostications offered by the augurs. Silva had no intention of disregarding any of them as long as they were quick about it. As he saw it, they could do no harm except waste time, so why not take the chance they might actually have some beneficial influence? Still, he was secretly proud that he had never canceled a military operation because some pip-squeak priest with his shaven head and white bonnet had forecast doom. In the event of a bird croaking the wrong tune, or the unfavorable entanglement of a pig's intestines, Silva preferred to proceed with the style of his long-ago predecessor, Julius Caesar. That esteemed general, upon landing at Adrumetum in Africa with his army, happened to fall on his face. His horrified officers and priests reckoned it a bad omen, but with great presence of mind Caesar turned it to the contrary. He took hold of the ground with his right hand and kissed it as if he had fallen deliberately. He announced in a loud voice, *"Teneo Te, Africa!"* (I take possession of thee, O Africa!)

Now, as he watched the priests dissecting a chicken while whispering their sibylline verses, he glanced at those who shared the platform that had been erected in the Legion's camp. There was Domitillia on his right hand. He saw that her eyes were half-closed as if the afternoon heat had made her drowsy. Silva thought that he should have postponed the ceremony, which was held expressly to honor Vespasian for his gift and to commemorate the visit of his daughter to Judea. The awning above their heads did little to alleviate the heat; in the evening there might be a sea breeze. Perhaps as darkness fell he might find a way to be alone with Domitillia.

See how your judgment has been swayed, he thought. His compulsion to spend as much time with her as possible had caused him to disregard the effect of the scorching afternoon sun and the consequent inattention of his legionaries who were formed in their cohorts before the platform. They were sweating beneath their helmets and armor, enduring for as long as they must this salute to an Emperor they had never seen.

Watching their faces, so many of them familiar to him, Silva knew a sense of almost overwhelming pride in their willingness to stand there so patiently while being parboiled by the sun. He resolved to keep his speech to an absolute minimum and to remind them that not only had they each earned this donative, but that the odor of further reward was already drifting across their ranks. Seven oxen had been slaughtered and legionaries who understood roasting had been at it since early morning—a rare treat of meat for his soldiers. He had also authorized the extra issue of fifty amphorae of wine, which should be barely enough for the thirty-odd centuries to which the Legion had been reduced. Sickness, death, retirement, and the assignment of five maniples to guard duty throughout Judea had reduced the Tenth to slightly fewer than three thousand men. Since there had never been any dispatch indicating Rome might send out replacements, Silva assumed the decline would continue.

For a moment he studied the face of Antoninus Valens, who stood in the front rank of the first cohort. He treasured his friendship with Valens, a bull of a veteran who had been with him since his days as a young tribune. Valens' mother, father, and total family were the Legion. He was getting on in years and claimed that he neither knew nor cared where or how long ago he had been born. Now he was obliged to wear a leather corselet over his woolen tunic, and Silva thought he must feel like a torch in the sun. Valens' chest was heavy with medals won in battle, a series of discs decorating a leather holder. One depicted a head with a wreath of ivy, another was engraved with the head of Medusa, another with a lion's head; all of them were proof that Antoninus Valens was as lucky as he was brave, else he would not have survived.

Near him stood Arrus Niger, the Tenth's eagle-bearer. Over his tunic he was wearing mail armor, and over that leather armor; he also wore nine medals. His right hand grasped the eagle standard, with the bird's extended wings wreathed by metal oak leaves.

Next to Niger stood Civilis Serenus, the standard-bearer. Ranking just below the eagle-bearer, he wore a special head-dress of bearskin, which Silva knew must be unbearably hot; yet such was the honor of the rank that Serenus had never been known to complain of either the bear's skull atop his head or the heavy fur of the carcass that was draped over his shoulders and hung down his back. Beneath the skin he wore a coat of chain mail. In addition to his standard, he carried a small round shield.

The apparel of his legionaries, Silva was reminded, had hardly been designed for the hot climates in which the Roman soldier was so often required to operate.

Silva could not resist glancing at Domitillia again. Her profile delighted him; the impertinent upward turn of her nose expressed exactly her fondness for challenge and independence. Her lovely lips were incredibly seductive even in repose. His eyes followed the line of her profile down to her breasts, so daringly revealed by the low-cut, nearly transparent gown she was wearing. She was, he thought, the kind of woman that men lose their heads over, and he was more than willing to take the risk. A sudden vision of Domitillia in the arms of her husband made him wince and turn his thoughts elsewhere.

Silva glanced beyond her to Egnatius Camillus, whose Praetorian duties required that he keep Domitillia under his protection at all times. Silva thought that he looked more like a handsome Greek than a Roman. He was staring at the glittering mass of men and biting at his lower lip. There was no expression in his eyes; in fact, Silva recalled, they were always devoid of expression. The man seemed a giant bundle of muscle and blooming health, a vivid and unfortunate contrast, Silva mused, to the surviving wreckage of his own body. Yet be not envious, old-young soldier, he thought. Camillus was like a great stag hound with only a mirror for a brain.

Julius Scribonia, who sat beyond Camillus, was another matter. While the priests continued with their tasting of the chicken's blood and shaking their heads in approval, Scribonia lounged in a chair that had been requisitioned from Silva's house, like all the others on the platform. His delicate fingers rose frequently to caress his heavy eyebrows as if he would tame them. He was obviously not listening to the priests, but his wary eyes lingered often on the faces of the younger legionaries. Once Silva saw him run his tongue along his lips in a provocative gesture, but was unsure if he was signaling an individual legionary or just expressing a thirst.

Scribonia reminded Silva of a desert hawk circling to find prey. When he found it he would pounce, and meanwhile his watchfulness caused everyone to instinctively avoid him. Silva wondered if Scribonia had any knowledge of the most secret message he had received from Titus—or was that why he had come?

Gallus Septicius sat at Silva's left. He was present, Silva decided, only in body, and there remained very little of that. He was humming softly to himself and twiddled his arthritic thumbs while he stared at the awning above him. Silva guessed that his thoughts were far removed from Judea, perhaps lost in anticipation of that other life in which he professed to believe. "You take the sons of Rome for awhile," he had said at last night's dinner, "and you mistreat them terribly. But when at last they all die, whether young or old, heroes or cowards, their treatment will be all the same. I heard a Christian talk that way once and decided his theory was puerile at best. Now I'm not so sure."

Silva thought that he would like to keep Septicius with him in Judea. Like the much-lamented Rubrius Gallus, he would be someone to talk to, a kindred spirit with whom he could discuss the theories of Pliny, the vituperative poetry of Martial or, since the building of the house in Praeneste had become such a preoccupation, how the red granite of Egypt might contrast with the white Carrara marble of the Italian Peninsula. Yes, Septicius would have been a good companion and an antidote for the loneliness that would certainly come when he sailed away with Domitillia in the morning.

Rufus Pedanius sat beyond Septicius, and Silva was willing to wager that he slept just as soundly in the Senate as he was doing at the moment. His fat hands were folded across his fat belly, and his fat chins rested one upon the other like a black-smith's bellows. He breathed deeply and an occasional sub-dued snore escaped his lips. Silva found himself speculating on what his soldiers must think of the dignitaries assembled around him. As a female and, moreover, the daughter of the Emperor, Domitillia would command automatic respect, but the others? Silva thought that if he were standing there cre-mating in the sun, he would be praying for the gods to poison the lot.

At last the priests were done. They displayed the entrails of the chicken first to Domitillia, who wrinkled her nose and looked away, then to Silva, and finally held up the bloody guts high for the troops to view. The priests announced that the signs were favorable for the immediate future of the Tenth Legion under the command of the great General Flavius Silva, and that the return voyage of Domitillia would come to a safe ending. They nodded in unison to Silva, indicating that he could now proceed. As he arose a series of hearty cheers hailed his name, "Silva! . . . Silva! . . . Silva! . . ." The chant continued for so long that Silva decided enough was enough. If Domitillia or anyone else now doubted his popular-ity with his legionaries, they must be deaf.

Disregarding the advice of Geminus, who had recom-mended that Silva wear his breastplate with the head of Apollo flanked by twin dolphins and his helmet of brass with red feathers sprouting from the crown, he had chosen to wear only his scarlet tunic and skin-tight pantaloons for this day. Signifying his respect for Domitillia and the occasion, he wore a wreath of oak leaves and acorns on his head, the *corona civica*. It had been awarded him by Titus and made the wearing of any of his other medals superfluous.

Silva raised his right hand and smiled upon his troops. He began to speak easily, almost in a conversational tone, and soon he had them laughing and whistling their approval as he told them how a cunning Jew had sold the Centurion Crispus a hillside cave loaded with sequestered gold. The story about Crispus, a popular centurion who rarely used his club on inferiors, delighted the legionaries because he considered himself very astute in financial matters.

Silva followed with a tale about another man of great popularity, the Decurion Longus Avso, who was given to boasting of his powers as a lover. It seemed that Avso was on guard duty at the ramparts of Caesarea one night when he was approached by an artful Jew who told him that the granddaughter of Cleopatra was living clandestinely on the hills east of Caesarea. According to him, she had observed Avso in the streets of Caesarea and had expressed a burning desire to share her couch with him. The Jew's description of her lures and sexual skills were so vivid that Avso was soon beside himself with desire. There was one condition. Avso must submit to circumcision or Cleopatra's granddaughter would have nothing to do with him.

"And now," Silva said with a nod toward Decurion Avso, "if any of you have been wondering about the perplexed appearance of our friend Avso, be tolerant of him. The invitation to demonstrate his abilities is now a month old and still pending. But the Jew says that Cleopatra the Third, or whatever she calls herself, is not going to wait forever. So Decurion Avso is torn by indecision. Is he or is he not going to be the first Roman soldier in history to allow tampering with his standard, or should I order him to Britain to cool off? You must ask yourselves, can the proud Tenth Legion afford to keep such a naked freak on our rolls?"

There were howls of denial mixed with hearty laughter and demands for the smiling Avso to prove he had not already submitted to such a disgrace. They may not remember anything else I say, Silva thought, but at least those utterly fictitious stories might remind them that their general was not out of touch with the common soldier.

After they had quieted again, Silva told them that he was well aware of their longing for their homelands, ". . . but a soldier's home is his helmet. As long as the Jews continue to remain quiet, we'll have an easy life here. At least we're not freezing in Germany or Britain. And we know from the past few days' experience that we're not forgotten men. Our glorious Emperor is a soldier himself. He's your friend and mine, and as long as the men of the army are treated with the respect they so richly deserve, then the Roman standards will continue to rule the world."

And *that*, Silva thought, was enough grandiose rhetoric to last them for a long time. What his legionaries really wanted to hear was something he could not discuss, at least publicly. Their basic troubles lay in the long terms of service demanded by the Roman Army. Men were enlisted as young as eighteen and were likely to serve for more than twenty-five years. Thus the best of their years belonged to an organization that ignored their human instinct for marriage and family. The Roman Army frowned on all permanent sexual relations in fear that such entanglements might overly pacify the troops and interfere with the mobility of the Legions. Legal marriage was prohibited, but the army did look the other way at *focariae*, a consummation of male and female who were bound to each other in every way except by law. Since most Roman soldiers served on the frontiers, attachments to the local women were inevitable and the creation of families resulted. Then came the complication of inheritance—not that there was ever much for the common soldier to pass on. Since illegitimate children were barred from inheritance under Roman law, the father could only make them heirs by testamentary deposition, and they became liable to the five-percent inheritance tax.

Now, very suddenly, Silva realized that his long practiced pose as a unique comrade in arms with his legionaries carried many hypocritical elements. For sure, he had sometimes fought with them side by side, he had campaigned with them and shed his blood along with theirs. But once the battles were done, what happened? Flavius Silva, a knight of the Roman Empire, moved instantly into another style of living. His food and lodgings were the best available in the conquered territory.

If he wished, he could turn the mundane business of the Legion over to his staff and depart at least temporarily to Rome or any other place where conditions might be more agreeable. Even of greater importance was the army's attitude toward marriage for officers of high rank. It was tolerated if not encouraged—for what little good it did him now, he thought ruefully. There would never be another Livia. Her place in his heart remained like a complete dream, a magic intermission in his loneliness that had taught him to taste the acid of regret. It had left him with the lingering guilt that he had not cherished her enough.

Stumbling along toward the conclusion of his address, his thoughts became a jumble and turned unaccountably to the plight of the stalwart men whose upturned faces reflected their trust in him. I am their one visible god, he realized, the beginning and the end of their normal day and sometimes of their very lives. They ask for so little. They are tough and rough, but they are not brutes. I love the bastards. They will kill and be killed for me.

Unlike so many of the other Legions, the majority of the men in the Tenth had been born and raised on the Italian Peninsula and were Roman citizens. Most had seen all the flowing blood they cared to see, indeed so much after Masada that even the veterans were sick of it. The majority wanted to be sent home as fast as possible, but this could not be. They dreamed of a home, a woman to fill it, and a bit of land to call their own. Silva knew that if they were required to fight more battles, less than half of them would ever realize that dream.

Silva also knew that an army surrounded by peace could become a dangerous organization. The longer the peace lasted, the greater the discontent, with a consequent erosion of discipline. Worse, the manifestation of mischief to relieve boredom would become ever more attractive. The only way to ease the tension, and that method in itself might lead to mutiny, was to work them like the slaves they had supposedly conquered. Silva was mindful that some Jews, who were not themselves impressed into hard labor, were laughing their heads off watching soldiers of the Tenth working in the sun on the baking roads while they, the conquered, took their ease in the shade. The Jews could not understand that the manual labor, the road patrols, the rotation of watches, the gate guards, duty in the baths and granaries, and even the street-cleaning were part of a hidden battle against the evils of idleness that could infect large numbers of virile men. Nor, he thought, did the legionaries themselves understand why this life was so hard.

As far as Silva was concerned, if their home must be in their helmets, they deserved a wife or a consort to polish it—assuming they could find one. It was now becoming obvious that the Jews had developed a subtle revenge on those who had come to rule their land. Few Jewish women except the harlots and other female pariahs of Hebrew society would have anything to do with a Roman soldier, much less form a permanent union with him. Silva noticed a new restlessness had spread through the ranks, and he often wished that the Tenth was stationed in Britain or Gaul where the native population was more willing. He had spent many hours trying to find a solution. He had even considered the shipping out of women from Rome. But what kind of women would leave the Italian Peninsula for the uncertain life of a camp follower, bound to a man they had never seen? And if they arrived en masse, as they certainly must in any sailing craft, the chaos would become uncontrollable as the strongest took the best and the fighting among rivals spread through the ranks.

Silva resisted the impulse to tell them that there could be no solution to their natural urgings unless the Jews could be persuaded to soften their attitude. He knew there was no gain to be had in raising false hopes. He switched themes quickly to rescue his address from total collapse. This was a notable occasion and a suitable time for the announcement of honors within the Legion. The soldiers of the Tenth would now bear witness to certain promotions within the noncommissioned-officer ranks.

"Livilius Octavianus of the first cohort second century, and Domitius Celer of the fourth cohort first century, promoted to deputy centurions . . . Cassius Rufus to orderly sergeant . . . Fabius Faber of the second cohort to senior noncommissioned officer liaison with the general staff . . ."

While Silva was reading off the long list of promotions and awards, Julius Scribonia leaned across the arm of his chair and spoke softly to Camillus. "I would steal your attention one moment," he said in a voice just above a whisper.

Scribonia was at last convinced that his assignment to this expedition had been providential. It had been arranged by Domitian for reasons he had not troubled to explain. Since he could not possibly have foreseen that the reunion between his sister and Flavius Silva would be so enthusiastic, he must have had some apprehension about Silva and the donative itself.

There was certainly something brewing even if its exact nature was still obscure. Who was toying with whom . . . and why? Silva was known as a favorite of Titus as well as a popular soldier within the Legions. And it was also known that Domitillia was particularly fond of Titus. All of which did not bode well for Domitian.

Scribonia allowed his imagination to blossom for a moment. What if this entire donative expedition was merely a screen to conceal a program of power development, the details to be carried back to Rome by none other than Titus' sister? Now, before it was too late, perhaps he should look behind the pageantry and try to discover what certain people had in mind for the future. Even a little knowledge, Scribonia thought, could sometimes become a priceless jewel on the lips of the possessor.

"There is a small favor I would ask of you," he said to Camillus, who turned his handsome head and favored Scribonia with one of his frigid smiles.

"Of course, dear Scribonia," he said. "If what you say can't wait, then I should hear it. Perhaps when we dine . . . ?"

Scribonia leaned further toward him. "No. Now is the time. In fact, after we have eaten I must ask you to be lax in your duty."

"I'm afraid I don't understand."

"It is a matter of loyalty to our glorious Emperor."

"I'm even further mystified. No one has ever questioned my loyalty."

"Of course not. We of the *frumentarii* are aware of your record. Still, there are others . . . and one must keep a careful eye on them."

Camillus wrinkled his heavy brow and pursed his lips, a habitual gesture designed to impress any viewer with his concentration on the subject at hand. "Of course," he said, then added, "one must always be alert."

"Then we are in agreement," Scribonia said. He glanced at Silva, who was still calling off names. "I've reason to believe that an unhealthy situation exists or is about to exist, and I must solicit your aid in stopping it. You'll appreciate that anything I suggest is in the utmost confidence."

"Of course."

"Be so good as to look straight ahead at the troops, dear Camillus. It would be unwise for us to appear in deep conversation during this ceremony. Listen carefully and you will soon understand why."

Camillus resumed his vacant staring at the troops and nodded his head.

Scribonia said, "I know it is your duty to keep Domitillia under your constant protection, but after we have dined tonight, I must ask you to find some need to absent yourself for some time . . . long enough for your charge to relax in her new sense of being unguarded. If I am correct in my suspicions, she will soon be escorted away from our company by a very important individual. I must ask you to ignore their departure and can assure you that no harm will come to your charge . . . although the seed of great harm to the Empire may be sown. It is my duty to see that this poisonous flower does not thrive. If you agree to proceed as I have requested, please place your right hand on your knee. "

Scribonia watched carefully and saw Camillus wrinkle his brow again. After an apparent inner struggle, he slid his right hand down to his knee. Scribonia smiled and turned to give Silva his fixed attention.

That evening, soon after the planet Jupiter rose above the eastern hills, Rufus Pedanius pushed at the wart on the side of his nose and exclaimed that even if all this could not be classified as a feast, it was certainly a very charming picnic that their host had arranged to celebrate their departure from Judea. Silva had selected a small ravine that gashed the landscape and fell down to the sea not far from his house. There Domitillia's party had assembled with the officers of the Tenth Legion. Since there were not enough couches in all of Judea to dine in the customary Roman style, the guests were required to sit on the rocks or the ground while they ate off plates commandeered from residents of Caesarea. For officers of the Legion the unique outdoor gathering was reminiscent of being on campaign, although it was much more luxurious with burning torches everywhere to illuminate the scene, and there was far more food and wine than they had ever known during actual service. Stacks of Mediterranean mullet, cooked in bay leaves and seasoned with thyme, and layers of octopi cooked in oil were served. There were not enough stuffed doves to go around, but a huge supply of sweet red oranges made up for the lack of birds. Chunk-style biscuits had been baked by a handful of Jewish cooks who had survived the war and had been assigned to the occasion. The guests munched on small hills of goat cheese, shrimp nestled in peppers, olives, and dates. Those who had been in Judea since the surrender had not seen such plenty for a very long time, and they were quick to thank Silva for his generosity.

"Just don't become accustomed to it," he warned his officers. "And remember, it was not I but the daughter of our commander in chief who inspired these pleasures."

As a consequence of such an unusual repast the guests remained relatively mobile, moving back and forth from wherever they might be to the supply tables for delicacies that particularly struck their fancies. They also spent some of their time chasing down the curiously inept Jewish slaves for more wine. They were outspoken in their opinion that the gentiles of Caesarea had erred in not slaughtering all the Jews, because the buggers would never learn how to serve civilized people.

The enclaves of both parties found entertainment and pleasure in the exchange of thoughts, memories, and experiences between those recently arrived from Rome and those who had been away for so long with the Legion. Even the Praetorians unbent enough to express their admiration for the Tenth's extensive participation in the conquest of Judea.

Rufus Pedanius was in his glory with batches of young officers gathering around his plate, while he chewed happily and expounded on his hard work in the Senate. He pressed ever more frequently at his nose wart as if it were a button designed to activate his mouth. He insisted that he was pleased with the growing number of freedmen who were engaging in Roman commerce all over the homeland, but he confessed that he was worried about their increasing tendency to take over jobs in the Roman bureaucracy. "In truth," he said after a moment of sucking the taste of the Mediterranean sea from his fingers, "I'm not concerned about much of anything except the welfare of the *proletarii*. They offer nothing to the state but their children, yet they all must be taken care of somehow." He chuckled again and peeled the shell off another shrimp. "Mark you, young sirs, it is the newly rich who are the least likely to share their wealth with the class they've so recently abandoned. There are many rascals among these new businessmen, and I would not be altogether surprised if they eventually brought Rome down around our merry heads." He was joined in his boisterous laughter by most of the officers around him, for the notion that Rome might some day falter was so absurd there was nothing to do but find amusement in the prospect.

Gallus Septicius was also very popular with the military guests; the older officers were particularly interested in his classical erudition, and his brief poetic recitations held them spellbound. He quoted Propertius: "Ghosts do exist. Death does not finish everything . . . the pale phantom lives to escape the pyre . . ."; and then Horace: "Oh place me where the solar beam has scorched all vendure vernal, or on the polar verge extreme."

Sometimes as he held his audience enchanted, Septicius drifted into elegant Greek. Those officers who failed to understand him were obliged to pretend they did until he pointed a bony finger at one and challenged him to repeat what he had just said. There followed much good-natured laughter as might be reflected in the classroom of a favorite tutor, and to their unanimous delight Septicius joined in their joshing of the officer caught in bilingual pretense. Later he astounded them with the news that Vespasian intended to grant the petition of Johanan ben Zakkai the Jew to start a school of Judaism in Jabneh. While none of the officers spoke against the proposal, their reaction was anything but enthusiastic. One, a bold fellow from Tarentum, inquired if such a move might not inspire the Jews to new rebellions. He was instantly reminded that the Emperor was his commander in chief and knew what he was doing.

Julius Scribonia also came in for his share of attention. He had a way of closing his eyes for long periods as he spoke, then blinking rapidly before a turn of phrase. The total effect on his listeners was such that the legionary officers who had been away from Rome so long became convinced that whatever he would say next must be profound. He became positively jolly as he spoke of the new construction projects in progress at home. He offered a vivid description of the enormous amphitheater Vespasian had begun and told how he intended to celebrate its opening with a solid month of games and gladitorial exhibitions.

Since Egnatius Camillus was a Praetorian and therefore considered in quite a different category than the other officers, and because his constant attendance upon Domitillia somewhat isolated him from the other guests, he was left to his own devices. He spent most of his time sitting on a rock behind the little stretch of sand where Silva and Domitillia had established a relatively private dining area. Camillus ate tremendous portions of everything available, while his vacant stare remained fixed on some invisible object in the twilight sea. Because of the Praetorians' relatively gaudy uniforms, soft duty, and much higher pay, relations between members of the Praetorian Guard and legionaries had never been warm. A more sensitive man might have felt like an outcast, but Camillus apparently had more on his mind than he cared to share with anyone.

When it grew dark and only torches illuminated the ravine, Camillus belched heavily, stood up, and stretched his magnificent body toward the stars. He sniffed at the night sky as a huge hunting dog might follow the scent of some nocturnal creature. He left the rock, and walked slowly upward toward the narrow entrance of the ravine.

Julius Scribonia, who had situated himself some distance from the others, watched Camillus' departure until he vanished. He then took his time in transferring his attention to Silva and Domitillia. He had not long to wait. He smacked his lips in satisfaction as he saw them rise and stroll side by side through the vociferous company, pausing now and then for brief conversational exchanges as if they had no real destination, and then moving on to the next group. They lingered momentarily at the supply table where they chose a handful of cherries, then moved casually down the ravine toward the sea.

Scribonia had been talking with a pair of officers about the need to police the crowds of foreigners who had descended upon Rome in the hope of sharing the wealth. "Barbarians most of them," he sneered. "The majority are lousy with lice and every other form of vermin. They are undoubtedly the cause of our last plague . . ." Suddenly he excused himself on the need for urination. "Forgive me, if not my bladder," he said as he turned down the ravine toward the sea.

Holding hands, intertwining their fingers in slow sensuous movements, caressing for a moment, and then squeezing their palms together in gentle signals of affection, Silva and Domitillia strolled along the beach. Their way was vaguely illuminated by the flickering light from the imposing watchtower that stood at the end of the harbor mole. From their vantage on the beach they could distinguish the three huge statues and the pillars on the left of the entrance. Silva spoke softly because the sea was so calm it seemed appropriate to keep the tone and match the subtle hint of the wavelets. "It's hard to believe," he said, "that Herod built Caesarea. He must have been an interesting man."

"The same Herod you told me built a palace on Masada?"

"The same. The Jews tell me that he was trying to show Augustus Caesar they could build anything here, which is how the place got the name. And I suppose Herod was right. Certainly the temple he built to old Augustus must be admired. The aqueduct is the product of very superior engineering and the drainage system is operated by what little tidal power there is. All very clever and farsighted. One should never discount the resourcefulness of the Jews."

"Do you hate them?"

"No. I've been obliged to kill many of them in the line of duty, but usually with regret . . . not because they were Jews, mind you, but because I take no satisfaction in eliminating brains and talent. I was sick after Masada, as sick of myself as I was of the Jews, and I'm not sure I shall ever recover."

"Would you want to stay here?" Domitillia asked. She halted and looked up at the brilliant stars. She raised his hand slowly to her lips, then lowered it again. "You didn't answer my question."

"I was thinking . . . wondering if perhaps I really should go to Africa. There's so much to do here . . . and my Legion is here."

"There's much to do everywhere in the Empire. We desperately need men like you to make certain the African Legions are for Titus."

"None of them are like the Tenth."

"I understand. But if Titus ordered you to another post, would it make you unhappy?"

"No. Your brother is my friend. Whatever he might want me to do when he becomes Emperor would be my pleasure."

"I've sent a message to my father suggesting you spend some time in Rome."

A long silence followed. "Why did you do that?" Silva asked finally.

"Are you angry with me?"

"No. I'm just wondering if you're running the army."

"If you're near, then you can be of great help when the time comes. Don't worry. When we meet in Rome I'll pretend I hardly know you."

"I'm not sure I can be that close to you and behave myself. It's difficult enough right here."

Studying her face in the faint light, he realized how utterly he had given himself to her beauty. It made little difference if he lost his kingdom here in Judea; some day he would lose it, anyway. Silva rubbed at his bad eye and smiled. He said, "I've never quite trusted those poets who sing their silly love songs, but I'm beginning to wonder if there's not some wisdom in them. They sing of difficult things, but they usually win in the end, and I like that. There have been two women in my life . . ."

"Tell me about them."

"No. They're ghosts now and are entitled to their privacy. Still, when I'm very lonely, as I have been out here, I sometimes call on them to show themselves and the surprising result is that they do. Of course, I could have had too much wine . . ."

"Can you touch them?" She took his hands and held them gently.

"Sometimes it seemed almost possible."

"Have you talked to them?"

"No . . . but not because I had any feeling I couldn't. I'm a coward and they might answer back, which would convince me I've gone mad." He paused, then added, "You're laughing at me?"

"No. But you don't talk like a soldier. I admire a man who honors past loves. It makes me believe he would value my love. I have need of such a man in my life."

"What about your husband?"

"I need a man I can respect. I'm not a child any longer, Flavius. I don't want to be patronized and harmonized by a man who considers me as an occasionally interesting trinket in his warehouse of playthings. I'm a full-grown woman now and I'm longing to give my passions to a man who considers me more than his handy slave. I don't care if he's still in love with a hundred ghosts, as long as he returns my devotion with the same energy . . ."

She hesitated, then said very softly, "I wonder, Flavius, . . . if you're not that man."

Suddenly he bent to kiss Domitillia and she opened her lips to him. "I want you," she said simply.

He dropped his hands slowly downward from her face until he found her breasts. Their mouths remained locked until, gasping, they parted momentarily. Being so familiar with each other by now enhanced their pleasure. He was thrilled again by her touch and silken smoothness. She uttered a laughing growl. Silva pressed hard against her, and Domitillia moaned softly with her pleasure. Even the slightest movement multiplied their passion.

Still holding each other tightly, they sank to their knees in the cool sand. Finally, he lowered her until she lay outstretched, and he eased himself down between her legs. He entered her and they echoed each other's gasps of excitement. "My love!" she whispered.

At last Silva fell away from her and they lay side by side looking up at the stars. "I am yours, beloved General," she said breathlessly. "I'm yours like no woman has ever been before. For me no one else in this world really exists except you. I hope you'll remind yourself of that after we sail away . . . and assure yourself that it's not just a pretty phrase."

"I would like to erect a single column on this beach," he said.

"You just did." She laughed.

He joined her in laughing and said that he had always loved

her naughty humor. "Since there are no trees to carve our initials in, I'd build a real column right here. The dedication would read, 'To D.V. and F.S., who waited too many years—'"

"What a charming idea!" The voice came to them out of the darkness, then Scribonia appeared. "I must say," he went on, "that I could hardly have expected our host to provide such unique entertainment as the sight of two such handsome people rutting in the sand."

Silva leapt to his feet and ran to Scribonia. He reached out with both hands and grabbed him by the neck. "You prying bastard!" He pressed his thumbs hard against his carotid arteries to cut off the flow of blood to his head. Scribonia dropped to his knees and Silva shook him violently. His every movement was the coordinated action of a professional warrior.

Domitillia called out to him, "Please stop! You're killing him!"

Scribonia's eyes were closing and his head waggled ominously. His choked words made no sense.

"This bastard will never see anything again!" Silva grunted.

"Let him go! Please!"

Silva relaxed his grip momentarily and threw Scribonia to the sand. He kicked him in the head, then put his foot on his neck. "There's no reason why this miserable bastard should live!" Silva bent down and seized Scribonia by the ears. He gave his head a violent twist and felt all resistance leave his body. Silva was sure he was dead.

He arose slowly, still panting for breath. He grabbed Scribonia's feet and dragged him into the water. He turned him over until he was face down and gave him a final kick. Then he hurried back to Domitillia and took her in his arms.

"We'll have to get away from here. If I know that man, he'll have arranged to be seen by others before he came to us."

He led her back up the ravine at a fast walk. "Is he dead?" she asked.

"Yes."

"I never realized how fierce you are."

"I've been a soldier a long time."

Domitillia remained silent as they climbed back toward the flickering torches. When they emerged into the light she said,

"Let's hold up a moment. I have to catch my breath. I have to think."

Silva took her in his arms and held her tightly. "My heart won't stop pounding," she whispered.

"Try to appear as if nothing has happened. The others will be watching you."

"How can I help myself? I can't keep my hands from trembling. Murder and adultery on the same evening? I'm not made of stone. I think the stars are not pleased."

"I did what had to be done."

Domitillia made a deliberate effort to calm her breathing. She touched at her hair, trying to make sure it was in place, and brushed at the sand on her gown. "I wish I had a mirror," she said. "No . . . no, I don't. I might see something new and ugly."

Silva said, "Just remember that I love you. Sooner or later someone was bound to kill Scribonia. There would be no future for us if he lived."

"But how are we going to explain—?"

"If anyone asks about him, say that he kept complaining about his health. Maybe he had a bad liver. No one will really care what he died of."

"There we go. We have to start lying and there will be no end to it. Flavius . . . dear Flavius, I'm not sure I can carry this off. What will happen tomorrow when we are supposed to sail? How can I explain his absence?"

"It won't be necessary. When you've rejoined the others, I'll go back to the beach. I'll arrange for his body to be found in his room at dawn. He simply died during the night. We can bury him here with full honors . . . or you can take him back to Rome."

"I've always been such a poor liar."

"Try to remember that Scribonia was a master at it and would have rejoiced to see us both crucified. He didn't know the meaning of pity, so spare your tears."

After a time Domitillia regained her composure and said that she was ready to face the others. "I will think only that we'll be together again soon . . ." She attempted a smile. "In Rome," she added.

They held each other and kissed their farewells. Then she turned away from him. He watched her make her way up the ravine until he saw her silhouetted against the torches. The sound of many voices greeting her drifted down to him as he made his way back to the beach. There was so much to be done now and he must do it by himself. Not even Geminus must know what really happened to Julius Scribonia.

When Silva reached the beach he turned to his left as he had done with Domitillia. He walked rapidly toward the beacon fire in the harbor tower. When he came to the place he had first embraced her, he halted and studied the wavelets. Here, yes . . . right here. This was the exact location.

He squatted, the better to see along the fringe of wavelets licking at the shore. With the light from the tower in the distance, anything along the water should be outlined clearly. But he observed nothing except the flat, dark water.

He straightened and walked away from the water. He retraced his steps twice, exploring the sand until he found the area he knew would confirm his location. Yes, the sand had been disturbed here. Here they had been together beneath the stars.

He decided he had made a mistake and had walked too far toward the harbor the first time. Still, Scribonia's body had to be in a direct line toward the dark sea. He walked hesitantly toward the water, then halted. Here in the sand were the marks of their shod struggle—not much fight in the man, really. The bastard had been like a limp goose. But where was he?

Counting, he walked fifty paces to the left. He became increasingly uncomfortable and knew an old churning in his intestines that he had not felt for years. Could Scribonia's body have floated out to sea? He considered it impossible in so short a time. He had left his head in the water, but most of his body had been on the beach, which was quite flat. He tried to convince himself that it was unreasonable to suppose the body had slid into the sea. The effect of the puny Mediterranean tide in such a short time was negligible—and yet the body was gone.

He must make cautious inquiries of the local fishermen. Was there some kind of strong undersea current along here?

He walked rapidly back toward the mouth of the ravine, then retraced his steps from the beginning. Everywhere he searched the starlight was sufficient to reveal his own footprints in the sand. But there was no Scribonia.

Gradually, he began to question whether he had actually killed Scribonia. Had he failed to break his neck? His certainty wavered as he tried to reassure himself. The body must have rolled over in some postmortal spasm and drifted away. By the gods, the man was like a snake, his parts twisting after death.

At last, he started back toward the ravine. He walked slowly although he knew he had been absent much longer than he should. Domitillia had been right—now he would have to invent a series of excuses that must match whatever she had said.

He was encouraged as he climbed the ravine and the sounds of the party became louder. Obviously, they were having a good time. Perhaps they had not even noticed his absence. Or Scribonia's?

When he came to the edge of the torchlight, Silva watched his guests carefully for a moment. Domitillia was just leaving with Camillus at her side. The others were bidding her good night with as much dignity as the wine in them would allow.

Silva was relieved to see that Scribonia was not among those still present. Of course not, he thought; Scribonia had drifted out to sea.

Without doubt.

SIX

THE EMPEROR VESPASIAN, Pontificus Maximus, four times consul, stood on the parapet of the Capitoline Hill and looked down upon the Circus Maximus. The sun had not yet risen although the sky was aglow with its promise as he sought to bring order to his thoughts. Perhaps, he reasoned, I am too small a man for the job . . . perhaps any man is too small. For from the very ground upon which he stood so strangely uncertain of himself all manner of edicts, plans, proposals, condemnations, and mandates flowed like a flooding river. This was the center of the world. It was said that fifty million, perhaps even sixty million or more people, were utterly dependent upon the will of Rome.

Vespasian found the numbers so incomprehensible that he sought refuge in trying to visualize the geographical territories rather than the masses occupying them. How unbearably impertinent, he thought, to suppose one man could digest such overwhelming facts and still avoid a sense of confusion. One should husband the energies of the mind rather than scatter judgments like seeds of grain thrown in every direction. Rome was the mother of the earth and therefore must be protected against her enemies within as well as against those who would cheer her downfall. A wise soldier maintained his vigilance even after victory was at hand and avoided celebration until the last foe felt the sword. Hence parsimony and conservatism must now be the rule; the loose squandering of the national treasury must be permanently halted. That was the trouble with trying to include the Senate in any governmental decisions. It was all very well to include that bunch of rebels in minor affairs, but how could any reasonable man expect several hundred individuals, especially senators who were mostly men of considerable wealth and determination, to agree on anything? While they argued, time laid a flat hand on results.

Vespasian saw the senators now in his mind's eye, exhorting each other in their special tunics with an oblong stripe of purple sewn to the forepart. The stripe was particularly broad to distinguish the wearer from mere Equites, who wore a narrower one.

Of course, he thought, there were some valuable moments to be enjoyed during the meetings of so many intelligent Romans, but there were also whole days of utter nonsense delivered by windbags of incredible endurance. Why wouldn't they understand that good government, particularly when applied to colonies, was as little government as possible?

The secret, he decided, was to urge the natives of every land, even the Jews, to go their own way—as long as they paid tribute to Rome. The proof, he thought, was in the soothing effect of time. After so many years and so much shedding of blood, the vast majority of the colonists liked and respected Roman law because they knew it to be reasonable, and they knew the law would be backed by overwhelming force if necessary. *Jus* and *Lex*. Those who were still inclined to defy the law also knew that the Roman Army was unforgiving of the slightest hint of rebellion. The historic result was peace and sometimes even gratitude for the keepers of the peace. Even now, when assuredly his own last battle had been fought, he marveled at the simplicity of the theory. It was a method for the mind to chew on and savor on such a morning as this. The view of the city spread out before him was tangible evidence that Rome was almighty; confidence in one's strength, he thought, led to tolerance at a profit.

The problems here at home were more complex than those abroad, and certainly the Senate was often at the root of the trouble. Once the magistrate had offered a sacrifice to that god whose temple had been chosen as the most appropriate meeting place for the day, the senators seemed inspired by the smell of frankincense—and then the mischief began.

Vespasian blinked at the milky sun and wished he would

stop hurting. The hurt is all through my bones, he thought, and every dawn it becomes worse. Maldopolis and Vocula, the two Greek doctors imported to attend upon his ailment, were a pair of fools. They typified the snobbery of all Athenians toward all Romans; they were convinced that because certain similarities were evident in the two cultures that *they* were the originators of all science and art. Poof! The Greeks were the originators of buggery and a few other contributions of dubious value.

Yes, he thought, some Greeks were passable artists and even capable doctors, but did that give them license to praise their dusty and decaying Athens as the cultural center of the universe? They should realize that they were essentially just another Roman colony—and at outrageous cost to the imperial treasury. As for their medical recommendations, how dare they suggest that an application of mercury poured into an open vein would bring a cure? More likely, a quick end to the present Emperor through loss of his fast-thinning blood! Vespasian allowed himself a wry smile. There were knives enough anxious to open the veins of a Flavian without giving the Greeks a free hand.

He sighed. How could he be so fatigued at the commencement of what was scheduled to be a busy day? A reunion with Domitillia was scheduled for the second hour. She had returned via Ostia in the middle of last night and was eager, thanks be to the gods, to see her father and tell of Judea. The mere thought of Domitillia pleased him. It was such good fortune to sire a daughter so full of spice. Indeed, if she did have an infatuation for Silva, it would soon pass and no harm would be done if no one else knew about it. Silva was not the sort to tarnish the brilliance of his sword with petty scandal. Petty? If the daughter of the Emperor was involved, nothing could be regarded as insignificant.

He turned away from the view and walked slowly back toward his simple quarters—kept simple amid the splendor of the palace because he wanted to be known as a man of the people and not some Tiberian-like tyrant who removed himself from the human race. Remember, he reminded himself, it is the Roman people who rule the Senate.

Really? Who were these vicarious masters but an odd-lot collection of sheep who would follow any leader who promised to increase their purses? The people rarely if ever knew what was good for them, and if the senators' unending motions were a true reflection of the people, then chaos, not reason, would rule the land. It often seemed as if the senators could speak as long as they liked—the most loquacious mouths always pleading for yet another filling of the water clock, another and then another—until nightfall ended the session.

Once in a while, common sense prevailed and a particularly obnoxious clown would be silenced by the noise and shoutings of his fellow senators. Remember the uproar against Catiline when he used abusive language against Cicero? Even the deified Julius Caesar had his problems with the Senate. Once when Cato tried to force the abandonment of a decree by wasting all day with his speech, Caesar, who was then a consul, ordered him to be taken away to prison. The whole house arose to follow Cato, a situation so embarrassing to Caesar that he was obliged to recall his order.

All long before my time, he thought grumpily; but he hoped the Senate would see fit to formally approve of Domitillia's mission in Judea. Perhaps they would pass a decree, *Eos recte atque ordine Videri fecisse.* And while they were at it, they might have the wisdom to praise the generosity and foresight of one Flavius Vespasian.

The Emperor paused momentarily for a final survey of the city. He could see a ribbon of morning fog still clinging to the River Tiber. He could see the Mons Arentinus, where both Titus and Domitillia had houses; the new road that joined the Via Appia, and one of the southern gates in the city wall. From where he stood the Forum was obscured by structures surrounding the palace, but much of the city was visible. A heavy layer of smoke from the morning cooking fires caused the tops of the hills to appear as if suspended in midair, yet he could make out the swarms of people already crowding the narrow streets. Like himself, he mused, those were the early risers. The majority of Romans were not quick to greet the day; when at last they set about their business, it would be almost time for their lengthy midday meal. Spicy foods—none of which his stomach could tolerate—were the fashion now, and it distressed him to think that while the profit in essential grains was meager, the spice market was booming as never before. Those who dealt in those commodities, nearly all imported from the East and Africa, were reaping a fortune.

The smoke, he thought, softened the reality of the city where too many people were crowded into countless warrens of apartments, each leaning against the other for support, a jingle-jangle of construction hastily assembled after the great fire. Since then, plague had twice swept through the population and no one knew how many had perished. Yet the actual numbers of people who flocked to Rome were increasing at an alarming rate, and native-born Roman citizens were fast becoming the minority.

"So be it," he sighed. Rome would survive even though so many immigrants from the east had brought their disregard of time along with the rest of their baggage, and their casual attitude had affected every Roman citizen. Was there anything more irritating, he thought, than a tardy supplicant? They should know that the person empowered to grant their wishes could only believe that they didn't very much want what they asked for.

Long ago the Romans had divided their day into two parts, *ante meridiem* and *post meridiem*, according to the midday passing of the sun through the zenith. Then they had divided the two parts again, making *mane, ante meridiem, de meridie,* and *suprema* to mark the arrival of evening.

Damn the idiots! Since the influence of the Orientals had become so prevalent, no one in Rome was ever on time. It was considered rude, even impolite, to appear for an appointment at a stated hour. Promptness was considered a fault and not a virtue.

Vespasian warned himself against intolerance and tried to smile as he remembered that of all the Romans he knew the one with the least care for time was his daughter. Indeed, if Domitillia promised a meeting it might be fulfilled the same day . . . and then it might not. Likewise, his son, Domitian, was so careless of his hours that he often failed to appear at all. He was a problem, that son, a porcupine of a young man who lived by his own rules. May the gods help the Roman people if he ever came to the throne.

But thanks be to the gods for Titus, he thought. Ask any Roman, who was the most popular young man in the city? Titus. Ask any soldier who they cared for. Titus. Ask any colonist, with the exception of the Jews, to identify the most trusted Roman. Titus. The gods had smiled upon the Flavian family from the day Titus was born. And he was almost always on time.

At two hours by the huge water clock in the atrium, Egnatius Camillus led ten of his Praetorian Guards to the reception chamber where Vespasian would be awaiting his daughter. Because of her relatively diminutive size, Domitillia was obliged to walk very quickly to keep pace with her escort. Despite the clinging chill of the morning, she wore a gown especially chosen for the occasion. It was fashioned of a material rarely seen in Rome and had been smuggled at great expense from Dura in Mesopotamia. Some enterprising Levantine had brought it from the other side of the world. The filmy material was said to be made by worms, and its incredible smoothness and viscosity clearly outlined every feature of her body.

Domitillia had pondered on the matter of her dress ever since leaving Judea. She wished the gown she had chosen had been available for the eyes of Flavius Silva. It was impossible to predict what her father might like, she had decided, but one aspect of his nature was certain. Despite his age, he liked his women well dressed and appealing to the eye. She thought it reasonable to suppose the same enjoyment would apply to his daughter.

As for her husband, Marcus Clemens, the man had not appeared to greet her on arrival at Ostia. Thanks be to the gods, or to whoever engineered his absence! A message had been left for her advising that he had been obliged to go stag hunting with Domitian near Amiternum. Of course, what Domitian wanted, Marcus conceded—including, she supposed, a battery of harlots and enough young boys to content them for the length of their stay. Eventually, Marcus would return, dragging his soft and pouchy carcass to the nearest couch and vomiting in the ferns of the peristyle. Just as he had done the last time and as he had repeated with astonishing regularity every time he had been keeping company with Domitian.

Even at this important moment the thought of her husband's behavior made her vaguely unhappy, although it was not because he might have been naughty. There was no place in her heart for bitterness or the censure of others; indeed, she was hardly in a position to criticize anyone. But it did seem a shame that Domitian and Marcus, two young men so richly endowed with the good things in life, would seem so determined to destroy themselves. How different they were from a man like Flavius Silva, who had lived a hard life and appreciated the most simple pleasures. There had been that Christian, Paul, who had warned against the vicious effect of possessions; but then he was a mystic, at least half crazy, and had got what he deserved.

Her father was standing before a huge mosaic that had recently been completed. It depicted the city of Rome geographically and the principal endeavors of the people in each sector. A fringe of gods surrounded the scene, and Domitillia wondered if she should tell her father that the total effect rather diminished him. One should always be careful about the presentation of oneself, she thought. A king should always arrange to appear as unquestionably a king, and humility had no place near a throne.

He came toward her, smiling and holding out his hands. She was shocked at the ravages his disease had inflicted upon him in so short a time. The famous chin was a trifle slack, and his powerful neck, a feature he had passed on to both Titus and Domitian (but not to his daughter, thanks be), seemed ever so much thinner, as did the whole of his frame. His eyes were still alert and questioning, but they were pouched in wrinkles of gray flesh. There was a forlorn stoop to his posture. She was horrified to see that he seemed to be having trouble keeping his head steady. "My beloved Papa!" she cried, trying to ignore all she had seen.

He took her in his arms, held her briefly, then with a flick of his hand sent Camillus and his Praetorians away.

"Welcome home," he said as he led her to the pair of couches he employed for his most intimate meetings. "You're on time," he said, chuckling, "or am I dreaming?"

They laughed together and she said that her eagerness to see him had almost caused her to be ahead of time.

He reached for her gown and fingered it thoughtfully.

"What's this?"

"Silk. Do you find it tantalizing?"

"Oh, yes. I've heard of it. I've also heard of the cost."

"Papa, when are you going to learn that money isn't everything?"

"The same day you become aware that there is never enough of it."

Again they laughed and Vespasian said that the Jewish sun had given new color to her cheeks and that she was without doubt more beautiful than any woman in the Empire. "Marcus Clemens is a very lucky man," he added in a tentative tone. "I assume he is pleased to have you back?"

"Perhaps."

"What do you mean by that?"

"Marcus is away with Domitian. Hunting, I'm told."

"Ah?" A long silence followed and Domitillia saw that her father was preoccupied. His disease is tormenting him, she thought; to ease through these first moments together she should urge him to speak of his health. She told him that to her eyes, which were much keener than his own, he was the handsomest man in the world. "You now have the mature look . . . the dignity of a true king, the sort of man ladies find irresistible. But I'm worried about you. You do look tired."

Vespasian pursed his lips and pulled at his knobby nose. It was no wonder, she thought, that artists loved to sculpt her father; all of his features were in harmony with each other despite their individual prominence. He needs another Caenis, she thought—that woman who had been his mistress for so many years. Her recent death had been like a part of her father dying. Only Domitian had refused to recognize Caenis' beneficial effect upon her father, but then his attention had always been on himself anyway.

"I just look tired," Vespasian said. "As this face of mine has been pickled by the wind and sun for nearly seventy years, you can't expect to see a ripe fruit. Rather, you're looking at an old melon that has been kicked around the marketplace and should be thrown out with the garbage."

"Don't talk that way, Papa. All Romans revere you."

"We also revere gods who have been long dead. And we create legends about them." He looked away from her and studied the black marble statue of a young Egyptian woman, standing near the entrance to the atrium. "The more I look at that woman, the more she excites me," he said slowly. "Tiberius Alexander sent her to me from Egypt. Where he stole it

I don't know, but it does seem to fit well with the reconstruction I've done to this place. Maybe Alexander thought that a stone statue was all I could enjoy at this time of my life. Strange, how much I've been thinking about Alexander these days . . ."

As his voice drifted away Domitillia thought that this was far from the kind of reception she had expected. So far not one question about Judea or the donative—and, praise the gods, no hint of his feelings about her relationship with Flavius Silva.

She waited for his attention to return to her, but he continued to stare at the statue as if he lusted for the Egyptian woman, and yet the expression in his eyes was of something much more distant. "Did I ever tell you," he began, "the truth about how I happen to be occupying this palace?"

"I only know that you've given too much of yourself to remodeling it after the fire . . . not to mention the whole city. If it weren't for you, Rome would still be in a shambles."

"I was not referring to that kind of reconstruction. Did I ever tell you the truth about how I came to be Emperor? There's a twist on the tale that the Legions spontaneously decided I was the man for the job. Anyone who would stop to think how far apart the Legions were scattered would know that was a fabrication, but then few people interrupt their daily schedule with thinking. As a consequence, there you are one day . . . the Emperor . . . Are you listening?"

His eyes still avoided her and she thought it was as if he had suddenly left the room. His body was still sitting on the couch, but his mind . . . ?

"When Nero had the good sense to kill himself, we all knew there would be a lot of trouble. The time and the situation were ripe for opportunists, and three of them jumped at the chance—Galba, Otho, and finally Vitellius. They were fools who would have ruined the Empire. But then I was not so altogether different. Something had to be done about our civil wars. Your uncle, Sabinus, was prefect of the city at the time, and he kept me posted on events . . . Mucianus was governor of Syria and the two of us decided it was time for us to come to the rescue. Mucianus didn't care about the throne for himself. He said it was too restrictive on his private life. Now that he's dead, I can tell you that he would rather have been a woman than a man, and he behaved accordingly. But it was Tiberius Julius Alexander who really set the stage; did you know he is a Jew?"

Domitillia wondered if she should start her report by telling her father that although the local gentiles had killed most of the Jews in Caesarea, others were now arriving and the effect on commerce and, of course, taxes would be very beneficial to Rome. Yet he seemed unready to listen, or had he completely forgotten sending her on an important mission? Was this history lesson more important than the attitude and morale of the Tenth Legion and the problems of Judea—as related by that priceless Roman, Flavius Silva?

"It was Alexander who persuaded the Egyptian garrison to swear allegiance to me. To this day I marvel at how he did it . . . Mucianus came along with twenty thousand of his troops from Syria, and from then on I knew Vitellius could never keep the throne. Just to make sure, I moved directly to Egypt and took over the grain supply. It seemed to me that if I had to, I could choke off the grain for Rome, and maybe Vitellius would give up without a fight. It didn't work out quite that way . . . things seldom do . . ."

Domitillia heard a new quaver in his usually strong voice, and he became nearly inaudible as his words seemed to drift across the room.

He rubbed at his brow and at last looked into her eyes again. "Forgive me, Daughter," he said. "I wander. As all old men I dwell too much in the past. Now tell me about Judea."

"The trip was a success. I believe all who went with me all agree to that. But have you been told about Julius Scribonia?"

"Ah, yes . . . Scribonia was his name. I remember feeling poorly about the time you left and Titus was very busy. I asked Domitian to appoint someone to keep his eye on things. It seems he chose well since the fellow is one of the *frumentarii*. I'm not particularly fond of their ilk, but you just don't send off that much money without some kind of insurance. Septicius and the others are fine gentlemen. . . . It's just that I've learned I trust people more if they are being watched by someone I don't trust."

"He died."

"Ah?"

She thought her father seemed visibly shocked. Perhaps

there might have been a better way to make such an announcement. In her desire to have it over with, she had been too hasty. Now it seemed best to steer away from the subject as quickly as possible. She saw him pull at the knob of his nose again, and she hoped he had already forgotten what she had said.

"I thought Scribonia was a relatively young man. Did a Jewish disease strike him?"

"I don't think so . . ." There it was, an equivocation if not quite a full-bred lie. It occurred to her that this was the first time in her life she had found it expedient to deceive her father.

"He died a natural death?"

"Yes . . . I'm quite sure."

She thought unhappily that she was becoming very clever with her phraseology—reporting a fact as if she had been witness to a fact. Greetings to a neophyte liar.

"You brought his body back with you?"

"No."

"What was done with it . . . rather, with him?"

"I . . . I don't know. I never realized how important he was to you."

"He was not important to me, but he was a Roman of some standing and I will be asked what happened to him. I suppose I can depend on your friend Silva to be sure that he was buried with the proper honors?"

"We left before there could be a funeral. My captain said we had to sail that morning because of the wind. I'm sure that Flavius did what was necessary. He's a very good man for you, Papa." That at least was a truth.

"So you suggested in your letter." He paused a moment and looked at her steadily. "But is he good for you?"

She could feel her heart take up a faster beat. If she answered, she must dodge and twist when she so longed to be straightforward.

Vespasian continued to seek her eyes as he said, "I'm having trouble understanding you younger people . . . which, considering the situation, may be quite reasonable. What kind of a family are we becoming? Your brother Domitian takes too much wine. Your brother Titus brings his Jewish mistress here to Rome and makes no attempt to conceal their relationship.

Now you, a married woman who I thought had better sense, are engaged in a dangerous flirtation with a man who is admittedly a good soldier but nothing more. And may I remind you that he's not your husband."

"It's not a flirtation, Papa," she said simply.

"Very well, an infatuation . . . whatever you want to call it. You cannot continue it."

"I'm not in love with my husband. I never have been."

"That's not the point. Marcus Clemens is an extremely rich man. We need his funding on many projects. The Flavian family must be above reproach, or we can't hold things together. Scandal is an insidious piece of machinery capable of multiplying itself. You must think beyond yourself. A man like Helvidius Priscus in the Senate would dearly love to learn of your affair. He wants social revolution; he wants to overthrow the whole imperial system and go backward to the days of the Republic. We must not give him the weapons to slit our throats."

Later, Domitillia wondered what had cut through her reserve and allowed her to declare herself with such vehemence. She knew she was being unfair to her father and to the tradition of her family, but the words poured from her and she was incapable of halting them. She thought to reach for her father's hand, but instead she stood up suddenly, and in spite of the mixture of hurt and anger in her father's eyes she raised her voice defiantly. "I don't give a twit about the future of the Flavian family if it depends on what other people think of my behavior or my brothers'! I am not the property of Helvidius Priscus or any other members of the damned Senate! And if Rome stumbles over the conduct of your daughter, them Rome is weak and sick and needs a thorough washing!"

Vespasian pointed his finger at her and she saw that his head was shaking more than ever. "You are an *adultress!*" he shouted. His voice echoed across the room. "You know the penalty!"

"I also know that I'm young and full of the love of life. Just to please you and my brothers and the silly Senate, I have been chained to a man I don't give a damn about for almost two years! Do I grow old with him just because I'm your daughter? Do I spend the rest of my life with that lout . . . or until I'm so old he throws me away. . . . Do I deserve that penalty? Go ahead and have me executed if that's the custom you want to follow. It's a better death than the one I've been living!"

Suddenly her voice broke and she began to sob. She sank to her knees before Vespasian and seized his hands. "I love him, Papa. Try to understand that I love him more than my life. Please . . ."

There followed a long silence. She could hear her father's heavy breathing, and she knew he was attempting to quell his anger. She crept closer to him until her head touched his robe. She moved his hand to wipe away her tears. "I'm sorry, dear Papa," she murmured. "I don't want to hurt you. You are my god, but I want to live the rest of my life with Flavius Silva."

At last she felt his hand move across her head. It was such a gentle gesture that she found the courage to open her eyes and look up at him. She saw instantly that he had regained his composure; the appearance of vagueness was gone, his jaw was no longer slack, and his head remained steady. She sensed that he had made a choice between Emperor and father, and she rejected the urge to tell him the full truth about Scribonia.

She withdrew from him slowly, fascinated at the change that seemed to be possessing him. The genial, philosophical man who had greeted her had vanished; instead, the image of the Empire appeared to be reflected in his powerful face. She knew suddenly that if she told him about Scribonia, his wrath would be directed at Flavius Silva.

Vespasian took a deep breath and spoke as if he were addressing a stranger. "Go to your house and stay there," he intoned. "You are to speak to no one except your slaves . . . and your husband when he returns. Now leave me until I can find the wisdom to decide your future."

SEVEN

MOST SECRET
From Titus—*Imperator Designatus* and Praetorian Prefect (via special courier).

To Flavius Silva—Commanding Tenth Legion Frentensis. Judea.

Consider this your signal to proceed immediately with your mission in Africa. You will contact the commanders of each Legion stationed there as previously directed and assure yourself of their loyalty to me, the legal heir to the throne.

I regret my brother's unfortunate ambitions and I cannot impress upon you enough the importance of having the African Legions sworn to our side. Through various ploys Domitian has now persuaded the First Alaudae and the Twentieth Valeria, in the Rhineland, to his allegiance. I hear that he also has the Fourth Macedonica and the Sixth Victrix, in Spain, and I suspect he will soon have the Third Gallica, in Syria, at his disposal. Thus you may appreciate that we are in very real danger of being overwhelmed unless we can challenge him with a superior force.

My father is fading fast. He often asks about you. Let us join in this effort to see the work of the man we both admire preserved. The future of the Empire depends on us.

I am planning a triumph to honor my father six weeks

hence. I hope that your task will prove easy and swift, because I know you would like to be present to honor him yourself.

I look forward to our reunion with great anticipation. Guard yourself well. If Domitian hears of your doings (he has ears everywhere), he will stop at nothing to assure your failure.

This day, when the wind had shifted to the east and brought with it the stunning heat of the desert, General Flavius Silva had finished with his staff conference by midmorning. Now he must hurry through a host of final details before his departure scheduled for tomorrow s dawn. First, the troublesome matter of Sullius Piso, a veteran legionary who had worked his way upward through the ranks, serving first as *librarius*, then *tesserarius*, *optio*, *signifer*, and recently as a centurion, had to be settled. Piso, a handsome man of thirty who had displayed quite extraordinary zeal in battle, had somehow made contact with one of the local Christianii sects and as a result had apparently undergone an almost complete change of character. He would not confess how he had encountered the Christianii or where, but he did repeat to the point of Silva's nearly unbearable boredom phrases he had picked up from the Jews: "The Lord is our God. The Lord is one . . ." It seemed to be his only response to the random questioning of Silva's staff.

When Silva asked Piso how he could quote the Jews in the same breath with the Christian sect, since apparently they were so at odds with each other (as were all the other sects in Judea), Piso said that they worshiped the same god and that Yeshu'a, the founder of his sect, was a Jew.

"Indeed? Then how was it this holy man you identify as Yeshu'a became an adversary of the Jews? Do you have the gall to propose he was one of us?"

"He was not an adversary of anyone."

"I fail to understand you," Silva said, rubbing at his bad eye as if the gesture would clarify his thinking. His mind was still preoccupied with Titus' letter, so he had trouble following Piso. "Are we talking about just one holy man out of the thousands who roam this land? Are you asking us to believe that there was something so special about him that he managed to addle the brain of a good Roman officer?"

"The Talmud simply identifies him as *Yeshu'a of Nazareth*. That's about the same as *Joshua*. The Greeks pronounce it *Iesous*."

"Answer my question directly! And don't insult my local knowledge by telling me that the Talmud is a Hebrew book. I know it. Have you become a Jew?"

"No, Sire."

"I simply cannot comprehend," Silva said, "how a man of your intelligence and background could allow himself to listen to such nonsense delivered by some fakir who's been dead for many years. What about the Sicarii, or the Pharisees, or the Sadducees, or any of the other zealot sects that still infest this colony? Why didn't you listen to their gibberish? You were at Masada. You know how insane the Jews are. What happened? Tell me you have fallen in love with some native woman and I'll try to understand, but just to take this up on your own volition is incredible. Confess now. Did some local female get you into it?"

"No, Sire."

"What do you suggest we do about you? Obviously, you can't continue in your present command." Silva thought that of all his centurions Piso was the one he would least like to lose. Time and again the man had proven himself reliable, he was popular with his men, and he possessed great personal charm. In every aspect except this silly surrender to a renegade religion, Piso stood out as a fine example of a Roman soldier and citizen.

Geminus, who stood next to Silva, whispered that perhaps a good scourging with a bastinado might bring Piso to his senses. Metilius Nepos, the assault weapons officer, suggested that Piso be dismissed from the Legion, prohibited from making any contact with other legionaries, and left to his own devices in Judea, where perhaps his fellow Christianiis might keep him from starving, since the Jews would certainly not.

Silva had been of a different mind since the beginning of the inquiry. To dismiss Piso not only would be awkward locally, but might ultimately bring disgrace to the Tenth Legion. And Piso was too stalwart a soldier for any physical assault to be effective. He was brave and determined; the spectacle of an officer like him suffering punishment at the hands of a lesser man would only distress his fellow officers and possibly lead to outspoken resentment among the troops. It had also occurred to Silva that Piso was exactly the individual he was looking for. Once off the hook in a tolerable way, he would do precisely as he was ordered; and if warned to be discreet, he would be as much so as he was now.

"Centurion Piso," Silva began, rubbing at his bad eye again as if a massage would relieve his frustration, "your behavior in this matter is most regrettable. If allowed to go further, it might seriously embarrass the morale of the Tenth . . . a situation you will recognize that we cannot permit. It strikes me that you need fresh air and a chance to restore your common sense. Once you've had a chance to review your defection—or shall I say folly?—I hope that you will apply for reinstatement and once again become a useful officer."

Silva made a quick survey of his staff and saw agreement in their eyes, for everyone felt sorry for Piso. He was like a man who had contracted one of the innumerable diseases prevalent in Judea, a battle casualty without the clash of armor. They understood and sympathized with him, for there was hardly a man among them who had not been afflicted with some local sickness in one form or another.

"Therefore, Piso, you will transfer your century to that eligible legionary who your men will elect immediately. You are to be sent to a different environment for recuperation over a period of the next three months. Geminus, see to it that immediate transportation is arranged for Centurion Piso's assignment to Rome. It is unimportant whether by land or sea. Piso, report to me just before your departure." Silva paused, then said sharply, "Dismissed!"

In a moment he was alone. At last, he thought, he had found a trustworthy courier to take the letter he had just written to Domitillia.

My beloved,

I stood long on the terrace, watching the sail of your ship becoming smaller and smaller until finally it disappeared over the horizon. The best part of my life sailed with you. For some reason, I find it very difficult to weep with only one eye, but I managed. If this sounds like I'm feeling sorry for myself, forgive me. I am and with a grand excuse.

Before you came back into my life, I walked alone in this world and I found it a terrible place to be without love. Now I view every day as an excitement and I continually anticipate our next meeting. Now I am making final preparations and am leaving for Africa tomorrow. I have seen to it that the affairs of the Tenth are quite well in hand; we have only the usual garrison problems and those not too many, thanks be to the gods. I suspect I will not be too much missed. There is a festival in August, Consualia, on the nineteenth according to my calendar, and I will try to arrive in Rome about that time. Somewhere I once heard the fete was in commemoration of carrying off the Sabine women . . . which might be appropriate under the circumstances. You *are* a Sabine, unless I'm mistaken.

I know you must be troubled about the disappearance of our overly inquisitive friend. Place your fears at rest. There is indeed a current running along that particular section of the beach, sometimes quite strong. My only regret is there was not time to place a coin on his tongue before he sailed away on his private voyage.

If ever time hangs heavy for you, go please to Praeneste and view the progress of my home. The architect is Antoninus Mamilianus, who is a freedman and a clever architect only some of the time. The contractor is Horonius Flaccus, a jolly, noisy fellow of deliberate cunning who holds my testicles in ransom. He is a born thief and knows that if I replace him now, the present tradesmen working on the project, along with several talented slaves he assigns to the job, must also be replaced with inevitable changes upon changes and the expenditure of enormous amounts of money. (You already know that my share of spoils from Jerusalem were pathetic and there is little here as yet to overload my purse.) Of all the jobs in the Roman Army, I suppose mine is the least lucrative.

Please ascertain that the shade trees are planted along the western perimeter of the property, since I dislike frying in the afternoon sun—there's plenty of that sort of thing here. I am anxious to keep everything as cool as possible after such a long spell of heat. Seventy percent of my soldiers have a rash of one sort or another generated, we believe, by our armor rubbing against sweaty skin. We have lost nine men in the past year to heat-stroke.

It is almost beyond my wildest hope that someday you may share the house in Praeneste with me! Your father has always been a sensible man, and if he could be persuaded to our cause, then it should be easy enough for him to annul your marriage or somehow arrange a divorce that would be satisfactory to Marcus Clemens . . .

There was much more to the letter, mainly expressing his total devotion and fear that she might suffer some hurt because of her involvement with a mere soldier. In his mind he composed a postscript:

This letter will be delivered by the Centurion Sullius Piso, who you will find an engaging man despite his current religious befuddlement. He comes from a good family in Sardinia and I assure you he is absolutely trustworthy.

There was another letter that had been waiting upon a suitable courier. It was addressed to Flavius Titus, *Imperator Designatus, Praetorian Prefect:*

My dear old comrade, greetings. I want to assure you that your sister has been a joy since the moment she set foot in Judea. What an utterly enchanting woman she has become! I find it impossible to relate her to the sprawling, pigeon-legged youngster we once knew.

Domitillia will post you on the situation in Judea and my efforts to keep these people at peace. They profess their yearning for tranquillity, but if they can't kill us they often turn on each other, and there are times when I despair of cooling their pugnacity. Your own familiarity with their nature may make it easy for you to understand my occasional frustration.

These days, with your father ailing and so many demands on yourself, I realize that you cannot concern yourself too deeply with this colony. Be assured that the Tenth Legion is quite capable of the job assigned to it.

While we would wish for more replacements and better food, we are battle-ready at any moment. Discipline and morale in the ranks are both high, and I am blessed with a particularly able staff of officers.

The gentiles of Caesarea killed every local Jew they could lay their hands on soon after Masada. This massacre was not of our doing; indeed, we had not even arrived here as yet. I held a conference with the leading gentiles and castigated them for wasting manpower. It would now appear my admonitions had some effect, since many Jews who fled and thereby survived have returned and are living in apparent harmony with their ex-enemies. A strange people.

I depart for Africa tomorrow and will do my utmost to carry out your desires per your directive concerning the Legions stationed there. When I reach Carthage I will take ship for Rome and report to you. I rejoice in that possibility.

In closing, let me tickle your humor with a quote from Petronius: "Pretend I'm dead. Say something nice about me."

Old friend, the world is yours and I am your servant.

That afternoon when Centurion Piso returned to him on the terrace of his house, Silva handed him the letters secured and sealed in a leather pouch. "You're a very lucky man, Piso. Your punishment could have been very severe. I hope you'll justify my faith in you and return rehabilitated and ready to serve the Tenth as I know you can do."

"I'll do what I can do," Piso said. Silva thought he detected a note of resignation in his voice. Could it be that this fine young soldier was incurably demented or so determined to ruin himself that nothing could stop him?

"Take my advice," Silva said, "or drink a bucket of hemlock. Your family, your friends, and your comrades in the Tenth will never understand how you could reject an opportunity like you now have just because some local fakir promised you the moon."

"As far as I know, he didn't promise anyone anything."

"Then all the more reason to forget the whole unfortunate business. . . . Now as to this pouch. You are to guard it with

116

your life. If it appears you're in the slightest danger of losing your life, destroy it. You will have no difficulty in delivering the letter to Domitillia if you mention my name. Titus may take longer, but you met some Praetorians when they were here and you could ask for Egnatius Camillus as a last resort. If you can catch him when he's not preening himself, perhaps he will find time to ease your way."

They exchanged a smile of understanding and Silva offered his hand. "Good luck," he said, "and have a good trip. Say hello to the Circus for me. The races should be starting soon."

After Piso had saluted and left him (without a word of thanks for my mercy, Silva thought), he became almost unbearably homesick. Why had he not become a merchant or a lawyer and so return to a true home once work was done? Anything but a soldier, that strutting stiff-backed bureaucrat, that minion of every ruler since long before the founding of Rome. Oh, honors—there were aplenty! A sop to the conscience, a salve to the wounds in the mind that would never heal, a recognition of deeds performed in the service of one vicious mob against another. Deep in the pancreas, he mused, somewhere between navel and bowel, an invisible informant warned the bravest soldier that he had made a mistake. He discovered that he might be about to be killed. He was about to become just gristle and bone in a foreign land; his honors, his courage, the way he talked and sipped his wine forgotten forever. Britain was not home, Cilicia was not home, nor was Gaul, or the Rhine, neither Farther nor Hither Spain, Syria, Illyricum, Numidia, Macedonia, Parthia, or Egypt. It was no life for a wise man.

He faced the sea, so very blue this afternoon. At least he had not drawn an assignment like poor Agricola, who had just been appointed Governor of Britain. At least he was not charged with chasing bunches of foul-smelling hirsute savages through the woods, as Agricola would be obliged to do. Poor Agricola. His daughter had married a young man named Tacitus, a literary fellow with a very loose regard for facts.

As an antidote to his forlorn mood Silva left the terrace and climbed up to the atrium. There he ordered Epos to prepare his bath and to bring his scraper, since the oil he had applied after yesterday's massage had not been entirely removed from his skin.

While he waited for Epos to return, he went into the peristyle and disrobed. Then he lowered himself into his dry bathtub, closed his eyes, and tried to lift his spirits by recalling some of the poetry of Lucan. The man must have been quite extraordinary, he thought. He had been capable of scorning dignity, yet he was able to cause some men to throw away their lives for a principle—including his own when he made the mistake of antagonizing Nero. It took a bold man to write a work such as *Pharsalia* when there were countless other subjects less controversial than the civil war. Was Centurion Piso of the same hardheaded sort? Certainly Lucan had not been one of the Christianii, but he had demonstrated the same stubborn lack of judgment; and when caught in his rebellion he at least had the grace to open his veins.

It was the same kind of people in obverse, Silva reasoned, who believed the Roman Army must be supreme over all other agencies of the government. There was room for doubt about such a principle; holding it up for inspection did not necessarily mean that a soldier was disloyal either to the Empire or to himself.

Apologies to Mars, he thought; should any general of a Legion entertain such thoughts? The same boredom, the same ennui that was so dangerous to the men in the ranks was now infecting him! Come now, these were all trouble-making thoughts bound to surface in a professional soldier when left without a war to fight. But what to do with one's mind, which could not be slipped back into a scabbard like a sword and withdrawn again only when necessary? How many times could a man read that amiable, hypocritical Seneca's *Epistulae Morales* without feeling vaguely patronized despite the twinkling beauty of his Latin? Caius Secundas and his oceans of books? After plowing through a few of them you were left with a sense of inadequacy. "I'm a soldier," Silva muttered to the blue sky framed by the upper perimeter of the peristyle. "I'm not a scientist, a philosopher, or a politician . . . or even a very bright man."

But he was certainly bored almost beyond toleration. Something had to come to his rescue.

When Epos arrived with the hot water, Silva felt a sense of relief. At least he could talk to Epos; he could say anything under the sun he pleased since his lack of a tongue guaranteed his total confidentiality. As Epos began to massage his neck, Silva said, "Here I am with the morals of a billy goat and the life of a priest. Disgraceful! For lack of escape the juices of my testicles roil and boil. They're like a steaming stove pot and my penis becomes more atrophied as he raises his head and searches in vain for satisfaction."

If only he could settle for some local bawd, he thought, be she Jew, Arab, Egyptian, or Greek, his discontent would fade away and it might be easier to accept the role of an unemployed killer.

"Would you agree, Epos, that I've killed far more men than any gladiator? I've even killed women and children, if not with my own hands, at least they died by my orders. Are these perilous thoughts for a soldier, Epos? Is it wrong to suppose there might be something wrong here? Stop your silly smiling, my tongueless lout, and answer my questions."

Perhaps young boys might be the answer? Why did so many Romans prefer dalliance with their own sex? Was it because they mimic the Greeks and fashion says they must copy them in everything? Or is it because they escape the fickle twists of females?

"That's not my style, dear Epos. Be it bawd or boy, I'm ill suited to casual copulation. For I'm in love, Epos, hopelessly, insanely in love with the most enchanting, delightful female imp in the Roman Empire."

Silva turned slightly in the tub and held up his right leg to examine the old spear wound. Hot water always caused the wound to turn red and ugly, but since leaving the desert the pain had been quite tolerable. His Achilles tendon, broken when his horse, Fury, took a fall, was another matter. The Greek doctors had cut into the leg and tied the strands together, or that was what he had thought they were doing while he arose and fell in an ocean of pain. So the limp. It was embarrassing to move about like a spavined horse, but Domitillia had said she didn't care, and certainly there was no one else who might.

Domitillia! Her name passed through the lips like a melodic phrase from a poem. Domitillia! The stance of that woman! One instant she was the mischievous little girl, the next a mature woman unafraid to risk her life.

"What next, Epos? Domitillia does not just enter a room. In

a room of ten people she glitters like a star, while the others become satellites. It would be the same with a thousand people. Did you notice, Epos, that there is a dimple in her left cheek that dances when she laughs? Did you notice the way she walks? Did you hear her throw an unpleasant subject away that other women might consider worth chewing on? She said her husband was unfortunate, that when he was forsaken by the gods he sought a mother. And what did he find? A set of nice teeth, a close connection to the throne, and a bottom that sashays when she walks."

Silva looked directly into Epos' eyes. "I'll tell you, Epos, that Domitillia has no match in the civilized world!"

Silva grunted with pleasure as Epos' fingers found a sensitive spot in his neck. He sighed his content with the moment and said, "Epos, let's dine well tonight. Let us now plan the menu . . . as usual, for just one. One very happy general, who if he cannot be with his beloved, has at least discovered her identity, which is more than most men can claim. Let us celebrate that triumph along with a solo festivity commemorating the fact that the general is alive and reasonably sane. . . . No, that last may be an exaggeration."

Silva twisted in the tub and searched Epos' expressive eyes. There were times, he thought, when the slave almost seemed to understand him. He took one of Epos' hands and placed it between his shoulder blades. "There," he said, "rub there."

As Epos complied, Silva continued, "A feast conceived in the mind might be even more palatable than an actual repast. Suppose we commence with a fine fish, a fresh mullet, say, and we'll sauce him with liguamen prepared from sprats or mackerel, say . . . then a side dish of cheese and onion spiced with Persian asafetida to give them pungency. Next? Now what next, dear Epos? Shall we say a fat hen drowned in wine that has been well peppered, or better, a duck whose final squawk is the signal that he has been precisely done. Shall we add some pomegranates from Libya surrounding a tender kid? Why not, Epos? We have only to summon such images in our mind and our tongue begins to slather and our belly ache. We might as well play such games, because in this land, which has been abandoned by every god in the Pantheon, we'll be very lucky to have a biscuit and a glass of rancid wine for our feast tonight."

Silva splashed some water on his face and tried to recall the unique pleasures enjoyed by most Romans at their baths. Never in the history of the world, he thought, had there been such devotion to hygiene and such a sense of deprivation if a daily visit to the baths was not possible. The Empire could float away thoroughly cleansed on the money spent in the erection of baths everywhere except Judea, where the legionaries made do with various ingenious makeshifts. The baths were institutions created for the comfort of Romans everywhere else. Now soaking in his own makeshift, Silva closed his eyes and thought how fine it would be if he could go first to the *apodyterium,* where he would remove his garments, then to the *unctorium* where, if the bathhouse were properly tended, his body would be anointed with oil, even as Epos was doing now. Next, he would pass into the *caldarium* for a warm soak and then to the *laconicum* for a steam. Afterward, he would enter the *tepidarium* and stay until he was cooled. Finally, if sufficiently robust, he might jump into the icy *frigidarium.* No. No, Flavius Silva. Why destroy the soothing mood, why upset the subtle joys of a true sybarite by thrusting one's carcass into arctic waters? Let the hearty ones jump up and down and gasp and pound their chests and holler their bad jokes at the top of their lungs if they pleased. The screeching echoes of their voices as Fonteius called to Dillius and Dillius to Valerius, who passed the word to Julius, was sometimes more than any meditative man could withstand, unless one understood that the vigor of Roman citizens and therefore of the Empire was so often confirmed through the mouth.

When he had finished his bath and Epos had scraped him thoroughly, Silva glanced at the lowering sun and wondered what he would do until it sank into the sea. How could he force himself to think of anything but Domitillia? His one good eye was so weary of reading that he could barely see the script. By the gods, he must contrive to do something else with his brain besides this dwelling on an unavailable woman! At least it would be a relief to get away from this place. Alexandria? He had never been there. Even Egypt would be a relief from this Hebrew monotony.

Since a suitable display of his medals would be important when he talked with officers of the African Legions, he was stowing them in his campaign kit when Geminus came to him, a solemn look on his face. Silva saw that he crossed the terrace with an unusually ponderous pace, like a rhinoceros with sore feet, he thought.

"Sire," Geminus began. "I have an unpleasant report."

"Someday you're going to surprise me with the opposite."

"There's trouble brewing in the town."

"Well, unbrew it." Damn it, Silva thought, he had been at least reasonably content watching the sun go down and communing with the spirit of Domitillia. Did Geminus deliberately choose this time to wreck his tranquility? Despite his hardness Geminus had much of the fretting mother hen in him and seemed to relish the delivery of bad news.

"Three legionaries have been killed," he said abruptly. "Calpetanus Rantius of the first cohort, Julius Cordus of the same, and Vettius Bolanus of the second cohort."

"What happened?"

"The usual. That's five men in the last two months."

"I asked you what happened."

"The Jews did it."

"Why?"

"The men went a-whoring and when they were mounting, the Jews came and rammed their knives up their rectums and then slit their throats. The whores are said to have cheered. It was a bloody mess, Sire."

"Have you caught the Jews?"

"No, Sire. They have disappeared. They may not even be residents of Caesarea. No one in the town will talk except an elderly gentile who was in the house at the same time. He says the soldiers were drunk and weren't satisfied with the Arab whores. They wanted Jewish women. When they were told there were none available, they hauled three women off the street and raped them. A mob gathered and the consequences were predictable."

"Where was the patrol? Why didn't they put a stop to things?"

"Decurion Priscus was in command. At the time of the incident he and his patrol were handling another trouble about four streets away. Apparently some Jew had been selling food that hadn't been blessed by the rabbis and saying it had been done. Another mob formed when the argument got hot, and they were tearing down the merchant's shop. According to

Decurion Priscus, they were all about to kill one another and he had his hands full quieting them down."

"Priscus should have let them have at it."

"Agreed, Sire. I told him that. But about the legionaries? What do you want to do?"

"Find the men who did it. March them through town and herd a few hundred Jews along with them. When you reach the center of town, stake them out and set them afire. Be sure the spectators understand exactly why you're doing it. Next, pass the word through the ranks that the next legionary who is found guilty of raping any woman—Jew, Arab, or whatever —will be crucified."

Silva saw in Geminus' eyes that he was distressed. The good man took everything concerning the Tenth so to his heart, and it was certain that he did not consider rape, particularly of any conquered Jews, to be more than a very minor matter.

"That's very severe, Sire."

"It's necessary. We've got to convince the Jews that we're not beasts if we're going to make this occupation a profitable enterprise, which I will remind you is precisely why we're here. We cannot accomplish our purpose by killing Jews or fucking their women or destroying their property, or in any way using force at random. Now that the war is over, we are the peacekeepers. We must govern ourselves as well as them by Roman law."

"I could round up a half dozen young Jews who looked like those who did it, and no one would know the difference. They'll burn just as well."

"The Jews would know the difference. They are the people we want to impress . . . not ourselves. Revenge does not bring gold, Geminus, only more hate."

What pompous words from Flavius Silva, he thought. Who was this stranger so full of the law and mercy? In former times, before the influence of that vixen Domitillia, he would have agreed instantly—round up half a dozen Jews, no matter who they were, and set fire to the rascals. That would teach the populace a lesson and put a stop to any further interference with their betters. Or would it?

Perhaps it was her lips, he thought, the way she screwed them up and tilted her head when she questioned something he had said that did the trick, or it could have been those hands, so expressive, matching the dash of her every movement. Some total, irreversible magic she had left behind was still in charge of Flavius Silva.

". . . I can't guarantee we'll find the real culprits," Geminus was saying, yet Silva barely heard him. He was listening, he realized, to another voice, and what his deputy had to say was of relatively little interest.

Geminus shook his head unhappily. "It will be like looking for six special grains of sand in the desert, Sire. We may never find them. Meanwhile, we have three murdered legionaries."

"See that their kin are notified that they were killed in action . . . which will not be an untruth."

"Should I close down the whorehouse?"

"No. We are powerful enough to be tolerant."

He was trying to remember; was that provocative mole on her lovely right thigh or her lovely left?

Geminus hesitated, then spoke softly, "Sometimes, Sire, I don't understand you."

"Sometimes, dear Geminus, neither do I."

Bemused at the mood that seemed to obsess him, he clapped Geminus gently on the shoulder and, smiling, turned away.

EIGHT

A S THE NEW PRAETORIAN Prefect in addition to his
appointment as *imperator designatus*, Titus Flavius Vespasianus found his duties and obligations becoming extraordinarily heavy, for many who could not arrange to see his father
were convinced the outwardly jovial Titus might further their
projects. Thus they paid court to him, and even if they lost
their immediate cause, they reasoned that a further acquaintance with the future Emperor would be a good investment.

Although Titus' official residence was in the palace on the
Capitoline, he kept a much smaller house in the Mons Aventinus district and thus assured himself a greater degree of privacy. Here the Jewish queen, Julia Berenice, dwelled with
him except for a very brief period when he had the temerity to
install her in the palace. And here on this very morning he had
reluctantly resolved to dismiss her from his life.

Berenice was a formidable woman, tempestuous, impul-
sive, and proud. For a moment he reflected on his mistress,
realizing she was the only woman he had ever loved. Now she
was showing a certain plumpness about her hips and a fullness
about her breasts that often ruffled his temper. He had understood she was an ever unwilling witness to the contest between her weight and a fondness for fine foods. Still, no one
who had been favored by her black eyes and utterly engaging
smile would deny her continuing beauty. She made it easy to

forget she was ten years older than himself. She was, he thought, a most peculiar joy.

As the daughter of King Agrippa, the Roman satrap who had ruled over southern Syria and northern Palestine, Berenice had done her utmost to stall the Jewish revolt against Rome before it began. She had claimed many times, Titus now remembered, that she knew victory for the Jews was impossible. A female prophet? Or just a witch? She was like the Jewish General Joseph ben Matthias, who called frequently at this house. Like him she had thrown in her lot with the enemy and had done very well for herself.

Titus managed a half smile. The rise of his remarkable Jewess had not been easy. Gossip about Berenice began the moment she set foot in Rome and never ceased, since she herself provided such delicious material. He thought that the poison of her name had been compounded and had thickened like roe along the tongues of her enemies. It was soon confirmed that she had been married three times and was said to have had at least three steaming affairs before she came into his arms. It was also rumored that she had had an incestuous affair with her brother Agrippa, who was quite as pro-Roman as his sister.

"Ah, yes," Titus smiled wistfully, but the gossips of Roman society could not bring themselves to disregard her considerable fortune. Money dictated; money spoke in a muffled voice, but it was always authoritative. The Flavian family had not ruled long enough to acquire great wealth, and Berenice knew it. She understood the need for money, and she knew the penalties of power, since she had been close to it since birth; she valued power not for itself but as a tool by which various beneficial things could be accomplished. "Where else could I find such a woman?" he whispered to himself. "Where else can I find a woman who loves me rather than what I can give her?"

Titus was acutely aware that his valuation of his mistress was not shared by the Senate or the nobles of Rome. They feared that once Vespasian had passed on, his son would be tricked into making "his Oriental strumpet," as they called her, his queen. And this might be. How amusing it would be to shock the wives of the prominent in Rome with just such a choice! Let their gossiping tongues suck on that for awhile.

Let their jealousy of her beauty sour their addled brains while they tried to compete intellectually with the one woman who understood the complexities of the Empire.

As if her success with the Flavian family were not enough (there was whispered gossip that even Titus' father yearned to bed her), Berenice was said to indulge in loathsome sexual addictions that would soon drive her lover mad. Perhaps. She did have a way of draining him, a style to her copulation in which she often became the aggressor. She would begin with various titillations—a touching of his parts ever so delicately until it was like a breath of wind passing over them. Then her tongue would descend, flicking like an adder's, teasing, exploring, promising until the whole of his body trembled with desire. Then her lips would close on him, very slowly at first, postponing the risk of explosion. Until at last she would straddle him and take him into her; there, true enough, delicious madness began.

Even Domitillia had fallen under the spell of this strange woman. She had not been long in Rome before the two were spending an occasional afternoon together, sometimes at the Theater Marcellus if the performance was appealing—they both preferred the laughs of Plautus to Terence—or simply enjoying an exchange of their rather strong opinions at either of their houses. Domitillia's brickworks was the largest in Rome, and Titus was pleased that its management offered countless opportunities for an exchange of opinion between two such exceptionally active women. It was Berenice who had suggested that the endless rebuilding of Rome would be better served if every brick Domitillia sold was impressed with her logo, thus identifying her superior product.

The fact that the two women were neighbors on the Mons Aventinus made such meetings convenient, but Titus thought that an even stronger force held them together. They were both given to an arrogant disregard of what others said about them, and they shared an independence of spirit that shook the average Roman male to his toes.

Titus sighed heavily. As it was going to be a painful morning, he had managed to procrastinate sending for Berenice until noon. He had at last concluded that he could not simply send her packing. He could not bring himself to dismiss such an extraordinary woman through one of his deputies; he must do it himself lest he lose not only her but her respect. He had prowled the house like a wounded stag for an hour until he had finally gathered his wits and resolved to summon the woman who had shared his past three years.

While awaiting her arrival, he canceled what was left of the day's appointments and called for his harp. Had fate not intervened and brought his family to the countless imperial responsibilities, he knew he would have been inclined to do nothing at all. He would have spent his time at the games or the theater and at such dalliances as each day might bring. He was sure he would have been quite content spending odd hours composing music for the harp or singing amusing little ditties to its accompaniment. Unlike Nero, whose silly artistic pretensions Papa had often described, Titus held his own talent in low esteem. "I've not a very keen ear," he would say, laughing, "and my fingers become ten thumbs when I'm plucking strings."

Titus played at his harp purely for the joy it gave him, and hoped that his efforts were not intolerable to others. Now, as Berenice approached, he nestled his cheek against the strings of his instrument as if it would provide a protective fence. He said, "This is not going to be a very pleasant day for either of us."

He saw that she must have been expecting to be called and had probably been so tardy in responding to his invitation because of the time required to fix a caplet of flowers in her hair and adorn it with an elaborate collection of precious stones. He became aware that she was wearing his favorite scent, a musky Oriental concoction with a name he would never find the gutturals to pronounce. She had obviously prepared herself for this meeting with great care and he wondered how she had anticipated it. But then, he recalled, she had always been witchlike in anticipating the principal events in his life. Indeed, she had prophesied that a man like Diogenes would someday choose a packed theater to denounce their relationship and thereby cause a public uproar. The man had been properly flogged for his temerity, but it was doubtful if the punishment had any effect on the crowds of cynics who seemed to have taken charge of the city. He wondered if she knew that only last week a second individual, a certain Heras, had so overstepped the bounds of propriety in respect to the royal family, particularly the continued presence of herself, that Vespasian had ordered the man beheaded? There was real trouble brewing in the capital, and he knew the seed of it now stood defiantly before him.

He waited for her to speak because she looked like she might, but she remained silent. He thought, she is not going to make it easy for me; her eyes are looking through me. Her eyelids were painted black to contrast with the fashionable white paint applied to her face and the deep maroon of her lips.

Avoiding her eyes, he examined the strings of his harp as if to find fault and struck a few notes experimentally.

"Did you bring me here in the middle of the day to hear music?" she asked. She spoke Greek, which annoyed him because he had never had an easy relationship with the tongue, disliking its labyrinthian phraseology.

Damn it, he thought, she is smiling; she knows very well what I have to say and is going to make me squirm for it. "The Roman people," he began, "do not approve of our relationship."

"What a shame, if not a surprise. I have been led to believe that you represented the Roman people."

"In a way I do. But my father is still our Emperor."

"And, of course, he still disapproves?"

"I regret his stubborn attitude, but he's an old man."

"And you go along with whatever he says, no matter what he says?"

He had never known her voice to be so cold. "Now . . . now. I'm simply compelled to inform you that we must make some other arrangements."

"Why?" Her voice lacked its usual melodious quality, he thought, and her eyes had become venomous.

He regarded her as he might an approaching thunderstorm. He saw the deep hurt in her eyes and questioned whether he could continue with what he must do. By all the gods, he had so loved this woman! And that passion refused to die.

Watching her now, she seemed like a wounded deer. The defiance and anger in her eyes were replaced by confusion and disbelief. He longed to reach out and take her in his arms, but if he so much as touched her he knew that all his resolve would be lost.

"As you know," he managed to say, "Papa is fading fast. It seems incredible to me that I may soon be sitting in his place."

"I've never thought it incredible, rather . . . a certainty. And now you want to be rid of me?"

"No! I do *not* want this to happen!" His voice rose nearly out of control.

"Oh? You do *not* want? You spineless hypocrite! You limp penis of a man! You slather over my body, you steal from my brain, you creep to me on your knees when you need comfort! *You do not want?* But your precious Papa whispers a word and off you go running to do his bidding!"

"Cork your mouth, woman. I don't have to listen to this."

Berenice shook her head furiously and the precious stones in her hair danced in the reflected light. "What if I refuse to go?" she demanded.

"I suppose . . . Well . . ."

"After almost four years, you're asking me to pack my kit and take to the woods like some old camp follower you hope will die on the trail? Then I suppose you'll marry some silly-ass Roman matron who will be more acceptable to your dear citizens than a Jewess?"

"I have no such plans."

"Then spare yourself a venereal disease or going to bed with a flounder. Or both."

"I appreciate your concern."

"You are full of shit." Although the tone of her voice remained modest, he saw her eyes ablaze, and he thought, now it comes.

She said, "You're the *imperator designatus*, yet you allow an assortment of fatheads and their brainless wives to dictate your personal life. I'm disappointed in you. To what remote part of your Empire are you sending me?"

"Would you consider Numidia? The climate there is salubrious and Carthage is a nice city. I could come to visit you."

"How touching. And how strange it is that a man has just come to me from Carthage. He has been trying to sell me some information he thought might be very valuable. If I'm willing to pay his price, he insists that no member of the Flavian family will ever dare to antagonize me. "

"Who is that man?" Titus asked without caring. He was so relieved at the apparent collapse of Berenice's fury that his attention had already drifted.

"From my lips you would be the last to learn. Worry about him, my former love. It becomes you."

Titus groaned. By all the gods, why had he fallen in love with a woman who could never share his throne? To keep her at his side would mean fighting mountains of opposition and prejudice for the rest of his reign—and perhaps even losing it. This is agony, he thought, because I still love her. But he said, "Although I know I'll miss those times when your tongue was much softer, I understand your displeasure. I'm sending you away because of obligation . . . not desire. All arrangements for your departure and such goods as you care to take with you will be made by this afternoon. To avoid any embarrassing scenes with the locals, I'll assign an escort of Praetorians to your party. I suggest you proceed to Ostia tonight. An envoy will be dispatched immediately to Carthage with instructions to appropriate a suitable house for you and your staff. Of course, I'll always be willing to make your life there easier if I'm asked."

"How generous of you, great Titus Vespasianus. This lowly Jewess will always appreciate the faithful heart and the integrity of a true Roman." She paused and a half smile crept across her sensuous mouth. "Perhaps someday you'll also know the joys of vengeance."

Berenice turned quickly in her jeweled sandals and walked away. She marched directly to her rooms, which comprised the most gracious part of the house. There she summoned Letitia, her most trusted slave, and told her she must go at once to the headquarters of the *frumentarii*, which were located just to the north of the Theater Marcellus. "You are to ask for a man who calls himself Julius Scribonia and give him this." She tore a ring from her finger, a Persian piece depicting the god Mithras, which Titus had given her. She handed it to Letitia. "Here is proof that you come from me, because the man Scribonia commented on it. Tell him to go at once to

Ostia and wait for my arrival tonight. Tell him I am interested in acquiring the item he has for sale."

The concerns of the Empire troubled Titus more than he cared to admit. As his father deliberately faded more into the background and spent more time at his country estate, it sometimes seemed that the world had just been waiting to transfer its weight from Vespasian to his own broad shoulders.

The balance of trade between the colonies and Rome was a particularly obtuse problem that seemed to defy a practical solution. Titus complained to his staff and used the name of his guardian god. "By my genius! We send money all over the world like a farmer casts his seed . . . but nothing grows. Every salesman in the world knows we're suckers for things we can get along very well without. Yet if I chop off the imports, the Roman people will throw me in the Tiber. We can't seem to make anything or export anything except soldiers and the law . . . which makes it easier for our colonists to send more and more."

Vespasian had also expressed his concerns about the trade deficit and its inevitable effect on the future of the Roman economy. As usual, Titus had been politely attentive to his worries; but Domitian had yawned and belched and played at killing a fly during his father's long recitation of numbers.

The *annona*, free distribution of grain to the poor of Rome, now included a third of the city's population, and more than a third of the supply came from Egypt; North Africa supplied nearly all the rest. Vespasian reminded his sons of the riots that had occurred some nine years previously, when bad weather had prevented the arrival of grain ships. "We can't have that sort of thing happening again," he insisted.

Vespasian reminded his sons that the port of Ostia was the busiest in the Empire. The wharves were groaning under the weight of fruit from Syria, of nuts, nard, glass, and every conceivable luxury. Asia Minor sent everything from oysters to carpets, while the Greeks sent timber, marble, perfumes, and statuary. Ivory, obsidian, and apes came from East Africa; and slaves from West Africa, along with elephants, camels, and various beasts destined for the gladitorial contests in several arenas and the soon to be completed Coliseum. Gaul sent timber south across the Alps along with vegetables, cheese, poultry, and cattle. Britain sent hides for the fashioning of legionary armor and tin, which was so important to the smithies; the savages of that gloomy island also provided lead and some slaves of dubious quality.

Vespasian warned his sons with one of his typical homilies: Rome represented one huge open mouth and the stream of export was of corresponding size to the anus. "Our hunger for all sorts of nonsense increases every day. We are breeding a whirlwind," he grumbled.

With the problem of Berenice solved at last, Titus tried to dismiss her as completely from his mind as he had from his presence. There were so many new problems to be faced. He brooded on them now as he listened to the former Jewish general, Joseph ben Matthias, who had displayed such remarkable common sense that he had given himself up after the siege at Jotapata. As a result of his expediency he was now living comfortably in Rome and writing a history of the wars in Judea. From the beginning of that enterprise Titus had encouraged him; having been so heavily engaged in the wars himself, he wanted to make sure Joseph had his facts right. The two former adversaries were dining alone in the government house that Titus had provided.

"You keep a good kitchen," Titus said as a pair of slaves removed the remnants of a Melian crane and brought in a roasted kid from Thrace.

"With thanks to your bounty," Joseph nodded. He pulled a sliver of meat from the roast and popped it into his mouth as assurance to his guest that it was not poisoned. Titus smiled in acknowledgment and asked if he was going to include military technique in his lengthy record.

"To some extent, Sire. I've just completed an essay on your Macedonian phalanx versus the mobility of more open formations."

"The trouble is that when we don't use the phalanx, we require more cavalry to protect our flanks."

"True. But the effect of the phalanx on the morale of both sides is very strong. I'd keep it if I were you."

"We have no intention of abandoning it altogether. Unfortunately, the army is convinced that foreign auxiliaries are disposed to break and run at the last moment, which can be disastrous."

Titus found it difficult to keep his thoughts on military matters. As soon as the meal was finished he must meet with his staff and assign at least two of them to a pet project of his father's—the founding of chairs in literature and rhetoric, one in Greek and one in Latin. Then the Armenian ambassador was due at the palace for a discussion on developing more mutual trade. Later, there was a delegation of merchants who wanted financing for an expedition to a country called Shansi.

Titus twisted off a crisp piece of the kid's skin and chewed on it thoughtfully as he watched Joseph duplicate his gestures. He liked the man. Jew or not Jew, he thought, Joseph ben Matthias was an individual of great wisdom; what he brought forth from his Oriental mind should always be heeded. "I'm a soldier at heart, but I'm not much involved with the army these days," Titus said almost apologetically. "Now I'm beset with a thousand other problems, and I can't say my father didn't warn me."

"You are irreplaceable, Sire."

"Sometimes I wish it were not so."

"However . . . may I suggest that you are in a delicate situation?" Joseph licked the gravy from his fingers, wiped them on a napkin, and then held them up rigidly as a counting device. "For example, there are about four hundred thousand slaves in and about this city. I'm sure you realize what might happen if they all joined together? Even with your Legions and your auxiliaries, you have only about a hundred and fifty thousand men. It takes only a single spark, Sire, and the whole house can burn down."

"Both my father and I have given the matter considerable thought."

"But not Domitian? Suppose one day your brother decides to challenge your right to the throne . . . and enlists such vast numbers to his cause? Perhaps he might even try to discredit you and even your sister . . . what then? I hope you will forgive my speculations, Sire, and I'm certainly in no position to find fault with the Flavian family, *but* . . ." Joseph arched his heavy eyebrows, humped his shoulders, and spread his hands with an air of finality.

"Fortunately, my brother is not a rabble-rouser," Titus said easily. He thought that here was an opportunity to explore a totally different and brilliant mind when the project that now so obsessed him was revealed. "I've a surprise for you," he began. "I've been seeking some way to reassure all Romans and hopefully dissolve their immediate discontents. At the same time, I want to lock their confidence in the Flavian family. What do you think of a magnificent triumph celebrating the whole illustrious career of my father?"

Joseph smiled. "You are very shrewd, Sire. May I suggest that you badly need an affair of such magnitude."

The following morning Titus conferred with Sextus Frontinus, the head of the Rome Water Department. He had just taken charge of the utility and found what he described as incredible corruption everywhere in the system. Just after Frontinus, eight senators fulfilled appointments—each with requests for money. "We're already suffering from the financial plague," Titus told them, "and money is going to be the death of us. Our purse is thinning, along with our blood."

The rest of the day and the day after were devoted to the enormous preparations for the event Rome would never forget. All haste must be made because of his father's health. Now that she had returned, Domitillia must be launched on whatever preparations she must make. Domitian must be hauled out of whatever brothel he happened to be favoring, washed, sobered, reminded of his responsibilities to the family, and otherwise included in the mighty tribute to their father. All government employees were to be granted three days' holiday, and all citizens of Rome were urged to decorate their houses and flats in an appropriate fashion. There were thousands of details, most of which were already in the capable hands of his staff. Yet there were still so many things to be planned. It was to be a traditional triumph as established by Augustus himself, and it had not been easy to persuade Papa that he deserved such attention. He had at last agreed "for the good of the Empire." Since Papa was such a stickler for detail, it must be arranged that all of the twelve bands of musicians were in the correct sequence, and the bearers of trophies carefully chosen for their physical beauty. Among thousands of other details.

It must be—for Vespasian, for Rome, for the Empire—the grandest day in history.

And one other detail, he reminded himself: Flavius Silva had not yet reported on the mood of the Legions in Africa.

Should there be the slightest question as to their loyalty or even if it was split between himself and Domitian, the true significance behind any triumph would be false. It was obvious that Papa intended the power of the throne to be consolidated again in a single individual. He knew that the instant death took him the ambitious would come from all directions; some were even capable of raising armies to their cause. Unless a powerful individual held the throne, the Empire could be plundered in a matter of months. Even the tragedy of another civil war could be repeated, and all that Papa had worked so diligently to achieve would be lost.

This triumph, Titus insisted, must be more than an obligatory recognition of the deeds performed by an ailing old man. It must be genuine in every aspect. Papa must be showered with glory in his last days. The people should be convinced that the gods always fought on the side of the Romans.

Poor Flavius Silva, he thought; you poor minor general upon whom so much depended. It was going to be extremely difficult to transfer power peacefully if Domitian had such a loyal soldier at his command.

NINE

IT OCCURRED TO Domitillia that if the truth became known, she would not be allowed to wear the *stola*, that lovely and provocative gown that reached to the feet. For the stola was forbidden to courtesans and to women condemned for adultery. As she instructed her seamstresses exactly how she wanted the fringe fashioned and specified the material she preferred and the intensity of the purple dye, she could not avoid some sly satisfaction with the way things had turned out. It was not so much the anticipated beauty of the gown, which would take the better part of a month to complete, but rather the comforting realization that she was deeply in love with Flavius Silva and had declared herself to the highest authority in the land. Now she found it possible to sympathize with her father's anger; it was to be expected of his stodgy generation.

Bless his magnanimous heart, she thought. He had lifted the restriction on her association with people other than that slob, Marcus, who was such a limp excuse for a husband. Every time she saw the man, he reminded her more of an overcooked cabbage. She had not seen him for days and that, she reasoned, was so typical of their marriage that her adulterous thoughts and actions were purely theoretical. But this was not the time for regrets or any of the other sour lemons of life.

She held a mirror to her face and saw the rejoicing in her eyes. This was an altogether new woman, a woman deeply in love, she thought. The effect on her whole image was startling. Where there had been a sardonic smile, she saw a blossoming of youth again. There were overtones of exuberance in her eyes, a merriment and warmth she had not seen for a long time.

"Hello," she whispered to the mirror. "Greetings to the renewed Domitillia, the most decadent, outrageous female in Rome."

She tipped her head from side to side as if to see a different aspect of herself. Yes, she was Flavius Silva's woman now, and that was infinitely pleasing. It might also bring the roof down on her head.

What a brainless, exciting vision! Poor Domitillia, lying there on the marble with bits of plaster in her hair. Poor Domitillia, laughing her way to paradise on the arm of a soldier who was far more than a mere warrior. May the gods smile upon Flavius Silva! And may the smile upon the lips of his partner reflect her total love.

Soon there would be further excitements to pass the time while she waited for a reunion with her Flavius. Soon the capital of the world would be decorated with all the joyous trappings imaginable; and all for the other man she adored—dear Papa. Her place in the grand parade would be somewhere behind him along with her brothers, but whether she walked or rode in a vehicle was still to be decided. There were committees for everything, and those persons in charge of transporting members of the Flavian family and their various relatives by marriage—such as Marcus Arrecinus Clemens, if he could stay sober long enough—were still arguing over style and position. One overly enthusiastic committee member had suggested the Emperor's daughter ride one of the elephants. The prospect at first amused her but she eventually declined. She was damned if she was going to be bounced around atop one of those monsters while wearing a stola that cost a fortune and could not be appreciated except when viewed at full length.

"And besides," she had told the committee member responsible for the notion, "elephants may not be beautiful, but they are unbeatable competition. You think anyone is going to look at me when there's a genuine pachyderm ambling right past their noses? Put a doll on your elephant's neck! Domitillia is going to be down where she can be comfortable and seen."

THE TRIUMPH

The forthcoming triumph had already generated many odd developments. Viewing spaces along the route of the parade were being sold by those who lived in advantageous locations. The coins depicting Judea on her knees, which had been minted before Masada and were hitherto ridiculed as premature, were climbing rapidly in value. The market for a certain type of oatcake traditional to triumphs was already lively.

At last, she thought, the recognition Papa had so long deserved was about to be demonstrated in an unforgettable occasion. The parade itself would take most of the day and the attendant festivities would go on indefinitely. Never mind if holidays were fast devouring the old Roman devotion to hard work. There were holidays set aside for deities high and low —Jupiter, Apollo, Neptune, Mercury, Saturn, Bacchus, Juno . . . Venus, and a whole pantheon of gods. Her brickworks was now lucky to find a solid four days in a week to operate at full capacity; meanwhile, construction languished, the number of unemployed was beginning to exceed the number of persons working, and nothing of pure Roman origin was done very well. For almost every endeavor the practice of going to foreigners, whether freedmen or slaves, was rapidly increasing. It was, as the saying went, "the only way to get anything done." But Papa's triumph was different, Domitillia decided. He was a living god.

There were two flaws in her current euphoria, and she tried with all her will to put them aside. One was the obligation to be civil to her husband. The other was the absence of Berenice! How very much she missed her companionship. Since her exile she had written long and tearful notes both to Titus and Papa, all of which lay about her dressing rooms, unfinished and undelivered. For Domitillia could not for the life of her discover a sound argument to keep Berenice in the capital. Unlike the Christianii who were harassed in Rome, the Jews were tolerated and even allowed to prosper. Still, that indulgence went only so far and most assuredly did not extend to the outer fringes of power. Berenice's closeness to Titus had doomed her from the beginning. But how she longed for the woman's wit and wisdom!

She was thinking about Berenice when a slave came to her and announced that an officer of the Tenth Legion waited upon her. She instantly cast away all reserve as she ran through her house in the direction of the atrium. Such was her haste that her sandals slipped on the polished marble flooring and she nearly fell as she rounded the last pillar of the peristyle. She was still breathless and flustered when she greeted Centurion Piso. "Welcome!" she said in a voice that echoed throughout the house. "Welcome, as you've never been welcomed before!"

It was all she could do to keep from kissing Centurion Piso. When he presented her with a letter he said was from General Silva, she could not restrain her tears. "You marvelous man!" she cried out, clutching the letter to her as if it might somehow escape by itself. "You've come all the way from Judea with this and I'm most deeply in your debt. You must stay here for as long as you please. There are countless rooms and anyone who has been selected by our dear friend, the General, must be our honored guest."

Piso smiled and she took an instant attachment to him. He was so stalwart, as she envisioned all men about Flavius must be, and she must force herself to consider his needs before she ran off to the privacy of her chambers where—dear gods, all of you be thanked—she would break the letter's seal.

"I don't wish Your Highness to keep the impression that I was selected," Piso said easily. "I was given little choice."

Domitillia hardly heard him. "Ah? Is your general all right?"

"Quite, Your Highness. As you know, he is a remarkable man."

"Oh yes, I do! You must need refreshment and food."

She clapped her hands for a slave, who came running. Today, she thought, this glorious day, everyone in the house of Clemens was running. And none would run as fast as Domitillia, once her duties as a hostess were done. She would race to read her letter.

She told the slave to see to Centurion Piso's every need. Then she said to him, "I'm thirsty for news of Judea and your general. Please ask for me when you are rested and fill my need to know all that has happened since my departure."

Later, after Domitillia had devoured every word of Silva's letter innumerable times, she could no longer wait to see Piso. So she sent him word to join her for a cup of wine in the peristyle as soon as possible—or sooner, she chuckled to herself. Oh, great day! For a little time it seemed as if her incomparable Flavius was right beside her.

After Piso had satisfied her yearning for news of events in Judea—a fig for events anywhere in the world, she thought; it was Flavius she wanted to hear about—he explained how he had been obliged to serve as the courier of Silva's letter because he had accepted the beliefs of the Christianii.

"And you swallow their principles?" she asked in some amazement. "I've heard a few friends discuss the cult . . . these things alway seem to start with the aristocracy and I'm afraid I don't understand them. What's all this about loving your fellow man? Is that belief for men only? It sounds like something the Greeks or our homosexuals would foster."

"By no means. Male and female are considered equal in the eyes of God."

"That's refreshing."

"We believe there is only one god."

"So I've gathered. Well . . . well. It would certainly be easier than all the bowing and scraping we do to our own collection of gods. What does yours look like?"

"I don't know."

"Then how can you address him? How can you make sacrifice?"

"Sacrifice is unnecessary. And God is everywhere. You can see him in everything from a tree to a fish."

"That seems somewhat ridiculous. You must admit it does," she said mischievously. Who cared what was ridiculous? This man had recently been in the presence of Flavius. Nothing else really mattered.

"Sorry, Your Highness. I cannot agree."

"You're a stubborn man, Centurion Piso. Explain to me then how you can be a soldier and love your enemies."

"It's difficult. It troubles me . . . that's why I'm here."

"Ah? But your general expects you to return to the Legion. If there's fighting in the future, what are you going to do? Lay down your sword and kiss your enemy? I don't think Rome will last very long if that kind of spirit infects our troops."

"There would be no fighting if we all lived by the principles of the Christianii."

"I didn't hear that, Centurion Piso. I've suddenly gone deaf. You are an interesting man and, I presume, loyal to

Rome and to your Legion. But some might consider your thoughts as dangerous, even revolutionary. I'd dislike seeing your handsome head on the end of a pike. Don't you realize that people in power are always worried about losing it?" The slightest deviation from what they think is right can send them into spasms of suppression. You'll do well to mind your tongue, Centurion."

"I appreciate your concern, and . . ." he smiled, "your patience."

Domitillia held a finger to her lips momentarily, then said, "Let caution guide your words, Piso. I hope the time will come when I can ask you more questions."

"I'm at your service. I hope there will be time for me to visit my family in Sardinia for a few days."

"Go to Sardinia and leave word where you can be reached."

As Piso saluted and turned away, she thought to tell him something he apparently did not know: Titus had advised her that he had ordered Silva to proceed to Africa and then with all speed to Rome. She changed her mind. It was not her business to relay military orders to anyone.

As he had done these past several months, the beggar astounded his audience with feats of legerdemain. His skill at pulling small stones from the ears of spectators and his rapid shifting of three nutshells with a borrowed coin under one, left him, as it had done throughout his long journey, with satisfied patrons and a tidy enough sum to make it through the day. So it had been in Crete and in Sparta and in Sicily; each place well worked until the inhabitants grew weary of him. Thus had he lived and paid for his passage bit by bit, starting with nothing whatever and at last making the port of Ostia so close to home.

As any man in fear for his life, the beggar was alert to every threat whether real or imagined. Except for his necessary performances, he did his best to remain inconspicuous. His clothes were rags, he was repulsively filthy, and he spoke only in the tongue of the streets. When asked his nationality he claimed to be a Thracian.

The beggar had proved his extraordinary cunning by managing to avoid all Roman patrols en route to Ostia. Now he relaxed his guard, since there were friends nearby to whom he was of considerable value and who were powerful enough to save his skin if necessary. This crisp morning, with the fog still lingering along the mouth of the Tiber, he was almost joyful in giving his last performance. He had persuaded his spectators to wager among themselves on the outcome of his shell game, while he himself "bet the house." Since he controlled the movement of the coin beneath the three shells, he always won, but these fellows, saying much for their proximity to the city of Rome, were lavish in their wagers. By noon, when the fog began to lift, he had enough to buy a place on a wagon bound for the city.

As the heavy vehicle drawn by two oxen groaned and thumped over the uneven paving stones, the beggar was most pleased to contemplate his present situation. Like the appearance of the sun, which now shone so gloriously upon his unkempt beard and bronzed face, his fortune had finally improved. The terror of making a mistake, the near certainty of being recognized for someone other than what he pretended to be, was over. Had he not been so cautious his mere manner of speech would have betrayed him; had he but once sought the comforts that he had so long enjoyed, suspicion would have begun and word of his possible identity passed along. While in the Orient, that would certainly have been a disaster, but even as he worked his way westward there was always the off chance he might be recognized.

When the wagon passed through the Ostian gate of the city during the early evening, the beggar breathed a heavy sigh of relief. For now he could throw away the name Gabba, which had served him since that terrible night in Judea, and resume his own identity. The gods had been kind and he resolved to make suitable sacrifices commemorating their protection.

Near the middle of the city he eased down from the wagon and turned into the Clivus Pullius. He walked along it jauntily, careless of how his rags flapped with his movements. When he came to a blue door recessed in the street wall, he halted, took a deep breath, and pulled the bell rope. He waited nervously until he heard the shuffle of feet and saw the door open a crack. Beyond it he saw the dark eyes of his beloved Spanish boy.

"My dear!" he said smiling. "I've come home!"

He saw the fear in the Spanish boy's eyes just as the door

was slammed in his face. Then the door opened again, a crack—then a little wider. "Let me in, you silly boy. Don't you recognize your very own Julius Scribonia?"

Late that night, after he had bathed and perfumed himself endlessly and plucked at his beard until it was at least somewhat neater, when at last he had held the Spanish boy in his arms and listened contentedly to his piquant phrases, he found his attention drifting from his momentary paradise and focusing on the details of his miraculous escape from the beach at Caesarea. Although he had reviewed that night countless times, he was surprised at how much he had almost forgotten. He had returned to consciousness while still lying in the water, pushed himself to his feet, and stumbled along the beach until he came to a bramble bush. Utterly exhausted, he had crept beneath it and spent the balance of the night. When his mind had returned to its normal orderliness, he realized that he was the sole possessor of priceless information that might result in a compounded increase in his personal power, in addition to being remunerative.

It was while nursing his bruises under the bush that he came to several logical conclusions. First, to stay alive he must disappear. Next, Vespasian would have little choice but to banish his daughter forever if told of her adultery. There was monetary worth in that knowledge.

Now? He must remain inconspicuous for a time, cutting his hair and beard and placing a ring in his earlobe. This would suggest to anyone who saw him in the streets that he was one of the fashionable Greek doctors. He would first report to Domitian and, with his consent, deliberately avoid the offices of the *frumentarii*. Meanwhile, he could commence the grandest ploy imaginable; little by little he would drop hints in just the right places at just the right times that Julius Scribonia was alive. Where? Somewhere. Most delicious of all would be the ever-growing torment of both Domitillia and Silva while they waited for the ax to fall.

He smiled happily and toyed with the Spanish boy's hair while he envisioned the future. "Your dear friend and master will be a very rich man before I reveal their disgraceful behavior."

For a time when the Spanish boy pressed against him, Scribonia even went so far as to visualize Domitillia trying to explain to the Senate how she could have been rutting on a beach with one of the Empire's most noble generals and moments later stand witness to an attempted murder. Was she another Messalina or Livia? Had that licentious pair set an entrapment whereby their sexual lust was enhanced by the sight of another man's blood? Would that not be the ultimate insult to the throne? Such inviting thoughts and the many ramifications that reality might bring seemed sweet reward now that he was safely home.

The Spanish boy attempted to fondle him, but he said, "Keep your distance, pretty thing. I've been sweeping the streets of North Africa with my pudenda and probably have acquired diseases hitherto unknown to mankind. The lice on my once-gorgeous body were the size of rhinos, and my breath stank of old goat cheese. I guarantee you, pretty thing, that the great Julius Caesar made a mistake when he took Africa. He should have junked every settlement in the land instead of only a few. Alexandria is an asshole, Carthage is an asshole, and so is every hamlet in between. I came hither on a Phoenician ship that was the ultimate cesspool; it kept afloat only by an inexplicable whim of the gods. Give me a week to cleanse my poor self, and I shall become once more the most succulent love you've ever known."

Scribonia was in such a frenzy to achieve his new character that he paid a barber fifty sesterces to cancel all his previous appointments and attend upon him alone until the job was done. After cutting his hair short as a senator's, the barber began treating the hair on his face and body with a series of poultices called dropax, which he guaranteed as a depilatory. He finished the project with his tweezers, plucking the hairs one by one from Scribonia's entire body, including his loins. His client endured the modest torture for hours, insisting all the time that he was immune to pain if it brought cleanliness. The barber cleaned his ears with vinegar and recommended a series of prune physics to flush Scribonia's reluctant bowels. He also suggested the chewing of mint and beeswax to polish the teeth. In the end Scribonia examined himself naked in the barber's mirror and smiled. "You naughty boy," he said to himself, "now no one will know you."

Later, he viewed his collection of togas with regret. They were the mark of a prominent and influential Roman of at least the equestrian class, and whether they caught the eye of approval or of envy they called attention to the wearer. But he must store them away. From now on, or at least until the culmination of his plans, he would wear only the simple tunic of the Roman citizen.

Scribonia had not fully appreciated his passionate attachment to the Spanish boy until the same afternoon after he had left the barber and returned to his house full of anticipation for play. "Pretty thing," he murmured as he caressed the boy's heavy locks, "how my tactile senses have longed for the texture of your skin! It's like the silk of China and it smells of myrtle. When you part your lips it is like unlocking a treasure chest . . . I can hardly wait to enjoy the sensations within. In other words, I'm in love with you, dear boy, and I do hope you feel the same about me."

Since the boy spoke not a word of Greek, in which Scribonia had chosen to recite his attributes, he was disappointed in the lad's lack of reaction. Didn't he realize that his patron would soon become one of the most powerful men in the Empire?

It was only when all their efforts failed to arouse Scribonia that the boy began to laugh at his impotence. Furious, Scribonia slapped the boy and sent him sprawling. Then he began to slap him repeatedly. When his terrified yelping ceased, Scribonia took him in his arms and apologized. "Excuse my wretched temper. It's just that I've so much on my mind these days. I must prepare myself to see Domitian tomorrow. Such concentration drains one, and events are collecting that are beyond my most outrageous fancies. Were I to stay up planning for a month of nights I could not conceive of more favorable timing. Our beloved Emperor, that paragon of the stupid military mind, is soon to be given a triumph. Honors will be piled on honors, gifts and felicitations will flow from all over the Empire, then joy and exaltation of the royal family will be unbearable. Pufferies and bullshit will mix with trumpet blasts in such a vainglorious brew it will be weeks before anyone comes to their senses. Yes! This will be the time to strike! You will see, pretty thing. We'll make love while scandal rips the Flavians to pieces and Flavius Silva is fed to the animals."

This time Scribonia chose to speak in Latin, so the Spanish boy understood his words if not their potential.

"Timing," Scribonia added. "The importance of timing must be brought to Domitian's attention again and again."

The boy was bored with Scribonia's orations and his interest drifted to a flute his master had brought him from Africa. He puckered his lips around it and made a tweedling noise. The gesture caused Scribonia to sigh heavily. Such a lovely boy! Why must his ambitions drive him to anything more?

That very night at the port of Ostia, where he had so recently arrived in rags, a resplendent Scribonia booked the best room at the inn. He then boarded the ship designated to take Berenice into exile. What a difference in this vessel and the wretched bucket that had been his transport!

Berenice sat cross-legged on a couch in the small after cabin. She greeted him coldly. He saw that her eyes sparkled in the oil light, but she was squinting at him. The old bitch is nearsighted, he thought; or was she preparing to pounce? Still, he found her quite beautiful in her way, and he understood how a man like Titus could be so taken with her. Now, if all went as planned she would have a chance at vengeance.

Scribonia bowed slightly and handed her the ring she had sent him. He thought it rather graceless of such a rich woman to take it back, but then what could be expected of an Oriental?

"What would you sell me?" she asked.

"Information of the utmost value. Something no one else will know. And it will be very valuable in, may I say . . . your present dilemma?"

"I do not buy unseen goods."

"How wise of you. While I cannot open the box until I'm paid, I can at least show you the key. Suppose this information concerned a member of the imperial family and a noble Roman? Suppose it could be extremely detrimental to the Flavian house if it became generally known? Suppose it might be useful to you in your future relations with the throne?"

Berenice's eyes narrowed even further. What female, Scribonia thought, could resist such temptation?

"What price have you in mind?"

"Ten thousand sesterces."

"Leave my sight. I find your perfume revolting."

Scribonia smiled, but he made no move to depart. "May I

remind you, dear lady, that information is power? In this case it is of far more worth than I'm asking for such a very private acquisition."

"I'll offer you a thousand just to be rid of you."

"My hearing is impaired, so I'm sure I've misunderstood you. As a man of means I am unaccustomed to dealing in sums as small as ten thousand, but in this case my sense of values was compromised because what I have to sell would be more useful to you than to anyone else."

"Two thousand and get out."

Scribonia gave a great show of patience. "Dear lady," he whined, "I cannot believe you're unaware of the circumstances . . . or are they too simple to be appreciated by one who was in their midst until very recently? We have an emperor who is so close to death he may have left us even as these words are uttered. He has designated one of his sons to succeed him. You have been, shall I say, well acquainted with that individual. The other son does not view this succession with enthusiasm. In fact, he will fight for what he considers his right the moment the famous papa is dead. Need I remind you what will happen then?"

"Three thousand and not an *aes* more."

"Lady, we are on the verge of civil war. Brother against brother. As far as the Roman public is concerned, the slightest factor can tip the balance between their support to one man or to the other. They want only a leader they can trust and admire."

"They have that in Titus."

"Very generous of you, dear lady. Particularly in view of your present . . . difficulty? Perhaps to rectify matters all you'll need in the future is a weapon against the Flavian family." Scribonia sighed. "I'm uncomfortable with bargaining, so I'll pass it on to you for a mere five thousand sesterces." Scribonia turned as if to go. "Very well," she said. "Speak."

"Not until . . ." Scribonia smiled. He held out his hands.

Berenice took up a tiny silver bell and at the first tinkle a middle-aged woman appeared in the doorway. Berenice told her to bring five thousand sesterces, and while she was gone Scribonia related his version of the disgraceful behavior of Domitillia and Flavius Silva.

When Berenice handed him the bag of coins, she asked, "Who else have you told this to?"

"No one. Surely you recognize its exclusive value."

"I do. I also recognize a rat on this ship. Will you take him away instantly or shall I?"

Scribonia found the weight of the coins did much to soothe his dignity. His step was deliberately jaunty as he left the cabin and continued so as he made his way through the streets of Ostia. Just before he reached the inn he patted the bag of coins, which he carried tucked under one arm. Five thousand sesterces was exactly what he had intended to settle for, and it had certainly been an easy night's work.

Suddenly, two huge men who looked like sailors appeared out of the darkness and blocked his way. He was about to protest when a coarse cloth was thrown over his head and secured tightly around his throat. It smelled strongly of urine. The bag of coins was jerked away and his hands were tied behind him. It was done so expertly and swiftly he had no chance to protest. A hoarse voice said, "The lady found your goods were faulty."

Quite as suddenly as he had been confronted, Scribonia realized he had been left unhurt and alone. Although his hands were tied loosely, it seemed an eternity before he managed to free them and remove the filthy rag from his head.

Scribonia spent a restless night at the inn. He blamed himself for not employing bodyguards to escort him through the streets, as most Romans of substance found it expedient to do. It had been sheer carelessness, but the distance between the ship and the inn had been so short he had not anticipated any difficulty.

Perhaps, he thought, that Oriental bitch had done him a favor. She had discouraged him from wasting his talent on the likes of her and steered him toward a far more valuable target. From this night on he would devote himself utterly to developing his tenuous acquaintance with Domitian. He would gamble on the odd horse and win.

TEN

SILVA HAD ORDERED his horse Fury to be prepared for a long arduous journey—its hooves trimmed and legs looked to—and the saddle, bridle, and all mounted accoutrements, including his regular service sword, placed in readiness. He decided to take two of his staff officers, Attius, a young Eques, and Larcus Liberalis, who was also young and equally fit. He instructed them to select ten of the most deserving troopers in the auxiliary cavalry to accompany them.

Geminus growled his displeasure at such a choice. He said that the most deserving legionaries of the Tenth would certainly and rightfully complain they had been discriminated against, and he didn't like to be left with them.

Silva's reply was curt. "You never like being left with anything, but I'll give you an answer for them. If any legionary feels that he can buy a horse and learn to ride while we move along at a fast pace all the way to Carthage, then he's welcome. But we won't play nursemaid. If he falls behind, he'll be left to the mercy of the locals—if any."

Since most Roman legionaries did not know one end of a horse from the other, Silva was certain there would be no volunteers. He was equally convinced that if he could manage to make Carthage in less than a month, then the relatively short sea crossing to Ostia should put him in Rome in time for the Emperor's triumph.

When they rode southward at first light, Silva did not even look back. As Fury settled into his long route-march pacing,

Silva prayed to all the gods he could think of that he would never be ordered to return to Caesarea or any place else in Judea. He thought that he had been so long in the land that he must be half Jew, by osmosis if nothing else.

They trotted along between the sea and the hills to the east and so found relative comfort in the cool of the coastal strip. There were occasional fields now brilliant green with the spring. Silva became even more invigorated as he realized that in spite of the fact he was temporarily riding in the wrong direction he was actually bound for home. To the east of his little party he knew that the sun was beginning to hammer on the Judean desert. Over there beyond the intervening range of hills was Masada baking in the desert heat. And there, somewhere in that wasteland were the ashes of Sheva, the Jewess who had done so much to open his mind toward other people.

He breathed deeply of the morning air and glanced over his shoulder at his twenty-man escort jouncing along with their helmets glittering in the morning light. They were mounted on the most stalwart of the cavalry's horses, and he listened for an instant to the melodious clinking of their equipment and the occasional laugh of excited troopers mixed with the snorting of their mounts. They are like boys suddenly released on holiday, he thought; but then, so am I. No doubt they would all present a different picture when they finally rode into Carthage, but for now the stimulus of exploration invigorated every man.

"Attius!" he called to the already perspiring young man who rode at his side. He knew that his voice was full of enthusiasm and saw the same vitality reflected in Attius' eyes. "I've a wager for you. Five sesterces we make Alexandria in seven days!"

"Easy money, General. I'll make it eight days no matter how hard we ride."

As Silva extended his hand to seal the bet, Fury shied at the quick and unusual movement, nearly unseating Silva. They both laughed heartily at his awkward recovery. "A surer wager," Silva said to Liberalis, who rode on his left, "is that we'll all eat standing up until our butts get pounded back into shape."

They came upon Gaza by nightfall. The centurion in command of the small detachment stationed in the town was greatly surprised that so august a personage as Flavius Silva would pause even briefly at his outpost. He made his guests as comfortable as his limited facilities permitted. He reported that the Jews had given him little trouble during the recent months, although there had been some grumbling about the new tax on grains and the share taken to feed his men. He also advised Silva to be wary as he rode south and west. While it was unlikely he would encounter any of the desert people who were a murderous lot, they did occasionally make plundering expeditions up from the Sinai and would not be in the slightest deterred by Silva's little party. "May I offer some advice, General?" the centurion asked.

"If my brain is not as weary as my rump, perhaps I'll hear it well."

"Should you see them approaching, run in the opposite direction."

Silva smiled. "I assure you, Centurion, that almost all of the fight has gone out of me. I have a very fast horse, and after spying even a lone figure with a menacing look in his eye, I'll be the first of my party to disappear over the horizon."

Since both men knew this was far from the truth, they laughed and were content with each other.

Although he moved stiffly on the following morning, Silva marveled that his spirits remained so high; he was delighted with the challenges of a new day in the saddle. Was it just that he was westbound for home? Was it the prospect of seeing Domitillia or the knowledge that after so much frustration and bloodshed, all of which had accomplished very little as far as he could tell, Judea might remain just an uncomfortable memory?

Flanked by Attius and Liberalis, with his troopers in line of trail behind, Silva led them through Gaza, then to Pelusium, thence through the marshes of El Quantara, and on to Tanta. On the eighth day, they came upon the city of Alexandria. Silva paid his debt to Attius and made another wager—that they would make Cyrene in ten days. "I'll make it twelve," Attius said, grinning. Silva said he was the worst pessimist he had ever known, with the possible exception of Geminus.

Since the time of Julius Caesar and even long before, every educated Roman held an irresistible fascination for Egypt.

Alexandria, with its double harbor, polyglot population, busy streets, and itinerant travelers from all over the Mediterranean world, offered an exotic lure that Romans found intoxicating. Flavius Silva and his little band of troopers felt an extraordinary excitement as they approached the outskirts of the city. They were weary and smeared with the dust and sweat of their long journey, and their horses' heads remained down more than up, but when they saw they had less than a few miles to go, they increased their pace and the soft clatter of their gear became staccato. The troopers knew that units of two Legions, the Twenty-second Deiotariana and the Third Cyrenaica, were stationed in Egypt. They hoped their comrades in arms would steer them via the quickest route toward the lascivious delights that Alexandria was said to offer. For Silva had promised three days' rest for horse and man, only one of which need be spent on repairs of their equipment and reprovisioning.

Silva disliked arriving unannounced and with such a small party, so he called a halt just outside the eastern gate and made his rather bedraggled men groom themselves and their equipment until he considered they were at least arriving with the best face possible. He knew that the governor would be only an Equite; it had been so since the deified Augustus proclaimed no higher rank could represent Rome in Egypt. He hoped his prospective host would recognize that although his troopers were auxiliaries, they were attached to the famous Tenth Legion and should be treated accordingly.

One evening not long after they had left Gaza, Silva had gone to the troopers' camp fire and at their request had told them something of Alexandria. There, he explained, Cleopatra had captured the heart of Julius Caesar, and there also her flirtation and eventually tragic romance had grown into an affair that shook the world. His troopers became enthralled as he described how Alexandria had been the scene of Marc Antony's triumph after the Parthian campaign, and how, after his defeat at the Battle of Actium, he had sailed up the Nile with Cleopatra toward their mutual suicides. To Silva's great satisfaction he had to plead total exhaustion before they had let him go.

They rode in good order and absolute silence through the crowded streets of Alexandria. Silva was pleased that his men were not jabbering like so many arriving pilgrims. They were awed, he knew, by the extent of the city, its busy atmosphere, and the hordes of people swarming through the streets. There was little wonder, Silva decided, that the Roman administration was said to be still having trouble setting things straight and right in Egypt. The traffic of wagons, chariots, carts, horses, and donkeys in the narrow streets was chaotic. Everything lacked the relative discipline of Rome, and the city seemed overwhelmed with people of every conceivable birthright. During one of their frequent halts for space to pass, Silva recalled an old saying, "Never let an Alexandrian slip between your back and a wall." Judging from the look of those jostling each other about him, Silva thought there might be some substance to the phrase.

General Petronius Niges commanded the Twenty-second Legion, and Silva knew him as a brave man always complaining of his pay. He was rumored to be so engaged in fattening his purse that he disregarded both the discipline and welfare of his men. Money then, Silva thought, might be the key to his loyalty!

When they found the headquarters of the Twenty-second Legion, Silva was disappointed. The barren, comfortless building was located at the harbor in an area of huge warehouses full of grain bound for Rome. Units of the Twenty-second Legion were assigned to guard the grain, but lassitude and a general indifference was apparent from the moment Silva spotted the first legionary. There was certainly none of the smartness he insisted upon in the ranks of the Tenth. Those men on post stood any way they felt like, he thought; some were actually sitting down. Silva warned himself against being too critical when he met with Petronius Niges. The loyalty of his Legion to Titus, however ill-mannered, was essential and could not be won by antagonism.

At the gate Silva was met by a decurion who took his time about saluting an obviously superior officer. When Silva told him to advise the commander of his arrival, the decurion said he was absent; "gone to Memphis for a look about," he answered with a smirk. Ordinarily Silva would have had the man reduced to the ranks and put in chains for a month or longer if his impudence remained, but for the sake of his hard-worn troopers he hesitated to inaugurate their arrival with any sign of impatience.

"Then send me your vice commander," Silva ordered. "Instantly!"

The decurion suddenly seemed aware that Silva meant what he said. He disappeared beyond the gate and returned almost immediately with an overage tribune who barely troubled to salute. Silva was sure that he was drunk, but decided to hold his temper until his requirements were met to his total satisfaction. His ruptured ego could wait; the needs of his men came first.

"I want your best accommodations for my men, including access to your baths and provisions for their mess. I also want suitable quarters for my two officers and myself." He caught the centurion's roving eyes and added, *"Now!"*

"You'll not want to go to the general's house. He's down with the fevers."

"I was told he was out of the city."

"We always say that when he's indisposed."

"What do you mean . . . indisposed?"

"You'll find out for yourself."

Silva was becoming increasingly annoyed.

"I don't give a damn who's down with what. We're tired and want baths. We'll stable our horses here and feed them ourselves." He crossed his arms and leaned forward on the neck of his horse. "Tribune, whatever your name may be, a label I remain ignorant of because of your failure to report yourself according to regulations . . . I am the Commander of the Tenth Legion, among other things, and I advise you to heed my words. I assume you've been in the Twenty-second for a long time and must have seen a certain amount of action. That does not excuse either your appearance or your behavior. Now, if you don't provide quarters by the time we're done with our mounts, I'll see to it that you'll lose your rank, pension, and whatever lands may have been granted you. Therefore, I suggest you move your ass smartly and find us the best in Alexandria."

Silva dismounted and handed his horse to a waiting trooper. He turned his back on the tribune and walked across the street with Attius. They stood on the fringe of the harbor and looked at the lighthouse near the entrance. Silva tried to remember the name of it, but failed. He said to Attius, "I think that's the place where Cleopatra first seduced Caesar—or so the story goes."

Attius said, "A lot of things seem to happen in this city. If we think we have troubles in Judea, we could do worse. I remember my father telling me that the last time the people of Alexandria got excited, fifty thousand were killed, mostly Jews and Greeks."

Silva looked out across the busy harbor where so much of the world's maritime commerce came. He was more fatigued than he had been in years, his bones ached, and he was hungry. Most of all, he longed for a real Roman bath and all that went with it. He rubbed at his bad eye with his fist and hoped he was not coming down with the fevers. He sighed. "I was hoping for a better reception. These Twenty-second Legion louts are about as hospitable as the Britons."

He had barely finished his complaint when he heard a step behind him and turned to see the tribune. Silva thought he had an evil, cunning face, but at least he appeared more sober. He said, "Your men will be quartered up on the ridge with the Twenty-second. I've found a place for you and your officers in town. It's all I can offer at the moment. You'll be staying with Magadatus. He's a Jew."

"A *Jew?*" Silva was hoping he had heard the man incorrectly. "Yes, Sire. Alexandria is more Jewish that Egyptian, you know. Magadatus is their ethnarch. Not a bad sort as Jews go."

Soon afterward, Silva, Attius, and Liberalis were led through a narrow street to a high wooden door set in a formidable wall of brick and plaster. A slave led them into a cool garden where a fountain bubbled softly. An elderly man wearing a black cloak approached them, his hands clasped behind his back. "I bid you welcome," he said in Greek. "I am Magadatus, the son of Saul, and the ethnarch of the Jews in Alexandria." He held up a cautioning finger and smiled. "Don't look so distressed. We're not as bad as we may seem to you. And I hope you're not as bad as your reputation."

Silva became rigidly polite when he introduced himself and then Attius and Liberalis.

"I know much about you," said Magadatus. "I knew you were coming."

"How? We only left last week."

"Some people come by ship, which moves swiftly by day and by night, General. And in Alexandria everyone knows everything that happens whether it actually happened or not." He smiled again and Silva experienced an immediate sense of appreciation for the man.

"We wish to avail ourselves of your baths and we would like some food," Silva said. "Of course, we'll pay what's within reason."

"General," Magadatus replied with an open display of controlling his patience, "this is not an inn. You will be my guests . . . if not honored, at least there will be no charge."

Was this fellow chiding him? Silva wondered. In Judea, of course, this would never have happened. Should any Roman soldier, much less the commander of the Tenth Legion desire shelter and food, he simply moved in and took it. If he had a choice, the owner would have disappeared and not returned until the Romans had left. Here in Egypt, which was just as much a province of Rome as Judea, here standing before this man Magadatus, Silva became somewhat embarrassed, although he could not imagine why. It was as if Magadatus stood in judgment of him. "Well, well," Silva said nervously, "we can't accomplish much just standing here."

Magadatus hesitated while he looked Silva up and down. As if I were some sort of ragamuffin brought in from the street, Silva thought.

Magadatus made an exaggerated circle with his lips and said, "Oh? I cannot agree, because at first meeting we see very clearly into another person. We will never see that same male or female in the same way again. A thousand different factors will go to work almost instantly and from then on, our vision is clouded. A tone of voice, a flick of the eye, an odor may forever erase our first impressions. Heroes become villains. Enemies become friends or vice versa. Now that you've had your platitude for the day, perhaps you will follow me to further refreshment."

Magadatus set off through the garden. He turned into a low arched gate where a mockingbird cawed noisily, and he advised his guests to remove their helmets. "You will disturb the other birds," he explained. "They know that only strangers wear helmets."

"Do you have any parrots?" Silva asked.

"One. I have named him Cicero, but it is a misnomer. He rarely talks."

"I like parrots," Silva said.

"Do you, now?" Magadatus said coldly. He did not bother to look back at his guests.

They passed through a narrow tunnel and emerged in another garden centered around a lovely pool constructed of Egyptian black marble. "For your pleasure . . ." Magadatus said with a wave of his hand. "Your sleeping rooms are just beyond. Unless you expect to be murdered because you are in the house of a Jew, you may leave your helmets and swords by your couches. They will not be touched. Now, it will not be long before the sun sets. I pray then. When I am finished, you'll be sent for and we'll have something to keep you from starving."

Magadatus glanced at the pool. "You will not pollute the water. It comes from the Nile and is changing constantly. I'll leave you alone now, since a prolonged association with Romans might pollute me."

When he had left, Attius said, "By my blood . . . he's a testy fellow, isn't he?"

Silva shrugged his shoulders and said that there were two kinds of Jews: those who were testy and disliked Romans, and those who were meek and disliked Romans. They had obviously encountered one of the former.

"He must be a very rich Jew," Liberalis said. "I didn't know there were any left."

Silva thought that apparently anything was permissible in Alexandria.

Later, when they were greatly refreshed from their bathing, a servant came to them and beckoned them toward the atrium. They followed and soon entered upon a room decorated with elaborate mosaics.

Magadatus sat cross-legged on a rug in the Oriental fashion. Another man with a scraggly beard sat on one side of him, and a boy sat on his opposite side.

Magadatus beckoned them to seat themselves on the pillows surrounding a huge bronze tray. Speaking in Latin, he introduced the bearded man as the priest Pappus, the son of Macheras, then called off the names and ranks of the Romans without hesitation or error.

Silva was instantly taken with the boy, who regarded him coldly. He could have sworn, he thought, that he had seen him before. There was something about his eyes, or was it the alert tilt of his head that caused him to appear so defiant? He wondered why Magadatus had deliberately failed to introduce him, and when they were seated he asked, "And who is this young man? Your grandson?"

"No."

Silva waited for a response, but Magadatus kept his silence while he solemnly poured wine for his guests. Silva kept looking at the boy and decided he must have been about twelve years. He was unusual, Silva thought; there was a certain dignity and poise about him that was so rare to youth.

Silva spoke again to Magadatus, "I asked you a question. Who is he?"

Magadatus answered carelessly, "Since you have already met, I hardly thought an introduction necessary."

"We've met? I don't follow you."

"He is Reuben, son of Eleazar ben Yair."

Silva felt the cutting edge of Magadatus' voice like a knife in his abdomen. Masada! Yes, Masada. There was a boy on the mountain who had survived . . . a tough boy who had fought and bitten a legionary. The rest was vague in his memory; the aftermath was almost entirely erased because he had been so drunk that he had no idea what was happening. Now a series of unwanted visions came flowing back with the force of a flooding river. He shook his head trying to drive the memories away. He saw the boy watching him, and his penetrating inspection compounded his uneasiness.

What is happening to you, Flavius Silva, General of the Tenth Frentensis, Governor of Judea, man of so many military honors there was no longer room for all of them on your chest? How is it that this sophisticated citizen of the greatest Empire the world has ever known should feel like cowering before a youth who, had he been a Roman, would still not be eligible to wear the toga virilis? Are you gone mad with too much bouncing of the brain atop a horse?

Silva could not find his voice at once. He looked at Attius and Liberalis, both of whom seemed to have a sudden need to stare at their bent knees. Finally, his eyes met those of Magadatus, who said, "As I told you, General, sooner or later everything is known in Alexandria, and your reputation preceded you. For example, we're aware that you made a certain pledge to this young man."

"I do not recall—"

"I will for you. Five children were brought before you after the fall of Masada. They were the only survivors. Reuben was one of them. Because of some inexplicable change in your stone heart, you suddenly decided that four of them should be cared for by a rabbi and this one should be sent to Rome for an education. The ship carrying Reuben came here en route to Rome. He was lonely and could not understand the language or what was happening to him. He left the ship and went to the nearest synagogue, where he concealed himself until the ship had sailed. Then he came to us, and eventually we heard the whole story. What do you suppose should be done? You massacred a lot of defenseless people."

Silva knew a sudden desperation. Vision after ugly vision returned to him. He was angry with himself for feeling obliged to suffer the accusing eyes of Magadatus, and he was angry with the boy for appearing so serene. He tried to keep his words measured and his voice factual. "We did not massacre those people. They were a lawless rabble who would be alive today if they'd used their heads!"

"Instead of their hearts? Their heads would have been yours for separation from their bodies, a fact you know better than I do. Why do you think they killed themselves?"

"They were crazy."

"They believed in something. Don't you believe in anything, General?"

"Yes. In my duty."

"Even if your duty means the deaths of helpless people?"

"They were not helpless! They were armed to the teeth! They would have killed us as easily as—"

"They were the ones who died."

"We did not kill them. *They killed themselves!*"

Silva could not believe his voice had risen to such a high pitch. All of the resentment, the regrets, the frustrations, and the woes he had known at Masada now suddenly seemed to have gathered in a heavy ball and rolled over him. He tried without success to draw himself up and regain his confidence, but it was lost and he knew it. "I . . . regretted Masada . . . very much," he whispered. "I wish it had never happened."

A long silence dominated the room. Silva hung his head and rubbed very slowly at his bad eye. An involuntary groan escaped him, and he was astounded when Magadatus reached across the bronze plate and patted him gently on the shoulder.

"And I regret ruining your digestion," Magadatus said softly. "Perhaps you will recover your appetite if I tell you that Reuben has made fine progress here. He now speaks excellent Greek and fair Latin. He reads every day in Alexandria's fine library. He writes and declares himself with particular wit and clarity. Perhaps he will become an orator. Although I never had the privilege of meeting his father, I'm told Reuben displays the same courage and determination. In a way, you are responsible for his progress."

Silva stiffened his back. There were times, he thought, when every man must give in to his secret weakness no matter how hard he fought it. He remembered once when he was a young centurion, perhaps too young for his rank. It was in Upper Germany and for some strange reason he had decided to spare the lives of a handful of Chatti after he had put the balance of the band to the sword. His excuse had been that they were needed about the camp of the Twenty-first Repax, but he had nearly been cashiered for his un-Roman conduct. Ever since, he had disciplined himself against sudden sentimental compulsions. He had always tried to warn himself that they had no place in a professional soldier's emotions.

Now he looked at Reuben once more and this time with better control of himself. And he thought that Reuben was indeed a fine looking lad in spite of his Jewish heritage. He found the challenge in his dark eyes irresistible. As for resembling his father, that was total conjecture. Except as a diminutive figure yelling insults from the high battlements of Masada, he had only seen Eleazar ben Yair once and that in the middle of a dark night. Their brief encounter on the side of the mountain had hardly favored close inspection.

"Reuben," he said bluntly, "your father was a brave man."

"I know that."

"What is your ambition?"

Reuben glanced at Magadatus, then said quietly, "To kill Romans."

Silva attempted a laugh. "You certainly sound like your father, who also had some unproductive ambitions. There are many who would say your resolve is rather out of date. We've brought peace and order to the world, and most peoples appreciate it. Troublemakers are out of style." That last was perhaps a bit hypocritical, Silva thought, but it seemed to fit the moment. Without plentiful adversaries the need for the Legions would soon cease, and he would be unemployed.

"Tell me," he asked, keeping his voice light, "assuming there would be an inexhaustible supply of Romans to keep you busy for the next thirty years, what else appeals to you?"

"Agriculture. I would like to be a farmer."

"At my place in Praeneste we're experimenting with dwarf elms to train our vines. Have you thought about growing grapes?"

"I've thought about all the things that God has given to the earth. They are all an expression of God."

"He has been long with the priests and rabbis," Magadatus interjected. "Perhaps too long."

"You jumped ship instead of continuing on to Rome as I ordered. Would you continue on now if given the chance?"

Reuben looked at Magadatus and then at the priest. Silva thought from the look in his eyes that no matter what they might say, he was his own man. He was not asking permission to do anything; he was simply giving them a chance to comment if they pleased. During the long silence, two Numidians brought in a large plate of lamb cuts, onions and peppers, and a bowl of pungent gravy. They also brought a huge loaf of coarse-grained bread, which Magadatus passed for tearing by his guests. He refilled their wine cups and murmured a brief prayer in Hebrew. Silva thought this quite a useless ceremony, since no suggestion of a sacrifice had been made and no gods were visible.

Magadatus signaled that they should commence eating by dipping his own chunk of bread into the gravy and, after first taste, grunting his approval. He carefully broke off three stems of grapes from a bunch on the bronze plate and tossed one each to Silva, Attius, and Liberalis.

Silva focused his good eye on Reuben and watched him chewing thoughtfully. The silence remained until he said, "I asked you a question, young man, and I expect a response."

Reuben stopped chewing and swallowed solemnly, then met Silva's penetrating examination, and wiped his mouth. "What could I find in Rome that I can't find here?"

"More education, for one thing."

"Better or just more?"

"They are the same."

"I don't agree."

Silva asked himself what in the name of the gods inspired these people to such feistiness. Throw them a stick and they'll break it in two. Try to help them and they spit in your eye. He said, "I'm thinking of education in the broader sense. You would meet many Romans in the city, hopefully without feeling the urge to kill them. You would see many things, including how our government works. Perhaps you'd even come to understand why a relatively small number of people control the world . . . and find your own place in that world."

"What are you proposing, General?" Magadatus asked.

Well, what *was* he proposing? Why waste words delivering a lecture on the glory of Rome to this youth who hated even the sight of a Roman nose? Silva thought that if he was becoming enchanted with the sound of his own voice there were posts for ambassadors all over the Empire. It was quite conceivable that if he decided to resign from the army, he could join the colonial service and say polite nothings to all kinds of people who were not listening. Then why should he expend any effort at all on this youth—Jewish or otherwise?

Suddenly, it struck Silva that he knew why he was so anxious to achieve some sort of relationship with Reuben. In the last few years he had expressed increasing interest in the welfare of young legionaries, those who were having trouble adjusting to the extremely hard life of a Roman "mule," those who were just homesick, and particularly those wounded in line of duty. And it had come to him that with all the honors he had won, his one marriage had been barren of issue. He had heard other men talk of their sons and had envied them in secret, although he was not quite sure why. Only recently he had recognized that what he wanted almost more than anything else in the world was a son. He had told himself that his yearning was no more than a selfish, narcissistic desire, a need for someone in whom he could mirror himself and observe, someone he could assist through known perils, someone to carry on the line. Yet every young man he had come in contact with had a family of his own, and where they were located made little difference. They existed as a family entity; whether they were hated, loved, or just tolerated, they remained the most priceless force in everyone who hailed from the Italian Peninsula. First family, then land, the two revered essentials in any true Roman's life.

Now, Reuben had aroused that same sense of need, and Silva pleaded secretly for his approval.

Reuben was looking straight at him. His stare was uncompromising. "What happened to your eye?" he asked.

"A Gaul didn't like me and he had a sharp knife."

"Have you killed many Gauls?"

"Yes."

"Don't you tire of killing people?"

"Yes. I'm still waiting for an answer to my question—"

"And I'm waiting for an answer to mine, General," Magadatus interrupted.

Silva hesitated. "What I am willing to propose," he began, marveling that at a time like this he should volunteer for new burdens, "is that I become Reuben's sponsor until he's of age. He could stay at my place in Praeneste and be tutored as necessary. He would become a member of my household, not as a servant or slave, but as my guest for as long as he chooses to stay. I would see to it that he receives the best my means will afford. Perhaps in the future if he wishes to involve himself in agriculture, he could improve the quality of my grapes. I would treat him as . . ."—Silva shook his head in disbelief at his words—"as my son."

A stunned silence followed. Attius and Liberalis again found it necessary to inspect their knees. The priest sighed heavily and scratched furiously at his beard. Magadatus studied a mosaic on the ceiling until finally he lowered his head and said to Silva, "Do you give your right hand to that?"

"I do," Silva answered without the slightest hesitation.

ELEVEN

THE EMPEROR VESPASIAN could not remember when he had spent a more irritating day. He had risen at first light, and although every bone in his body seemed to cry out in protest, he was full of enthusiasm for his anticipated journey to Reate. There, in the countryside where he was born, he had always been able to find tranquility and contentment. This time, more than ever before, he longed for a rest. Perhaps, he thought, I will snooze all day and drink and fart in the manner of old men who have little else to do. Perhaps I will walk if my gout permits, or I will just sit and watch the shadow of each day creep around the sundial. I will do all that until some damned courier arrives with news of something I must attend to, and there will go my peace until the matter is settled. At least Titus would be taking care of the daily problems of government; yet there were still a few things he could not handle by proxy.

Now, on this morning, Vespasian was reminded that one of the worst ways to start a day was with an obligatory address to the Senate, which had been scheduled just prior to his departure. It should have been a simple chore, a defense of Julius Agricola and his campaign in Britain, which admittedly was not going well. The tribesmen there were as stubborn as ever, vast amounts of money had been spent on the conquest, and, as far as the senators could see, nothing had come of it. They insisted that the campaign had not enriched the treasury by so much as a sesterce when the sums were all added and the minuses subtracted, and that there were better things to spend Roman money on at home. Despite his self-appointment as censor, which gave him supreme command of the Senate, Vespasian had found himself actually pleading for patience. One day, and not long hence, he insisted, Britain would justify its cost in blood and money and become another jewel in the Roman crown. Meanwhile . . .

He had been in a difficult position, or he would never have been so conciliatory. Only recently two senators, Aulus Caecina Alienus and Titus Clodius Eprius Marcellus, had been discovered as the principal plotters in an attempt to kill him and eliminate the throne. Before sentence could be passed on them, both men committed suicide, and the aftermath of their deaths had left the Senate with particularly bold displays of resentment. Even those senators most loyal to the Flavian family were distressed when two of their own were condemned.

Irritation upon irritation! Damn this need to pacify a collection of baboons! How was it that out of a hundred and forty-eight senators, he had personally appointed fifty-five and was still having trouble with that semisacred body. The mischief originated, he thought, in their being all of the same class— "men of honors," or *honestiores*—and they stuck together like a swarm of bees. It took at least a million sesterces to qualify for a senatorial appointment, and all other Romans were considered *humiliores*. Thus the senators were members of a club with an unspoken bond between them; if they all decided to vote one way, only the censor could persuade them in a different direction.

It might have been worth his trouble if the Senate had accepted his reasoning on Agricola and Britain, and let that be the end of it. Yet no sooner than he had thought the storm over Britain had been at least temporarily quelled, the matter of his proposed triumph arose without any forewarning. The senators had again tried his patience when he attempted to explain that he did not want a second triumph, since he had done nothing spectacular to deserve it, and the idea was particularly repugnant to him because several years back he and his son, Titus, had been accorded such tribute after the conquest of Judea.

To his dismay several senators he had allowed to speak

became almost violent in their endorsement of an additional commemoration of his accomplishments. They claimed that at this time the Roman public needed heroes they could see and applaud. They pointed out repeatedly that the image of the Flavian family was now dull, and they inferred quite boldly that while the expedition made by Domitillia was admirable, the reputation for greatness about the throne had been tarnished by the peculiarly parsimonious attitude of the Emperor himself. The clunkheads! They themselves were all so rich they had forgotten that all treasuries, including that of the Roman government, could be exhausted if squanderers had their way. As for an excess of frugality, what about the countless construction projects in Rome and elsewhere, financed by the government and employing thousands who would otherwise be sucking straight from the tits of the treasury? What about the Coliseum and his favorite, the Temple of Peace?

All to the good, the senators agreed, but there had to be more of the same. A triumph would focus attention on a great leader at a time when there was an atmosphere of uncertainty and the population was becoming restless. If they had a glittering symbol paraded before their eyes along with suitable reminders of all he had done for the Empire, the public would feel united under a strong leader, and the subsequent benefits to all Romans would be incalculable.

These were difficult arguments to challenge without showing what would only be misinterpreted as hypocritical modesty or, worse, appearing completely unaware of the times. Ah, yes! When a man was six months shy of seventy years, he began to wonder if he was so addled he might be unfit for any job! Although they dared not speak out, it was obvious that several senators would be happy to see Flavius Vespasianus turned loose in some distant pasture and forbidden to enter the gates of Rome. There were even some wags (or were they serious schemers?) who whispered that things would be a lot different when Domitian came to the throne. Domitian? They knew very well that Titus was his designate.

At least he had achieved a single victory out of all the palaver that had insulted such a beautiful morning. The celebration in his honor would be conducted under the Augustinian specifics, but would not be formally referred to as a "triumph." This hair-splitting concession, he was certain, would be violated constantly until the affair was done, but at least he had managed to divert an uninhibited splurge.

There was one other factor inspiring the whole affair that everyone present recognized, but no one mentioned. And that, he thought wistfully, was the unequivocal fact that he was dying. The senators were in understandable haste to honor him further; it was much more exciting for everyone if they had a living symbol rather than a corpse.

I should be touched, Vespasian thought, and would be if I were a simple citizen. But everything I do, including going to the baths or the toilet, affects another Roman, and consequently most of this concern is born of either desire or need of protection. The cynics will be laughing their heads off.

When at last he left the Senate, the sun was already past the zenith, and he encountered further frustrations to his day. For a man who was supposed to be on his way to the funeral pyre it seemed that his person was overzealously guarded. Outside the Curia, a whole maniple of the Praetorian Guard awaited him, and the mere sight of their pompous splendor vexed him. Their duty was to protect the Emperor of the Roman Empire, an assignment they followed all too assiduously. They not only guarded the palace and all other buildings of any significance on the Capitoline, but they also covered all public appearances and travel arrangements of any member of the ruling family. As if that were not enough, they had developed a very efficient system of internal information. Very little happened in Rome or elsewhere that did not reach the ears of the Praetorian command; all informants were encouraged to bring whatever they knew to feed the Praetorians' boundless curiosity. The guards were also prone to seize and torture a reluctant informer until the information they sought was forthcoming. It was a nasty outfit, Vespasian thought, and all the more annoying because of their glittering armor and the red cockades sprouting from their helmets.

Worst of all, the Praetorians were not to be trusted. He would not be the first Emperor who was unseated because some other man had persuaded them that they would be better off under him. Where were the Praetorians when Galba, who admittedly was an idiot, was torn from the litter in which he was riding and promptly beheaded? The Praetorians had listened to Otho, another idiot although a senator, who accepted

Galba's bald head without a qualm. Wishing to display it to the surrounding mob, Otho held it high by thrusting his thumb in its mouth.

Vitellius had discharged all of Otho's Praetorians and had formed a huge new corps that he thought would be loyal to him. Altogether he had sixteen thousand Praetorians, yet where were they when Vitellius himself was dragged naked through the streets of Rome by a horde of drunken legionaries, tortured and slain, and his remains tossed into the Tiber? Claudius—how well he was remembered—obviously regarded the Praetorians with even less enthusiasm. Although at first he had tried to bribe them in thanks for the throne, he later ordered one division to fight panthers for the amusement of the public. Unfortunately, the panthers lost. Nero, similarly inclined, ordered a Praetorian unit to fight four hundred bears and three hundred lions. He managed to be rid of a few, but it was not long before the Praetorians avenged themselves. Nero, who was so obligated to the Praetorians, was eventually sentenced to death by the Senate, which also needed the outfit. He became a suicide only to thwart his potential murderers. Indeed, the Praetorians, who fancied themselves as kingmakers, were inclined to foster the opposite.

Now, reviewing his own actions since he had found himself sitting uneasily on the throne, Vespasian decided that he had acted wisely. Fearing another Sejanus, that scoundrel who had so commandeered Tiberius, he had appointed Titus as prefect of the Praetorians. Titus seemed to have kept them reasonably well behaved. But just in case Titus himself might be deceived, or worse, become influenced by veterans of former regimes, Vespasian had cut down their cohorts from sixteen of a thousand men each to a total of four thousand men. Most were new to the outfit; in this way he had tried to destroy all associations with the past. Then, as if the ground were not completely covered, he had established a separate and most secret organization known as the *frumentarii*. They were very few, but carefully selected and trained to conduct themselves entirely independent of the Praetorians. As he had hoped from the beginning, the two outfits frowned upon each other and soon became rivals in their dedication to the imperial household. Very little occurred among the Praetorians that the *frumentarii* did not know, and they in turn were under constant surveillance by the Praetorians. All scum, Vespasian thought, expensive and wasting a great deal of energy . . . but they were sometimes useful.

The moment he left the cares of the senators and emerged from the Curia, the Praetorians surrounded him and escorted him to a reasonably comfortable sedan chair. By the gods, he had wanted to ride a horse to Reate and not be bounced around by four smelly slaves who had no idea how to keep in step and so ease a journey that would take at least two days. But the Praetorians would have none of a horse—"too dangerous," they had insisted. The streets of Rome were full of villains who would welcome so easy a chance at the Emperor's life, and the roads in the countryside were not much safer. Nonsense, of course, but the suggested danger did exist and caused the Praetorians to be all the more important. The world, let alone a poor dying Emperor, could not act without them. Thus he, Vespasian, ruler of the world, had reluctantly agreed to ride in the sedan chair.

He took a moment to glance at the afternoon sun and admire a team of mares' tails whipping across the clear blue sky. He knew it would be long after dark before his entourage would come to a halt. Perhaps the Praetorians had a point. If he were on a horse, an assassin could slip out of the darkness, pull him off the horse, and thrust a knife into his heart before anyone could shout a warning.

A mounted unit of twenty *speculatores* preceded the procession as it left the Curia and made its way along the narrow alleys converging on the region known as the Subura. One hundred Praetorians on foot marched alongside and to the rear of the sedan chair. There were constant cries of "Make way . . . make way!" because the traffic in Rome at this hour always seemed to peak and occasionally became nearly impenetrable. Vespasian was reasonably comfortable despite the waves of pain that surged through his bones, but he managed to stifle his groans lest they be heard over the clatter outside. The Emperor should not feel pain, he believed; even if he did, the world should never suspect it.

Vespasian saw that they were passing from dark to light and back to the shadows again, a contrast in light caused by the tall and rickety apartment buildings, some with six and seven stories perched precariously one upon the other and teeming with *plebs*. The buildings were ugly, dirty, and dangerous; they were a constant fire hazard and their filth was a disgrace. But where else, he thought, would the poor live?

Vespasian looked out frequently and was rewarded with glimpses of another life between the shoulders and heads of his armed escort. Despite the perpetual reminders of abject poverty, he sensed that here was a vitality and bumptious energy altogether missing from the relatively sterile area of the Capitoline and the further reaches of the city, where the rich lived in a sort of armed exile.

Domitillia's bricks might be better used here, he thought, rather than to construct more government buildings, which only served to shelter an ever-increasing number of bureaucrats. There was laughter here, fights, screams of ecstasy, and wailings of grief. There was perpetual noise, sometimes almost overwhelming, all mixed with the stink of defecation, the aroma of cooking, the barking of dogs, and the bawling of the newly born. These were sounds and sights for an old and lonely man, he thought; but he did not envy the people who lived in Subura. Perhaps in another life, he mused . . .

He knew he was responding to the rhythmic movement of the sedan chair, for gradually his cares were being soothed and he began to dream while still awake. As his eyelids became heavier, he had trouble focusing on the scenes outside the windows, yet he saw himself clearly as he glided gently through another life. He saw himself as an unrecognized figure come to this part of Rome to desport with the legions of harlots licensed to practice between the Viminal and Esquiline, and he was utterly without care either for the opinion or the fate of the world. He saw himself discussing the balmy weather with the vegetable vendors in the Forum Holitorium, and the freshness of the lamprey with the fishmongers in the Forum Piscarium. He saw himself in argument with the butchers and in debate with the booksellers, barbers, and countless artisans, all of whom had varied opinions on that estimable man, Titus Flavius Vespasianus. Gradually then, the scene outside became subdued, he found he could no longer keep his eyes open, and by the time the procession passed through the Porta Salaria and left the city behind, he was snoring softly.

THE TRIUMPH

* * *

On the same evening that the master of the Roman Empire was jouncing along steadily northward, Julius Scribonia presented himself to Domitian. He had heard through one of Domitian's freedmen, who had heard it from a reliable household slave, that their master had returned from a hunting expedition in a nasty mood because no game had been taken. Scribonia had meticulously developed those sources that provided him with information, which he now reviewed. After considerable trial and error in establishing his system, he was proud that there was hardly a single Roman family of any consequence with whom he had failed to create at least some link. Slaves, freedmen, or relatives (disgruntled ones preferred) were all willing to talk if it was even hinted that one of the *frumentarii* was listening, and sometimes the odd sesterce would produce golden nuggets of intelligence. That these were not always used to the benefit of the *frumentarii* themselves was of little concern to Julius Scribonia. He passed on information for which he had little use and kept what might serve him. Thus he carried in his handsome head a full storehouse of facts, gossip, rumors, and accusations, all of possible value when the need arose. He now knew the weaknesses and foibles, strengths, and monetary wealth of Rome's elite. He knew from the slaves in Domitian's bath that their master's eyesight was poor, which undoubtedly contributed to his occasional fits of disorientation when awakening from his postbath nap.

Ever since his miraculous return to Rome he had been thinking about Domitian. While the thin thread of their acquaintance hardly offered intimacy, Domitian would at least see him and it would be his task to capture this important man's attention and hold it. Toward better things! The bureaucratic life in the *frumentarii* was not for Julius Scribonia. The pay was meager and the opportunity for a notable career insignificant. Stay close to the real power, he told himself repeatedly, even if it's only the second best. If the rumors were only half true, Domitian was certain to make a bid for the throne. The time to join him was now when he needed help.

Never mind that Domitian was capable of almost savage behavior when thwarted, as he was said to be after an unsuccessful hunt. Could Domitian, the young aristocrat who claimed the sight of blood made him ill, now lament the lack of it? The riddle only confirmed that he was a man of wild contrasts. At heart he might be a lamb, Scribonia reasoned, although no self-respecting ram would trouble to fuck such a mealy, balding creature. He could not bear jokes about baldness and was writing a book about hair. Did that make him an authority or was he really writing of unrequited love? The contrast would be more amusing, Scribonia decided, if he were not said to be capable of instantly becoming a tiger with a malicious set of fangs snapping at everyone in sight. Unlike his brother, Titus, or his sister, Domitillia, he had a very limited sense of humor.

Assuredly, there was some risk involved in approaching Domitian just now. Still, any audience with so temperamental a man as Domitian was touchy—all the more so if his mood was foul. Do not forget, Scribonia cautioned himself, there was always opportunity when all others ran the other way. Witness the poets Martial and Statius who fawned upon Domitian's yearning to hear his virtues lauded. They were rewarded handsomely for their epigrams, but this was nothing compared to the wondrous situation that Julius Scribonia might soon enjoy.

Scribonia wondered if Domitian's very complexity might not work in his favor. The man was a public prude, yet his private wantonness was so shocking that even the most jaded citizens of Rome shook their heads. It was said he enjoyed plucking the pubic hairs of various concubines one by one and saving them for later inspection. Would that be in his book? He was accused of being a sexual animal who lusted for young eunuchs as well as women. Thanks be to the gods, for if he were so inclined he would not disapprove of one who detested females. He chuckled at the licentious tone of Martial while condemning the pantomime performances in Rome as being an insult to the morals of the city; the poet, Scribonia decided, was the sublime hypocrite.

Scribonia planned to lay his foundation on the solid rock of masculine illusion. Since the mind was the ruler of all rulers, he intended to play upon Domitian's primal urges as he might pluck at the strings of a harp. Thus he called upon Valerius Cordus, the finest potter in the Subura. "I want you to make a special flask," he explained, "and we will both disregard the cost. It must be fashioned as no other flask has ever been turned before, and somewhere on its surface the word 'Syria' must be engraved. You will provide with it a stopper that will fit the mouth so exactly no sealing will be necessary. Altogether, one must regard it as a thing of beauty."

"I can't guarantee that," Cordus objected with a shake of his head. "Some people like much ornament, others simplicity. I make a red flask and you like blue. Then where are we?"

"We place our faith in Valerius Cordus, who is incapable of an ugly creation."

"I thank you. It would help if I knew what you were going to put in the flask. If it's a gift, I should know the sort of person who will be the recipient. A man or a woman?"

"Neither. A god. Within the flask I'll preserve a certain nectar that revives the senses."

"Are you a doctor?"

"Of course."

"Then why trouble with beauty? An ordinary flask would do. The creation of beauty always costs money and not always in proportion to itself."

Scribonia allowed himself to appear slightly annoyed. "My dear man," he said, "if I want economic wisdom, I'll go to the bankers. What I'm after here is a flask, which I will thank you to manufacture with exquisite taste. Do not delay, and remember it must not resemble any other flask in the world."

The following week, when Valerius Cordus grumbled about the extent of his labors and charged him outrageously, Scribonia knew that it would have been far more economical to have kept the acid off his tongue. Even so, he was enormously pleased with the flask. It had an unmistakable phallic suggestion about its shape, and the mouth had a hint of that female aperture, which he considered disgusting but here was exactly suitable.

Next he went to Junius Afrinus, a wine merchant to whom he was unknown, and asked him to recommend the worst wine he had ever carried in his vast stock.

"How bad do you want it? I have some in the rear of the shop, a shipment from up north that will scorch the thorax and perforate the liver. I call it the vengeance of the Gauls."

"It sounds too tasty for what I want." Scribonia favored the wine merchant with his most winning smile.

"There's an epidemic of rats in the city. I've some wine that

I swear is made out of their piss. You can have it for nothing if you'll take it off my hands."

"I accept," Scribonia said, "providing you guarantee it's nonpoisonous."

"I can guarantee that whoever drinks it will be alienated from you for life . . . but will not die. On the other hand, I have a rare Thasian that would suit the finest table for a mere one hundred sesterces an amphora."

"I'll take them both," Scribonia advised while he signaled for the Spanish boy to do the carrying. He was well aware that he was being charged double for the Thasian, but such was his euphoria with the progress of his plan that he was in no mood to object.

The next step was more delicate and difficult. After tasting the first wine himself to be sure it was hideous enough, he washed away the taste and odor with a long swallow of the Thasian, and sighed in contentment. He took another long swallow, the better to fortify himself against the task of getting the rat urine down Domitian's throat. The last thing in the world he wanted was to have anything happen to his chosen mentor, but certainly any member of the Flavian family, let alone one in line for the throne, would never be permitted to drink anything unless it was first tested by a slave. If the slave survived, there was a decent chance a gift would at least be tasted. If the slave died, then the donor might save a great bother by opening his own veins.

The hook here, Scribonia thought, was to make this dreadful liquid irresistible to Domitian. There was a way he was sure it could be done. Domitian himself must demand the stuff be poured for him even if the testing slave made a face when it slipped across his tongue. The answer lay in the ancient axiom that anything that was good for a man must taste awful, and anything that was bad must taste good. Hence a secret love potion smuggled out of Syria and delivered to Julius Scribonia during his recent visit to Judea, a precious liquid capable of rendering a man more potent than his wildest fantasies *must* be repulsive. How much was consumed was of no consequence, although Scribonia had decided small doses would be appropriate. In a week, say, there was bound to be some stirring in Domitian's loins and he would naturally credit the wine Julius Scribonia had brought him.

One made oneself indispensable in various ways, Scribonia thought, and any keen student of past Roman dynasties knew that eventually a Sejanus would join every royal household.

Domitian was playing at gammon with his friend Marcus Clemens when Scribonia was ushered into his presence. The husband of Domitillia was not very bright, but Scribonia warned himself against displeasing him, since he was a notorious gossip. How interesting it would be to detail for Marcus Clemens how he had been cuckolded by a certain Roman general, but the time was not now. His presence was inconvenient, although perhaps fortuitous. Scribonia found it exciting to visualize the scene when Clemens told his darling wife, Domitillia, that he actually saw the man she had thought was dead. Oh, for the joy of watching her face at that moment! What a delicious predicament! And no errant general to come to the rescue.

"Good day to you, dear Scribonia," Domitian said with a tolerant smile. "Where in the world have you been keeping yourself? Everyone else came home weeks ago. At least I'm now reassured that the reports of your death were false."

"One wonders how such rumors are conceived. I appreciate your concern, Sire. But I am interrupting your gammon."

"We're stopping anyway." Domitian tossed the dice into Clemens' lap. "My opponent, the richest man in the Empire, has run out of money."

Scribonia decided to take a chance. He bowed, and smiled benignly on Marcus Clemens. "You're a brave man to play against such a skillful prince."

"Mind your words," Domitian said. "We do not have princes in this government."

Scribonia saw that Domitian was blushing, a peculiar tendency for which he was thought so remarkable that all the male elite of Rome attempted to do the same thing on occasion. Blushing had become so much the fashion that many went so far as to pinch their cheeks to create the proper hue.

Scribonia also saw that Domitian was pleased and interpreted his reaction as a signal to go further. After living in the shadow of his illustrious brother for so long, he thought, it was past time for Domitian to share in the gravy. "Then may I say, Sire, that if there were a prince of the Roman Empire, most certainly you would be the most honored one."

"After I'm dead . . . ho-ho." Domitian chuckled.

Scribonia vowed he would twist the testicles of the slave who had passed on the information that Domitian was in an ugly mood. He was much relieved when Marcus Clemens rose and said he must be off—Domitilla would be waiting, he explained.

Oh, *would* she? Scribonia thought. Dear, dumb husband: your adulterous wife is waiting for Flavius Silva—and who knows how many others? It's habit-forming, you know. No doubt she's had a go with a gladiator or two, or more likely some Greek doctor attending her pretended ills, or a handy eunuch who can guarantee her conceptual immunity. You're married to a carnal enthusiast, or did you know? *I* know because I was there!

When Marcus Clemens had departed, Domitian slipped down in his chair and caressed his bald head for a moment. He seemed to have forgotten that Scribonia was still awaiting his attention. He yawned expansively, displaying what Scribonia considered a mouthful of seriously neglected teeth. Surely the man must have access to some of the remarkably clever dentists who operated in the city. There were several who manufactured quite convincing false teeth.

"What brings you to my house?" Domitian asked in the middle of his yawn.

"Fortune, Sire. Yours . . . not mine."

"You talk in riddles."

"All of us are subject to the whims of fortune, and I'm happy to say that my own astrological signs have never been in better juxtaposition. I was set upon by several individuals in Judea and left to die on a beach. I credit the planets with engineering my survival."

Domitian displayed minimal interest, but he asked politely, "What happened? I didn't send you out there to be killed. You were supposed to keep your eye on those people who tagged along with my sister. They were running around with a lot of money, and I find it hard to believe they were all honest men."

"I made certain they avoided temptation, Sire."

"You've taken so much time getting back here that my interest in the whole expedition has evaporated. I understand that the donative was paid, and while I personally disapprove of such bribery, if it makes my father happy, so be it."

"Unfortunately, the donative was used by General Silva as a tool for his personal glorification."

"So? It only proves that anyone who can afford it can buy a Legion. I assumed from your lack of other communication that there were no special problems. Where have you been all this time . . . lying in the sun with some lusty Jewess?" Domitian hesitated, then laughed. "No. Of course not. Not you."

Domitian waved his hand in dismissal, and for a moment Scribonia thought all was lost. He must do something to recapture the man's slippery attention!

He rushed into an invention he had planned for a much later date. "I beg your forgiveness, Sire. Because of my uncovering a very serious treachery, an earlier return was impossible."

"Explain."

"May I ask how well you know General Silva?"

"We were tutored together in our earliest years. I've rarely encountered him since. He was always much closer to my brother."

"Do you trust him?"

"As a class, I don't trust soldiers, but I suppose he's as loyal as any. I remember him as somewhat on the stuffy side."

Never in his life, Scribonia thought, had he stood so close to the brink of an abyss. Domitian's reaction to what he must say now could be catastrophic. Yet the man was yawning again and must be brought to heel. "Sire," he said evenly, "it is my distasteful duty to tell you that General Flavius Silva has seduced your sister."

Domitian's yawn collapsed. During the long silence afterward, his eyes narrowed and he passed through a display of blushing. He worked his sensuous lips vigorously, and a wildness came to his eyes. Suddenly Scribonia realized he had struck a vital note and was momentarily terrified.

Domitian leaned forward and seized Scribonia's necklace. He pulled Scribonia's face so close to his own that Scribonia could smell the wine on his breath. His normally well-modulated voice became a growl. "Do I understand you correctly? You claim that Silva and my sister—"

"Remove these eyes if they lied to me, Sire. They witnessed the copulation. It was Silva who tried to kill me. He wanted to blind me forever!"

Domitian reached up for his hair and brought his face below

his own. He shook Scribonia's head viciously. "You saw them? You saw them consummate . . . ?"

"Yes, Sire." Scribonia tried to keep the quaver out of his voice. "If Silva left his seed, Titus will certainly appoint the firstborn of the family his successor. Need I emphasize where that leaves you, should anything happen to Titus?"

Domitian's breathing became so rapid that Scribonia thought he might be experiencing a stroke. He began panting like a wild dog and the color of his face changed from pink to crimson. Domitian gulped for air, then shoved Scribonia violently aside. He emitted a high animal cry, overturned the gammon table, and sent the pieces flying. He screamed invectives at the sky and the garden, and seizing a vase of flowers, threw it as far as he could. It smashed against a marble column of the peristyle; the noise seemed to give him so much satisfaction that he picked up a small statue of Mercury and repeated the action. Moving safely out of reach, Scribonia realized he was witnessing one of Domitian's notorious fits of temper. They were not epileptic, it was said, but they transformed the normally lethargic man into a ruthless murderer. Scribonia thought that he had never felt so alone.

"That bitch!" Domitian screamed. "That loathsome bitch! She planned it! She hates me! She has schemed against me for years! She has turned my father against me! She has turned my brother against me! That whore has turned the whole family inside out!"

Domitian took up a fast pacing back and forth. He seemed to have forgotten that Scribonia stood watching him, but his screams subsided into a low muttering: ". . . that Silva . . . that glamorous, handsome, fucker-boy . . . I'll see to it he pays for his cock with his head."

Suddenly, as if his temper had drained him completely, he sank into his chair and his rigid body became limp. He wiped at the perspiration that had collected on his face and stared at Scribonia in an almost friendly fashion. "What are we going to do about this?" he muttered.

Scribonia was greatly heartened by his host's use of the word "we." He ventured in his most soothing voice, "Let us wait and see if indeed there was a conception."

"But that will be too late."

"No. May I presume you will leave the solution to me?"

"Very well . . ." Domitian confirmed his words with a careless gesture. "Poor Clemens . . ." he added, "the poor fool will have a little bastard under his roof."

Scribonia thought he saw his chance. It was time to put things back in orderly sequence. A series of misgivings flashed through his mind like thunderstorms, but now at this very crucial moment the unlikely diversion, the surprise, could be exactly what was needed to cement this new relationship. After a temper tantrum, one must find new amusement for a child.

He began easily, "Not only did I survive in Judea, Sire, but another wonder occurred there that may be of some interest to you. I met a wealthy Syrian . . . the ugliest man I've ever seen. He was fat and quite dirty even for a Syrian, but he was surrounded by a harem of the most adoring females. They worshiped the very ground he walked upon, and when I asked how this could be, the Syrian declined to reveal his secret unless I shared it with you."

"Why me?" Domitian was still preoccupied, but Scribonia was certain he saw signs that he was coming around.

"He was in Rome at the time of Vitellius and knew of the noble and courageous work you did during the strife in the city. He thinks it marvelous that a mere lad of eighteen did so much during such dangerous times and credits you with saving his life."

"I remember nothing of the sort."

Since the Syrian was fictitious, Scribonia realized suddenly that he had created an unwanted problem for himself. He had thought Domitian would have dismissed whatever he was supposed to have done on the Syrian's behalf as yet another compliment, but now he wanted to know more details. The terrible civil war of that time, when Vitellius was trying to escape mutinous troops wild with blood and plunder, had also involved the young Domitian. "Perhaps my Syrian friend gave you the credit for someone acting in your name, Sire. I well remember everyone was very confused then. At any rate, my friend thinks you saved his life, and he's been eager to offer you some recompense ever since."

Scribonia took the flask from behind the balustrade where he had placed it so carefully on his arrival. He set it down ceremoniously before Domitian, who glanced down at it, then reached out and touched it with a bare foot.

"What's in it?" he asked skeptically.

"A gift of a powerful nectar, Your Grace . . . of unbelievably bad taste." Scribonia allowed his last words to fade away slightly as if the strength of his voice was lost in awe of the substance.

"Why bring it here? Does your Syrian friend know of its foulness?"

"Yes, Sire. There's a compensating factor that allows one to almost ignore the taste if one allows the mind to drift toward more pleasant matters during the swallowing."

Scribonia was prepared for at least some peevishness to be aimed in his direction, but he detected none.

"You must know I never touch anything that comes from outside unless it's tested first. Otherwise I should be dead long ago. As for this"—he prodded the flask with his foot—"why should I trouble to even test it?"

"Because of its power. Be sure that you lock up the slave whose tongue first receives it and . . ."—Scribonia leered mischievously—"see that the poor man has a female to share his imprisonment. When you are satisfied that he is anything but dead, then may I suggest you swallow some yourself? Soon your standard will be flying very high and the woman who is impaled upon it will worship you for the rest of her life."

"It's some kind of aphrodisiac?"

"No, Sire. Aphrodisiacs are drugs born of legends, unacceptable to the intelligent. There is nothing dubious about this liquid, although I recommend you tell the slave what is expected of him. He should not be chained with thoughts of hovering death or anything else to intimidate him. At best, Sire, the subsequent performance may amuse you."

"I would rather do than observe."

"That's exactly what the Syrian had in mind. Thus, in his Oriental way did he intend to express his gratitude."

Domitian smiled and Scribonia thought he saw anticipation in his eyes.

"I am also most grateful to you," Scribonia said, "simply for being alive. Your presence graces Rome and the Empire, but I'm distressed that your talents lack full employment. May I make a frank comment on that, Sire?"

"Make it brief. My feet are giving me trouble again and I want a massage."

"Sometimes our world can be changed when we see ourselves through the eyes of others. New ideas blossom from us when, only moments before, we thought ourselves marooned in a desert. We all need something or someone to return the echoes of our thoughts. That is the avenue of any new approach to a problem." Scribonia took a deep breath and added, "You would make a much better Emperor than your brother."

"There are those who would agree."

"Titus is in excellent health," Scribonia assumed his most casual air. "But what is the situation if he's unable to take the throne? There are always accidents to be considered, Sire. We must all recognize that as long as we are mortal, only the gods can shape our lives."

Domitian bit at his underlip and eyed Scribonia as he might regard a new species of human being. He hesitated, cleared his throat, and said very slowly, "There are times when you do seem wise, Scribonia. Come and see me tomorrow in the evening. I would speak more with you."

Domitian rose and walked past Scribonia as if he did not exist. He left the flask in place, but Scribonia would have staked ten thousand sesterces that it would be sent for soon.

TWELVE

DOMITILLIA MADE IT a practice to hold a day of *pro-festi* for herself at least once a week. It was then that she visited her brickworks and not only exhibited herself as a reminder to the slaves and freedmen who labored there that she was neither an absentee nor a careless owner, but she took an active part in trying to improve the product. Rome was a brick city and her works made all manner of bricks, mostly red in accordance with the dye chosen by Domitillia herself, but some gray bricks when that hue was available. Her constantly smoking kilns produced common bricks, capping bricks, feather-edged bricks, and buttress bricks, which had a notch at one end.

Domitillia derived a special pleasure in discussing the strength, texture, and variety of size in the bricks with Aponias Afrinus, the manager. He was a young and sharp-witted freedman who had once been briefly enrolled in one of the gladitorial schools and had resigned because, as he declared with a smile, he "loved money, but detested being killed."

Domitillia chided him about his biceps. "It would seem to me, Afrinus, that you could kill any of the best with your bare hands."

"Not me, Your Grace. The sight of blood has always made me ill."

"I'm surprised they would let you go."

"They were glad to be rid of me. They were afraid I would ruin the school's reputation."

Like most ladies of good family, Domitillia was not partial to the games, particularly those involving gladiators, and she attended as seldom as possible. Yet an occasional appearance of the imperial family was thought mandatory. Only Domitian could be counted upon to show himself. For a moment she thought about her younger brother; poor Domitian, he had so little else to keep him out of mischief. She thought he must just sit through every day waiting for the sun to fall out of the sky. It was not good for a man like Domitian to be so long idle.

When she had finished discussing the overabundance of holidays with Afrinus and how they always interfered with the prompt delivery of clay, she returned to her house. There she intended to write a letter to Flavius Silva, even though she knew that he was on the move and would probably never receive it. So much the better, she thought; I can let my heart sing.

She was surprised to find a small party waiting for her, one of whom removed his woolen cap and introduced himself as a sea captain. "I come from Alexandria," he said, mouthing his sibilants in the manner of most seacoast people. "I've brought you a present, and a bundle of trouble he will be, I dare say." He reached out, took the hand of a dark-eyed boy who stood resolutely beside him, and said, "Here is Reuben. He's a Jew and he won't let you forget it."

Domitillia was puzzled until she remembered a portion of Flavius Silva's most recent letter. It had been included, she recalled, among those few lines she had not read forty times: "I went to the Bank of Seuthes and Son and arranged through their partner bank in Rome for the financing of one Reuben, the son of Eleazar ben Yair who led the people on Masada. Begging your forbearance, I ask that you would see to Reuben as you might a favored relative. You may find him somewhat resentful, even sullen at first, but he warms eventually . . ."

"Oh, *yes!*" she said to the captain. Smiling upon Reuben, she bade him welcome. The boy did not display the slightest interest in her although his eyes were very busy examining the surroundings.

The captain explained that he had decided to bring Reuben

from Ostia personally because they had sailed through a most terrible tempest. While all of his crew and passengers had been sick unto death, Reuben had not left his side for a full day and a night. "I've never seen anything like him. He seemed to be enjoying himself. Once when I was sure we were about to lose our mast, I saw him shake his fist at the eye of the storm. He shouted something in his own barbarous tongue, and later when I asked him what he said, he answered me that he had told the storm—if you're trying to scare me, it can't be done!"

The captain tapped his big fist on Reuben's shoulder and said sourly, "Some of our young Roman boys should pay heed to this tough Jew."

Domitillia told herself that now was as good a time as any to practice being a mother. She extended her hand to Reuben. He stepped back instantly and frowned. "I just want to welcome you," she said, "and congratulate you. How lucky you would be if General Silva decides to adopt you."

Reuben remained fixed in position and his black eyes said nothing.

"Don't you agree?" she asked.

"No."

"Why not? The general is a most marvelous man." What a joy, she thought, to know the pleasure of saying so aloud—to anyone . . . anywhere.

"My father is dead," Reuben said quietly.

"I know. My own father is dying, but we can't live with the dead."

"I'm not a Roman, I'm a Jew."

Mothers, she reminded herself, must learn patience. "Someday you may return to Judea and help bring it back to prosperity."

"We would never have lost it if you Romans had left us alone."

Flavius, my darling, she thought, your generosity is buying you a lot of potential trouble. But she thanked the captain, who touched his forehead respectfully, placed his hand on Reuben's head only long enough for him to twist away, and left.

Domitillia wondered if her smile was as fixed as she thought when she reached again for Reuben's hand. He jumped backward to avoid her, and she thought he was like a wild animal. "Just follow me," she said, wondering if her smile had taken on the stiffness of an actor's mask.

Reuben reached to the floor for his tiny flax bag and followed her along the peristyle. They turned at the very end of the house and nearly collided with Marcus Clemens. He was disheveled and red-eyed. His jaw hung slack. He staggered backward, and for a moment Domitillia thought he would fall down. She knew at once that he must have spent the night carousing with Domitian.

"What . . . what's this?" he mumbled as he eyed Reuben.

"We have a guest. He may be here for some time."

"Why? We don't want children here." Marcus Clemens leaned forward to better examine Reuben. His lower lip crept out in a pout and he shook his head in disapproval. "He looks like a Jew."

"He is. He will also be the adopted son of General Silva."

"What is this? Has Silva gone crazy?"

"On the contrary. I wish I could say the same for you."

Clemens was silent for a moment. He rubbed at his mouth and the stubble on his face, then suddenly he shouted, "Get him out of here! Take him from my sight! I will not spoil my days with having to look upon a Jew in my own house!"

"I refuse. He will be our honored guest."

"Listen to me, woman," Clemens snarled, his voice falling away to an ominous growl. "I don't care whose daughter you are. I've had more than enough of your rebellious nature. *I* am the master of this house! And *I* say how this house will be run, and *I* say how you will behave. Now you damn well do as I tell you or I'll wreck that pretty face forever!"

"You wouldn't dare touch me."

Clemens lunged at his wife with his fists doubled. But the blows he intended fell short in two wild swings because Reuben had thrown himself at his legs. Seizing him about the ankles, he hurled him to the floor. Clemens' head struck the marble with a thump and he rolled onto his side. Before Domitillia could catch her breath, Reuben had pulled a knife from his flax bag and straddled Clemens. He held his knife to Clemens' throat and looked up inquiringly.

Domitillia pulled Reuben away quickly. For a moment she thought her husband might have been killed, but then she saw a flicker of his eyelid and heard him groan. "Quick!" she gasped. "We must get away from here!"

She grabbed Reuben's hand and ran with him back toward the atrium. "I'll put you in my own rooms. He never goes there."

When she had caught her breath and entered upon the privacy of her chambers, she sent a pair of slaves to look after Marcus Clemens. "He is drunk," she explained. "See that he finds his bed."

Then she pulled Reuben to her and gave him thanks.

Silva did the best he could to smarten his appearance before meeting with Petronius Niges, but his tunic was already travel-worn and the leather of his armor cracked and dry. He decided against wearing his helmet or his ceremonial sword. Let greedy Petronius Niges know that he was not the only officer in the army who led an austere life.

Considering that Niges had no warning of his coming, Silva thought their first hour went off rather well. They met in a dilapidated building that served as the Twenty-second Legion's command post. Silva was appalled at the filth he saw inside. Even Niges' aide who had come to fetch him from the immaculate house of Magadatus was ill-kempt, slovenly of posture, and strolled rather than walked. Did he saunter into battle as well? That is, if the man had ever been near a battle. Silva thought that he more resembled a Gaullic shopkeeper and it amused him to speculate on how long he would last in the Tenth Legion. Geminus would have him scrubbed and polished in moments, and assigned to so much extra duty he would regret the day he was born.

Niges actually seemed to be pleased to see him, and Silva found it pleasant to talk over old army times, their friends scattered throughout the world, and the difficulties of two campaigns in which both of them had fought. Yet as soon as he inquired about the strength of the Twenty-second and its morale, he saw Niges become uncomfortable.

"Why are you so interested, Flavius? I should think you have enough trouble with your own Tenth. I hear you've had a time for yourself these past years with the Jews."

"All is quiet now. I'm interested in the Twenty-second because we need your loyalty. It's as simple as that."

"You say 'we'? Who is 'we'?" Niges was a huge man grown so overfat that the rumples of his chins draped themselves around his jaw like the jowls of an old bull. His arms and legs were fit for a giant and were very hirsute. His eyes, Silva thought, were the only small features about Niges' massive physique. Were they really so small, or just of a normal man's size and in comparison appeared out of scale?

"I must ask, dear Flavius, on what authority do you inquire as to the details of my Legion? I've had no directive to pass on any information."

"Do you need a direct order to assure your loyalty to the throne? Come now. We're old comrades. In the event of Vespasian's death, may I assume you will stand fast under the banner of his legally appointed heir?"

"Of course. Why not?" Niges made a sweeping gesture with one of his big hands as if physically dismissing any other possibility. "What would you have of me, Flavius? You want me to sign something in my blood?"

"I'm on my way to Rome and I want to be able to tell Titus that he has no fears about the reliability of the Twenty-second."

"How could there by any question?" Niges appeared to be astounded, but Silva was sure he saw a new spark in his miniature eyes. The new look made him uneasy.

"How about the Third Augustus?" Silva asked. "What is their condition?"

"I do not command the Third. That is Cassius Paetus' problem. The Third is so scattered all over Africa it falls on us to be the only solid unit. And for that very reason, dear Flavius, may I point out that our worth is invaluable. It would be hard to set a specific price on it, but perhaps a man of your reputation could reach a satisfactory figure."

"I'm not sure I understand you."

"Flavius," Niges sighed in a heavy demonstration of patience. "As you say yourself, we are old comrades. Let's not loiter through this. I assume you're in haste to continue your journey. Surely there is something in this for you, and I would not like to think that you might have become selfish in your advancing years." Niges' little eyes narrowed until they almost disappeared in the moon of his face. He forced a flat laugh. "I know of the donative to your own Tenth Legion, and since I take it as an obvious reflection of your influence with the throne, I suggest you use it again and see that we of the Twenty-second are also rewarded for our long and faithful service. I will be reasonable, since I assume even the designated emperor has financial limitations. Would you say that a modest reimbursement of, say . . ." Niges paused, closed his eyes completely, tipped his massive head back, and seemed to be napping. "Would you say . . . that a million sesterces would be unreasonable?"

Silva stood up quickly and struggled to hold on to his temper. "I would say that any monetary price on your loyalty would be as worthless as the condition of the Twenty-second appears to be. Your troops are a slovenly and ill-disciplined rabble. They have not fought in so long that they've forgotten how. You set a sales price on yourself and your army of vagrants. I will tell Titus exactly what I think you're worth!"

Niges frowned, then emitted his flat laugh again. "Flavius, remember where you are. Except for the Third's territory around Carthage, I run Africa. I would be most unhappy if even a minor accident befell you. Why don't you come back tomorrow and we'll discuss this matter in a more reasonable fashion? Give yourself a chance to think about it. Meanwhile, for your safety I'll provide you with a loyal escort."

"I have an escort."

"But not enough. The way to Carthage can be dangerous. It changes with the mood of the Africans, who do not always view us with approval. Fifty men should do nicely . . ."

"I don't want them."

"But I do—for your own welfare and that of your men. Surely you would not deny me this chance to prove my loyalty to Titus?"

Niges' little eyes became fixed on his guest. "Of course," he smiled, "it could be that Domitian might wish to place an even greater appreciation on the noble Twenty-second."

Silva turned quickly and left before he entirely spoke his mind. It occurred to him that he had done something completely foreign to himself; he had left the presence of a fellow officer without the formality of a salute.

THE TRIUMPH

* * *

Silva marveled at the quality of the Egyptian paper on which he was writing. Long the masters of papyrus, the Egyptian industry had now developed new ways to press, glue, and cut the leaves of the tree until now the product seemed to invite inscription. The manufacture of this new luxury was becoming one of the land's major exports, and because of its flexibility and smoothness Silva found it all the easier to ease himself into the company of his beloved.

Flavius Silva to Domitillia:

Greetings. I've been so long in Judea that I've become a country bumpkin and am impressed by all that is here to see. The harbor has miles of wharves, and ships are constantly coming and going. I find the other tourists most interesting, since they come from everywhere to view the pyramids and temples of Thebes. Unlike Rome, the streets are wide enough to accommodate the traffic generated by some 800,000 people (according to my host, a Jew named Magadatus).

Unfortunately, I've not been inside the administrative buildings that were originally constructed by the Ptolemies. For the same reason I've also missed viewing the body of Alexander the Great, who founded the city. He is exhibited in a case of glass and his remains preserved in honey.

These Alexandrians are of every race and religion under the sun, and aside from a few murders every day, they seem to live in relative harmony.

The Legion stationed here is a raffish lot who seem to have been absorbed by the local atmosphere of indifference to official rule and a general attitude of let be what is to be. Magadatus tells me that some forty percent of the population here is Jewish, which may be the reason it does not fall to pieces. After so many years living among them, I have recognized that their one quality (aside from a certain intellectual capacity) is determination. It seems to me that when a Hebrew mother launches a son, some of her womb goes with him as a shield against adversity, and thereafter he survives where others fall by the way.

By now Reuben should have arrived. Eventually I intend to install him at Praeneste, at least until he is old enough to wear the toga virilis, at which time he may do as he pleases. I would also hope to one day make that dwelling sublime by sharing it with a wife.

I have had some difficulties here with my mission. Unavoidable and regrettable. However, tomorrow we should be riding west with all speed. I am driven with the anticipation of your father's triumph, having missed the first some years ago, and certainly no Emperor had ever deserved it more.

Until our next reunion, may the gods smile upon your grace.

Your friend,
S.

Silva reread what he had written lest he find something that might betray them if the letter fell into the wrong hands. Finding nothing, he could not resist adding a postscript.

. . . Magadatus (my host) invited a certain Philo to come eat with us last eve. He is a very old man and is highly situated in the export trade. He talked in a way I found difficult to comprehend. Aside from the usual Jewish stand that theirs is the one and only god, he claimed that it is a mistake to view any god as existing in the human form. His god, he explained, is more of a spirit and is everywhere, like a ghost, if I understood him correctly, and causes all things to occur, including the transformation of matter. If I have that only half-right (what he expounded), then it seems to me he sounds much like our Stoics . . .

Silva was interrupted by Magadatus, who entered his room without troubling to announce himself. A fierce-eyed parrot was perched on his shoulder. "You are leaving tomorrow and I find it difficult to let you go without a parting gift. You are a rare Roman."

Magadatus pulled the bird from his shoulder and handed him to Silva. "He will not leave your shoulder unless he's displeased with you. He has been a good friend to me and I've told him to be the same for you. He may repeat a phrase that translates, 'I hate Romans.' Do not discipline him for his prejudice. He says it only in ancient Hebrew and no one will understand."

Silva placed Cicero on his shoulder and then did something he would never have believed he might do. He reached out for Magadatus' hand and pressed it gently between his own. "I have learned much from you," he said. "My sword is sheathed in your kindness and wisdom."

Silva had not the slightest intention of calling again upon Petronius Niges. When his anger had left him, he decided that a Legion led by a scoundrel would be more of a detriment than a help, and he was sure Titus would agree with him. The answer was to make as graceful an exit as possible. It struck him as significant that he would trouble to bid farewell to the Jew, Magadatus, and not bother with a fellow officer.

He alerted Attius and Liberalis that they would not be departing at dawn, but soon after midnight, and they must see that their little party was victualed and ready to ride in every respect. They slept only a few hours, and long before the sky grayed in the east they passed out of Alexandria at full gallop. Once in the countryside they slowed their horses to a long trot, and then every five miles to a walk. When they were breathing more easily they resumed their speed again. By noon, when the sun blazed down upon them, they had reached a hamlet where they watered their horses and refreshed themselves with vinegar water. Cicero had protested violently at his unstable perch on Silva's shoulder during the ride, but now after his head was bathed in cool water from the village well, the parrot ceased screeching and responded to the tender caresses of his new master.

They were congratulating themselves on evading the company of any so-called escort that might have been provided by Petronius Niges, when Attius called Silva's attention to a dust cloud on the horizon. They waited until they saw that unmistakably the dust trailed a column of Roman cavalry. "By the gods," Silva smiled when he saw how heavily they were armed and provisioned, "this will be interesting."

A centurion commanded the detachment, and he saluted Silva with a halfhearted attempt at smartness. Then he groaned as he slipped clumsily off his horse and stood reeling in the sun for a moment.

"We've come to assure your safety," he grunted, waving his hand at nearly one hundred of his men. "By order of General Niges."

"How thoughtful of your General," Silva said, enlarging his smile. "We bid you welcome, so just tag along."

Silva glanced at the column and saw that the legionaries were already bleary-eyed with fatigue. They looked fat and soft and were overloaded with all manner of gear. Utterly lacking in discipline, they removed their helmets as they pleased and lounged over the necks of their horses. Worse, he thought, they were babbling complaints like a tribe of old women. A few had dismounted and lay stretched on the ground.

"Very well," Silva said. "We're off." He mounted his horse quickly and saw his own men do the same without a spoken order.

"But Sire!" the centurion protested. "We need a rest."

"Really? You've only begun. Off we go." Silva squeezed his legs and his mount gathered herself instantly. She set off at a fast canter and, glancing back, Silva saw the dust rising behind them. "Nice to have company!" he shouted at Attius.

For the rest of the day and well into the night Silva maintained the exhausting pace. Twice the centurion caught up with him and pleaded for at least a brief halt. His men were falling farther and farther behind and were threatening mutiny.

"Pity." Silva smiled. "But it's important we carry on. You should have brought harder troops."

The next morning, long before sunup, Silva had Liberalis rouse their own men, and they rode off while nearly all of the centurion's detachment were still asleep. Late that day, as they were approaching Matrûh, they looked back and found the landscape as barren as when they had passed through it. They never saw the centurion or his men again.

Throughout the following week they rode with only short halts to recover the strength of man and horse. After five days they began a great loop along the coastline, which took them to the north of the Jabal Mountains and at last to Cyrene. Silva had intended to pause a few days there, although Magadatus had warned him that the city was not to be compared with

Alexandria. Yet the moment he passed through the outer gates Silva sensed a hidden antagonism among the population. Later, the Roman prefect told him that the natives were obsessed with the idea they should be full Roman citizens in return for their taxes and did not seem to understand that granting such a designation was impossible.

The prefect was a gaunt man who said he was suffering as usual from the fevers, as he had since the first week of his arrival in the colony. Silva was not pleased with his grudging hospitality and the man's manner of snarling at most everything. Nor did he approve of the style in which the prefect declared, "I tell the buggers they're very lucky to have Roman law and, if they want, a chance to serve in a Legion. They don't remember that before we came they were at one another's throats night and day. Were it not for us, they would have exterminated themselves long ago."

Silva resisted the temptation to tell the prefect that he should consider himself lucky if only because he did not have to deal with Jews who would make the average residents of Cyrenaica look like doves. He wondered how many other prefects were scattered around the Empire who knew little of how to manage a colony and would never learn. The only reason they survived was the constant presence of legionaries. In Judea there had been Felix, who had governed with incredible cupidity, and Albinus, who threw people into prison with the elementary understanding that they would have to pay him personally to be released. Florus had been the worst of all, plundering and murdering until a civil war erupted between the Jews, some of whom begged for patience to tolerate the monster, while others saw open rebellion as the only solution. Florus rounded up almost four thousand of the rebels and killed them. The next day he went right back to his looting. No wonder Judea was so poor when Silva had finally come to office.

The best of Romans did not emigrate to the colonies except as the occasional tourist or as part of a military unit. The best stayed home. The others, the countless civilians who made up the bureaucracy of all the colonies—the tax collectors, the grain inspectors, the magistrates, lawyers, freedmen, merchants, and even the prefects—ranged from second- to tenth-rate individuals. Once arrived in a colony or province, they soon discovered that their power was nearly unlimited, and employed it against rather than for the natives. There was this vast resentment, not only in Cyrenaica, but in Mauretania, Dacia, Moesia, Thrace, Macedonia, Galatia, and Syria; even that first of the Roman conquests, Sicily, still fumed at mandates from Rome.

After so much blood had been sacrificed by his friends and contemporaries, Silva found it rather discouraging that what they had fought so gallantly for was now left in the hands of so many incompetents. If the annual revenue of the Roman State was really the one and a half billion sesterces that he thought, then certainly something better could be done about the quality of colonial representatives.

They left Cyrene and their snarling host as soon as they were resupplied and had a night's rest out of the wind. For this was the season of the haboob, the strong winds that swept across the middle deserts of Africa and filled the air with a fine dust. Now the sun became a dim orb, a yellow hole in the iron sky, while the relentless wind tore at the nerves of all men, natives and visitors alike. In spite of the heat, Silva and his party wore their helmets and wrapped their faces in pieces of muslin cloth they had bought in Cyrene. Only their unhappy eyes were visible behind the cloth. They cursed to themselves because the wind sucked away their words and made communication impossible.

At night, when they made camp along the route, they were sometimes obliged to share the shelter of a cliff or a ravine with a caravan of camels or mules, or a mixture of both. Silva thought their drivers were an evil-looking lot who smelled as bad as their mounts. Then he caught a whiff of Attius, who was standing beside him, and laughed. Romans or Africans, he thought, all men stank who marched so far. He told Attius to post guards until daylight, "lest they slit our throats while we dream of baths to come."

The necessity to post sentries was annoying because those on duty were cheated of half their sleep, and the rest halts on the following day became longer. Impatient with the delays, Silva stood the longest of the night watches himself and ordered his legionaries to sleep. He fought off his own drowsiness by holding long conversations with Cicero, and by puzzling over the stars and what meaning the positions of the planets held for his future.

On some nights he thought mainly of food and found himself pretending he could taste pheasant, boar, mullet, sturgeon, and oysters such as he had enjoyed in Britain. He thought long on Domitillia and how somehow, someday, some year—before it was too late—they must be together. Perhaps he could become a bureaucrat in some distant land? A good one; Upper Spain was not so unlivable, or perhaps Gaul if the post was not too far north. But the idea was ridiculous! The former commander of the Tenth Legion shuffling accounts in some remote village? Vespasian would have apoplexy and would never allow his daughter to be carried so far away.

As they continued westward, the land became more barren and devoid of other humans. They came upon Leptis, where they lingered for a day, and admired the numerous construction works in progress. Then they rode toward Oea and passed into Numidia, where they encountered a caravan of slaves bound for the markets in Leptis and Alexandria. The caravan master, a crafty-eyed, emaciated man, seemed to have been waiting for their encounter. He tried to sell Silva a pair of Numidians he claimed were unmatched for strength. The man spoke a little Greek and Silva said to him, "You're starving them to death. They'll not be worth their bones when you reach Alexandria. What's your price to spare one from the buzzards?"

"Two thousand sesterces for the best in the line," the master smiled, "and my guarantee of no disease."

Silva looked down the long line of black men who were lightly chained together. They were big men, true, but there was hardly anything left of them. He thought they must have come a long way. "Where did you steal them?"

"They come from Gaeta and they're the very best to be had."

"You've brought no females?"

"I don't deal in females."

"Why not?"

"Because every man's taste is different. Fat or thin, tall or short, the buyer always wants what you don't have." He frowned at Cicero, who was stamping about on Silva's shoulder. "I don't like parrots. Obviously, you do."

"Where's Gaeta?"

"It is a land beyond the sun. Twenty-six days marching."

"Are there Romans there?"

"No. And there never will be."

Silva was amused at the caravan master's cockiness and found it difficult not to admire the man. He was alone in an uninhabited area with at least a hundred men who would probably tear him to pieces if they found the chance. In his way, Silva thought, the man was a conqueror of considerable dimensions. He could not avoid comparing him with some of the lazy Roman bureaucrats he had met along the way.

"I don't want your human garbage," he said, "but tell me of the way to Carthage. What can we expect?"

The caravan master waved his hand along the horizon as if he owned it. "More of nothing until you are nearly there. Then you'll see a rich land where there are innumerable women to soothe you. Take my advice and provide yourself with a fine slave to polish your body."

Silva laughed—the first time that he had done so in several days. "You take my advice," he said, "and fatten your herd before they all expire. Then you may get one tenth of what you're asking . . . when and if you ever reach Alexandria."

Silva was about to turn his horse away when he was surprised to see the Arab seize his reins. He pressed himself tightly against the horse's foreleg and beckoned Silva to lean down to him. Silva's first instinct was to knock him aside, but then he changed his mind. Those eyes, he thought, are informing me he has something important to say.

The Arab glanced furtively at Attius and Liberalis, who both waited a few paces away. "Can you hear me, Sire?" he whispered.

Silva leaned down further, his curiosity aroused. "Be quick," he said, "about whatever you want."

"How would the general like to be a very rich man?"

Silva chuckled. Now the scoundrel was going to try to sell him his entire parade.

"I'm serious, Sire. There could be a million sesterces deposited in your name at the bank of the brothers Pettius when you arrive in Carthage."

"Obviously, I've underestimated the income from the slave trade."

"There are better things." Now the Arab's whisper took on a rasping sound as if what he must say was choking him. "Think of it, Sire. One million sesterces and you would have to do so little. We are alone here in the desert. No one need know of our meeting, which is why I was chosen to place this magnificent offer before you."

"What is so little? And while we're at it, how did you know we were coming?"

"My current employer has the fastest sailing ships in the world."

"And who might he be?"

"I'm not at liberty to tell you, but perhaps you can guess if I explain that *if* there is a contest in the near future, you will not commit the Tenth Legion to support any party, and when you reach Carthage you will do your utmost to persuade the Third to do likewise. There is nothing unreasonable about that. When the time comes, just do nothing. It's so easy . . ." The Arab allowed his whisper to fade away as Silva leaned down until their heads were almost together.

"And how much would be your commission?"

"Nothing from you, Sire."

Silva hesitated and tried to appear as if he was making a momentous decision. He glanced at the slaves, then inquired if the Arab had the key to their chains.

"Of course not, Sire. That would be very foolish of me. Those people would kill me if they thought I carried one. Tricks of the trade, General . . . just like soldiering. I keep my distance from them."

Silva nodded in understanding and stood in his stirrups. "Attius!"

"Take six of our men and tie this filthy whoreson hand and foot. Then bind him in the middle of that long chain . . . and be quick about it."

The Arab tried to run away, but Attius reached down, grabbed the hood of his burnoose, and hoisted him off the ground. As the Arab howled and struggled, Attius was joined by six men who carried out his orders. Moments later, the Arab was on his knees, bound firmly amid the column of his astounded slaves.

As the slaves began moving toward their master, Silva raised his hand to his escort and called the order to continue their march. He did not look back. There was no need. He knew the desert would have new bones, and he knew his own would be added unless he was extremely careful.

THIRTEEN

DOMITILLIA SPENT THE best part of Reuben's first day
in her care trying to make him understand that if he was
fortunate enough to become a Roman citizen, he would enjoy
all the rights of inheritance. She had called in her lawyer who
had explained that Reuben might be classed as an *arrogatio*. It
would then be necessary to propose a bill to the people, which
was an uncertain and cumbersome process. A better course
would be for Reuben to become an *adoptio;* since Silva had
no children of his own, the law said he could avoid the loss of
his rights and of his name at death if he adopted the son or
daughter of another man. The praetor, or president, of a province or simply a magistrate, could conclude the formalities in
a single day. Then his name would become Reuben ben Yair
Silva Nonius Bassus, which would be quite a mouthful.

After the lawyer departed, Domitillia chatted with her chief
gardener, a garrulous man, and by the time they had finished,
it was noon. These were the hours she found most difficult,
for the preoccupations of the day were not enough to keep her
mind from rattling like a dice box with thoughts of Flavius
Silva. She had even reread bits of the *Aeneid,* hoping to find
some solace, and the same went for Ovid and his *Metamor-
phoses,* which she found too mechanical for her taste in spite
of his occasional brilliance. Indeed, nothing she had read and
nothing that her astrologer had revealed seemed to soothe her
sense of standing on the edge of a volcano. It was strange how
easy it was to forget that she had a husband. There was no

predicting what he would do if he knew the truth. Although discreet flirtations were a part of Roman society, many of the people she knew took a hard view of actual adultery; the woman involved could expect to be made miserable for the rest of her life.

Now she could not seem to overcome her sense of guilt. It was discouraging, she thought, how easily she had convinced herself that she had a perfect right to fall in love with Flavius Silva. Her will insisted that she would not hesitate to sacrifice all of her status for even a brief period with Flavius. But would Domitillia, the human being with so many frailties, who was so vulnerable to new ideas, and whose basic nature had become so strongly sensuous it might better suit a harlot —would she thumb her nose at the whole world and be content with only her devotion to Flavius Silva? Or any other man?

Centurion Piso was waiting for her in the atrium. She had sent for him to come from Sardinia and await his general's arrival, or so she had excused herself for taking him away from his family. She knew that what she really wanted was to talk about Flavius with someone who knew him. She wanted to discuss any facet of the man: his laugh, his daily activities. Did his eye trouble him and was he embarrassed about it, or did his leg pain him? She wanted to hear about his time in the army, his bravery in combat, how he stood in the estimation of other men, and who were his closest friends. She wanted to know about his more regular habits, which must have required some adjustment when the daughter of the Emperor was with him. She yearned to hear of anything that might relate to the subject that so obsessed her. While she realized that a mere centurion could not possibly know the more intimate details of his commander's life, she hoped for something, even a few crumbs from a man who at least knew of his tolerance.

Piso stood very erect, his glistening helmet clasped to his chest, his self polished as well as his segmented armor. He bowed his head slightly at her approach and took her extended hand. "You have filled this beautiful day with honor," he said.

She laughed warmly. "How long have you been rehearsing that bit of eloquence?" she asked.

"From the moment I left Sardinia."

"I regret pulling you away from your family, Centurion, but

your general will be arriving soon and I thought it best you be on hand."

"Of course, Your Grace."

"Where are you staying in Rome?"

"The Praetorians have put me up in their barracks."

"That's too far away. You'll be more comfortable here. Are you aware that my father is soon to be accorded a second triumph?"

"Yes, Your Grace."

"Most of the Flavian family will be in the parade, and I'm weary of Camillus and his pompous Praetorians. I intend to ask your good general if you may be assigned as my escort. The Tenth Legion should be represented strongly. Between now and the time of the triumph I hope you will supervise the construction of the various standards, making sure the letters inscribed on them are correct . . . and—I believe you call it *vexillum*—the flags of the cavalry? Then isn't there a red flag displayed when some important ceremony is about to take place?"

"The red flag means to prepare for battle, Your Grace."

"That sort of thing should be visible throughout the parade. The standard for the Tenth Legion should be prominently displayed near General Silva, who I hope will arrive in time to join in the ceremonies."

"We'll need a silver eagle holding a thunderbolt in its claws. It's fixed to the end of a spear. In battle it marks the location of the commanding general."

"Very well. I'll see that you have funds for its making. Now, my brother, Titus, is attending to the trumpeters and all manner of other displays. He has left this sort of thing to me and I need help. The time is growing short and the artisans are slow. Many have never made a standard before and need authority. Will you accept?"

Piso bent his head and said he would be honored.

"But your religious convictions? Can you compromise with such a display of military might and conquest?"

"I had ample time to think in Sardinia, and I've decided to return to the army, the Tenth Legion, if General Silva will allow it."

"Are you sure?" Domitillia discovered that she was divided between her loyalty to Silva and a certain disappointment that

Piso seemed to have surrendered his principles. The Christianii, she had always heard, were extremely pigheaded. Like myself, she thought.

"Yes, Your Grace. I'm sure."

"But what about . . . what happens if someday you're required to discipline some of your same faith?"

"I'll pray."

"To whom? To Mars . . . Jupiter? They'll all be represented in the parade."

"I'll pray to my God . . . the Christ."

"And how will he be signified? Or does he have his own standard?"

"If it rains, he'll be there, and if the sun shines, he'll be there."

"If it rains, the whole thing will be postponed. You can't have the Roman Emperor looking half drowned. Do I gather then that you've not abandoned your religion?"

"Never, Your Grace."

"Good for you. Then you still swallow that story about your god rising from the dead? If so, I recommend you be much more discreet about it. I would hate to see your handsome head in a basket. Put it all down as a temporary affliction . . . as your general was tolerant enough to do."

"I will try to be more discreet."

"I'm confused about what you Christianii really believe, but I do know that legends have a way of finding new homes. Long ago the Egyptians claimed the same sort of connection for their Osiris-Serapis. Doesn't that make you just a little uncomfortable?"

"No."

Domitillia studied his eyes for a moment and found no sign of indecision. She said, "After you've settled in here and have your new duties in hand, I'd like a further discussion on the subject. Perhaps you can relieve my confusion."

There was a grand peristyle extending nearly the full length of Domitillia's house, and she saw Reuben trotting between the columns. He was whistling as he made a figure eight pattern around them, appearing and disappearing as he rounded each one. She beckoned to him and he came warily toward them. His solemn eyes fixed on Centurion Piso, he halted while still at some distance from them.

"Here is Reuben," she smiled. "He is staying with me until General Silva arrives." She thought she saw bewilderment in Piso's eyes, so she added, "The general is taking Reuben into his household and I'm merely his temporary custodian."

"I know you," Reuben said, looking hard at Piso. "You were at Masada."

He started to turn away and Domitillia called to him. "Now, Reuben, you must be as tolerant of us as we are of you. Centurion Piso means you no harm."

"All Roman soldiers smell like camel piss."

"Reuben! I will not have that sort of impudence in this house!"

"Throw me out in the street then. Am I supposed to bow down to a man who killed my family?"

"I expect you to be courteous at all times. You will soon be part of a noble Roman family and it behooves you to behave accordingly."

Reuben said something in Hebrew, directing it at Piso, and there was no warmth in his tone.

Domitillia whispered "patience" to herself and asked what he had just said.

"Do you want it in Latin or Greek?"

"Either. In the future I'll ask you to refrain from using Hebrew while we are together."

"Very well," Reuben answered in Greek. "I said that if the centurion is a homosexual, like so many of the other Roman officers, he should keep his distance from me. I told him to go fuck himself."

"Reuben! Go to your room this instant!"

Taking his time, Reuben turned on his heel and walked away slowly.

Domitillia fought to control her powerful urge to burst out laughing. Oh, poor Flavius! What has he done? She was obliged to look at the floor when she said, "Please accept my most profound apologies, Centurion Piso. We must remember that the young man comes from quite a different culture and has not been long with us."

She looked up and forced herself to meet Piso's eyes. She saw only amusement there and knew at once that this tall young man was worth trying to save even if he persisted in openly declaring his beliefs.

"It strikes me," Piso said, chuckling, "that your young guest is rather stubborn."

"Yes, you two would make a pair. A Jew and a Christianus . . . both of you deaf and blind to the real world."

Later, when she began the ceremony of her bath, she wondered if here amid such luxuries, a real world could be found. Seven of her slaves stood in their usual positions around the huge bathing pool, which had been especially designed for her by Pontius Gallicanus, the most sought-after artist in the city. He had caused small and exquisite statues of Mars, Pan, Odysseus, and Zeus to be placed around the perimeter of the pool; and her slaves, standing still as if they also were fashioned of marble, waited to attend her.

There was Faustina, who would clean her ears with vinegar. She was a Macedonian and Domitillia always had trouble remembering her name. There was Phalea, a new slave who would apply poultices to her armpits and, by tearing them away, remove unwanted hairs.

There was Arria, unquestionably the world's best masseuse and a very amusing woman as well. Near her stood Helvia, who waited with a new gown for the evening. She was a simple Gaullic woman who guarded the most simple covering as if it were a cloth of gold.

There was Julia, who would do her hair, brushing a lock forward in a wave and then piling up a rampart of curls created with her hollow iron, which was already glowing on the coals. Julia was always alert to the latest trend in fashion, believing correctly that the Emperor's daughter should please herself and not those who imitated each other.

Also waiting was Drusilla, a beautiful girl who mixed her cosmetics in alabaster bowls. Using lanoline as a base, she created a wide variety of color combinations. She used ocher to tint the cheeks red and antimony powder to outline the eyes in black and to emphasize the eyebrows. Sometimes she suggested touching the temples with a hint of blue (there was something saucy about it, she said), but lately Domitillia had been reluctant to create any more provocation than she could avoid. At least for awhile—at least until *he* arrived. Then Clodia, who prepared the most divine perfumes from a large collection of liquids and unguents, would be much busier than she was now.

Yes, this was the real world, but the suspicion that it would soon change drastically was now confirmed with the positiveness of a thunderclap. She knew at last why her behavior had been so eccentric of late—her appetite jumping between nil and ravenous, her passion insatiable for boleti, mushrooms, and pistachio nuts. She had waited apprehensively for more signals, and now in her bath the awful supposition became undeniable fact. She had missed a second menstrual flow and she knew a different real life had begun.

Of course, she could consider an abortion. It was common enough among the noble and the wealthy women of Rome— only the poor had more than a few children—but who could be trusted to perform the operation on the Emperor's daughter? No. Never, never, *no!* She thought, I want the man I love to live beyond his years. Together we are forever . . .

She glanced down at her belly, as she often did these days. There was still no sign of any enlargement, but now she knew it must come. Oh, Flavius, dear Flavius, what have we done? Should we celebrate or commiserate for this new life that is our very own?

The evening sun had been nearly obliterated by the smoke fires of Rome when Julius Scribonia saw Domitian approaching him in the garden. Scribonia coughed discreetly lest he have trouble locating him between the hedges.

The household majordomo had taken Scribonia here, ushering him to this expansive terrace commanding a fine view of the Palatine in the distance, with the twisting streets of Subura below and the Mons Oppius to the southeast. The house itself stood resolutely on the summit of a hill, a fitting shelter for the future Emperor, Scribonia thought, if a trifle severe.

He preferred a more lavish use of the Oriental in dwellings occupied by the wealthy. How else could one impress others? While he was willing to concede that Roman architects, still inspired by the examples and writings of Vitruvius, had absorbed Greek design and often improved upon it, he was not sure he approved of the simplicity of the newer Doric columns. Where was the fluting? And the Ionic capitals that topped the pillars were monotonous in their regularity, all appearing identical no matter the position of the viewer.

Although most Romans of taste exclaimed over the beauty

of those open spaces, which were as much a part of their houses as the rooms, Scribonia found them sadly lacking in utilization when the wary Roman sun lost heat to winter. The exposure to the elements, so delightful in summer, was difficult to exclude from the rest of the house when the bitter winds cascaded down from the Alps and turned all Rome into a *frigidarium*. The portable charcoal heaters were of small comfort during the dreary months, and the best refuge was the baths, where at least one could enjoy the benefits of central heating. Perhaps that was why the rooms in the average middle-class house were so small, particularly the bedrooms. The energies of ordinary Romans took them out of the house during the day, first to the baths, and then to one of the innumerable Roman restaurants, which ranged from simple stalls where food was taken while standing to more elaborate establishments where chairs and even couches were provided. Like their Oriental and African neighbors, most Romans were irregular eaters, taking food only when they felt the need.

What was left of the power in the sun painted Domitian's house a dull maroon with the areas in shadow turning a rich purple. All quite fitting to majesty, Scribonia thought, smiling to himself. He had been studying the sky and saw a band of sapphire green melting into a lush blue as his eyes followed upward to the zenith. There, some childish-looking clouds seemed to have lost their way home, and Scribonia congratulated himself on having regarded them with such poetic appreciation.

The future Emperor of his choice was a handsome man in many ways, he thought; he was tall and possessed of a unique bearing not to be found in ordinary men. Yet the man was devoid of humor. Unlike his brother, who thrived on humor, a joke played or spoken in Domitian's presence was almost impossible to visualize. As Domitian approached, Scribonia noticed that he was still having trouble with his feet, for he walked as if there were sharp stones in the grass. He must ask about his feet, he thought; there was no surer way to capture a man's attention than to request a report on his health. If the description of ills and afflictions went on long enough, as was usually the case, the questioner could seek out the other's mood, or if nothing else, plan his own next holiday. Actually, listening to the report was against the rules of the game, except when a future Emperor was talking.

"Ha!" Domitian shouted, while still at some distance. "I see you are here as requested."

Scribonia bowed, rather too deeply, he thought later. "How could I do otherwise?"

"I like people who keep their word and are on time. That's rare in Romans. I've also developed a great fondness for our Syrian friend."

"So? Then you were impressed with the performance of your slave?" Scribonia was astonished when Domitian actually winked at him before answering.

"Indeed. I completed the experiment by giving him his manumission."

"How appropriate of Your Majesty."

Domitian suddenly turned fretful. "Don't use that address to me, even in private. You know better."

"My apologies. I was merely practicing for what must one day be." Veer away from that mistake immediately, Scribonia thought. Remember the man's duality. "May I be so bold as to inquire if you sampled the potion yourself?"

Again the wink. Scribonia wondered what the world was coming to. And yet another wink!

"I have. Dreadful stuff . . . positively nauseating. But . . ." Domitian paused and studied the sky as if he had detected a speck in its porcelain clarity. "It's a pleasure to discover one is still very much alive."

"Of course. I'm pleased. So will be the Syrian."

"Can you buy more of the stuff?"

He is panting, Scribonia thought, absolutely frothing at his chops, bereft of his reason in his desire for more of the worst wine in the world. Behold one of the most powerful individuals in the Empire just about ready to go down on his knees for a swallow of absolute swill. And where did this obscene scum originate? With J.S. no less, Julius Scribonia, who should perhaps buy up the world's supply or make his own. One may easily neglect the customary chores of the vintner. Why bother mixing this stuff with the yolks of pigeons' eggs, or even bunging the barrels? Forget fermentation or inclining the casks. Boil the junk until it was sufficiently rancid, then dilute the shit of a female Gaullic dwarf in the residue and take the product directly to market. Testimony of its worth would be provided by the great Domitian himself. There was a fortune to be made.

And the price? How much per drop? There was no way to charge for the inspired selection of time that had caused J.S. to bring such an elixir to Domitian's attention at just the right moment in his sexual history. There was now no way to convince him that once his mind had been firmly set on a certain physical accomplishment that he could have found the same effects after a cup of water—and with a much better taste in his mouth.

Here, indeed, was opportunity actually pounding like a battering ram on the door of his future. How Domitian underestimated J.S.! Did he think Julius Scribonia would be so crass as to allow the slightest taint of money to foul this ever so delicate business? Absolutely not! This was a service, friend to friend.

"Your Grace," he said, "I would not know the price."

Did one cut the clover before it was yet ripe? This was an "ape and sack" drill according to the fashion set by Nero, who certainly did not attempt the parricide of his mother, aunt, and a few other assorted relatives all at the same time. The custom was first to administer a whipping, then tie the victim in a sack and see that he had for company an ape, a snake, a rooster, and a dog. The wiggling package could then be heaved into the sea, or for want of an ocean, into the nearest sewer.

Above all, he thought, one must be cautious and alert to any signal of wavering when dealing with the mighty. This was a time to be wary of suspicion rising in Domitian's heart, if beneath that ample bosom there actually was one. The greatest care should be taken to dispel all doubts; it was quite permissible for J.S. to appear hopeful of prospering by association with a prominent Roman, because all rich and powerful people expected such behavior and had long ago learned to accept it. What displeased them was the notion that they might have paid too much for something, or had been persuaded to take some action that might prove embarrassing.

"I suppose the cost of the liquid is high," Domitian was saying.

Ah, how remarkable, Scribonia thought. In a single week

the mind of Domitian had transformed him from an ailing, frustrated, and skeptical man into a roaring bull. But what did this prove? Just as the appearance of wealth creates the reality, the conviction of sexual prowess did the same. All hail Caesar—and while one is at it, do not forget His Excellency Julius Scribonia!

"The actual cost is unimportant, Sire. Our Syrian friend is a man of considerable taste and I can't imagine him sending you anything cheap. Allow me to inquire—"

"Never mind. I want a lot more."

"But, Sire, certainly you have enough?" Raise the gods, Scribonia thought, was the man gulping the stuff constantly? "I wouldn't take too much," he continued. "As a matter of fact, I remember our Syrian friend recommending once a day is quite enough. Otherwise, it might have an inverse effect."

"I want to give a party for some special friends . . . invite them to have a few cupfuls and see what happens."

Scribonia could see the "special friends" now. If ever a noble Roman knew every harlot and concubine in the city, as well as the most amusing homosexuals, then Domitian was that individual. "Be sure," he said, "to warn them of its properties."

"Why? It should be more interesting if they remain innocent of what might happen."

Wrong, Scribonia thought, all wrong. There was no way to be sure of the timing; Domitian's guests might be in the wrong mood, or even more damaging to the reputation of this marvelous elixir, quite satisfied with themselves. Their minds might need a bit of prodding as well. "I cannot agree, Sire. They will receive the maximum enjoyment if they are able to anticipate the result in others and, of course, observe their performance."

Domitian laughed. "I'm beginning to think you're a bit of a genius! By the gods, Scribonia! You're absolutely right. I can see it now." He hesitated, then still chuckling in his delight, placed a finger alongside his nose. "Why don't you take charge of planning the party? It seems you have much imagination."

Scribonia resisted the temptation to cheer. . . . He was winning. Domitian mischievous? Incredible? "I will do the best I can, Sire. Are there any restrictions?"

"None." Domitian's eyes were gleaming.

"It may be frightfully costly. My imagination sometimes overdoes things."

"Let it run free."

"May I choose certain entertainers who I believe will please you?"

"Of course. What's the nature of their performance?"

"Both erotic and exotic. When should I plan this festivity?"

"The night after my father's triumph. I'll have had quite enough of solemnity and the glory of the Empire by then."

My wildest dreams, Scribonia thought, could not have envisioned such rapid progress toward a distant goal. The man in charge of a prince's pleasures was bound to be thought of fondly, and a wise man could feel his way upward from there. Salute! To Julius Scribonia who was already clawing his way to finer things from the bureaucratic ranks of the *frumentarii*. "If I may ask your help on one matter, Sire . . ."

"Don't ask me who you should invite. I'm weary of the same old faces and butts. I want to be surprised with new girls, although they need not be virgins."

"And boys?"

"Of course. Both must be free of disease or I shall chastise you most severely."

Scribonia could easily envision how severe his punishment might be; if Domitian was not too angry, he might just be banished for life. Still, there were times when even the most cautious gambler was obliged to take risks.

"Now," Domitian said, and Scribonia saw quite a different mood come into his eyes. "I have rather bad news for you. Your friend, Flavius Silva, is en route to Rome and has been invited to appear in the triumph. I would hate to have you die between now and the night of the party. I'm sure I would find the uncompleted arrangements irksome."

"Yes." Scribonia caught at his breath. So near and yet so far. "It would be a great inconvenience for you."

"That's partly why I sent for you. I intend to provide you with a brace of bodyguards . . . rough fellows to look after your welfare."

"I'm most grateful, Sire."

"Silva's activities in Africa distress me. I dislike working through the *frumentarii* because too many people learn things that are none of their business. Therefore, it has occurred to me that you might detach yourself from that organization and serve me as an individual. Do I interest you?"

"Totally, Sire. I'm yours to command."

"Any breach of confidentiality will of course result in your immediate demise. Is that clear?"

"Perfectly, Sire. "

"I regard the future with certain misgivings. One of them is Flavius Silva. I sent a courier with instructions to make him detour on his way here, but the method he chose was unsuccessful. Apparently, Silva is not interested in money."

"Possibly true, Sire."

"Yet at this critical time I'm convinced Silva's presence and influence among others might be disastrous for the Empire."

"For the Empire. Of course, Sire."

"I would not be disappointed if some accident befell him, and I propose that you see to it. You will be provided with ample funds or whatever else you require to accomplish your purpose."

Maybe, Scribonia reasoned, my future ruler is not as stupid as I believed. Has he chosen me only because he knew I would have a personal vengeance to drive me, or has he even bigger projects on his mind? "Sire," he said, "you may be sure my devotion to the task is total."

Now, Scribonia decided. There would never be. another chance like this. *Now!* The sun had vanished and the twilight lent an air of secrecy and confidence to the garden. Far below in Subura the rattle of wagons on the stones mixed with the continuous bumble of thousands of voices proclaimed the existence of another world far from these airy heights. Now was the time to share the priceless secret with Domitian, for nothing binds a friendship more solidly than mutual stress. Yet one must proceed obliquely, thereby avoiding even a hint of mere gossip. "Sire, it was my misfortune . . . by pure accident I happened to discover that your sister is pregnant."

The silence that followed was deep and ominous. Domitian became livid, then paled. His head shook slightly and he rubbed at his baldness as if to stop it. Suddenly, he advanced on Scribonia and encircled his neck with his big hands. The pressure in his fingers was light, but the suggestion that he might decide to cut off his wind was certainly present. Scribonia cautioned himself against showing any resistance lest he provoke a greater use of force.

"If you are lying," Domitian said through his teeth, "a thousand bodyguards won't save your hide."

Scribonia pretended to choke and felt a slight easing in Domitian's fingers. "Sire, I would have no cause! I worship you and only regret that what I had to tell gives you unhappiness. If you please . . ."

Domitian released his grip and stepped back half a pace. He looked at Scribonia as if he were judging a new statue to go with the many others in his garden. "So?" he said at last. "My little sister is producing yet another heir to the throne . . . fathered, I suppose, by Flavius Silva?"

"It is probable, Sire."

"And if Silva should be persuaded to back that child with a few Legions—"

"Only Titus would stand in your way."

"How did you come by this information? Is nothing private anymore?"

"Not in the lady's bath when one of the slaves is willing to speak. When the throne is yours, Sire, you will require much more information, if only to protect yourself. I would be greatly honored to provide it."

"Would you, now?" Domitian said. Scribonia saw a sly new crinkle of the skin about his eyes. The man changes like a chameleon, he thought, and a dangerous chameleon at that.

Domitian's voice dropped to a whisper. "I would not be so sure that my brother would stand in my way, either as protection or foe. What happens when my father dies? What happens if Flavius Silva, the hero of Judea and the soldier's soldier . . . what if he has sired a son and decides, in his interest, to rally a few Legions about himself instead of the rightful emperor? If my sister spawns a son, Silva's loyalty could be easily bent by such a slut. He and his Legions could be upon us before we are prepared. It has happened to Rome before . . . again and again . . ."

Domitian poked a finger into his mouth and began to massage his gums as if to soothe his thoughts. "But I speculate," he said. "I see dragons under the bed, and there is no need of it. By the time the child is born, our fancy General Silva will be only a memory . . . as will be so many other things."

Scribonia was compelled to make a questioning comment, but decided against it, for—deliberately or not—Domitian had just revealed the existence of some plan that might change everything. How to become a part of it was a new and mandatory challenge.

Domitian shook his head and his eyebrows shot upward. "We must be extremely cautious. Let us pretend even to ourselves that the child was sired by Marcus Clemens, who will no doubt be thrilled to learn he could sire anything, except one sesterce after another. I can foresee all manner of detrimental results if this becomes generally known before the triumph. Do you agree?"

"Exactly, Sire." Scribonia could hardly contain his sense of elation. Domitian had actually asked his opinion. The way was clear now; he had only to keep a leisurely pace and walk a direct line toward becoming this future Emperor's closest adviser and confidant.

"You haven't spoken to anyone else on this matter?"

"No one whatsoever."

Domitian smiled, but Scribonia thought the gesture was closer to a display of fangs. Those teeth, dear, dear; call in the best dentist immediately and have him make repairs.

Domitian said slowly, "That was very unwise of you, Scribonia . . . because I could have you slain and the secret would die with you. One might say it would be a duty to my family."

"It never occurred to me that I might be condemned by you, Sire, so of course I'm utterly at your mercy."

If Domitian had so much as a drop of warmth in his blood, then the sense of helping the helpless might lead him away from his victim. A sage once said, "Let a man extricate you from difficulty and you have gained a faithful companion."

"Ease your fretting," Domitian said as he smiled. "I like a man who trusts me. Now, as it happens, Marcus Clemens will be arriving shortly for dinner and a bit of gammon afterward. If you would care to dine with us . . . ?"

"Certainly, Sire. How very kind of you." Indeed how kind, Scribonia thought, as his right hand made an involuntary pass at his throat.

"Of course, we will say nothing further of this matter,"

Domitian cautioned. "And everywhere you go, keep that facile tongue of yours from wagging. Is that understood?"

"I've never understood anything so clearly, Sire."

One night, after they had left the desert behind them and knew from the relative lushness of the land that it could not be far to Carthage, Silva lay on his back staring up at the stars. Despite his exhaustion, he found sleep eluded him. He was thinking about Magadatus the Jew and was surprised how the man kept recurring in his thoughts. In many ways, he decided, Magadatus and the young philosopher Epictetus, whose views had apparently taken Rome by storm, were much the same. They spoke of a single god who had some kind of a pattern to which all things and beings are subject. Magadatus had said, "You are responsive to God whether you like it or not . . . ," which was almost exactly what Epictetus claimed. According to that theory, could his relationship with Domitillia be the working of this mysterious and invisible god?

Silva considered his wounded leg, which after a long ride always gave him pain and was particularly vicious about it tonight. Epictetus had advised that the human race enjoyed only temporary ownership of anything, including such personal parts as a leg. He held that it was wrong to resent the loss of its normal use; you should be grateful the leg was still there, and if it had been lost entirely, then you had merely given it back to the universe.

Silva shook his head. He lowered himself until his face was level with Cicero's; the parrot regarded him gravely from his perch on a saddlebag. "Your friend is not very bright, Cicero. Flavius Silva Nonius Bassus is inclined to explore too much. Neither Epictetus nor Magadatus has said that what will be, will be, only that all matters, down to the most minute detail, are part of a vast organization commanded by a single god. Is that god male or female? They don't say. What does the god look like? They don't know. When did the god live? Always, since the beginning of time. If for some reason I lose my house in Praeneste, then I'm not supposed to regret it. It was only borrowed, anyway, and possessions can be a curse. That house of dreams is a curse?

"Cicero! Clarify things for me! Borrowed from whom? Peculiar people like Epictetus and Magadatus claim I'm only the temporary proprietor of the vines surrounding the house. Indeed? Then who is the real owner? Suppose I want to leave the vineyard to Reuben. What then?"

Silva rolled over on his side, hoping the stars would no longer captivate his good eye. Should he now dismiss the inadequacy of his other eye as simply part of the pattern set by a single god who refused to be identified?

Maybe Vespasian was right in wanting to be rid of all philosophers. They were troublemakers given to uttering puzzling phrases that were too often misinterpreted. Like Magadatus and Epictetus, they were given to tinkering with the law. They would not concede that *Jus Natural vel Naturale* is what nature or right reason teaches is right. They wanted all to be loose and flexible, or obedient to the will of their entirely imaginary god, and therefore, it seemed, like the cohort of a Legion uncertain of its orders, they invited defeat.

Silva told himself, as he had many times before, that a government that was successful should not be harassed; in this case, Vespasian, when he was trying to do a good job. Rome was order. The law and the army held the Empire together like masonry. The edicts of the most insignificant praetor in a small town were directly related to the Emperor and to some extent the Senate, even if the official did toy with his interpretation of the law.

When at last Silva began to drowse, he vaguely recalled a demonstration of Roman law that, at the time, impressed him as both proper and sensible. It had happened years ago when he was still a young tribune. For some reason an urban prefect had been killed by one of his slaves. The law said that in such an event all of a master's slaves must die. It so happened that the victim had four hundred slaves, and although there were pleas for mercy even in the Senate and a great outcry among the public, all of the slaves were executed.

It was comforting to know the law still applied, because Nero, whose view on the personal property of others was eccentric to say the least, had gone so far as to appoint a magistrate to hear the complaints of slaves claiming to be abused. Vespasian, who had served under Nero and had known the man, said that while his eyesight was very bad and he squinted constantly, his beliefs were very farsighted. To this day some of his precepts were still an influence on Roman society.

The law of Rome was marvelous, Silva thought. The *Licinia Cassia*, for example, which stated that a tribune for the Legions would be chosen by a consul or the praetors and not by the people. The people did not know of one Flavius Silva Nonius Bassus, but two praetors did. Presto! A new tribune—and a long career.

Then there was the *Tutoribus*, which legalized the appointment of guardians for the orphans of Rome. The law had been extended to cover the provinces, which should make it easy for Silva to adopt Reuben officially.

Let the lawyers of the city become rich, as they certainly were; their presence at ten times any fighting soldier's pay was a clear sign that at least a pretense would be made in following the law.

He glanced at the rumples of darkness that were the bodies of his slumbering escort. Because they were Roman citizens, the law said that every man in his little dust-worn party had the same rights. The law said that Flavius Silva Nonius Bassus was no better than his lowest-ranking legionary. And that, he thought, was as it should be.

On the twenty-seventh day of their long ride, Silva and his escort came upon the outskirts of Carthage. They halted at the village of Hammamet, and such was their relief at the coolness from the sea and the bountiful tree shelter that they were reluctant to press on. Anxious as Silva was to enter the city and meet with Cassius Paetus, the commander of the Third Augusta, he concluded that they could not possibly reach their destination before nightfall. Better to spend the night here, he decided, tend to their gear, and so appear as smart as possible in the morning. Besides, as Attius pointed out, they had not found another campsite that had a soothing vista of the Mediterranean, extensive green grasses for their half-starved mounts, and certainly the most friendly inhabitants they had encountered. At dusk the leading man of the village, accompanied by several elders and their women, brought them dates, tangerines, and fresh bread.

Soon after their departure when darkness had fallen, an old crone approached Silva and Attius, who were trying rather unsuccessfully to restore some degree of polish to their helmets. She spoke to them in a barely intelligible Latin, but Attius, who had a smattering of Arabic from his service in Syria, finally understood that she needed help of some kind and was pleading with them to follow her. She kept shuffling backward and returning and pointing toward the trees behind them where, he gathered, she had a dwelling.

Silva was not sure whether it was his frustration with his helmet or his overwhelming sense of relief at having his goal practically in sight that prompted him to rise and follow the woman. She was cloaked in black and nearly disappeared against the darkness of the trees. Only her toothless mutterings made it possible to follow her. Attius, who decided to join them, said he thought she said something about leprosy, and he hoped he was wrong. As they climbed a low hill, Silva said that at least they were having a different kind of exercise.

Soon they came upon a small house standing clear and white in the starlight. The old woman kept mumbling and beckoning and pleading until Attius said he had changed his mind. Now he suspected she was trying to lead them to much-younger women.

"Damned hospitable of her, but I'm not interested," Silva said, though he wondered at how true was his lack of interest. You're becoming an overrighteous fellow, he thought; no wine . . . and no women. Was this a new kind of sickness?

"I did understand one thing," Attius said. "She thinks Romans can do anything and will help her."

"That's rare enough to make the climb worthwhile."

Within the dwelling a single oil lamp partially illuminated a barren room. The old woman put a finger to her rumpled lips and gestured vigorously at a dark, open doorway. Attius hesitated, then entered the doorway. "Curiosity," he said, "has gotten to me."

"That's what she's counting on, I'd guess."

Even as he spoke Silva knew he was right. For the old woman moved to the lamp and pinched out the flame with her fingers. Immediately he felt a sharp pain along his collarbone and he sank to the floor under the weight of another man. He called out once to Attius but heard only a grunt, and then he forgot all else in his struggle for survival.

His opponent was not a big man, but he was powerful. He

wore leather armor and had a knife. He had struck for Silva's throat and missed in the darkness.

They rolled across the floor, kicking and twisting. Silva tried desperately to keep the knife from descending again. He smelled the man's foul breath and felt the nubs of his hard leather armor pressing against his own simple tunic. A fool, he thought; he had been a fool to let down his guard even for a moment.

Somewhere in the darkness about him he could hear Attius and what he assumed must be another attacker. Silva knew a flash of hope. Apparently there were only two.

He had no idea how long he struggled with his adversary, but he knew that his strength was fast running out. He had tried everything he had learned in his long years of soldiering to be rid of the man and gain the knife, but nothing had succeeded. And suddenly he was convinced that the man was not a native. He was either a professional bent on killing him or a legionary.

The realization so angered him that he revived momentarily and managed to shove the man's head to the floor. As he did so he heard the other man call out, "Strabo!"

Despite his fierce grip, Silva's man spun away from him and jumped to his feet. As Silva started to arise from the floor, he heard a fast scuffling of feet . . . and then silence. He waited, exhausted yet poised for a counterattack. At last, over the sound of his own gasping, he heard Attius say, "General? Are you there?"

"Yes. Are you all right?"

"I think so."

Still winded, they moved outside and stood beneath the stars. The silence was so deep they could hear the gentle lashing of the surf in the distance. "I wonder," Silva said at last, "what that was all about?"

"I have something for you," Attius said. He handed Silva a knife sticky with blood.

"Your blood?"

"No. His."

"It's a Roman knife. Was your man wearing Roman armor?"

"Yes."

"Let's get out of here."

THE TRIUMPH

On the following morning Silva and his party entered Carthage. We are a fine show, Silva thought bitterly, sorely in need of repairs. There was nothing that could be done for Attius' black eye and the deep purple bruises that made his face look like an overripe pumpkin, and the cut along Silva's shoulder was superficial but messy. There was no doubt that the knife had been directed at his throat.

Why? Silva was puzzled as to the identity of their attackers. Niges was an avaricious man and had no doubt been disappointed, but there was no benefit to him if a murder had been the result of the ambush. Was Attius also included? It made no sense. Chance? There had been no attempt at robbery and the men of his escort had been such a short distance from the ambush. Someone, then, knew that he was en route to Carthage.

Most puzzling of all was the sudden departure of the enemy. Had Attius' man just panicked because he had been cut? And the old hag? She had vanished the instant the lamp had been extinguished.

Silva thought he should have rounded up the villagers and threatened to kill them all if they failed to produce the old woman. But his entry into Carthage and the smarting of his wound seemed more urgent.

Just inside the south gate of Carthage, so new it was still under construction, they were met by Cassius Paetus, commander of the Third Legion, Augusta. He was a skeleton of a man who immediately apologized for obvious ill health. "I greet you from the threshold of my deathbed, old friend. I have the fevers and possibly worse."

Silva had not seen Paetus for years and was shocked by his appearance. Great bags hung under his rheumy eyes and he sat his horse like a withered cornstalk. Yet his smile was as warm as Silva remembered it from their time together in Gaul. He asked about Silva's leg, which he recalled had been a sorry business in Gaul, and when he observed Silva's new wound he insisted they make haste to his quarters where legionary doctors could tend it. "I have two excellent Greeks," he explained. "They can fix anything."

By afternoon Silva was bathed, his wound and bruises cared for, and his temper at his own stupidity in following the old crone subdued. Cassius Paetus had busied himself all morning and was full of information. The old woman was unknown in the village. The house had been abandoned because it was said to be plague-ridden. And indeed, two legionaries of the second cohort had deserted the day before the attack and one was named Strabo. Their decurion had seen them in conversation with a seaman during the early afternoon, but the seaman could not be found. There the trail ended. "But I assure you, dear Flavius, we'll find the fellow and prompt him to answer a few questions. And if the natives don't kill our two deserters should they take to the countryside, we certainly will."

They speculated briefly on the possible causes for the defection of the legionaries, but were unable to reach any logical conclusion. "Quite obviously someone with considerable power or money, or both, would like to see you dead," Paetus said. He passed his nearly transparent hands across the unnaturally protruding veins at his temples and added "The legionaries each had a bad record and the Strabo of the pair had been a gladiator. I suppose we'll never know why he suddenly decided on a retreat."

"It was certainly not my doing," Silva said. "I was out of strength and brains."

"But not luck." Paetus smiled.

They then fell to discussing the delicate question of the Third Augusta's position should a conflict develop after Vespasian's death. "Ah, my friend," Paetus said, "there already is a conflict and anyone who fails to recognize it must be blind."

"I've been isolated for a long time . . . perhaps too long," Silva said. He wanted to avoid the appearance of pressing Paetus into declaring his allegiance; better if he volunteered. He had already seen enough of the Third to know that on the whole they were a fine Legion, not up to the Tenth, of course, but worth more than their weight both in neutralizing Petronius Niges and his hapless Twenty-second, and holding them at bay if they sided openly with Domitian.

Paetus, whose sick eyes were still intelligent, made it easy for him. "I give you my right hand that the Third will remain loyal to Titus . . . as long as I'm in command. The problem is that I may not outlast Vespasian."

"Nonsense," Silva lied. "You still look like a youngster. I suppose the ladies of Carthage are always at your feet?"

"Haw! I'm their ideal grandfather. You'll see that tonight."

The more the Emperor Vespasian talked with the locals in the region of Reate, the more he became convinced that his affliction might be the same as had cursed so many of them. An epidemic of syphilis was raging through the central and northern provinces on the Italian Peninsula and had struck down noble and commoner alike. On those rare occasions when he ventured from his villa, Vespasian was repeatedly accosted by his subjects, who knew him as a generous and kindly man. In their view the Emperor was possessed of certain mysterious powers that would allow merely a drop of his spittle or the caress of his hand to heal their multitude of infirmities. This magic was rumored to include symptoms resulting from the plague. His supplicants were mostly peasants and none of them knew that their Emperor himself was affected; they took his teetering pace and spinal slump merely as evidence of his age, which was now approaching seventy.

Wherever Vespasian went during those late spring days, he was accompanied by a trio of Greek physicians who had banished meat from his diet and persuaded him to accept hydrotherapy treatments, for he was becoming increasingly difficult to handle. They also advised him to bathe frequently in Lake Cutiliae; when he complained of the water temperature at this time of year, they insisted that the chills were good for him.

Vespasian spent long hours staring into the distance and brooding about his beloved mistress, Caenis, and how her death had subtracted from his enjoyment of life. His philosophy of love, which he displayed an increasing willingness to discuss with anyone handy, was favoring more and more his conviction that the same standards of devotion and faithfulness should apply to men as well as women. This was quite a change, his more knowledgeable visitors thought, remembering the bevies of concubines that had once been his only lavish indulgence.

Vespasian read little these days although he sometimes engaged himself in something of Pliny's because of his certain comments on the dreary business of dying. He wondered if Pliny was right in describing death as the supreme reward after a life always filled with grief and trouble, and after which there was nothing.

Despite such doleful views, Vespasian found them strangely comforting, along with what he considered even more bizarre observations. A fasting man, for example, could kill a snake by spitting into the creature's mouth. Anagallis juice could be helpful before an operation for cataract. Fruit will fall from a tree that shelters a menstruating woman. Pliny was somewhat of a fakir, he suspected, but what he wrote was often amusing. At least his works represented some escape from the relentless progress of his ailment; a disease so withering that it was possible to envy the squadron of lepers who camped outside his house in the hopes of experiencing a cure through some form of imperial osmosis.

Vespasian found that he was given more and more to brooding upon his imperial predecessors. It was as if they had suddenly come alive and paraded before his eyes in steady progression. A few lingered longer than others and interrupted their pantomimes long enough to almost convince him they were about to speak. It was a strange pageant, he mused, because with the possible exception of Nero, who had once been his commander in chief, he had never given any of them more than a passing thought.

He had personally experienced so much history and had met so many notables that he held tales of past events in low esteem; as witness that fellow Josephus who was manipulating past events of the wars in Judea and twisting the facts to his own design, so that his revelations bore little resemblance to what actually happened. But Titus was pleased with his work, and perhaps it would all be properly resolved.

Did those promenading ghosts of other emperors mean that the disease had begun to rot his brain, as some said it would? The specter of Nero seemed to be of much greater substance and clarity than the others, but then he had known the man and liked him. Of course, he had been foolish at times and altogether too vain, but then modesty had little place in an imperial household. Nero had done the Empire a great deal of good in many ways; some of his extravagant legacies still graced the capital.

It was quite peculiar, Vespasian mused, how he managed to discipline his thinking and keep the imperial images in proper sequence. They refused to be summoned and appeared only when they chose to appear, not before or after. This made it difficult to credi one for his contributions while stripping another of legends. Why did Tiberius hide himself on a rock in the Tyrrhenian Sea, cut nearly all the thongs of command, and leave the ministrations of his government in the sticky hands of underlings? What really caused a man who had been a splendid soldier and had commanded armies in Illyricum and Pannonia with memorable success to make so many mistakes when he became Emperor? Was the same thing happening to another former general, Flavius Vespasianus? Tiberius, however, had lived a long time—until he had seventy-nine years, or so it was claimed. He was the one who said that handling an army was like holding a wolf by its ears. Alas, the truth was sometimes buried with the dead. And his son, Titus, was hardly an ordinary underling.

There was Julius Caesar, another soldier who was never officially proclaimed Emperor, but had himself declared perpetual dictator. No one could argue with his enormous talents, and the conspirators who had slain him had, in Vespasian's opinion, been so hasty that they committed their act without regard to the possible effect on the Empire. Fortunately, Augustus came along and prevented what might have been a debacle.

Caligula occupied his own mysterious area in Vespasian's mental procession. A pity so little was really known about the man, although the records seemed determined to emphasize the sinister. Caligula also had his troubles with the Senate, but had been far more severe than his successors in dispensing with the opposition. He came to the throne because of support from the Praetorians, and it had not been long before he realized he was their captive. Caligula's solution was brutal and a reflection of his wretched youth spent largely in the company of his mentor, Tiberius. He obliged Macro, the Praetorian prefect who had put him on the throne, to kill himself. Yet it was said that Caligula had been an extraordinarily charming man.

Two rules for an Emperor, Vespasian thought, if he hoped to leave this world without help from the knives of others and with some honor. Keep the armies busy; along the Rhine or the Danube would do, since the savages who inhabited the surrounding lands were basically unconquerable and were such resourceful ruffians that the Roman officers needed no further challenges. Keep the Senate talking and so thwart the chances of their remaining silent long enough to take any action and thus undo things already accomplished. The rest was simple if tiring. A smile, a frown, a sprinkle of ordinary wisdom stolen from some obscure sage who was never credited, a well-observed groan of humility in accepting this great honor, et cetera, and—presto—one became Emperor.

At high noon when the sun was at its warmest, Vespasian liked to walk in his modest gardens with terraces leading down to the shore of the lake. He ordered his household to stay away from him at this time and included his ever-present Greek doctors in his dictum. There would be no approaching the Emperor, nor was he to be interrupted regardless of the circumstances during this chosen period of solitude. What he really wanted to do was talk to himself, a habit he had become partial to during the past few years. Was it oncoming senility? He was not sure, but he was well aware that if he was observed mumbling his way through the shrubbery, rumors would fly and he would soon find himself elected to the pantheon of the insane.

It was during these midday sessions that Vespasian set a pace which he considered appropriate to an old soldier, without overtaxing his fading strength. The legs went first and then one's cock, he thought; or was it the other way around? Whatever the case, both were infirm now, leaving only the questionable mutterings of a sick old man.

This day the dispatches that were brought daily from Rome by fast courier informed him that the Tiber was overflowing again and causing extensive damage. Something should be done about it because some senators were complaining that enormous sums were being spent on the Coliseum to provide games while the river washed the public's food away. But do what? The Tiber could be a powerful stream, and thus far in its history the attempts to control it had met with little success.

Another report stated that a bust of the deified Caesar had been taken from its pedestal in the temple dedicated to his name, and all attempts to apprehend the thief had failed. The idiots in the three urban cohorts who policed the city could not find the Forum if their lives depended on it, he thought. Titus should discharge the tribune in command and someone should put the *frumentarii* on the job. At least they would know that a single thief could not carry off such a heavy and cumbersome prize. It had to be an organized band of rascals, and thus all the easier to track down. And who, he thought, would trouble to steal that bust?

There was a further and very detailed summary covering the repaving of the Forum with travertine marble. Damned expensive, but necessary if only because it kept a great many laborers out of mischief.

Thousands of bricks had been ordered to do certain rebuilding about the Temple of Peace and some surrounding structures. That was very good news because the temple was a Flavian family project. If Domitillia's works furnished the bricks, what was wrong with that?

Another report dealt with the water supply in the city and started Vespasian conversing with himself: "There are eight damned aqueducts supplying the city with enough water to drown every inhabitant and now there is a huge clamor to build another. *Nine* aqueducts? The urinals of the city will be flooded if everyone drinks his share. And the money? There are just so many public slaves—about twenty thousand by last count—and they're all engaged on construction projects throughout the Peninsula."

Another report concerned the meat ration for the poor being limited to pork and distributed only five months of the year. Now the silly buggers want distribution continued right through the year. It's no use explaining they'll all poison themselves if they eat meat during the hot months. Their hands are out and their mouths open, and they are now in the habit of having both filled. There are experts at being poor just as there are experts in every other kind of survival. They know the best ways to cheat and take more than their share because they have devoted themselves to the problem, experimented, and learned from failure . . . and have become true professionals. They expend all their energies on winning against the system and have very little left for taking care of themselves. . . . Some of the colonies are the same way.

And yet another report that Scorpus the charioteer had won fifteen bags of gold in his last race. A pity, he thought, not to have placed a small wager on him. Noronius Helio wanted to know what the Coliseum should be called when it's finished. Would it ever be finished at the rate they're going? Why does it take so damn long to build anything? A man could die while waiting. How about Amphiteatrum Flavium? It has a nice ring and keeps the family name before the public.

More headaches. The Temple of Apollo and the Theater of Balbus need repairs . . . urgently. So do the streets that run through the ninth region.

Still, more reports, but good news for a change. The school system is working right. The business of providing teachers with a steady salary so they'll have some desire to teach their little rascals how to translate the ink of a cuttlefish into intelligent messages is confirmed a success. Take credit, Flavius Vespasianus. May the teachers remember your name after you're dead.

And what was behind that report from the *frumentarii?* It was a hinting, generalized message. His troublesome son Domitian was being seen constantly in the company of Marcus Arrecinus Clemens and that fellow Scribonia. What was *he* doing in such high company? Something had gone wrong with Domitian's upbringing . . . perhaps you were away at the wars too long. But then see how splendidly Titus had matured. Both bred of the same mother and father. And what had Domitian and Marcus Clemens in common except Domitillia . . . sister to one, wife to the other? The *frumentarii* report omitted any opinion. It was a sidewise glance. Beneath the flat expository words it suggested that something was not quite right. Very well. Clemens was a fathead and Domitian not much better. What do such men do in their spare time— which was all their time—after their lusts are settled?

Vespasian wondered if he was becoming too much out of touch with Roman affairs despite his efforts to remain alert. Perhaps he should die now and cause as little inconvenience as possible. Who loves an old man? His heirs, the Stoics say. This coming triumph will really be a funeral with all the mourners duly on hand to bid farewell. Among the floats in the parade there should be one depicting Charon and his boat, and he should be posed in the act of demanding money. One denarius to transport a pleb to the land of darkness, but one million sesterces for Flavius Vespasianus . . . yes, even in death, even in the land of darkness, nothing would be different.

As he forced himself to continue his walk at his old marching pace, Vespasian tried to ignore the muscle seizures in his legs by reviewing the honored guest list for the triumph. One name thrust itself repeatedly to his attention: Flavius Silva. It would be good to see Silva again; that young-old soldier was one of the best campaigners in the army, yet it was bound to be uncomfortable because of this business with Domitillia. The silly woman continued to maintain that she was in love with the man, but then what about son-in-law Marcus Clemens? Somehow Domitillia must be persuaded to behave herself during the time Silva was in Rome, or the scandal could ruin them both. Force must be used if necessary. The wife of Marcus Clemens, the daughter of the Emperor, must not allow a whisper to be uttered that might reflect on the Flavians. Domitian was bad enough, but he still had much of life ahead of him and might reform. There was no reformation for an adultress. Domitillia must do the same thing Titus had done when he got rid of Berenice. Or good soldier Silva must die.

He thought for a moment about Mucianus, who had done so much to put him on the throne. There was a man who preferred to be thought of in the feminine but who would not tolerate rivals to the man he wanted to see as Emperor. It was a good thing Mucianus himself was now dead. The melancholy bastard would not hesitate to kill Domitian so he would not rival Titus.

Now, Vespasian asked himself, where do I stand? He needed some sort of personal reckoning of his success or failure. How have you done, you old fart? Have you improved the Empire? The correct answer seemed to be yes. Have you made it more powerful and raised Roman standards? Yes . . . with some exceptions. Have you killed too many people in doing all this? Yes . . . too many Jews . . . and not enough Germans or Britons? The Jews were useful and could make contributions to the state if properly guided.

Count the dead. A very few. Helvidius Priscus, old friend who turned against you and objected to the dynasty you were trying so hard to achieve. He was dead before your order to countermand your own order arrived. Regrettable; yes, a sorry business, which it would not have been to a man like Mucianus. And then there had been Demetrius, who provoked the same temper. Fortunately for him, remorse had set in for Helvidius Priscus and you only warned him, "You're doing your best to make me order your death, but I don't kill dogs for barking."

Even now, there was trouble with those who seemed incapable of knowing when they are well off. Less than a month ago, Aulus Alienus and Clodius Marcellus had been caught plotting to end your life. Think of it. Two senior senators, both former friends, had been willing to betray the Emperor. Now, condemned by the very Senate they revered, they were being given the privilege of dying by their own hands. What were they waiting for? Why were so many people willing to lose their own lives in attempts to eliminate a leader who had only tried to do his best?

"Have I been too inaccessible?" he asked the noonday sun. He thought not. When in Rome, he took frequent walks in the Gardens of Sallust so that anyone who wanted to approach him could do so and say what they pleased.

At the end of Vespasian's pacing pattern there stood a statue of Jupiter. Now he halted before it. He addressed it as he might any adviser, "Tell me, wise one . . . that I took an empire that was in ruins and brought it back to life. Tell me that I have been successful in raising taxes enough to rescue us from financial disaster. Tell me I have a loving son who will continue the good works I've begun." He wondered if he should write his requests on a wax tablet and place it on Jupiter's knees as they had done in ancient times.

Vespasian shook his head and smiled at the statue as if he expected an audible reply. "Tell me I deserve to die in honor and in peace."

Scribonia watched Marcus Clemens snouting through the leeks and truffles that were heaped on the great bronze plate Domitian's slaves had set before them. There were also fresh sardines from the Tyrrhenian Sea, and Scribonia came near to expressing open disgust when he saw Clemens pop them into his mouth and chomp down on them like so many peanuts. Never, he thought, had he seen such a hog. First this, and then that . . . a fistful of grapes followed by a ball of Cappadocian bread dipped in olive oil and seasoned with hazelwort and ginger. Next, another foray into the sardines with a double finger helping of pike liver and lamprey roe to top off the mouthful. Scribonia, a meticulous and fastidious eater, found the spectacle revolting.

Domitian, he now knew, was hardly more delicate at taking nourishment. The man was much given to sucking noisily at any warm food, and despite the demonstrated health of his taster, he was inclined to sniff suspiciously at any new dish.

No matter. This was Scribonia's third invitation to join Domitian and Marcus Clemens at dinner, and he had no intention of souring his welcome. So much to know! Such priceless information as they shared with him created the impression that he now stood as a full partner in their schemes. If he wished, he supposed he could now have them both scourged and crucified by repeating only half of what he had learned. But he did not wish to. Here was the new Rome waiting to be realized with Clemens' money and Domitian's determination —and with my invaluable information, Scribonia reminded himself.

". . . let us say we can count on half the Legions in Gaul and perhaps a third of those in Germany. As I see it, we will actually need their allegiance for less than a month. But can we afford it?" Domitian asked.

"I've set aside ten million sesterces for that purpose," Marcus Clemens said between mouthfuls, "and I suppose more might be available if absolutely necessary. However, I am opposed to lavishing too much on the military. We must think of the Senate and set aside some reserve for their persuasion."

Domitian lunged for a shank of hare he had spied on the opposite side of the great plate. "Bugger the Senate," he said. "Swords make better speeches."

"I agree," Clemens said with a nod at Scribonia. "But I'm sure our friend here will back me in suggesting that once the throne is ours, the Senate will be much less troublesome if they are not ignored at the beginning."

Scribonia wished he were elsewhere, at least momentarily, because he was obviously expected to voice an opinion, and one never knew how Domitian might take the slightest disagreement. "I wonder," he asked the frescoed ceiling above them, "just how soon we should buy off a few senators?" There, that was safe enough, he thought. He had avoided a direct answer by posing a question.

"You'd better start lining up your candidates," Domitian said, "because you're the one who will be doing it."

"Of course, Sire. But I had thought you were sending me off to Africa to rouse the Legions there."

"Send someone else. I need you here . . . all the more so when my father dies. You will be charged with creating some deception to draw a good number of the Praetorians away from Rome on the night we strike. I can have access to my brother at any time that seems appropriate, and it's best for our plans. Since he obviously intends to usurp all power, I will have reason enough to proclaim him a traitor."

"You would kill him?" Clemens asked through a mouthful of roe. "Your own brother?"

"If he is a traitor to the Empire, and apparently he will become so . . . then it is my duty."

Scribonia was not sure if Domitian was taking himself seriously or merely testing their nerves. "It would seem to me, Sire," he said cautiously, "that that could become a very hazardous undertaking. It would be of no benefit to the Empire if we lost our true leader."

"Are you suggesting that I couldn't best my brother in weapons?"

"Of course not, Sire. I am merely concerned for your safety, as I hope to be for the many years of your rule. Allow me to think of a more convenient way to accomplish the task."

"Very well. But review it with me before the week is out. Time grows short."

"I agree," Marcus Clemens said firmly. "I'll have money in readiness for the African Legions, and my ships are standing by to transport them here."

"And Silva? The darling of his troops? What is to be done about him?" Domitian asked.

"If you please, Sire," Scribonia said quickly. "You must understand why I do beg that assignment also."

231

Domitian chuckled and glanced briefly at Marcus Clemens. "I do . . . oh, yes, indeed I do."

And I, Scribonia thought, seem to have inherited almost all of the action in this affair. And just as certainly, I shall be the last to complain.

FOURTEEN

TITUS FLAVIUS VESPASIANUS regarded his sister with the bemused air of a worldly man who had at last found tolerance his best weapon against disappointment. As always when greeting a guest, Titus behaved in a style quite in contrast to his reputation as a ruthless soldier and severe taskmaster. He was inclined to lounge in a chair rather than sit up straight, and his walk was a leisurely stroll rather than the quickened pace of a man determined to get something done. There was an amiability about him most people found irresistible; he laughed easily and smiled often.

As usual in the mornings, Titus' eyes were flecked with red, the result of his dedicated dissipation. He yawned elaborately while bemoaning his lack of will to conclude the preceding evening. His trouble originated in the very charm that had been his since birth. To be in Titus' presence was an experience so extraordinary some described it as "being with a man who glowed." Women of every existing status somehow found an excuse to frequent his house, and their pursuit of him ranged from the lyrical to the bawdy. His firm, yet sensitive lips invited their caresses, and it was not in him to refuse their offers. He managed without apparent effort to carry off the manner of a lazy man who had somehow found himself in a responsible position.

Yet those who underestimated Titus soon learned they had made a mistake. Domitillia knew of his deceptive easiness as she approached him. She knew that like his brother Domitian, he had a duality about him, although the dark side of his nature was not so predominant or nearly so threatening. Titus enjoyed enormous popularity with his troops and with the public, and he was careful not to despoil it. "Give me your attention," he would say when he was about to ask even the lowliest slave for something; or "If it doesn't inconvenience you" when he asked a nobleman to perform a disagreeable job. Titus had been a poor student, far outdone by his sister and Flavius Silva when they were all tutored together, but he had always been an excellent listener. As a consequence, he was able to display a modest amount of erudition that most visitors in his presence took for the natural heritage of a prince. He sometimes chided himself for giving a false show. "Sometimes I'm a pompous ass," he was fond of declaring, "and a good part of the time I don't know what I'm talking about."

While it was difficult if not impossible to be sure of Titus' feelings toward his countless friends and hangers-on, there was never any question about his loyalty to the Flavian family. He was fiercely devoted to his father and often served as a mediator between Vespasian and Domitian when the two were at odds. He adored Domitillia and had served as her protector and champion since their childhood days. They had perfected a marvelous signal system between them to converse with total secrecy even when surrounded by others. If they wanted to transmit information in the presence of the Emperor or Domitian, which they knew would cause unwanted friction, they resorted to an exchange of gestures secret unto themselves; a finger to the eye said, "I see it differently," a scratch at the throat said, "Hogwash, that's not the way it will be at all." They hardly knew themselves how the system got started, but it was a source of amusement during lighter affairs and a prime instrument of rescue at more public gatherings.

Now, on this morning when he had returned from his duties as prefect of the Praetorians, Titus fixed his smile on Domitillia and gave her welcome to his house. She greeted him with the salutation "old goat," a nickname dating from their teens when they were trying to appear older than they were.

They kissed briefly, a gesture Titus had sometimes been tempted to prolong, since he considered his sister one of the most alluring women he had ever known; but incest, even to a voluptuary of his caliber, was (he admitted to himself) just a bit more decadent than he cared to be.

"I've asked you to come here," he said when they had settled in the little room that he used for his most private entertainments, "because I so rarely get to feast my bleary eyes on you. By my oath, you're a pretty piece, and I can only wish there were more like you in the city. Do you realize this is the first time we've been alone together since you came back from Judea? It's disgraceful. You live hardly a mile away."

"Maybe if you can unravel yourself from the ten thousand females who drain your energy, you might have enough left to drop by and see me. I have a new Thracian cook who performs miracles in my kitchen, and someday when you've nothing better to do, I'd like you to visit my brickworks."

"How is the brick business? My informants tell me you've practically created a monopoly."

"Not so. There is so much competition I can't get a profitable price. There are times when I've thought to chuck the whole enterprise."

"That doesn't sound like you. Flavians don't give up."

"I won't. But you didn't ask me to come here to talk about bricks."

Titus chuckled and offered her a cup of wine. When she declined, he rubbed at his red eyes and said, "Bless you. Then I'm not obliged to join you. I'll admit to overdoing things a bit last night."

"You always do. It's a Flavian tradition."

"Not for Papa."

"Is life in the country helping him?"

"I would suppose so. At least he keeps a lot of couriers running back and forth. Two or three a day at least come here, and I can only guess how many he sends elsewhere. He still keeps his hand in things, but now when something goes wrong he has someone to blame . . . me."

"What do the doctors have to say about him . . . his condition?"

"A lot of mumbo jumbo. Like all doctors, they can't afford to say they don't know, and like all doctors, they must provide some cure. Whether it suits the ailment is an entirely separate matter. If there are three Greeks involved, as with Papa, the vagueness triples along with the damage. We have as good or better medics with the Legions. Speaking of which . . ."

Titus hesitated and Domitillia sensed that he was becoming uneasy, an attitude so rarely seen in her brother that she suspected at once this would not be just a sentimental reunion. "Yes? . . . You were speaking of the Legions?"

"One of our finest commanders is coming to the triumph. Or do you know?"

"Yes, Flavius Silva."

"Our old playmate, my comrade in arms . . . our friend . . ."

"I think it's very appropriate."

"Of course you do."

There followed a long silence while Titus looked her directly in the eyes. He knows, she thought; but how much?

"What do you mean by that last remark?" she asked. "I'm not sure I like the way you said it."

"I'm aware that your relationship with Flavius is in a dangerous stage."

"Look who's talking! Who gave you this information?"

"Papa. Then you don't deny it?"

"Why should I when your minds are already made up?"

"That's not the question. Your lover is coming to Rome. There is to be a huge occasion and all eyes will be fixed on the Flavian family. We *are* the Empire. We can't have our most glamorous member mooning over a mere soldier while her husband wilts on the vine."

"Marcus has been wilting on every vine he can find since long before I married him. And he will continue—"

"I'm talking actualities. We may know Marcus lacks quality, but the rest of Rome doesn't. So we have to do some playacting. We have to appear as if all is as it should be . . . especially in view of Papa's condition."

"Are you trying to hang Papa's welfare and survival on me alone?"

"I suppose I must."

"Well, think again. Flavius and I aren't going to disgrace you or anyone else. If my dear husband suspects some past indiscretion, it will not be because of our behavior."

Titus sighed and rubbed at his eyes. "I'm pleased you realize the seriousness of the situation. Our dear brother gives the family enough of a bad name without help from you."

"Or you. What is this—a morning class in acceptable manners conducted by a professor who has more concubines marching around than he can count?"

Domitillia warned herself to calm down. This was only her brother talking and he meant no harm. But had her husband also meant no real harm when, while soaked in wine, he had babbled of his scheming with Domitian? He had not mentioned anything of the same nature since, and perhaps his drunken imagination had simply eased his envy of better men. To tell Titus now, before she was absolutely sure, would certainly drive a terrible wedge between the brothers. No, she thought; nothing had come of Marcus' drunken ravings. Perhaps it would all fade away.

Titus was frowning. He said, "I gave up Berenice. Why shouldn't you make some sacrifice to the Flavian name?"

"Poor boy! You gave Berenice the heave-ho because Papa said you should. And what is your reward? The throne. Poor Titus . . . his best toy sacrificed to morality."

"Ridicule does not become you."

"The same goes for lectures on behavior from you."

"There is one other thing—"

"I can hardly wait to hear."

"As prefect of the Praetorians I naturally come in contact with the *frumentarii*. I understand you have a new house-guest."

"For once those miserable people have stumbled on the truth. I am the temporary custodian for Reuben, a young Jew Flavius intends to adopt. I'm sure he'll speak to you about it when he arrives."

"You have another guest. A handsome centurion? Apparently he was in some trouble in his Legion?"

"Are you also informed every time I go to the lavatory?"

"Now, now . . . keep your sweet disposition. We're not debating this matter before the Senate. I just want to caution you—"

"You keep your cautions to yourself! You can use them! You have no right to pry into my affairs!"

"How many affairs have you got going at the same time? How many more handsome young officers are standing in line for an invitation to your bed? Who do you think you are, another Messalina?"

Domitillia sat absolutely rigid for a moment, then very deliberately brought her arm upward and slapped Titus with all her strength. She hit him so hard he almost capsized his chair in recoiling. His face flushed with anger for an instant; then rubbing his jaw, he burst into laughter. He was still laughing when he explained, "By the gods! Do you know what the *hastati* are? They're our first-line troops, the fellows who first meet the enemy in battle. That's where you should be!"

Titus unbuckled the thin belt that encircled his tunic at the waist and slipped off the small ceremonial dagger he wore whenever he visited the Praetorian camp. "Here," he said, holding the scabbard and dagger toward her. "If you want to kill your brother, do it like a lady." He pulled his tunic aside, baring his chest to her.

She glanced at the dagger without removing it from the scabbard and tossed it back in his lap. "I don't want to kill anyone. I just want some understanding and not any snide remarks about my lack of virtue."

"After a wild punch like that, dear little sister, I don't care to pursue the matter any further."

"Something your precious informants neglected to tell you is that I've really intensified my exercises and am ready to take on a bear. I thought I'd better learn how to defend myself for the next time my husband assaults me. And if you haven't noticed, I'm also getting a bit chubby about the hips . . . it's that time in my life."

Titus groaned; he was at ease again. The affection they had always felt for each other warmed the little room. "Don't remind me about blubber," he said patting his belly. "A few months ago I discovered a farmer who feeds his pigs on figs. You can't imagine how good a paté of sow liver can be. Would you like to try some?"

"No, thank you. I'll remain pure."

They were smiling now and their animosity had vanished as suddenly as it had come. Titus asked, "Wasn't it Ovid who said that a pure woman was one who had not been asked?"

"I have only one lover."

"Rather selfish of you, isn't it? What do you propose to do when Flavius has to go back to Judea?"

"I was going to ask you not to send him back."

"Aha! Now the freedom of Roman women has gone too far. You want to run the army to suit the convenience of your affections."

"Flavius has been out there long enough. He deserves something closer to home."

"I agree. I'll take care of it. But you still haven't answered my question. What are you going to do about your unfortunate husband? Just walk away and leave him? Among other negatives, do you realize what that would do to Flavius' career?"

"I doubt if he cares."

"Flavius is not a rich man. What would you live on?"

"I have plenty."

"Unless Flavius has changed entirely, I'd be surprised if he'd be happy living on your money."

"Thanks for your encouragement," Domitillia answered flatly. "You don't seem to understand that Flavius and I were made for each other."

"I'm astonished that my sister, whom I've always considered an intelligent woman, would rest her future on such a trite foundation."

"I'm having trouble smiling through your cynicism."

"I'm not cynical, just realistic. How well do you know Flavius Silva? You go out to Judea, spend a few days with a man you haven't seen since childhood, and suddenly you can't wait to throw up your good life for him. If that makes sense, then Berenice and I made sense, and I wish she were here right now to reason with you. Are you aware that the army frowns on marriage and won't even allow it in the lower ranks? You're talking about mating with a man who is a born soldier and has been one since he was fifteen. He doesn't know any other way of life even if he thinks he does. You'd be bored stiff in six months—"

"I'm bored stiff now."

"—and you would always be a candidate to become a widow until the day he retires. The army isn't a social club. People get themselves killed in the army for a variety of reasons . . . the enemy being only one of them."

After a moment's consideration, Domitillia found it easier to smile. Her beloved brother was so typically male, so dear and protective, so hardheaded. She said, "Why don't you go down to the Forum and take the rostrum? Just stand there and spout old-fashioned chestnuts like you're doing now and soon enough you'll have a much bigger audience."

"If there's one thing I can't stand, it's a sharp-tongued female. Things must have been much easier in Republican times, before you women decided you should rule the world. . . . You took a bite of power pie and now you can't get enough. I'm not trying to reform you. . . . A little flirtation never hurt anyone, but I am trying to keep the Flavian family from acquiring any more scars than we already have. Now for the love of the gods, will you help me?"

"Revered brother . . . there is something I must tell you . . ."

It was almost out before she could catch herself. She saw that his attention had drifted momentarily, and she was grateful because her compulsion to tell someone, almost anyone, of her condition was so powerful it would not be denied. "Titus, are you listening?"

"Of course, of course."

"I'm pregnant."

His eyes brightened and a broad smile spread across his face. "Well, well. Congratulations. That should solve everything. Does Marcus know?"

"No."

"Why not? He'll be very excited."

"Yes, I suppose he will be. It's not his child."

Titus hesitated as the smile slipped from his face. He reached for the pitcher of wine, poured himself a full cup, and drained it. He slammed the cup down on the tray, peered at his sister unhappily and asked, "Flavius?"

"Yes."

"Kill it."

"I will not!"

As Titus sprang to his feet, she saw the other side of her brother take full command of him. His body became taut, his eyes cold, and the tone of his voice almost ferocious. Now she saw the Titus only the military knew, the hard, cruel soldier who expected his orders to be carried out instantly. His words lashed into her as if they were on the end of a whip. "You slut!" he yelled. "You would not only disgrace the family, but you would suckle a bastard who could possibly rule the Em-

pire? You will go to the doctors at once! You will have that
thing, which drains your sanity, removed this day. You will
make all arrangements and by this afternoon I must hear that
all is well. We will never mention this matter again . . . to
anyone . . . ever! When Flavius arrives you will inform him
that whatever your relationship has been it is now finished.
You have decided to return in heart and body to your husband.
A satisfactory display of your intention will be visible to all,
including Flavius, before, during, and after the triumph."

"I refuse."

"Do you?" Titus' voice became even more strident. "You
refuse the order of the emperor designate? You refuse your
brother who leans upon you to help him govern the Empire?
Very well. Unless I hear by tomorrow that you have complied
with my orders, you will be exiled to as miserable a place as I
can find. I will be more forgiving of your lover, who will be
allowed the choice of dying by his own hand, or I will see that
it is done for him. Now leave me. I'm sick of the sight of you.
I look forward to the time when your behavior will allow me
to erase the memory of this morning from my thoughts."

Domitillia arose and the confusion of her thoughts was such
that she turned the wrong way to leave the room. She found
her bearings almost immediately and turned again to walk past
her brother. She did not pause or look at him when she said,
"Farewell, Titus. I had hoped you would be the one person in
my life who would understand."

Then she was gone.

When Domitillia returned to her house, she sat in the peristyle for the rest of the morning, trying to gather her franti-
cally wandering thoughts. She called for her slaves to mani-
cure her nails and dress her hair. Afterward she inspected a
new delivery of lingerie, all of silk and designed to cover
those areas left open beneath her robes. She tied some silk
scarves across her face in Oriental fashion, which had lately
been adopted by many Roman ladies when walking the
streets. But she was instantly reminded that she had no desire
to appear seductive or mysterious to any man except for one,
and he would not care whether she wore a veil or not.

During the last of the morning Domitillia kept an appointment with her dressmaker, who had completed several new

formal gowns, most with embroideries of gold and silver thread. They all proved to be a rather tight fit around the waist in compliance with the current Roman fashion; she wondered how long it would be before they became useless to her. The dressmaker hinted that if Domitillia wished, she could let a little more room in a few of the gowns, but she declined. Did the dressmaker guess, or was a prospective first-time mother just so nervous that she thought everyone must know?

Her jeweler called upon her at noon. He was a diminutive man of such great artistry that he was renowned by the wealthy throughout the Empire. Domitillia had long thought he resembled an aged walnut. Now he had brought her a large opal, which he suggested would be displayed nicely as a pendant on a necklace of gold links.

"What would be the cost?" she asked indifferently. The material things of life had suddenly become so unimportant.

"Perhaps forty thousand sesterces," the little man said. "Perhaps more when I'm finished."

"How long will it take you?"

"Two months . . . maybe three."

In two days, she thought, she might well be on her way to exile. In two months none of her new gowns would fit her . . . in that time Flavius might be dead.

She dismissed the jeweler with the suggestion he come back after the triumph. Her thoughts then flew in desperation to her father. If he learned that there was even a possibility that a bastard child might some day rule the Empire, the thought could kill him. Titus had not mentioned when he would send her away. Would he allow her to appear at the triumph as if nothing had happened? Would she have to ride in the parade beside her supposedly adored husband to prove all was well with the world and all the Flavians? If Titus carried out his threat now, how was he going to explain the absence of Domitillia in the triumph?

Soon after the jeweler departed, mumbling to himself about the unpredictable rich, Centurion Piso came to her. His stalwart presence somehow seemed to restore order to Domitillia's thoughts.

After they had exchanged their usual formal greetings, she said, "I hope you're comfortable here."

"I'm ruined forever, Your Grace. For a soldier this is the soft paradise."

"And your projects for the parade? Are you receiving complete cooperation from everyone you must deal with?"

"There's been some trouble finding the proper Tyrian dye for the red banners and flags, but that's now solved. The manufacture of the effigies of your gods is progressing . . . Hercules, Minerva, Jupiter, and Mercury are already completed, with Venus and Juno and Ceres yet to come."

"And you find their creation distasteful. I can see it in your eyes."

Piso lowered his head slightly and stared at the floor. "The teachings of Paul allow only one god. All the rest are false."

"But that's what the Jews say. You're one of the Christianii."

"We're the same in many ways."

"Who was Paul?"

"A tent maker."

"Poof! And he leads you Christianii?"

"No. He taught . . . or shall I say, persuaded. He spoke sometimes of war and sometimes of love."

Domitillia found herself suddenly interested. "Can you tell me what he has to say about love?"

"He said, 'Though I have all faith so that I can move mountains, if I have not love I'm nothing. And though I give away everything that I am, and give myself, but do it in pride, not love, it profits me nothing. Love is patient and kind. It is not envious or boastful. It does not insist on its right . . . it never fails.'"

"Where is this man? How can I talk with him?"

"When you were a little girl, his head was removed by Nero. But he could not remove such thoughts."

Domitillia looked away from Piso. She found it difficult to meet his eyes, and her mind was a whirlwind of contradictions. Piso, she thought, spoke in riddles. Was he trying to confuse her, or was he just a little crazy? Still, those words of love . . . did Piso make them up or did some long-dead Jew really pronounce them? "Piso," she said, "I may be called away very soon and might be gone for some time. If it happens before General Silva arrives, I want you to stay here and look after Reuben until he comes. Will you do that?"

"I'll try. As you know I'm not, shall we say, his favorite uncle?"

"Do your best."

"Of course."

Domitillia pulled an emerald ring off one of her fingers and pressed it into Piso's hands. "If I should be away when your general comes, give him this. It was worn by my mother, for whom I was named. Tell your general what you've just told me . . . what that man Paul had to say. Tell him I will hold those thoughts for as long as this stone shall exist."

"You do me the honor of trust. It's a gift to humble anyone." Piso bowed, but his face gave no evidence of surprise. "Is it possible that you may be interested in some of the other things Paul said?"

"No. Not now. My thoughts are too tangled. . . . What about the torchbearers in the parade? Are there enough people assigned? We should have at least a thousand. Have you made all the arrangements?"

"I encountered some argument. The priests want to carry torches, but not if the slaves do. They say it would disgrace them."

"Poo . . ." Domitillia puckered her lips in a gesture of disdain.

"The priests are willing to bring incense and recite the usual incantations on your father's behalf, but they want carts to transport them and there are not enough suitable vehicles as it is."

Domitillia made a face. "We could think about commandeering the city's manure carts."

"I will explore that possibility," Piso said solemnly. "I'm told by one of Titus' tribunes that he plans to dispense with using any captives in the procession. There are not enough left alive to be impressive. Instead, it will be sufficient to display their swords, belts, and embroidered saddlecloths. The spectators will be far more impressed with the coins to be thrown at them as the procession passes. With your permission I will arrange for the turning of special bowls to hold the money. I presume Titus will furnish the coins."

"Well, I surely won't . . . and Papa? You know how he feels about throwing money away."

Piso smiled at last and said, "I believe he is a cautious man."

"Have you found the quota of medal winners, Piso? It's my idea and I'm not sure Titus will approve, but I should like to see them at the very head of the procession. It seems to me it would be like an announcement . . . here is a moment of supreme honor and dignity."

"Unfortunately, they can't be in the lead, since there must be at least a cohort of Praetorians at the head of the procession to clear the streets. They will be followed by the students in the gladiatorial school. As for the honored marchers, I have been lucky in locating four wearers of the *corona civica*, awarded for saving the lives of citizens. I've located only one wearer of the *corona navalis*, being the first to board an enemy ship. One lives in Ostia and says he will not march more than a mile because sailors are not born to walk."

"As long as he's marching when we pass through the Forum he can swim the rest of the way." She was not really listening; her mind was on Flavius Silva. Oh, my general, please hurry!

Piso was saying, "I've been disappointed in finding men who've won the *Corona Vallaris vel Castrensis—*"

"What in the world is that?"

"It's awarded to the first to mount a rampart. I managed to find two, both former officers, and they promise to be present. I've had no luck in finding a winner of the *corona vallaris*, the first to scale a wall. I'll keep trying. There will be at least two or three hundred other lesser award winners carrying spears without irons or flags. They will wear horns on their helmets, for example, if they fought in Germany . . . others will be wearing honorary bracelets, belts, buckles, and chains signifying their accomplishments."

"You've accomplished a great deal in the short time you've been here. I'm particularly impressed because I know your heart is not in it."

Domitillia heard a step behind her and turned to see her husband. An obligatory smile flickered across his loose lips, and he waggled his head in the way that always made Domitillia think of a rooster on the prowl. He said, "Aha, my dear, the beauty of this day becomes you as it does our special guest." He waggled his head at Piso but failed to smile. "I have no wish to interrupt . . ."

Piso said he was just departing and started to move away.

"Ah, but my good man, you must not be in such haste! At least allow me to thank you for your services toward my father-in-law's triumph. I gather that my wife would have been lost without your help. It's all very complicated, I'm sure, and takes a great amount of organizing. My own participation is minimal . . . poor in-law relatives, you know? We always sit considerably below the salt."

Domitillia saw that Piso longed to leave them, but was having trouble finding an excuse. She said to him, "No one seems to have considered the physical comforts of those in the parade. Has some provision been made for that? If we are involved for hours, something must be done about our . . . hygiene."

Marcus Clemens tittered softly and said that as far as he was concerned, he had never been able to take a leak when people were watching. Then he pinched his cheeks to imitate the Domitian blush and tittered again.

Domitillia ignored him. When Piso said he would see to the problem of hygiene, she indicated that he could leave. Then she focused on Marcus Clemens. "What's so very amusing, Marcus? Do you lock some special humor in your manly chest that might also give me cause to smile?"

"Who could help but laugh at the spectacle of a tall, handsome, and I trust, courageous centurion making arrangements for your pee pot. I find it a hilarious abuse of military might. I trust that for the glory of Rome, not to mention the Flavian family, that you will see to your own bowels."

"Marcus Clemens, you are disgusting."

"Am I? How now the bride who refuses to sleep with her husband? Perhaps I should play Vulcan and thereby find new entertainment for myself. And you be Venus so I can spring the trap."

"Just what do you mean by that?"

"Oh, pure one, perhaps you never learned that Mars and Venus committed adultery together and her husband, Vulcan, caught them in a net in such a way they could not change positions or escape." Marcus Clemens paused, waggled his head, and rolled his protruding eyes toward the open sky above the peristyle. His eyes rolled back down and fixed on her as he added, "After all, I'm bored with masturbating."

"Marcus! You're a pig!" Domitillia spoke slowly, but she tried to keep an even temper in her voice.

"Tut, tut, my dear," Clemens chirped. "Don't look so woebegone or I shall begin to speculate on who in Rome might someday accomplish the impossible by arousing your passions. I was merely repeating a rather lyrical anecdote I heard last night while dining with Domitian. A most amusing individual who suppered with us spoke mainly in Greek, and we fell to comparing Mars with his Greek counterpart, Ares, Venus with Aphrodite, and Vulcan with Hephaestus . . . or is that all too complicated for your pretty head?"

Domitillia's heart was pounding and she was having trouble controlling her breathing. Oh, gods, she agonized, if he knows about Flavius, nothing can save us.

"Never mind, my dear," Marcus said. "I just thought you might find the story rather poignant . . . as I did. Can't you visualize them in that net? Perhaps I didn't relate it as well as that fellow, Scribonia. I've never been much of a storyteller."

"Who did you say the man was?" If Scribonia was alive? If Marcus knew? If he had told what he knew?

"Julius Scribonia. Do you know him?"

Domitillia hesitated. To gain time for her shattered thoughts to become less frantic, she asked, "What does he look like?" She hoped she sounded as if she were simply trying to solve a problem of identity.

"Quite spare, dark beard . . . a homosexual. I believe he is or has been with the *frumentarii*. At any rate, I found him most charming. Domitian has really taken to him. I suspect he'll be spending more time with us. It's been a shame how your brother has been left out of things. He deserves ever so much better, but Titus and your father are blind to his qualities."

"Who are you talking about?" she asked vaguely. Now a dizziness had come to her and she was not sure whether it was simply a characteristic of becoming a new mother or because of what Marcus was saying.

"Your blood brother, Domitian. . . . When your father dies, he will have nothing. It's wrong."

Domitillia covered her eyes with her hands and started to move away. Scribonia? That loathsome man? "You must excuse me, Marcus. I think I'm going to be sick."

She half-ran away from him, continuing until she had left the peristyle. She turned into her sleeping room and threw herself on the bed. It was some time before she could control her sobbing.

FIFTEEN

IN THE LATE afternoon, General Flavius Silva Nonius Bassus stood on a high promontory overlooking the ports of Carthage. The now-hodgepodge city, which had long ago lost its glory, was spread out below, and in Silva's eyes it looked like a rat's nest, despite the efforts of the Carthaginians and the Roman immigrants to make it a decent place to live.

His vantage point gave Silva a view of the two harbors, a circular port resembling a huge pie and a rectangular port where a channel had once led to the open sea. Silva remembered reading about how Scipio had captured and destroyed Carthage; in the process he had closed that escape route only to find the Carthaginians had cut through another channel, which exited from the circular port.

In the distance, winding as a thin line to the southeast, was the same road he had followed as his party had approached Carthage. The hardships of that long ride and even the ambush were already fading in his memory. His mission was completed. Cassius Paetus had pledged the Third Augusta to Titus no matter what the circumstances. Good man, Paetus, he thought; may his appearance belie his true health.

Now all below was golden in the late sun, and history seemed to rise up and smite him in the face. "I'm sorry we couldn't see it during its better days," he said to the man standing beside him. He was a pleasant Greek whom Silva had met the night before at a small dinner the governor of Carthage had given to honor Silva's departure on the morrow.

They had established a common bond almost at first sight because the Greek confided his interest in military history, and Silva found he lacked the usual snobbishness of the cultivated Greeks he had met. He was called Plutarch, which Silva thought an unlikely name for a Greek, but it was not unusual for them to alter or change their names completely if pronunciation proved awkward for Roman tongues. Plutarch had said that it was his ultimate desire to write a book comparing the great Greeks and the great Romans.

"I suppose," he said after Silva announced that he was anxious to leave, "that you will be awarded some kind of special medal for your voyage?"

"Why should I?"

"Because anyone who must go to sea takes my profound sympathies with him. I come very close to dying once the dock is left behind."

At last, Silva thought, he had met a man willing to confess that he was not at heart a ho-ho Phoenician pirate. "I'm not much of a sailor either," he said. They found a pleasant camaraderie in their mutual distrust of the sea, and soon they were discussing everything from how Carthage had been destroyed over a hundred years ago to the relatively new rights of Roman women. The Greek told of Vespasian's recent establishment of a chair of philosophy in Athens. Silva said that he was astonished. "I thought he detested philosophers."

"Maybe he's just trying to keep them as far from Rome as he can since they've given him so much trouble in the past."

Plutarch sniffed the air. Looking down at the harbor he said, "I think the sailors find this place by homing on the stink." He was referring to the odor of the human dung that was used to fertilize the fields in the vicinity of the resurrected Carthage. Here, in the long ago, after ten days of burning the city, the Romans had cursed the site by drawing a plow across the rubble and pouring salt into the furrows, hoping to render the land barren forever. Present-day Carthaginians were doing their utmost to prove the curse no longer existed, but without much success, they agreed.

"This place reeks of legend and tradition in your profession," Plutarch said. "You people brought all kinds of mercenaries through here, Numidian light cavalry . . . Libyan archers . . . Balearic slingers . . . they all came through

Carthage. And down there in those rolling hills Scipio defeated Hannibal and left twenty thousand Carthaginians dead in the fields."

Silva had read the Emperor Claudius' book on Carthage, so perhaps, he thought, that was partly responsible for his disappointment. Claudius had led him to expect more. From their position, they could follow the course of good roads leading to the fertile Bagradas Delta and beyond to the caravan routes that twisted through the lush countryside toward Thugga, Thamugadi, and the mysterious deserts where no Romans ventured. Exceptionally stalwart slaves came from there and also from the jungle lands a great distance south.

The Greek waved his hand across the urban sprawl below and said, "Do you remember what Scipio said when he saw this city in ruins? We must realize that here was the capital that ruled most of the world for seven hundred years."

Silva said that his memory was poor for quotations and that his Roman education, mostly conducted by Greek tutors, had been neglectful of events in Scipio's time.

"Scipio compared Carthage to the fall of Troy, and then to the collapse of the Assyrians and the Macedonians, and he borrowed a bit from our Homer. He said, 'I am seized with fear and foreboding that someday the same fate will befall my own country.'"

Silva chuckled. "Are you suggesting that the Roman Empire is about to fall to pieces?"

"Do I detect a slight hollowness in your laughter? At least, you'll admit that history has a way of repeating itself."

"I can't even conceive of such a situation."

"Of course not. My people thought Troy was eternal. Now we're looking down on the revived capital of Africa, the seat of learning surpassed only by Alexandria."

"You've just disproved your theory. Carthage has come back."

"Shorn of an empire. We're looking at the empty packing case of a once all-powerful force. Think about it."

Silva pointed at the numerous ships in the harbor. They were of all types and sizes; some were said to carry as many as five hundred passengers. From Carthage there were regular sailings to Sidon, Tyre, Byblus, and Alexandria. The smaller craft traded to Leptis Magna, Utica, Bizerte, Bone, and Lixus.

"I'm thinking of my belly," Silva said grumpily, "for tomorrow one of those beastly things will take me to Ostia."

"Possibly the gods will have mercy on you and you'll drown. But don't jump overboard! It's bad form, particularly for a Roman general. Let the ocean come to you. And think of your friend Cicero. He'll need you."

Silva reached to stroke Cicero's chest. The bird was at his customary station on his shoulder. Now he clucked softly.

"I shall miss talking with you," Silva said to Plutarch. "Where do you go from here?"

"Who knows? I'm weary of Semites and these Carthaginians are not unlike them. Do you realize there are something on the order of seven million Jews in your Empire?"

"Now?"

"So I'm informed by those who have attempted a count."

"I've been so long in their midst that I've come to think of them as individuals rather than as a mass of strangers."

"Do you think that's good or bad?"

"I don't know. I'm not too sure about a lot of things lately."

"Anyone who would ride a horse all the way from Caesarea to Carthage is very sure of himself. That much time bouncing around on the back of a semiwild beast would cripple me for life."

"If I could find a horse that would gallop on water, I'd ride straight to Rome."

"Why are you so anxious to leave?" The Greek patted Silva affectionately on the shoulder. "It must be a woman for whom you'll suffer the agonies of the sea. How intriguing, but no fear I'll ask her name. Let me say that our discussion of women was superfluous. They rule the fields, the mountains, the seas, and the very skies under which we talk."

"You Greeks amaze me. You shift from bellyaches to world rule in a single breath."

"It's that very lack of fixed direction that's been our defeat and victory for you Romans. You are a straight line . . . we are a convoluted design. We are aesthetically pleasing. You are strength."

"I've never been able to follow the twisting trail of Greek philosophy."

"You might try harder, because if you can stay with it you would also understand that women rule when they please because of our sexual urgency. The wise ones play upon it as they would the strings of a lyre."

"And you, my friend, are unaffected by it?"

Now it was Plutarch's turn to laugh. "I have the resistance of a caterpillar to becoming a butterfly. I am linguistically incapable of pronouncing a negative in the female presence. Let those grand words remind you that I am a pure and simple sucker for any female who casts an eye in my direction. I envy any man who is in love."

"I hope to read your book when you're finished. I like the way you say things."

"May you live long enough. Masterful procrastination is another Greek failing. Any self-respecting Greek can think of a thousand ways not to do something, however small . . . unless, of course, there is money involved. Even then, he can delay indefinitely. The specter of actual accomplishment, of being able to say that it is done, strikes him as uncouth, as a rather vulgar moment that should have come to someone else. You must visit Greece someday and discover the art of smelling the flowers along the road to nowhere."

Silva wondered what the Greek would write about Vespasian if he managed to meet him. "If you want to write about a great Roman," he said, "why not Vespasian?"

"From what I've heard, he's rather colorless."

"Of course, I'm prejudiced. He made me a general long before my time . . . the youngest in the army. But you should recognize the many important things he's done for the Empire. I'm quite sure I could arrange for you to talk with him."

Plutarch's eyes brightened and he seized Silva's hand. "I would be most grateful. Before your coming ordeal, before the salt in your eyes matches the salt in the sea, please remember that men tire of love and economics long before they do of war. You are the most un-Roman general I've ever met. Somewhere soon, we must come together again."

They stood appreciating each other in silence for a time, squinting at the last of the sun. Finally, Silva said they should be going, since the captain of his vessel had insisted he would be finished loading his mixed cargo of wheat, beans, and legumes by the end of the day and would sail at once. They embraced and exchanged kisses on both cheeks. Silva said the time they had spent together had been enough to form a precious friendship.

"Farewell, new friend," Plutarch said. "May your woman give you a long leash."

Domitian took leave of his brother in an angry mood, as he always did. As usual, Titus had treated his blood brother like a supplicating relative hoping for a few crumbs to be tossed his way. The grand Titus! Titus the magnificent! The arrogant, domineering, stupid, ill-mannered spawn of their common mother had behaved predictably.

Domitian was still descending from the Palatine Hill when he decided that Julius Scribonia had assessed the situation in the Flavian family correctly. It was uncanny how that man had foreseen exactly what the arrangement would be when the Emperor died. Titus would take all. There was no question of a coregency or anything like it. Domitian would be just another Roman citizen and nothing more. "He is going to steal my birthright as surely as a common thief swipes a purse," he fumed at Marcus Clemens who walked beside him.

Clemens waggled his head despondently. "Are you sure your father hasn't made some decree, written or otherwise, that would guarantee a sharing of the throne?"

"I asked him once and he gave me the cold eye. The next time I saw him, he said he ought to do something about it."

"Did he?"

"Not as far as I know. The trouble is that anything written is worthless. Titus, as you may know, has long had the hobby of handwriting. He can copy almost exactly any script or signature. He's an expert at it and would not hesitate to forge any decree to please himself. I've been lax. Time is growing very short for Papa, and I'm not going to sit waiting for the inevitable."

They made their way through the Forum, enduring the crowds as if they were ordinary citizens. Yet they stood out from the multitude because, in proper respect to their audience with Titus, both were wearing togas. Their dress and purposeful manner caught many eyes, but Domitian's formidable marching was in harmony with the fury about his mouth and eyes. The combination caused most people to keep their distance.

Domitian said, "Scribonia was right. There comes a time when action is mandatory, and I think that time is very near."

"We must be extremely careful," Clemens warned. "We've already had two failures. Buying off Silva was a good move, but it was mishandled."

"It was not Scribonia's fault."

"I didn't say it was."

"Scribonia is waiting to hear if Silva is still alive. We have reason to believe he met with a fatal accident."

"Ah? Let's just not forget that Titus' spies are everywhere. I don't fancy my neck up on the chopping block."

"That's the chance you take when you cast your fortune and your future with the disenfranchised brother. Not very wise of you, dear Marcus."

Clemens made a rosebud with his lips as he always did on those rare occasions when he chose to speak out directly. The gesture was preparatory, allowing him time to rescind any statement that might later prove to be dangerous or embarrassing. After he allowed the rosebud to wilt, he announced with just enough force to reach Domitian's ears, "It's my belief that you'll not long be disinherited. With you on the throne and my wife at my side, no one can deny that we're the right people to rule the Empire."

Domitian grunted. He pushed past a beggar, knocking him down, and he shoved aside a drunk who came careening toward them. He had deliberately chosen to walk from his house to the palace. He could have asked for an escort of Praetorians, but that would have been asking something of Titus. He could have been carried by his slaves in his litter or ridden a horse, but that display of well-being would have given Titus reason to remind him of his affluence. If he was to be the poor brother, then he must play the role. He had hoped some of the stench of the streets might arrive at the palace with him.

As they passed out of the Forum and slipped onto the Clivus Orbius, there were so many pedestrians that their brisk pace slowed. Domitian decided he would take to his bath as soon as he arrived home. Rome was overcrowded to the point of idiocy, he thought. One breathed the foul exhalations of his neighbor's breath. As soon as he took the throne, there would be some mighty clearing out to do. He would tear down all these claptraps of buildings hanging together for support like so many poplars in the wind. These narrow twisting streets were infested with non-Romans of every breed, Christianii, Jews, Macedonians, Syrians, Germans who had been brought to heel, and a sprinkling of hairy Gauls. There would be a new and better world under the Emperor Domitian. These same people would see.

Soon they made their way through the Viscus Sandalarius, where countless sandal makers shouted the quality and worth of their wares. Coming into a much wider street, they continued more rapidly and with great determination toward Domitian's villa on Mons Oppius.

Clemens tried desperately to match the determined pace of his hero and was soon red in the face and puffing noisily. The conversation between them was hardly more than a monologue delivered by Domitian in erratic spurts, with echoing punctuations exploding from Clemens' fat lips. The rhythm of Domitian's words matched the steady cadence of his own progress. "I must see Scribonia this very morning . . . he'll know how much money we'll need and when . . . always talking about the importance of time . . ."

"Ah, yes . . . of course." Marcus Clemens fought for his wind.

"Titus has declared himself. . . . We know where we stand. . . . Can you imagine that decadent drunkard telling *me . . . me!* . . . his blood brother . . . that he alone will take the throne . . . that there does not exist any sort of document giving me rights to *anything* . . . not even the smallest province in Gaul or a muddy field in Britain? . . . Can you conceive of such patronizing shit as to say to me, Domitian, that perhaps when Papa dies, he, Titus, mind you, will try to find something for me? . . . Something *he* considers is not beyond my very limited ability and intelligence? . . ."

"The man is truly a beast . . . beast and thief. If it had been up to him, I would never have been permitted to marry dear Domitillia."

"Better perhaps you had not!" Domitian regretted his words immediately. The poor fat-assed idiot who was trotting beside him was still one of the richest men in the Empire and his funding was essential. If he told him what he knew about his wife, there would be a split and, as Scribonia was so fond of saying, timing was everything. A disillusioned husband was of no foreseeable benefit to the new Domitian. Indeed, as Scribonia had forecast, there would be a long and difficult campaign ahead probably requiring enormous sums of money before it reached a successful conclusion. Informers must be paid, ways found to circumvent or penetrate the heavy protection surrounding Titus, and even the Senate must be soothed beforehand. Thus, only could the groundwork be properly laid for the time when the Emperor Domitian would come into his own. "If Flavius Silva isn't already dead, we can't have him coming into Rome. Absolutely not. I have reason to believe that once here he would give us serious trouble. And Scribonia agrees with me."

Clemens puffed out his own argument. His face was beaded with perspiration. "Do we have to walk so fast?"

"Yes. I'm now convinced that Julius Scribonia is a brilliant man. I've a mind to appoint him my chief tactician . . . or something of that order. What do you think?"

"It's important that you surround yourself with good people now rather than choose in haste later. Then the opportunists will come flocking to your standard. Those who are willing to bind themselves to you now will be more reliable when you need them. But we must be discreet. Once our plan is discovered, it will be all over . . . for all of us."

"Sometimes, Marcus, you make remarkable sense. I want you to draw up a list of those who might join our cause. We need at least a few senators to prepare and deliver the first proclamation. . . . We must invest heavily in the Praetorians . . . find one or several high officers who will look the other way if required . . . and look our way if needed. We'll need several generals to bring their Legions to our service. There's no way of knowing yet how much harm Silva has done to us in Africa."

"The treasury, Sire. We must be sure the Legions are promised a donative in your name. Likewise for the Praetorians. And it must be done before anything else is attempted."

"I agree. It has been done exactly so before. But I'm the first to have his brother obstructing the way."

Domitian slowed his pace slightly so that Marcus Clemens could catch his wind. They turned up the road that led to Domitian's house. It was a steep incline and Clemens nearly came to a halt. He wiped at his brow with the sleeve of his toga and said that he was not accustomed to such exertions.

"You're in terrible condition," Domitian commented sourly. "Why don't you get rid of some of that fat?"

"My wife asks the same question."

His wife? Domitian thought. Should any disposition be made for her in this new hierarchy? The daughter of Vespasian hardly could be ignored. Scribonia would have the answer. Let him handle it—and her troublesome General Silva as well.

"When do you propose to accomplish this very major project?" Clemens panted.

"There must be a decent period after Papa's death. Then final preparations must be made, and then we'll strike."

"Sound. Very sound thinking."

"We are agreed that everything depends on secrecy. Mind your tongue everywhere . . . even around your wife. There are three who will know of this: myself, Scribonia, and you. If we are discovered, I'll know it has not been Scribonia who has talked."

"How will you know that, Sire?"

"Because greed rules him. With us he knows exactly where he stands."

At his villa in Reate the Emperor Vespasian sat watching the late spring rain and wondered if he was correct in his conviction that it always rained during the first week in June. He smiled wanly at the satisfaction he found in the rain because he recognized that he was like every other Roman in his love of the land; the sight of the plowed fields turning black with the moisture pleased him.

The rain prevented Vespasian's daily stroll in the garden, which had become a strangely precious event in his almost monastic life. But the chills were with him again and the Greek doctors had said it had nothing to do with his affliction. "I suppose," he told them, "that it doesn't make any difference what I die of as long as I don't exit on my hands and knees."

The Greeks, in the humorless manner of their calling, asked what his body position had to do with his admittedly uncertain future.

"It has long been my opinion that an emperor should die standing up."

He had lately asked the gods not to humble him with any of the positions of death he had observed during a lifetime of soldiering. "I don't want to be curled up like a fetus or sprawled on my back with the gas of my last meal still inflating my stomach. I want my mouth to be closed and not twisted in some final scream. Above all, do not permit my eyes to be open and staring like two marble eggs at those who discover me."

Now, for a moment all too rare in his days at Reate, Vespasian found cause to laugh. Suppose, he mused, I die with an erection? Still laughing, he slapped his cheek as if to reprimand himself. "You silly old bastard you haven't even known a senile sprouting in months, but I suppose as long as you can worry about it, you're not quite dead."

Later that day there was a great clattering of hooves in the courtyard and Vespasian knew the cause. He had sent for Titus, who arrived with a full complement of mounted Praetorians.

"You're soaking wet," Vespasian said as his favorite son approached. "You could have waited until tomorrow. There is not such urgency."

"Any request from you is urgent, Sire."

Vespasian waved him into one of the simple chairs that he kept as a reminder of the long gone days of his childhood when the villa was no more than a modest farmhouse. "We have some unpleasant matters to discuss. I'll not seem to be challenging you if we're both sitting down."

"If I've displeased you, Papa, then I can only express deep regrets."

Vespasian wheezed audibly and said in an apologetic tone that he had caught a chill and it had affected his voice. "But I want to listen rather than talk." He hesitated. He hated his suspicions, but they must be denied or proven if his thoughts were ever to rest again. He asked bluntly, "Where is Berenice?"

"At your bidding, I sent her away."

"Where?"

"Sicily."

"That's not far enough. Have you had any communication with her?"

"No, Papa."

"None at all?" Vespasian's hand trembled as he extended it to touch the armor of his son.

"She's written a letter to me, but I've not responded."

"And what did she say in the letter?"

Now it was Titus' turn to hesitate, and Vespasian saw that he was having a painful struggle within himself. And he thought, dear gods, the trouble men will make for themselves over a woman is almost beyond comprehension! My son, my son, the glory is already yours . . . you have only to pick it up and cart it off as you would a prize of war, but beware of stumbling along the way, beware of traps set by complex females for innocent adoring males. "What did she say?" he insisted.

"She said she was waiting for the day when she could return to my side."

"Of course. Particularly if it's on the other side of the throne. Tell her when you reply, as I'm sure you will, that Rome will never tolerate a Jewish queen."

Titus deliberately changed the subject. "You must take more rest, Papa, if you will have the strength for the triumph. I fear it will be rather tiring."

"It's going to cost a lot of money. I'd rather see the same funds directed toward the Coliseum. That will stand for a long time, while the triumph will soon be forgotten."

"Not so, Papa. Much of the city is involved in the preparations. The money expended will employ thousands of people. It will be the most magnificent triumph Rome has ever seen. The procession will begin at the Campus Martius and go from there along the Via Triumphalis, through the Circus Flaminius, and on to the Capitoline via various streets strewn with flowers."

"Sounds ridiculous and very expensive."

"Expense to honor you is of no matter, Papa."

"I can no longer march that distance, you understand?"

"Of course. You'll be seated comfortably on a great wagon with an awning above and certain decorations celebrating your career."

"Where will you be?"

"On my horse, near the head of the column."

"And Domitian?"

"Somewhere in your trail. It's not been decided."

"Domitillia?"

"As you would wish . . . either ahead of or behind you."

"I care not as long as she's satisfied. How is she getting on with her husband these days?"

"Fine. They seem very happy."

Vespasian was suddenly overcome with fatigue. He wheezed several times, cleared his throat, blew mightily into a handkerchief, and then farted. "I am not at all well," he said as if to justify the noise he had made, "and I'm becoming very tired. There are several matters I wish to discuss and clarify with you before my mind turns more addled than it already is. Quickly now because even my immediate time is limited and we must review our major concerns. What of the army?"

Titus took a small tablet from beneath his leather jerkin and studied it momentarily. "The Sixth Legion . . . that's the Victrix," he said, "is in Spain and in excellent shape. Morale good, local acceptance good, thanks to a fine disciplinary record."

"We have Caristanius Priscus to thank for that. I always knew he'd make a good general."

Titus continued. "In Upper Germany we've had some problems, as you already know. Like the Fourth Macedonica, something seems to influence the Legions we put there, and soon enough we have a rash of desertions and outright mutiny. The Twenty-first Repax is reported to be in reasonably good shape, but the Twenty-second Primigenia is a source of perpetual trouble. Cashiering individuals has not met with much success, so I'm thinking of doing it en masse. Extinguish the whole rotten Legion and form a new one."

"The ghost of Caligula will never forgive you. He raised the Twenty-second, you know."

"I did not, but possibly that's where the trouble started. Now in Lower Germany we have the Fifth Alaudae and the Fifteenth Primigenia. All is well there, although there are reports of dissatisfaction with pay. Nothing new and even my report is a month old. In Britain we have the Second, Ninth, and Twentieth Legions, two more than necessary, in my opinion, because I don't think we get enough out of Britain to justify the expense. Dalmatia has the Eleventh, and I'm sending the Fourteenth to beef them up a bit because they're expecting some action. Now in Egypt we have—"

Vespasian held up his hand. "I haven't the time for a full accounting. My bath waits. Just tell me of any problems."

"The Twenty-second in Africa has lost over two hundred men to the local desert tribesmen in the past year. I'm not sure what to do about it."

"Cashier the general. Who is he?"

Titus consulted his pad. "Petronius Niges. I don't know the man."

"I do. He's a scoundrel. Get rid of him. Send some young man out there who's got some fire up his ass and tell him to make the killing go the other way."

"Done, Sire. One last thing. I've been approached by several officers who want our cavalry to be provided with metal instead of leather breastplates. They say the extra shoulder pieces don't provide enough protection against a downcut."

"There are very few Romans in the cavalry, right?"

"Right. Except for the officers, the men are from everywhere . . . a very mixed bag."

"How much will metal breastplates cost?"

"Roughly about a half million sesterces."

"Not worth it. Next?"

"We are experimenting with a new design for ballistae. The arrows are short bolts and quite heavy and have an accuracy range of about three hundred yards. When I was at Jerusalem, our heavy catapults were sending fifty-pound stones as much as five hundred yards, and some of the bigger engines threw them seven hundred yards. But we needed something to back up the damage they did before we actually tangled with the Jews."

"I know. I was there, or have you forgotten?" Vespasian attempted a smile but found it difficult because his hurts were increasing and he longed for his bath. He made a vague gesture, passing the fingers of one hand across his brow, and asked, "What of the city? I'm not anxious to return. The noise distresses me."

"We had a collapse of a residential building and about two hundred inhabitants were killed. It was in Subura, about midway along the Argiletum."

"Those old buildings should be razed and new ones built. People deserve a decent place to live."

"Very few of the dead were Roman citizens, so there was not too much commotion. Meanwhile, I hope you'll approve of my plan to take Nero's old place, which was badly decayed, tear a lot of it down, and build a huge new public bath. We need one in that area."

"It sounds like a reasonable idea, but watch the cost. Our contractors have become expert robbers."

"The artists are still working on the decorations for the arch that you so kindly dedicated to my fortune against the Jews. There will be a full relief of my triumph and what I've seen appears to be very impressive. The style is somewhat different than we are accustomed to seeing, but perhaps that's an advantage. I've told the artists to take their time, do the job well, and stick to the truth. I don't want to be made beautiful." Titus laughed politely. "No one would recognize me."

Vespasian smiled. "You're overly modest."

"I'm trying to encourage more Roman artists. We're too much influenced by the Greeks. For the architectural designs around the new baths, I've told them to let their imaginations take charge and to forget the ordinary."

"Why not? All artists are crazy. Worse than philosophers. Tell me . . . what does your brother do with his time? He worries me."

"Be at peace about him, Papa. He'll calm down eventually. I've told him you had no intention of splitting the throne, and he seemed to accept the fact . . . albeit somewhat sullenly. As you suggested, I allow him enough money to live well, but not too well."

"Does he ever manage to have a serious thought in his head?"

"Now, Papa, don't be so hard on him. He'll mature. Right now his chief complaint seems to be that the Jews in the city have too many children and they won't stay on the west bank of the Tiber. He says if they keep breeding, they'll take over the Empire."

"Nonsense. They're too clever to want the headaches. Leave them alone as long as they pay their taxes. There are more important things to do. Such as win a bet on the blues, a luxury that refuses to come my way."

Titus laughed heartily. His father was well known for his faith in the blue chariot-racing team, which had so far made a very poor showing for the season. The greens had won almost every race in the Circus Maximus, which had seen victories even by the unlikely reds and whites. The blues, hitherto almost undefeatable, had been a sour disappointment to what seemed like half the population of the city; yet most of the blue devotees had, like Vespasian himself, remained stubbornly loyal. Chariot racing had become a complicated and extremely expensive endeavor, with large stables supported by rich men who continuously tried to outbid each other for fine horses, chariots, and drivers. Enormous sums were wagered on the major races involving two-, three-, and even four-horse events. Romans who could not afford to lose a denarius somehow came up with a pittance to back their favorites.

Vespasian snorted into his handkerchief again and farted as if to punctuate his disgust with the blues. "What's wrong with the blues?" he asked almost savagely. "How can they lose so often? Has anyone checked the manure of their horses? Are they being fed properly?"

"It's the drivers, Sire."

"Why? The blues . . . until last year at least, had the best drivers in the world."

"I don't understand why they can't seem to win, Sire. The fortunes of the track are always mysterious."

"Leave me then. A son who cannot predict the outcome of a race is no good to me."

"If I spent less time with judicial matters, I would have more time to learn about the races."

"The lawyers are becoming too much for you? Ah, how well I understand."

"If the magistrates make a decision and it displeases the defense, the lawyers come running to me for appeal. If I heard them all, I'd be doing nothing else. I think our juries are too large. It's impossible to find seventy-five people or even fifty to agree on anything."

"Why don't you simplify the system?"

"With your permission, I will."

"Then we've accomplished something for this day. Anything else?"

"I'm still having trouble with the farmers. They all want to grow grapes instead of grain. I point out to them that they can have some very bad years for the vine, as witness the Surrentinum the past year or so, but they see less money and more work in grain. Our cost of importing grain from Africa is putting an awful hole in our balance of trade. In fact, there isn't any real balance worth considering, and somehow we've got to change it."

Titus stared at the raindrops dribbling down the window-panes, which were of Egyptian glass and quite transparent. They were a symbol of his father's long rise to prosperity, for this house in which he had been born, and his father before him, had not been so protected from the elements in its life-time.

"I sometimes wish," Titus said forlornly, "that all I had to do would be to fight a few Jews . . . or Germans, or Dacians. Ruling is the hardest job a man can find."

Vespasian chuckled. "At last," he said. "I've waited years to hear you say that. Now I know that you understand what you're doing. I can die in peace now. See to the comfort of your escort and yourself. If I'm alive in the morning, I'll not delay your departure with bundles of questions, for I well understand that the working Emperor never has any real lei-sure."

Vespasian pushed himself to his feet and stood as straight as he could manage. He licked at his dry lips, wondering if he had said all he must say, and decided that perhaps he had said too much. The tongues of old men are too supple, he thought. They wag when they should be resting on the gums. They deceive their owners into believing that wisdom grows with their years, when in fact they are only discovering their igno-rance.

"Rest while you can, Son," he said, and turned away.

III

"Even bitter Juno
whose fear now harries earth and sea and heaven
will change to better counsels, and
will cherish the race that wears the toga."

—Virgil: *Aeneid*

> ("Quin aspera Juno
>   quae mare terrasque metu
> callumque fatigat,
>   Consilia in melius referet,
>   mecumque fovebit
>   Romanos, verum
>   dominos
>   gentemque togatum.")

III

SIXTEEN

WHEN FLAVIUS SILVA finally placed his foot gingerly on the wharf at Ostia, he vowed that he would make a sacrifice to Isis, the patroness of mariners who had escaped shipwreck. For in his estimation it had been a frightful voyage; the Mediterranean had been in a savage temper during the entire five-day passage from Carthage. He was exhausted from lack of food and sleep.

Soon after he had left Plutarch on the hill, Silva began a series of preventive measures against the perils of the sea. He obtained a myrtle wreath and a pair of honey cakes, which he placed in a small temple of Jupiter. He was not sure whether he should whisper his prayers to Jupiter as Pluvius, god of rain, Jupiter Fulminator, the maker of lightning, or as Jupiter Tonans, the thunderer. Hence he prayed to all three, just in case.

Afterward he prayed to Poseidon in Greek and his Roman counterpart Neptune in Latin, again just in case. And he finished by begging to all the gods he could think of for *pax deorum*, lest he offend some important dignitary. Finally, he faced the west where the planet Venus floated on the horizon, held both hands straight above his head, and twiddled his fingers two hundred times—all on the advice of a merchant who had consigned cargo to the vessel.

Once Silva had climbed aboard, a feat he compared unfavorably to scaling the walls of an enemy fortress, he humbled himself as Plutarch stood watching in amazement. Following the recommendation of the slave who had poured his bath at General Paetus', Silva lowered himself to his knees and bent down to kiss the planked deck. Stomping furiously for his balance and squawking for rescue, Cicero drew the attention of the entire harbor to his master's genuflections.

Unfortunately, Silva's tenuous confidence suffered further humiliation when the lines were cast off and the vessel got under way. Before they left the harbor, Silva placed Cicero in the scuppers and began vomiting over the side. Two days later, when despair had nearly overcome him, he groaned to Attius, "Where is my poor belly? I've lost it somewhere in the Mediterranean and we have to go back and find it."

Attius did what he could to comfort the general, but soothing words and boiling Silva's urine mixed with a few hard-won drops of his saliva, as recommended by the sailing master, failed to bring recovery. "Give me up for dead!" Silva pleaded. "Oh, god . . . gods of the sea . . . Neptune and/or Poseidon! . . . Stop the wind! . . . Stop the waves! . . . Stop the world!"

Silva's muttered complaints were viewed with tolerance by the crew and with dismay by those few of his escorts who were not too incapacitated themselves to care what happened. They feared he might make things even worse by cursing the elements, and they viewed Cicero's fierce imitations of his master as possibly supernatural. Was that damned bird the soul of some long-lost sailor?

The captain of the vessel smiled at the brilliant sun and remarked that this was proving to be one of the most pleasant voyages of his long career at sea. Silva overheard him and vowed to have him castrated if he ever came near a camp of the Tenth Legion.

Later, when the captain was of sufficient distance from Silva to be sure his words would be carried away in the wind, he swore that all Roman soldiers were born landlubbers and that he knew why they so rarely wept. The salt of their tears, he claimed, would make them seasick.

Attius was the only member of the escort who had not been sick. He smiled tolerantly when Silva had declared he should have joined the navy. Liberalis had remained on deck, comatose for two days, with salt spray spewing at him constantly. The leather of his armor was still black from the soaking.

"You look like some old hock of marinated camel," Silva said to Liberalis, "and I'll thank you not to tell me what I look like."

"You'll live, Sire," Attius said. "There is a small hotel here. Rest for a day and get some nourishment in you. I'll go on to Rome and make arrangements for our accommodations."

"Very well, Attius. You're in command for the moment. I think you should be an admiral instead of a tribune. I'm too feeble to go on."

They walked slowly away from the wharf and Silva did his best to keep his head high. He glanced back at his bedraggled troops who had left Caesarea in such proud style, and he saw that some thorough sprucing must be done before they entered Rome. They must shave, bathe, and divest themselves of their armor and weapons, just as he must, before passing through any of the gates. That was the law. Even the wearing of daggers was prohibited. However, the more cautious citizens often carried a writing stylus as defense against roving thugs in the night streets. The innocent-looking instrument could cause considerable damage; because of its small size it was referred to as a stiletto.

They had walked only a little way from the wharf when Silva saw a synagogue. He shook his head in disbelief and pointed it out to Attius. "Have we not been anywhere . . . or did it follow us?"

Although it was still early in the morning an unusually chill wind swept through Ostia. The streets were already crowded with people. It struck Silva that he was like a country boy. By the gods, he thought, I'm not going away again no matter what the army wants!

The hotel was comfortable and Silva went to sleep immediately. He was unaware that the proprietor of the hotel, who had received him with unctuous solicitude, had already dispatched his most trusted slave to Rome. The slave was to proceed without delay to the house of Julius Scribonia and advise him that a certain general had arrived. His message was important and he must be certain that he delivered it directly to Scribonia himself.

THE TRIUMPH

* * *

Even as the slave from Ostia passed through the gates of Rome during the late afternoon, Joseph ben Matthias, now at pains to be known as Flavius Josephus, agonized over the few paragraphs he had written during the first week of June. Ever since his surrender to the Romans at Jotapata his sense of shame had been somewhat eased by his continuing attempt to write a history of the recent war in his native land. The scanty information he had been able to gather on Masada particularly irked him, primarily because those Jews who defended it had all found the courage to take their own lives. Josephus had never been to Masada, nor had Titus, who had told him about it. Hence, the only information he had on the whole event was the quite dubious report of an addled old hag who had died soon after the fall of Masada. She claimed there were three or four children who survived in addition to herself. Josephus had been unable to determine their ages—were they infants or half-grown? Nor could he discover from this distance their eventual fate.

Josephus was a wiry, bright-eyed man, birdlike in his movements. He moved in quick little sparrow hops from place to place in his quarters, which had been provided by Titus. The emperor designate desired that he be near his own residence, thus easing their frequent communications. Therefore Josephus lived and worked in a section of a government house on the Clivus Scauri. It was sequestered and quite old, yet manned by eight excellent government slaves.

Josephus rationalized his acceptance of such relative luxury at the hands of his former enemies by constantly reminding himself that his work was even more important to Jews than to Romans. One day, perhaps while he was still alive, his writing might inspire his people. To that end he had begun his writing in Syro-Chaldaic, a language that most Jews understood, but he had soon switched to Greek so that Titus and other people of reasonable education could follow it. He wrote passionately and voluminously. There had been times when Titus, who had been so cruel and unforgiving at Jerusalem and was accountable for its destruction, asked him not to be so easy on the Roman troops or even himself. He said he wanted the truth, and Josephus, in his ebullient way, was quick to point out that the truth depended on who was telling it.

Josephus did not deceive himself as to who would read his words. They were intended for gentile readers as well as Jews. When he paraphrased the Hebrew Bible, he did so in a way that he hoped would help gentiles understand his people. The Jews, he reasoned, had kept a relatively common mind since long before the Diaspora and already understood.

Josephus would have liked to return to Judea for a time, there to further his research into the war, but he knew that because of his defection, his murder by someone whose mouth would form the word "traitor" would be only a matter of days.

Traitor or not, he was momentarily beyond caring, for his perpetual literary loneliness was about to be broken by someone he hoped would prove to be a most interesting visitor. Months previously, he had complained to Titus of his lack of reference to confirm his writings. Now, as if in answer to his prayers, Titus had sent a message in which he described a Centurion Piso who had actually fought with the Tenth at Masada. If Josephus cared to talk with him, he would make arrangements. Now, barely able to control his excitement, Josephus watched the water clock, which was reasonably reliable as long as the slaves remembered to fill the reservoir. It leaked, however, and when the fluid was all gone, time stopped—a situation Josephus found worthy of meditation.

Josephus' elation caused him to bound into the air when Piso arrived on schedule and brought with him a boy whom he said had survived Masada. He led them into the little room off the atrium that he had chosen as his place of work.

"We're honored to meet a man of letters," Centurion Piso said.

Josephus winked at Piso and held up a cautioning finger. "I didn't invent letters. The Egyptians and Phoenicians did. I am merely an unemployed general. Sometimes I write from right to left in the manner of my forefathers, and sometimes from left to right, as I do now. I don't think it makes much difference. It's what you say that counts, and I'm trying very hard to say the truth."

They sat down and Josephus exhaled his satisfaction with the moment. He waved his hand at the hundreds of scrolls that were stacked like cordwood against the walls. "My work," he said genially. "Little wonder I can find anything." He passed his fingers gently across a collection of stylus, wax tablets, papyrus, a parchment called *Palimsestos* on which erasures were easy to make, and bottles of cuttlefish matter he used for ink. He patted a pile of clean white paper and said it was called *Claudia* after the Emperor Claudius, who had by certain improvements in an inferior type, produced the best in the world. "Titus sends me stacks of this stuff, which no ordinary writer could afford. He says he wants what I have to say to last for a long time. I hope," he added, "that you will help me confirm certain facts."

Josephus looked at Reuben and said to him in Hebrew, "What troubles you so, son? You look unhappy."

"I am."

"Why?"

"I don't like the company of Romans or of Jews who live here."

Josephus glanced at Centurion Piso and saw that he did not understand their exchange. He knew a sudden foreboding. Was this sullen youth about to spoil things? "It's better than not being anywhere at all. Wouldn't you agree?"

"No. I come from Masada. My father and mother died there. The man who wants to adopt me killed them."

"From what I've been able to learn, they all killed themselves . . ." Josephus tried to put down his rapidly growing concern. Here was an opportunity he had longed for and it seemed to be dissolving. He decided to gamble. He reached across the table and selected a polished stylus. He regarded it thoughtfully, then held it out to Reuben. "Here," he whispered, still employing the Hebrew, "it's very sharp. If you believe what you say you believe . . . why don't you do away with yourself?"

Reuben studied the stylus, then raised his eyes to meet Josephus'.

"No. I have other plans," he said in Latin.

"So have I," Josephus answered testily. "And I won't help my people by dying. Neither will you."

Piso eased the tension by laughing and said to Josephus, "Bit of a handful, isn't he? Have patience. He simmers down after a bit."

"His Hebrew makes me homesick . . . slurs his gutturals like a true Galilean. Do I understand he is being adopted by one of your generals?"

"Flavius Silva. The best soldier in the army."

"And you? How is it that you're here? Did you come for the triumph?"

"I'm on leave."

A slave brought vinegar water in cups and they sipped it noisily.

"Egyptian vinegar," Josephus pointed out, "best in the world." He drained his cup and took up a stylus and pad. He puckered his lips momentarily and wriggled down in his chair as if to better handle the business at hand. "Tell me about General Silva," he said. "I'm aware that he was in command at Masada. I beg you to speak freely of the man. Titus has assured me there will be no reprisals for anything used in this work. To that promise he's given his right hand."

"Silva is no ordinary general," Piso began. "He is a complicated man. He can be gracious and he can be cruel."

"You're a centurion. I didn't think you knew the meaning of cruelty . . . or do I misjudge duty and custom in the Tenth?"

Piso grinned and said that he was also complicated, that he had experienced some inner changes in the last few years. He was not sure why. "If it were not for General Silva, I would leave the army."

"What would you do?"

"Maybe . . . spread the word of God."

Josephus swallowed and his ever-busy eyebrows shot up on his forehead. His stylus became fixed on the tablet as if it had slipped into a hole.

"What god?" Josephus tried to hide his dismay.

"The Christus."

"You're a Christianus?" Josephus mispronounced the term. "A centurion? I find this difficult to believe. How could you have fought at Masada?"

"There wasn't any serious fighting at Masada."

"Do your comrades in arms understand your faith?"

"No. And I'm not sure I do."

"This feisty young *zayin* you brought along; don't tell me he's joined the Christianii?"

"I was born a Jew and I'll die a Jew," Reuben said quickly.

"How will General Silva feel about that?"

"I don't care."

275

"He'll handle it," Piso said easily. "General Silva can handle anything he sets his mind to."

"I'd like to meet such a paragon of virtue. . . . But tell me about how you took Masada, everything you can remember. Then I want to hear what Reuben has to say."

"It may take the rest of this day and maybe more," Piso said.

"Impatience can ruin a whole story."

"And memories are tricky. Reuben, for example, will never understand why we had to take Masada."

Josephus smiled and held up his stylus. "Thousands of facts flow through this instrument, but even if I told it to say, 'I've found a way to turn iron into gold,' it would not be satisfied. There are three ways I can tell this story. I can tell it through meditation, which is usually both vague and dull; or I can tell it through imitation of others, which is the easiest. The best way is through bittersweet experience . . ."

Josephus kissed the stylus and held it poised above his tablet.

"I am listening," he said.

Julius Scribonia could hardly contain himself after hearing the news of Silva's arrival. He gave the messenger a bag of denarii, told him to be sure to spend it foolishly, and then hastened through his house to find the Spanish boy. He found him by following the sound of his flute. The pretty thing was at his practice time.

Although Scribonia had been worried about the boy's weight, he adored his rumples of baby fat. Now he had difficulty hoisting him off his feet and squeezing him to emphasize his glee. He kissed the boy when he could catch his lips and repeated triumphantly, "Oh, my lovely one, my precious thing . . . my true love . . . the time has come! I've only to conceive how best it can be done!"

The boy resisted Scribonia's fervent embraces, but he was no match for his lover's strength. He ran the length of the peristyle and disappeared into his room. His reluctance did not disturb Scribonia in the slightest. There was something about bringing the boy to heel that gave him great pleasure. He was so sweet-smelling always; nibbling his ivory skin was like biting into a fresh peach, and the cheeks of his rump were of incredible texture. His absurd little snits were only the emotional Spanish in him. He was priceless and far more beautiful to the eye than any toy the greatest men in Rome could find.

The first true love of his life, he thought. "I adore you," Scribonia sighed as he watched him retreating. "I love you more than I can ever say . . ."

For the moment when he stood alone, he was regretful and depressed. Then the importance of the day struck him, and his scribe was waiting. Ordinarily, he wrote his own letters, but the one he had in mind must be perfection in all its parts, since it represented insurance on his future.

Scribonia warned the scribe, a freedman he had used before, to take particular care with his lettering. He would soon realize the propriety of same when he heard the salutation.

"Julius Scribonia . . . to Flavia Domitillia . . . *se vales Bene est . . .*"

"That's an ancient greeting," the scribe protested. "Are you sure you want to begin in such an old-fashioned way?" The scribe drummed his fingers on the small boxwood writing table he had brought with him.

"I'm sure. It's a fitting greeting for the someday possible queen of the Empire."

"I think that is most unlikely, considering her two brothers."

"I'm not interested in what you think. Did you come here to argue succession with me or to copy down my words?"

"As you wish. Will you be long or short?"

"I shall be as brief as possible. That may be long."

"I hope I've brought enough pads. When I transcribe, do you want parchment or paper?"

"Paper, of course." Scribonia had thought to say, "Paper, you idiot," but changed his mind. This man was always obstinate, but good at his job.

"The paper alone will be three sesterces per page."

"I'm not interested in the price," Scribonia said through clenched teeth.

"You always have been before."

"Times have changed, even if you haven't. May I commence or is this to become a social visit?"

"In addition, my fee will be three sesterces per page."

"Humph. Why have you raised it?"

"As you say, times have changed. And if I were in the

mood for social chatter, I've no doubt it would be more agree-able elsewhere. The tax will be one sesterce. Vespasian will not be denied."

Scribonia favored the scribe with a thin smile. There was no use provoking the fool. Today, when all of the timings seemed to have come together in exactly the right juxtaposition, it was impossible to be unhappy with anyone. "You keep a tart tongue," he said. He stood up and began to pace back and forth in front of the scribe's table. All the while his hands kept busy scratching at his beard, twisting his eyebrows, and scratching at his crotch. When he found such activity distract-ing, he folded his hands behind his back and vowed to keep them there.

"If my reappearance in Rome surprises Your Grace, please be advised that the gods have been kind to me. It's as useless to deny their aid in my preservation as it is impossible to ignore the circumstances of a certain night in Judea that called for all the good fortune an innocent man could wish for. . . . No, strike that out. Make it . . . an innocent man could ex-pect . . ."

Scribonia was silent for a moment as a sudden wild desire for the Spanish boy passed through his loins. Later, he warned himself. This dictation could be of incalculable importance. "As Your Grace is fully aware, I was victimized on that night and left for dead. Alas . . ."

"Why don't you use the word 'unfortunately' here?"

"Because I like 'alas.' Shut up and tend to your scribbling."

"If you want to sound like an ancient Etruscan, carry on." The scribe shrugged his shoulders.

"Alas, what I saw that night on the beach refuses to be erased from my memory. I would like to keep it a secret be-tween us until I'm truly dead, because I developed a remark-able fondness for your charms, your intelligence, your beauty, and your kindness to us lesser mortals . . ."

Now be careful, Scribonia warned himself. This was no time for threats, but it was a unique opportunity for insinua-tions.

"In the course of my normal duties it has come to my atten-tion," Scribonia dictated more slowly, "that a certain general of our mutual acquaintance will soon arrive in Rome. You will forgive me if I presume you will see him. Be so kind as to inform him of my survival. Tell him also that I long to be a trusted servant of the Flavian family and have no intent to spread any word that might reflect unfavorably on you or him."

The scribe paused and said that he must sharpen his stylus. Scribonia waited, tapping the toe of her sandal impatiently on the mosaic he had caused to be laid at the entrance of his library. It was not an original design but copied from one he had seen in the atrium of a wealthy shipper's house in Ostia. It consisted of a perfect circle outlined in maroon stones and featured an enlarged phallus of black stones in the center. Scribonia had been disappointed that no guest who had come to his house had displayed the slightest sense of shock or even curiosity. He now considered the mosaic a waste of money.

When the scribe nodded and held up his stylus, Scribonia spoke in a tone to match the humility of his words. "My dear lady . . . even under the most excruciating torture I would keep your secret. I look to the future when I may someday have established even closer relations with your family and serve yourselves as I would serve the Empire—"

The scribe interrupted. "Do you really suppose anyone would give a dried fig for what you have to say?"

Scribonia pretended to be appalled. "Your impertinence is almost beyond my comprehension! Have you come here simply to titillate my boundless good nature, or are you determined to make me genuinely angry?"

"All of this is bullshit and you know it."

"By the gods!" Scribonia screamed. "I don't have to listen to the puerile opinions of a mere scribbler! I can write this letter myself!"

"Not in Greek. And that's what you want to enhance your pose of the highly educated man. I know you can speak it, but you can't write it . . . so shall we resume?" The scribe raised his eyebrows.

"You *are* a cocky bastard!"

"Anyone who has worked as hard as I have to obtain an education has a right to be. If you really desire another to record your words of wisdom, you might try Calestrius Flaccus . . ." The scribe picked up his tablet and began to fold his writing table. "You'll be more content with a servile hack even when you learn that his inscribing is that of a Greek peasant, or a Latin peasant, or whatever his very limited education allows. One thing is guaranteed. Whatever Flaccus has put down is certain to utterly confuse the reader." He stood up.

"Now, now," Scribonia said hastily. "Sit down, sit down! Please accept my apologies. I'm somewhat nervous over this matter. I want your talent to help me do this properly."

"In view of the addressee, I suggest you stay with the best." The scribe sat down and laid out his materials again. "You may proceed."

Scribonia folded his arms across his chest as if to contain his patience, and said, "May I suggest that Your Grace pass on to the general that any attempt at retaliation on his part toward ~~myself, however unjustified, would result in the gravest con~~sequences for both of you . . ." Scribonia held out a hand and waggled it at the scribe. "No . . . strike that last. Make it . . . after 'to the general,' write . . . it's my wish that he become my friend as well as yours, since I hold no bitterness toward anyone. The acquisition of my knowledge was purely the result of chance and I've never proposed to take advantage of it."

"Not much you don't," the scribe said. "You've never in your life let anything go by without turning it to your advantage. It must have been quite a party, and I don't even know your secret."

"And, my fine fellow, you never will. Now I want to end this in the most formal and proper way. Suggestion?"

"Deos obsecra ut te conservant, is the proper subscription to royalty."

"But that's Latin."

"Still proper. But I can translate it to Greek if you wish to be consistent."

"Do so then. And rid me of your presence as soon as possible."

The scribe was already picking up his tools. "Two things I've always admired about you, dear Julius: your taste in boys and your consistent resemblance to a famished hyena."

After the scribe had departed, Scribonia paced the length of the peristyle several times, brooding on what he had dictated and wondering if he had said enough. Only recently the *frumentarii* had learned of a series of clandestine meetings in the excavations below Domitillia's brickworks. It was reported that the meetings were led by a guest of Domitillia's, whose background was not yet established. There was also a boy guest (a new toy for Marcus Clemens?) with unverified background, although he was thought to be of Jewish stock. Of course, royalty could do as they pleased, and Domitillia was inclined to exercise all her privileges, but what would she be doing with a Jewish boy in her house? Did he have something to do with the meetings below her works? Thus far, no one in the *frumentarii* had been able to actually attend the meetings, but it was thought those admitted were either Jews, or worse, Christianii. Why would Domitillia have anything whatever to do with such rabble, much less afford them shelter for possible troublemaking?

Scribonia ran his tongue around his lips as if he could actually taste the line of thought that he had deliberately put aside until all other distractions were at rest. A most provocative report offered by the *frumentarii* had come to his attention late the preceding night. It was a castaway, considered of so little significance it was not even explored beyond a casual remark that had come to his ears. Like all reports, it was useless floating alone, but when combined with a need it became priceless. Perhaps, Scribonia concluded, it would now be possible to accelerate the time when Domitian would take the throne!

Was the sun shining upon Julius Scribonia? Was opportunity literally laid in his lap? Here was the awkward, dawdling *frumentarii* stumbling upon a fact so useful its full value might never be appreciated . . . except, of course, by J.S. Titus, the *imperator designatus*, who was known to visit a certain Matthias, a Jewish soldier who had defected from his own troops and now lived, at Titus' pleasure, in a government house. The man had even taken the name Flavius, presumably in honor of his patron, and he was said to be writing a history of the Jewish war.

What did this mean? Nothing of any great import to the average Roman, but to J.S. it could mean the end of an old world and the beginning of a new one. If Domitian were ever to become Emperor in the foreseeable future, then something must prevent Titus from succeeding his father. But if there were no Titus?

Until now the problem had always been the protective cordon that surrounded Titus constantly. He was almost never alone and even then, wherever he might be, a whole army of Praetorians was close at hand. Yet the *frumentarii* had reported that Titus always left his guards outside when he visited Flavius Josephus. He considered the government house so little known that he was safe from any intrusion, and his arrival there was always scheduled for nighttime. Apparently, he was devoted to the Jew's book and considered himself a part of its artistic creation.

Scribonia paused in his energetic pacing as an old Roman axiom came back to him: "No one ever believes an assassination is being planned until after it happens."

Very well. Let Titus' artistic ambitions flower. Let him be at peace with the Jew in a secluded house that could be entered with a minimum of risk. And let him eventually be found there . . . an honored and regretted dead prince.

It would cost a considerable amount of money, but there was always the ample purse of Marcus Arrecinus Clemens.

Scribonia licked his lips again in anticipation. His genius had not deserted him for an instant. Now at last, he was protected from any eventuality. With Vespasian joined to the gods and Titus out of the way, Domitian would take the throne. But suppose something happened to Domitian? Another accident . . . or just the providential workings of nature? Then it must be Domitillia and her child who would command the Empire. And who would be at her side? Scribonia allowed himself a smile of congratulations. Thanks to the letter he had just dictated, his insurance for the future was complete.

As if his mental gyrations had inspired his physical being, he felt a sudden surge of desire for the Spanish boy. He had departed in one of his snits, which must have passed by now, and after a few soothing caresses of his plump little cheeks, he would be anxious to indulge in more exciting fondling.

Scribonia started toward the Spanish boy's room. He moved on tiptoe, purposely swinging his hips in a hinting dance, clasping and unclasping his hands as if he were trying to capture a tiny bird. He opened the door with great care and peeked inside. There was the boy's bed and his pillow smashed against the wall, as was his habit. But the boy was gone.

Scribonia straightened. He was having trouble absorbing what he saw, and he reassured himself that the boy was incapable of vanishing into the mural of a garden painted on the wall. Then where was he?

He looked behind the door and saw nothing except a sandal lying askew. He turned about and quickly strode along the peristyle, calling the boy's name gently—and then more stridently. He turned back again and retraced his steps, still calling his name. He recognized the growing rate of alarm in his voice and forced himself to remember that the boy had no place to go except the house. He had no money and only a very limited knowledge of the city.

Scribonia moved quickly to the toilet, an unusually elaborate accommodation for a Roman house, with three positions cut in the marble and continuously running water, which carried waste to the city's sewer. The room was unoccupied.

He stepped outside. Instinct told him that the boy, his lovely Spanish boy whom he loved so passionately, had run away.

Scribonia's voice echoed throughout the empty house as he clapped his hands for his slaves. Two of the five he owned appeared. He questioned them without results, and they joined him in an exhaustive search of the entire house. When it became evident that the boy was not to be found, Scribonia dispatched his slaves to the streets. "Find him," he ordered in despair. "He who finds him will be given his manumission!"

When they left, Scribonia slumped down in a chair and sobbed. He thought that this great day, which had begun so fortuitously, had become the most unhappy day of his life.

SEVENTEEN

IT HAD BEEN Silva's intention to send Domitillia a message asking for a place of rendezvous convenient to her. Now that he was on home ground, her marriage to Marcus Clemens became very real, whereas in Judea it had been little more than a vague realization in his mind. He found it easy to remind himself that most Roman marriages were arranged by family elders who intended the resulting unions to enhance the position and fortunes of both families. Little love was lost between mates. Premarital courtship was uncommon; it was often true that the bride and groom had barely met before the marriage ceremony. Such arrangements were particularly common among the aristocracy. Hitherto, Silva had found it easy to assume that between Domitillia and her husband there was little more than a sterile relationship. Yet here in Ostia, while recovering from his voyage, he was beset with new misgivings.

Since Domitillia had no way of anticipating his arrival, there had been no message awaiting him, nor had he received any word from her in a month. During the interval, had she possibly reconsidered her bold adventure in Judea and allowed her head rather than her heart to rule her actions?

Silva was consoled by the fact that he must fetch Reuben and take him to Praeneste, an excuse that would demand a visit to Domitillia even if her husband was standing in the atrium. Nor, he reasoned, could her husband take any offense with such a legitimate reason for his calling.

THE TRIUMPH

Silva had barely awakened in the hotel at Ostia before his sense of discomfort about meeting with Domitilla was replaced by new concerns. Four mounted Praetorians arrived and their decurion presented Silva with a brief message from Titus.

Titus Vespasianus, *Imperator designatus* to Flavius Silva, General commanding Tenth Legion Frentensis. "Come to me at once. Make all speed. A fast horse is provided."

He had not expected a signature, since that was not the Roman custom except for edicts and other official documents. Yet there was nothing more, no welcome, no friendly subscript, no indication that Titus had issued more than a military order. Leaving his kit with Liberalis to take on to Rome, Silva broke his fast on a roll sprinkled with cinnamon, a chunk of freshly slaughtered sow seasoned with bay leaves and figs, much overboiled for his taste, and a glass of vinegar water. While the Praetorians waited, he ate hastily and was soon riding in their lead toward Rome. Cicero, squawking his usual litany, rode on his shoulder.

They rode at a canter even after they reached the streets of the city. Not until they were abreast of the Circus Maximus did their pace slow because of the heavy traffic of carts bound for what Silva was told would be Vespasian's pet project, the Coliseum. They threaded through the carts and swarms of slaves, tradesmen, beggars, plebs, Orientals, street merchants, and idlers until they were brought temporarily to a halt by the construction of a new triumphal arch, this one intended to honor Titus' victory in Judea.

Silva glanced at the arch and the partially completed frieze that decorated a section of it. He found little of interest in the depiction of military events of the campaign. He had been there and fought through the very battles the arch was supposed to commemorate. Now, somewhat to his own surprise, he saw little reason in preserving that long-ago past in stone. It was impossible to depict the heat of the sun broiling the carcasses of dead Jews and dead Romans. It was impossible to preserve the agonized screams of women who saw their men die, or the whimper of a youth in full armor lying prone and pale-faced, surprised that an arrow had found its way to his neck. Instead, of an arch, Silva thought as they turned up the Palatine Hill, there should be a monument of some kind to hold the cremated hopes of those who were slain. It should bubble with the fluid of their lost blood and give off an unforgettable stink, as did all battlefields when the killing was done. As they passed the arch and continued up the hill, Silva did not trouble to glance back at the new construction.

Titus received Silva in the Flavian house, which was still undergoing renovation from the fire of Nero's time and much new construction. It was a true palace now, with extensive rooms embellished by fine marbles and mosaics. After greeting Silva with a warm smile, Titus apologized for the volume of noise created by the more than a thousand laborers working on the place. He laughed and said that he could hardly wait to see the expression on his father's face when the contractors turned in their bills. He inquired about Cicero, still perched on Silva's shoulder, and Silva told him the story of his presentation.

"I trust he'll not launch into one of his long orations?"

"Unlike his namesake, he can be easily insulted. If you yawn in his face, he'll shut up."

"Splendid chap. I wish I had his company."

Silva hesitated, then made what he thought was a frightening decision. "Then, Sire, he's yours if you wish."

Titus waved his hand in dismissal. "No, no. I appreciate the honor, but I'll find my own friends."

Silva inquired of his father's health as Titus led him to a small room overlooking the western reaches of the city. "Here we won't have to shout at each other," Titus explained.

After they sat down in two ebony chairs, Silva said that he thought Titus might have put on a bit of weight since he had last seen him.

"Indeed I have!" Titus said easily. He patted his belly and shook his head. "I like everything that's bad for me. May I remind you, old comrade, that there's nothing like a war to keep you trim? Yourself now . . . you appear to be in fine fettle . . . a trifle emaciated, I'd say, but a few weeks in Rome will fix that. With any luck you'll have to waddle back to Judea."

"About that," Silva said uneasily. He found it necessary to caution himself that he was not speaking just to his old comrade in arms, but to the emperor designate. Since the power of the world was in the hands of this man who had once been his playmate, he must accept the fact that their relationship had changed accordingly. "I don't want to go back to Judea. I've had a bellyful of the Jews and their land."

Titus smiled tolerantly. "Oh, come now. You just need a rest and some variety. After you've enjoyed yourself here, you'll find it less than perfect. A little time in Praeneste with a few cold days of north wind and you'll be damned glad to get back to the Judean sun. Remember, it's not the land of the Jews any longer—it's ours."

"I wish I could be more convinced of that."

"By and by. How is your house in Praeneste progressing?"

"Coming along, I understand. The usual trouble with architects and contractors and my purse . . ."

"And of course, it takes forever. A man grows old just waiting."

"Yes," Silva said lamely. Was this why Titus had sent for him so urgently? Were they going to sit around and talk about a relatively modest little dwelling in which Titus could not possibly have much interest? "Your imperial duties seem to have agreed with you," he said to fill the rather sudden silence. "You have acquired a new dignity. You've always had it, but now it's been polished. It shines."

"Very fancy words, old friend." Titus looked out the window toward the Tiber. He seemed preoccupied. "I must suppose you know me as well as anyone. I find it hard to believe our faces were once smooth and our beliefs all intact. . . . It seems like another life. So many of our contemporaries are dead and we're still relatively young."

Was this why he sent for me? Silva wondered. He stroked Cicero's wings to ease his unaccountable sense of foreboding. Something was wrong. Titus was conducting himself according to the rules of friendship, but it was like a military drill with one limping man.

"Those were grand days. Sometimes I wish we could go back to that life. It was so simple . . ." Titus' voice faded and his eyes became wistful. "I wish we could both go back and stay there," he sighed. Now there was a new firmness in his tone. "But we cannot stay in one place. We must face up to certain responsibilities that have come to us with age. We must recognize that true friends are few and far between."

Again Titus paused. He gazed steadily at Cicero as if he

expected the bird to make some comment. "Flavius . . . reluctantly, I must refer to the matter of your association with my sister."

Silva fought to keep his composure. He *knew*. Here was real trouble and there was no escaping Titus' mood.

"Certainly you are aware that my sister is a married woman, that she is constantly in the public eye as well as that of the Senate, and that her behavior is a direct responsibility of the throne. Whatever she does—good or bad—creates a reflection on our family. For that reason alone your conduct appalls me. Had it been any other man, you may be sure I would personally butcher him. You've known my sister since childhood. You knew that she has always been a hoyden, a self-willed, vulnerable woman who gives her heart to anyone who applies, or any cause that strikes her as amusing. You have betrayed the Flavian family by bedding my sister as if she were a common whore, and in doing so you have betrayed the trust given you by the throne."

Titus' tone was unmarred by variation. It was cold metal, Silva thought, and terrible to hear. His thoughts raced through a thousand responses. All of them he knew to be wrong.

"Let me assure you that you may not be ordered back to Judea or anywhere else except the arena and *ad bestia*. I wonder how you will look standing there naked before ten or twenty thousand honest Romans while we turn a few leopards loose with you? Will you run? Or will you stand there and let them have at it? Probably I should put Domitillia in there with you. You dedicated lovers can die together . . . but that's quite impractical. My sister, the daughter of Vespasian, the greatest Caesar who ever ruled, cannot be exposed to dishonor and ridicule, nor can any public acknowledgment of her perfidy be encouraged . . ."

Titus snorted and stood up. "Now I see that you and your wretched bird are silent. Because there's nothing to say . . . right? Because you know damn well what you've done, and what is there to say to a friend whose trust has been so churlishly betrayed? Who do you think made you a general? Who plucked you from among the young tribunes and said, 'Here is a special man who will do us all honor on the battlefield'? What we did not know is how you would dishonor us in the flesh. If Domitillia were single, then the matter would be simple enough—you would marry her. But she is already married to another man who is honored throughout the city and who we now consider a member of the Flavian family. He is a very rich man who has contributed enormous amounts to our treasury. The last thing we want to do is offend him. But with your careless cuckolding you have done it for us. When he finds out about you and his adulterous wife, you would both be better off dead."

Silva was tormented by an almost overwhelming desire to unleash his temper and tell Titus that his love for Domitillia was pure and should be given the respect it deserved. He yearned to explain in the strongest terms he could command that there was nothing common about their affair; indeed, it had been the most uncommon. They had not indulged in any secret planning; nor had Domitillia deliberately betrayed her husband. They had been as surprised as they had been overjoyed to find themselves powerless to deny their love. He wanted to tell Titus how they had realized the consequences from the very beginning, yet their will to turn each other away vanished instantly at sight of the other. He wanted Titus to know how it had been that after an unbelievably short time their thoughts had become as one; their spirits had joined and were now locked together forever. No leopards could break his love . . . nor any man, including the Emperor of the Roman Empire. Yet railing at Titus would only aggravate him because he would be speaking a language he would never understand. With a snap of his fingers he could make sure that he would never see Domitillia again.

"I need you, Flavius. I need your friendship and if a knuckles-down conflict occurs between Domitian and me, I'll need your strength and support. I wanted you to ride close to me in the coming triumph because I thought your services to the Empire deserved such recognition. And now? With Marcus Clemens riding with his wife in the same parade? His *pregnant* wife? Honor and hypocrisy do not mix! This triumph will be the culmination of my father's life—"

"What did you just say?" Silva demanded fiercely. His pulse was pounding as he leapt to his feet. He barely restrained himself from reaching out and shaking Titus. He rubbed his fist in the socket of his bad eye and demanded that Titus repeat what he had just said.

"I'm trying to tell you how important this is to the welfare of Papa and our family . . . not to mention yourself."

"No, no! You said something about Domitillia!"

"You must know she's pregnant."

Silva groaned. "No . . . I did not know. We've had no communication for some time . . ." Suddenly, he wanted to escape from Titus, he wanted to go away and think, he wanted to find Domitillia and take her in his arms.

"I find it difficult not to assume that you are the father . . . unless, of course, my dear little sister was experimenting with other soldiers while she was in Judea . . ."

Silva stared at the floor and flexed his fists. He wanted to kill Titus.

"Here is the situation," Titus said, as if he were proposing a battle plan. "It is highly unlikely that Marcus Clemens would claim the child as his own, and we cannot present a nameless little bastard to the Senate and the people of Rome and simply shrug our shoulders . . . because *they* won't accept it. Therefore, I proposed . . . no, that's not quite the way it was put . . . I *ordered* Domitillia to have an abortion."

"And what did she say?" Silva's voice was husky with anger and frustration.

"She refused. I then did my utmost to explain how important it is that nothing disturb our father's triumph or his equanimity at this time. He's an old-fashioned man with an old Roman sense of right and wrong, especially when it comes to the Flavian family. Times may change, but Vespasian does not. No one can shake his belief in honor, duty, the family, and the Empire. If this nasty business comes to his knowledge, as eventually everything seems to do, I think it might kill him. So, I informed your lady friend."

"And what did she say?"

"She still refused. I had no choice but to give her a choice. She could have the thing aborted immediately, or be exiled to the most distant and uncomfortable island I can find."

Titus folded his arms across his chest, and his mouth took a hard set. "Now I'll also give you a choice. Sometime today or tomorrow at the very latest, you will see Domitillia and persuade her to abort. When that is accomplished, my order for her exile will be withdrawn. In time, when I am well established as Emperor—which could be many years from now—

she might even request a quiet divorce and I might be persuaded to grant it. . . . But I doubt if she would be much interested in you at that indistinct time. Because if you refuse to participate in this protection of the family and throne, I can only assume that you are an active enemy. You will be stripped of your rank and honors. Your house in Praeneste will be confiscated and sold to the benefit of the treasury. You will be condemned to fight *ad bestia* at the games that will follow the triumph. Do I make myself perfectly clear?"

Silva nodded his head almost imperceptibly. He could not find voice to defy Titus. What little reason remained to him warned against showing his temper.

"Now to the problem of deployment," Titus continued with the same severity. "I'll provide a place where you and Domitillia can meet discreetly and settle this business. Accommodations are waiting for you in a house that belongs to the throne. Only a few rooms are presently occupied by a Jew who calls himself Flavius Josephus. He's that fellow who surrendered to us and is engaged in writing a history of the war. You need not even see him, but once your principal purpose there is accomplished, you might enjoy contradicting various details in his work, since he's writing in Greek as well as in his own barbarous tongue. A Praetorian will take you to the house, where you will remain under personal arrest. Your mistress will meet you there as soon as she can make the necessary arrangements to conceal her identity. You will advise her that the same precautions must be taken when she goes for the abortion. She must appear to be merely the consort of a *pleb* or some such of low rank, and, of course, she must not use her regular Greek doctors."

Titus paused and watched Silva's eyes. "That will be all, General, which you still are . . . on my tolerance. Do not try me further."

Titus turned his back on Silva and stalked out of the room. When a Praetorian officer appeared and stood waiting in silence, Silva was still seething. He reached to caress Cicero, for he had never known such loneliness in his life.

Nighttime at Reate was difficult and extremely uncomfortable for the Emperor Vespasian. Then it seemed all the furies of his pains gathered in nocturnal lumps and moved from place to place throughout his body. Only his heart seemed willing to keep to its proper locale, although it often raced and thumped like a legionary drummer's call to arms.

Vespasian could find little to divert his thoughts during the long torment of his night hours. He tried calling musicians but found their music far from his taste, although they willingly played the tunes of his younger days. He sent for magicians and too easily discovered their manipulations. Despite his patronage of the escritorial arts, he was not a reader, so he tried storytellers and soon became bored. He had trouble tolerating their pomposity and overly meticulous diction. He even imported a troupe of dancing girls and actors from the city, but their suggestive gyrations and elaborate pantomime failed to arouse him. Finally, in desperation, he began to think of his accomplishments, an accounting that went against his modest nature, but at least gave him some satisfaction.

When he had come to the throne the Roman government was close to bankruptcy. Fully aware that the only means of rescue would not be popular, he had taxed almost everything not already subject to tax and raised the rates on those already taxed. He had managed by official penury and some confiscations to raise about forty billion sesterces, and once again established the government as a solvent force.

He had reduced unemployment by vastly expanding the public works on roads, rebuilding various temples, and creating the Temple of Peace.

He had injected much-needed new blood into the Senate by calling to Rome many members of prominent families who had long resided in the Italian hinterlands and were unspoiled by the follies of the city. He appointed many of them to the equestrian order and championed their qualities of rusticity and optimism when they were scorned by cynics in the assembly. Now, although the Senate remained his occasional adversary, the substance of their quarrels had usually been for the good of the Empire.

Brooding through the nights, Vespasian decided he was not so pleased with the ever-growing number of slaves on the Italian Peninsula versus the population of freedmen. As far as he had been able to ascertain, there were far more than a million slaves and they were breeding like rabbits, a habit even their masters were encouraging in the hope that volume would bring down their cost on the market. With the average price now quoted at about four thousand sesterces for an ordinary slave, it had become very expensive to get any work done. Slaves with specialties, such as scribes, teachers, artists, and just pretty boys, ran ever so much higher. There was nothing, Vespasian sighed in resignation, that he could do about it. He could only hope that the slaves would never realize how many they were.

Perhaps it was the limited quantities of hellebore his Greek physicians were prescribing for him, or his unsavory diet of barley slops and water porridge they called *ptisan*. Strangely, the long sessions he spent seated in his marble toilet became by contrast somewhat of an amusement when compared to his major suffering. His forced position and inability to control himself touched both his soldier's rough humor and his rural acceptance of man, soil, and nature. His distress in such circumstances reminded him that he was far from a god and that there were various things in the Empire over which he could have no more control than he had of his bowels.

Another problem was the infertility of the upper classes as compared to the fecundity of the poor. Abortions were illegal, but in Rome money could buy anything.

There were also the immigrating Greeks who were inundating the city and spreading out all over the Italian Peninsula. Such was the flood of their numbers, hastening to the profitable hive like bees, that hardly a single enterprise was established these days without a Greek somewhere involved. Even their language was threatening to supercede the traditional Latin; most communications were written in Greek. The Greeks were a busy, imaginative people, he thought; they were now displaying an almost incredible resilience by playing the role of conquerors long after they had been defeated.

Seated in his "thought chambers," as he sometimes referred to his toilet, Vespasian reviewed the population of Rome with such humor as he was able to muster. From this throne, he thought, I cannot rule for or against any of them. There were the Syrians who, like the Greeks, were into everything, including the banks. There were the Egyptians, who were certainly not lazy, but lacked the drive to make themselves wealthy. They were mostly artisans of one sort or another, and most lived in a colony they had established in the Field of

Mars. Except for petty thievery, they rarely gave anyone trouble.

There were the ubiquitous Jews whom Claudius had protected by law even after they had rioted. Vespasian thought it odd that these same people had continued to lead their normal lives in Rome while he had been fighting their brothers in Judea. They kept to themselves, spent too much of their productive time in their synagogues, and smelled of sesame and garlic. They were now, thanks to him, each contributing the half-sheckel they had been paying toward the reconstruction of their temple in Jerusalem to the rebuilding of Rome. The edict had made them furious, but he did not care. This was where they lived.

As for the moral stature of the Roman people, Vespasian concluded that there could be considerable improvement—or was he just an old man who had forgotten the delights of amoral behavior? Prostitution was legalized, the brothels restricted to decent hours, and the whores licensed (tax for the treasury!). The leaning toward pederasty brought to Rome originally from Asia Minor had flourished in the capital, and only the gods knew how many homosexuals now resided in the city. Passing laws against it was a waste of time.

Who should proscribe the sexual habits of other Roman citizens? Certainly, Vespasian thought, his own family would have been ostracized from society had they behaved in the same fashion three or four hundred years ago, say, in the time of the Republic. Here was Domitillia admitting she was in love with a man other than her husband and possibly committing adultery. Here was Titus, who had lived openly with the Jewess, Berenice, and now indulged himself with whatever females crossed his path. There was Domitian who, if reports from the *frumentarii* were to be believed, favored both women and boys to calm his impulses and was particularly given to group debaucheries. Where was the honor of the Flavians? Buried in a lonely and sick old man, a bag of bones perched on a marble toilet, a once-great warrior encased in a wrinkled and odoriferous hide.

Perhaps he should be embalmed in the manner of the Egyptians, he thought. He should be wrapped in honey, as Marc Antony was said to have done with the body of Hasmonean, the ruler of Judea. Suppose his physicians could wrap him in cloth soaked in resins and enough natron to keep him from rotting. Would premature embalming prolong his life or just his pain?

"I must not die quite yet," Vespasian mumbled to himself. "A triumph does not need a corpse."

Domitillia had decided that this was one of those days when she wished she had become one of the Vestal Virgins. She had stayed up much too late the preceding night listening to Centurion Piso talking about his god, "the Jesus," or whatever he was called. Apparently, that man-god had been understanding of another adultress, and Domitillia yearned for someone, anyone, who would wash away her lingering sense of guilt and appreciate that love between man and woman could not always be regulated to the convenience of society. It was all very interesting, but she mistrusted some of the customs and regulations that seemed to be part of Piso's faith. The Jesus seemed to be his only god, and somehow this worship of a single man who apparently had no real family background reminded her of what she had been told about the long-ago times when Bacchus was celebrated. Now most Romans met and spoke to the gods while alone. Gathering in numbers was dangerous; people became so carried away with Bacchus that wild orgies resulted and some of the participants were killed. The worship of Cybele had not been much better. The priests dressed in outrageous Eastern costumes and encouraged hysteria and self-mutilation among their drum-beating, flute-playing followers. Many people in Rome claimed the Christianii were inclined to the same sort of thing.

This morning, however, her real concern was for herself. While in her bath, she had discovered a trace of blood between her legs and was terrified something might have gone wrong with the child she bore. She must do something, for after Titus' ultimatum she had promised herself that the child of Flavius Silva must be as perfect as their love. Whatever its sex, it would not be left at the foot of the Column of Lacteria where so many female babies were abandoned.

Since she had refused an abortion, she thought that Titus would probably send her to Sardinia, a savage place with clouds of mosquitoes. Never mind. She would survive and her child would survive because Flavia Domitillia would be the best mother in the world. But if she lost the child . . . if this bleeding, however slight, should forecast the end of it or even its malformation, then who was guilty?

It was a pity, she thought, that she dare not go to a military *valetudinarium*, where the sick and wounded were given the best of care. There were no such hospitals for civilians, but there was a Greek doctor who was said to treat patients in his own home and sometimes, if they had enough money and appeared to be likely prospects for survival, would allow them to remain there until they were cured. His name was Xanthos and he lived far from the Palatine Hill, so it was very doubtful if he knew what the daughter of Vespasian looked like. She must disguise herself in such a way that he would never realize he was treating royalty. Toward that end she now put on a blond wig. It was the fashion of the moment to look like a Germanic tribeswoman.

She began the long business of making up her face in a way she hoped would alter it beyond recognition. She applied three creams mixed with finely ground barley meal, honey, and the froth of red niter. Each mixture was colored and applied separately; the maroon to her cheeks, the white to her jaw and neck, and as if to be sure no Roman lady was actually mistaken for a German, there was the black to emphasize her eyebrows. She brushed her lips with a lively red and, taking a deep breath, dared to regard herself in a mirror.

"Why, you flagrant hussy!" she whispered. She had intended to appear as the courtesan of a middle-class lawyer because she knew her speech would betray her if she tried for any lower identity. Had she overdone her appearance? "Perhaps," she whispered, as if she were enjoying herself, "perhaps things have not been so good lately . . . perhaps you've fallen upon hard times?"

She selected a cloak of modest fabric and dragged it along the peristyle in an attempt to dirty it as she strode to her waiting litter. She was delighted to notice that her household slaves glanced at her casually and then in wonder as they tried to place her. She passed Reuben, who cocked his head and asked if she was going to play in the pantomime.

"Why not?" she answered. "Our theaters could do with more spice."

Just as she had seated herself in the litter, Centurion Piso came bounding toward her. She pulled aside the curtains.

"General Silva is here," he said breathlessly. "I'm to take you to the house where he's staying."

Domitillia did her best to conceal her delight. She was tempted to change her destination instantly. But Flavius must be told about the child, and she must first be reassured that her fears were exaggerated. "The general will have to wait a few hours," she said.

"My orders are from Titus."

She was puzzled. Titus? Was he suddenly condoning . . . or condemning? "You must wait here." She smiled at Piso. "I'll return as soon as possible."

"I will say I couldn't find you."

"I thought lying was against the rules of your god-man."

Piso smiled and brought his fist to his left shoulder in salute. "Remember . . . he forgives."

Xanthos, the doctor, lived in a tawdry middle-class house near the Porta Latina. Since the traffic had not yet peaked, Domitillia's slaves made good time. She commanded that her litter be set down around the corner from the house, and she walked back to the entrance. When she entered the house she was tempted to turn around because the stench was almost overpowering. A man with a bleeding wound on his head was laid out on the floor of the atrium; he appeared to have ceased breathing. There was a confused-looking man whom Domitillia thought must be a carpenter or a cobbler, since an awl was sticking upright from his thigh. There was a tanner moaning over a series of dog bites along his legs, and Domitillia was reminded why such people were obliged to live apart from others. They bathed their animal hides with human excrement prior to tanning and the odor never left them. Mixed with the soft smells of a bakery next door were the strong scents of ointments made with goat grease, swine grease, zinc oxide, and frankincense.

A female slave approached Domitillia and, as if realizing instantly that she was a person of substance, indicated that she should follow her to a room near the rear of the house. There she was told to wait, a boring status Domitillia had so rarely experienced in her life that only worry kept her from departing. To curb her impatience, she began to examine the collection of containers lining the shelves of the room. There was quicklime, salt, salamander ash, and dung of swallow, wood pigeon, sheep, and lizard. There was myrrh vinegar, egg white, copper sulfide, alum, copper oxide, and pounded snails, all neatly labeled in Greek. And there was opium, which Domitillia had heard dispensed with pain.

She was beginning to wonder if this Xanthos was indeed an *archiatri*, a term that would identify him as a "responsible practitioner," when he entered the room. He was a tiny person, more dwarf than man, yet Domitillia was instantly impressed with his dignity and aura of efficiency. "Tell me your troubles," he said with a quick smile.

She told him of the blood and he shook his head sympathetically. He said that since she appeared to be a healthy woman he doubted if there was any serious trouble, but she must submit to his speculum if she wished to be sure.

Domitillia took a deep breath, vowed she would remain silent no matter what came next, and lowered herself to the couch in the corner. Xanthos called for the slave girl who had conducted her to the room, and she brought him a speculum. He appeared to be deep in thought while he warmed the instrument with his hands. To Domitillia's vast relief, she saw that the slave girl remained in the room while Xanthos asked her to spread her legs. Muttering solicitous phrases, he began his examination.

Moments later, almost before she was resigned to her embarrassment, Xanthos removed the speculum and stepped back. He explained in the same comforting voice that he had found nothing serious, but had washed her vagina with vinegar, which she should continue to apply for one week. He had found some irritation, which he had eased with an application of something called ephedron, a styptic made from a plant of the same name. Finally, he suggested that she wash herself regularly in cold water until the bleeding ceased. "Your breasts are still full, so I say for now that you need have little fear of miscarriage. It is the woman who is very thin or even of moderate health who might have trouble in the second or third month. Their cotyledones become filled with mucosity and cannot support the weight of the fetus."

Xanthos hesitated and a mischievous light came to his eyes. "And now," he said as if privy to a shared secret, "since you have gone to so much trouble to disguise yourself, I'll not trouble to ask your name."

"Floria Soranus . . . consort to the lawyer Bibulus."

"Nonsense. You are Domitillia, daughter of the Emperor, and I'm mystified at your coming here." Xanthos chuckled and added, "I have a full-sized brother who is also a medical man. He recommends wool plugs soaked in an astringent solution to avoid conception. Perhaps you should have paid him a visit before you came to me."

"You are very impertinent, Doctor."

"You will be pleased to know I'm also a keeper of secrets."

Domitillia held out a bag of sesterces. She hoped it was enough to keep this little monster from talking, although she supposed no one would believe such an incredible situation. Xanthos shook his head, smiled in open enjoyment of the moment, and said, "No, no, Your Grace. I'm proud if I can soothe your worries. I wish you only the best of life."

After she rounded the street corner and slipped into her waiting litter, she thought there were some things about this day that were going right. She thought about the little doctor most of the way back to her house. All of her life the Flavians had been wealthier than the average Roman family, and as a consequence were ripe targets for every exploitation. The price was always raised on anything a Flavian wanted or needed. After a time, she thought, it became endurable because there was no other choice; but secretly, deep within Titus and Domitian and certainly herself, there was an uncomfortable sense of shame. As far as she knew, no one had ever done anything for a Flavian during recent years without a heavy charge. All things were sold or performed for a price— and yet this little doctor . . . ? May the gods bless him and his work, she thought. She wiped away a tear of pleasure and for a moment forgot entirely that her future was hopeless.

EIGHTEEN

JULIUS SCRIBONIA FOUND his despair nearly intolerable. Despite the one thousand sesterces he had offered as a reward and the dispatching of his slaves to every likely area of the city, there had not been the slightest report on the whereabouts of the Spanish boy. Neglecting everything else, he and his staff had searched the Quirinalis and the Viminalis, which were relatively adjacent to his home, and had then branched out as far as the Campus Martius and the Mons Aventinus. But they had found nothing.

Scribonia had personally followed along the course of the Tiber, being as fearful that he might find something as that he might not. There had been a few false alarms when he spotted a boy of similar build and age. His heart had pounded with anticipation; then just as quickly, when he realized that his eyes were combining with his wish to discover the Spanish boy, his pulse subsided and his cry of joy was stifled. Gradually, as the third day of the boy's absence wore on, Scribonia knew that unless he managed somehow to divert his thoughts to other endeavors, he might lose his reason. Thus he went to call upon Domitian, thinking to share with him the discovery of the Jew, Josephus, now residing in a government house, and of Titus' clandestine visits to him there. Yet he must be extremely careful. Brother against brother was dangerous territory. Would Domitian agree that a murder was permissible? Would he be willing to take the responsibility of fratricide, or if there was any kind of public outcry, would he find a scapegoat? Say, J.S.?

Domitian was in one of his darker moods, and Scribonia almost wished he had not come. He was seated at his gammon table with a nubile young Macedonian girl who was winning the game. Scribonia concluded instantly that she must be a truly stupid female to have thus risked offending her always-touchy host. She could not have known, he thought, that Domitian's worst side was now faceup and might soon show the terrifying mask of his anger.

Domitian greeted Scribonia with a single raised eyebrow, but no sound passed his tightly compressed lips. He reached for the large hourglass on the table and inverted it. Then, seeming to forget the game, he watched thoughtfully as the granules of sand slithered down to the bottom of the glass. At last he sighed and grumbled, "Do you know what that is?"

The answer was so obvious that Scribonia sensed it would not be simple. What would Domitian like to hear? "It's a measure of time until you are on the throne, Sire," he ventured.

"It's more than that. It was a present from my brother, celebrating my birthday ten years ago."

"How appropriate, Sire." He hoped he had not given the impression of condoning anything Titus might have done.

Domitian scowled at Scribonia and then at the hourglass. "Indeed," he said, and then said it again. He reached across the table, seized one of the Macedonian girl's earlobes, and twisted it until she squealed with pain. "Luscious little twitch, isn't she?" he asked. "Marvelous skin. One is tempted to bite into it."

"Yes, Sire. There are times when a touch of cannibalism seems attractive." Scribonia saw to his astonishment that Domitian appeared to have taken him seriously. One could never predict the twists of the man.

"No, no, I'd never entertain such a desire. That's more my brother's sort of thing."

Scribonia kept his silence and wished he was elsewhere. He glanced at the Macedonian girl, who flicked her tongue at the air and ran it around the perimeter of her lips, then wriggled provocatively in her chair. He found the gesture repulsive.

"My brother is the monster, not I," Domitian announced as

if he were addressing a large body of people. Then he switched suddenly and continued as if he were talking to himself. "For example, this hourglass. That's not sand in there. What appears to be grains of sand are the cremated remains of one of the ten thousand Jews he killed in Judea to honor my birthday. All ground up to a fine powder, of course, . . . bones and all. He wanted to give me a keepsake of the occasion . . . *me,* who cannot bear the sight of blood."

Scribonia saw that the Macedonian girl either had not heard or had failed to comprehend. She was fiddling with her hair, and he wished he could hide behind some similar preoccupation. If what Domitian had just said was only half-true, then the Roman public had been badly deceived as to the character of their newly appointed leader. Not that any sensible Roman cared about the Jews . . . it was the *idea* of such a gift!

Scribonia glanced at the Macedonian girl. "Could I speak with you alone, Sire?"

"Something that cannot be shared with this little creature?" Domitian patted her bottom lightly. "Go away, small one. I'll eat you later."

When she was gone, Domitian looked after her and said that the strange and foul wine provided by their Syrian friend so raised his desires he was often driven to biting off more than he could chew. Then he chuckled and sighed and blushed—all manifestations Scribonia took as favorable to his presence.

"I wish to discuss a Jew with you, Sire. A certain Flavius Josephus."

"That fellow? I know all about him." Domitian ran his fingers gently up and down the hourglass. "My brother has some sort of an agreement with him. It is a puzzling relationship, since I understand the Jew was an officer in the Judean forces. He's writing a history of that war, and since Titus has not only endorsed the project but has quartered him in a government house, it's natural that he's going to praise him. I would suppose that my brother is going to be promoted as the son of Apollo if the Jew can't find a higher and more beautiful god, and his deeds will be greater than those of Augustus and Caesar put together. I don't like this . . ."

Domitian paused and stared into space. Scribonia thought he looked exactly like an emperor should, a noble head on a noble neck, a firm chin, an intelligent forehead; altogether a strong face if somewhat marred by a spreading graffiti of tiny pink veins. His hair was going fast, yet somehow the patches of baldness seemed to emphasize his air of dignity.

"It's obvious to me," Domitian intoned, "that left alone, this Jew is going to record a lot of prejudicial and inaccurate history. My brother will be exalted until he's immortal and I'll be ignored. This is bad for the Empire. I don't want Roman children to be taught that Titus was perfect and that his brother barely existed . . . if indeed I'm mentioned at all."

"A most grievous situation," Scribonia said solemnly.

Domitian transferred his attention from the hourglass to Scribonia, examining him as if he had never seen him before. "Now," he said, "we should set this Jew fellow to rights. Read what he has written and revise it according to the truth. See that he tells how Titus slaughtered and burned without just cause . . . tell the true story of the Jews' sufferings. More important, see that something is said of my actually serving as Emperor at the age of eighteen and then graciously handing the power to my father when he arrived in Rome. He should write down at least several pages concerning my poetry, which has brought nothing but praise from those who've read it. If he wishes, I'll be glad to furnish him with copies of my work to include in his manuscript . . ."

"Sire! May I suggest an even more useful employment of the Jew? Your brother confers with him frequently and always at night. He insists on being alone with him and dismisses his guards because the house is so isolated he thinks them unnecessary . . ." Scribonia pursed his lips. "Suppose the Jew, in a fit of anger . . . could no longer resist retaliation for the suffering his people have endured at the hands of his host? Suppose . . . ?"

Never before, Scribonia thought, had he so captured his patron's total attention.

"I believe I follow you," Domitian said very slowly. "You do have a way of solving problems. I will think about it . . ." Domitian's voice trailed away and Scribonia realized that for the moment he should not press him further. For here was a way Domitian could justify himself. Domitian, the second son of the deified Vespasian, had never served with the Roman troops anywhere except on a brief and fruitless march to Lugdunum after the rebel Civilis. He had been too late. The civil war had lost all momentum and he had returned to Rome without having accomplished a thing.

A pity, Scribonia thought, that his brilliant services were not available to Domitian at that time. The situation might easily have been reversed and he would be standing ready to accept the throne now. But rescue was at hand. Should an unfortunate accident befall Titus, the sacrifice of a single Jew who had taken revenge would be understandable to everyone.

Comfortable at last in a wing of the government house, Silva was removing a collection of nits from Cicero, who seemed to have acquired them in Carthage. "Poor fellow," he murmured softly as the bird was objecting strenuously to the operation. "We should consider it a miracle that we got out of the place without acquiring something worse. "

He pulled at a nit, a feather came with it, and Cicero screeched in outrage. "Patience, old boy! Save your voice to tell me what we're going to do about money? I have very little left. I could try selling the house in Praeneste, but that may take a long time. And then there's Reuben. We promised him an education and a proper bringing-up as a young Roman gentleman. What shall I do about him? Too many questions, Cicero. Give me some answers, preferably of an encouraging nature."

Cicero squawked obligingly and Silva patted him on the head. Cicero nipped his finger for his trouble. "Damn your manners, bird! Someday you'll go too far and I'll put you in the soup along with whatever finger I've lost."

Cicero snapped his head back and forth and clicked his beak rapidly.

Silva heard a voice behind him say, "Now you've hurt his feelings."

He turned to see Domitillia smiling. He opened his arms and she came to him, her embroidered slippers whispering across the marble floor. They held each other soundlessly for some time; then their mouths met and they remained lost in each other.

Silva had no idea how long they stood holding tightly to each other, but if ever he had felt fulfilled this was the time.

"You're radiant," he said. "You glow. You are more than mortal . . ."

"Drivel. But I love it."

"You're also sneaky. I didn't hear you come."

"I've been standing behind you forever. I didn't want to change the picture of you fussing over your friend. It was too much like the visions I've seen in my dreams. And now, you're real. I must touch you again to make sure." She reached up and slowly brought her hand down his cheek.

"*We* are real," he said, "and we have to stay this way." He held her at arm's length for a moment and his eyes followed the contours of her body.

She asked, "Why are you looking at me in such a strange way? What is this . . . a regimental inspection?"

"I can't see any difference . . ."

"Neither can I. But wait another month or two." There was a roguish sparkle in her eyes. "Congratulations," she added.

"Titus has told me. What do you want to do?"

"He wants to send me away permanently, but I doubt he will until after the triumph. He wants me in it. Otherwise, it would be too difficult explaining my absence, both to my father and the public."

"I understand." Silva wondered if he really did. He questioned whether he should tell her of Titus' other ultimatum? How do you explain to the woman you love that you're as good as dead unless she agrees to give up another precious life?

"At best, we don't have long," she said. "The triumph is eight days from now. The preparations are all made. I don't think Titus is bluffing, although his bark is always worse than his bite. But if I'm going to have the baby—and I am—he won't let me stay in Rome."

He saw the resolve in her eyes and wondered how he dared destroy it. "You're determined to have the child?"

"Absolutely."

"Will it be worth losing all that you have now? Everything?"

"What I have is nearly worthless to me. There is no price on our child."

"Supposing Marcus Clemens would be willing to claim it?"

"Flavius Silva," she said, frowning, and he saw that she was close to anger, "you can't be serious."

"I'm only trying to find out how serious *you* are. Because we have to make a decision." He told her then of Titus' threats, but he refrained from explaining that Titus would forgive him if he succeeded in persuading her to abort. Be damned, Titus, and be damned to his own career! He had known enough soldiering to last him forever. It was time to begin a new life. He knew that if he told Domitillia all that Titus had threatened, he was certain she would abort to save him. And there would be no living with that. There was another way . . . dangerous, perhaps even dubious of success. It would be like launching into a campaign without time to plan any of the logistics. They would have six, perhaps seven days at the most, to make preparations.

He spoke quickly as if his life depended on it, as indeed, he realized suddenly, it did. "If we're to be together, we must escape together. There's much to be done, but maybe we can stall until the triumph. Then there will be so much excitement and general tumult that what we do may not be noticed. Under my personal arrest I can do as I please for the moment. When your brother sends for me, I'll tell him matters are progressing . . . that you are unable to find a competent physician until after the triumph. I'll go to Praeneste, where I know the locals and can buy good horses without creating a stir. Send Reuben to me there tomorrow. Meanwhile, make no show of your departure. If Titus sends for you, do everything you can to avoid seeing him . . . pretend you're ill . . . anything. Is Piso still with you?"

"He brought me here."

"Good. Does he know anything of us?"

"I suspect he suspects."

"Never mind. On the night before a triumph the streets are always full of people very busy with their own celebrating. If you wear a hood of some kind they'll never notice you. Tell Piso to leave his armor at home and wear only the garb of a *pleb*. He is to bring you to the Praenestine Gate and proceed along the Via Praenestina for one mile. I'll meet you there, and Piso can return to your house."

"But Praeneste will be the first place they'll look for us."

"We won't be there. In the army we would say we're making a feint."

"Where are we going?"

Silva took her in his arms again and held her tightly. He said, "I think you're the only woman in the world who would wait until now to ask." He kissed her and gently maneuvered their bodies to the couch, where silently, almost as if nothing else mattered, they made love.

Afterward, while they lay in each other's arms and were still breathing heavily, Domitillia whispered, "Where are we going?"

"A long way . . . to Lusitania."

NINETEEN

TITUS WAS EXHAUSTED. For three days and nights he had been directing the efforts to calm and finally extinguish a fire that had ultimately destroyed the temples of Jupiter, Juno, and Minerva, along with a large number of buildings in the surrounding area of the city. Rome was the most prone city in the world to fires; one after the other had plagued the population for centuries.

When at last the fire had subsided, Titus staggered back to the Palatine Hill and threw himself fully clothed on his bed. He slept until midmorning when one of his personal aides shook him to wakefulness. "Your Majesty," he said gently, "your father has left us."

It was a moment before what Titus had heard penetrated his weariness. Then he arose instantly and began giving orders with the firmness and clarity of a man who had long prepared to face a crisis. His bath must be readied at once. Cinders, dirt, and smoke, he thought, had made him smell like a sacrificial altar.

Now, quickly—fresh tunic, his full dress armor. Horse at the ready and twenty Praetorians mounted and ready to ride.

A courier to Domitian with instructions to meet him at the Porta Salaria. . . . Titus hoped his brother had gone to bed early for a change; certainly he had never shown his face at the fires.

Another courier to Domitilla. No need for her to go to Reate; stay where she was. Details later.

THE TRIUMPH

Courier to the Senate . . . choose a distinguished officer for passing the word. Let the Senate announce it to the public.

All Praetorians on full alert and all other troops confined to barracks until further notice.

Snap to, now! The greatest of Roman Emperors is dead and his triumph will become his fitting funeral.

The ceremony would be scheduled five days hence, four earlier than the planned date of the triumph. All who were responsible for the various features of that occasion should be notified and must work day and night if necessary.

By order of the Emperor. No excuses tolerated. "By order of the Emperor?" Titus tasted the rhythm of the phrase in his bath as a slave massaged him with oil and then scraped it away. Everything would now be by order of the Emperor who sat stewing in his tub, filled with wonder at his lack of control over events. Of course, he had expected this to happen. . . . Everyone knew it must. What it all came down to, he realized all too suddenly, was that an Emperor was an exalted bureaucrat who could order people around, but not events. He could send fifty thousand men to fight almost anywhere in the Empire, yet he could not prevent a famine if the grain ships from Egypt failed to reach port. He could force his sister to undergo an abortion or his brother to forsake the grape, but he could not predict or prevent the events his edict would inspire. He could not control their certain hatred.

Titus sighed heavily. Papa alone would understand his thinking. Suddenly, all of their disagreements had dissolved. The sometimes annoying display of rusticity, which his father actually seemed to enjoy, was no longer a cause of ridicule. It was, or had been, a demonstration of an absolutely honest man who had his feet on the ground. Papa's devotion to duty, honor, and family—the cause of much cynical eyebrow-raising in times gone by—now became the qualities that made a great man. Even Papa's frugality had become a characteristic to view with pride. No one could squeeze a sesterce quite as dry as Vespasian, but note that the budget was balanced, or nearly so.

Hail Caesar! May the deified Vespasian live in our hearts forever. And may his son, Titus, rule with the same wisdom and forbearance. May he continue the Pax Romana and let events prove to be so favorable to the Flavian family the impression will be that Titus the new Emperor knew what he was doing.

When he had mounted his horse and started down the Palatine Hill, Titus was surprised to find that there were tears in his eyes.

"My sympathies," Titus said to Domitian when they met and rode on side by side.

"For what?" Domitian grumbled.

Titus failed to hear him over the clatter of the horses and said again, "As brother to brother, my sympathies. We have lost a great father and the Empire has lost a great man."

"You're full of pomposities this morning," Domitian growled.

"I can't help it. I can't believe Papa is really gone." Titus shaded his eyes as if to avoid the weak morning sun. He really wanted to keep his escort from seeing his tears. "I'll try to carry on with Papa's wishes. I hope you'll help me. It's a big job."

"Papa was aware of that, which is why he thought we should share the throne equally . . . as coregents."

"I never heard of that. It wouldn't work, so it doesn't sound like the kind of thing he would propose."

"He recorded it all on paper. He told me he did."

"Where's the paper?"

"I don't know."

Titus smiled. Of course, he thought; in his usual ill-timed fashion Domitian was attempting to make a joke. "Come on, Dom . . . you know that's bullshit. But Papa would want me to make you content. What can I do to satisfy you? And let's not argue while his bones are still intact."

Domitian avoided Titus' eyes when he responded, "Ho, ho! What a great and patient leader my brother has become! Suddenly. He'll bend down to toss a scrap of some kind to keep his brother quiet. What will we do with the poor fellow? Make him custodian of the lavatory flies? Or might I better employ him polishing my arch in the Forum? How about making him inspector of brothels? Now there's a job I'm sure he could handle without fucking it up!"

Titus squeezed his horse and plunged ahead. He had heard enough from Flavius Domitian. The man was demented.

THE TRIUMPH

* * *

The news of Vespasian's death spread rapidly throughout the Palatine and the Capitoline hills. By nightfall the ordinary Roman citizen was aware that a new Emperor would now take the throne. No one was surprised and many were saddened. Vespasian had proven to be a good Emperor, particularly after the unrest and carnage of the civil war. He had brought Rome back to its senses. Many were disappointed that there would be no triumph for the old man; hope that they might share in some kind of largesse was painful to cancel. Soon, however, when they learned the triumph would become the grandest of all funerals, a new excitement replaced the old.

Cynics and those in the Senate who had all along objected to the dynasty established by the Flavians now found new cause to speak their minds. They were opposed to the example of nepotism as demonstrated by the appointment of Vespasian's oldest son to the throne. They wanted the "best man" to be chosen as Emperor and selected on merit alone. Their objections went largely unheard, and the objectors were strangely lacking in conviction. They knew that when the qualifications were reviewed honestly that Titus was the "best man"; in their hearts they were satisfied that he would make a good Emperor. Certainly, he was popular with the people, and more importantly with the military. He had trained conscientiously for the job, and if he had been overly eager and inclined to encourage brutality in his Praetorians, they were willing to accept it as only a reflection of his firmness. He had proven himself as a successful soldier. The Empire would endure and prosper with Titus as leader.

Julius Scribonia kept his estimation of the future to himself. He wondered how much the seed he had implanted in his chosen leader might be germinating. Thus far, Domitian had given no hint of his feelings about using the Jew, Josephus. His duality of purpose had again manifested itself in his obsession with that dreadful aphrodisiacal wine, and he sought constantly for new erotic experiments. He insisted his friends drink the awful stuff while he stood by and watched the results. "Nectar of the gods!" he would exclaim and toss off a cup of it himself. Lack of the stuff enraged Domitian; he demanded the Syrian's head if he continued to supply others while poor Domitian went without. His tantrums did not subside until some slave girl or boy (usually provided by Scribonia) convinced him that he was still the greatest of lovers. Was the man truly losing his mind?

These were nervous times, Scribonia thought. No progress was being made toward the throne and the loss of the Spanish boy had been more devastating than he had ever imagined. He was in a perpetual twit these days; his own thoughts so addled that he had trouble focusing his attention on anything else.

Meanwhile, to guarantee his own durability by carrying out Domitian's every desire, he called upon Joseph ben Matthias. The man was a Jew, was he not? Thus there were a thousand ways he could be compelled to write what he was told. Domitian would be angered if the Jew rejected his suggestions, and that would be all to the good. Maybe he would authorize him to be sure that the next meeting between Titus and Josephus had more than the usual spice.

Josephus received him in the small section of the government house he occupied. At first, he seemed pleased at Scribonia's interest in his work. He said he had included Domitian in the very volume he was working on. Searching through the manuscript, he read aloud how Mucianus, upon entering the strife-torn city during the civil war, had stopped the mass killings. He then produced Domitian and recommended him to the multitude until his father should come himself. The people, being freed from their fears, made acclamations of joy for Vespasian to be their new Emperor, and kept festival days for his confirmation and for the destruction of the cruel Emperor Vitellius . . .

"That is all?" Scribonia asked, pretending shock.

"Yes, there is nothing more to say. Domitian was but eighteen in years. He really did nothing of note."

"How would you know? You were in Judea at the time."

"I've endeavored to learn as much as I can through countless interrogations . . ." Josephus thumbed anxiously through more pages of the manuscript. "Here! Here's another mention: While Titus was at Caesarea, he solemnized the birthday of his brother, Domitian, after a splendid manner and inflicted a great deal of punishment intended for the Jews in honor of him . . . for the number of those that were now slain in fighting with the beasts, and were burnt and fought with one another, exceeded two thousand five hundred."

Josephus smacked the manuscript page with the palm of his hand. "There you have a second mention of Domitian, and I'm still far from finished."

"I should hope so." Scribonia stood up and went to the table that held Josephus' piles of papers and scrolls. He looked down upon them contemptuously. "Do you like living here in Rome?"

"I do. By the grace of Titus, I live quite well . . . as you see."

"What *you* don't see is that the assumption of the throne by Titus, which we have witnessed on this very day, may be only temporary. You have been totally inept, inaccurate, and ill advised to mention Domitian so inconspicuously. I suggest you devote several chapters to him immediately."

"But there's nothing to say except that I've heard he drinks heavily."

"I will help you find things to say."

"I'm not interested in collaboration. I'm dedicated to completing this work alone."

"I assume that you would not like to learn someday that it had caught fire?"

"Are you by any chance threatening me?"

"By all chances. It is important that you write history as it was, and that must include a generous portion devoted to a truly great man—Domitian."

"I seek only the truth."

"The truth can be told in a thousand ways."

"Titus will not smile when I tell him of your visit!"

"I would not mention it if I were you. If you do, I will advise my colleagues in the *frumentarii* that you are involved in an assassination plot! They will pass the word to the Praetorians and the result is easily predictable."

Scribonia smiled. His growing sense of power over the affairs of the mighty was heady stuff. He thought that the time had come when he could afford to be both cool and gracious.

"Think things over, Jew. Allow your undoubted intelligence to chew on the matter. It would be a pity if a scholar of your supposed stature disappeared along with his work. It's so easy to explain the defection of a man who has already once defected."

When Scribonia departed, he passed along the peristyle of

the government house at a lively clip, for he believed that he had accomplished his purpose very handily. He was certain that Domitian would now be more prominent in Josephus' journals, or whatever they were, and he had mentally drawn a map of his quarters for use when the time came to see the exit of a new emperor.

As he passed through the atrium, his sense of satisfaction was compounded. There before his very eyes, as presented via a small latticework window, he saw something that brought his mincing steps to an instant halt. There, on the opposite side of what appeared to be a second peristyle, taking his ease beside a fountain, sat General Flavius Silva. "Incredible." Scribonia breathed softly. "And the man is unguarded."

His first instinct was to call the loathsome humanoids that Domitian had furnished him as bodyguards and order them to take Silva away. Then he revised his thinking. Titus was still the Emperor, albeit if only a few hours. The connection between himself and whatever happened to Silva would be too easily established. No, this was not the right moment. But it would come.

Scribonia allowed himself a few moments to study the man he hated so passionately. Handsome chap. Arrogant. Well muscled and proud. His skin was still bronzed from the African sun.

All of that would be changed soon.

As he approached the house in Praeneste, Silva was grateful that he had decided to do so in the late afternoon, when the sun was low. It cast a mellow light and clearly outlined the profile of the house, as well as the hedges marking the perimeter of his property. He caught his breath at the beauty of the land; indeed, it seemed he was viewing the same visions he had conjured for himself during the long and lonely periods in Judea. Uncanny, he thought, how exactly those visions now matched the real thing.

Attius and Liberalis had finally located their general through Centurion Piso, whom they had traced to the house of Domitillia. At the government house, Silva had explained that he was under his own arrest, but he did not say why. As expected, such splendid officers did not ask. At his request they brought him the only horse they could find on such short notice, a spavined, elderly beast with mule ears and a habit of sighing heavily when asked to move. Thus it had taken most of the day to reach Praeneste.

The home that had almost been his stood on the highest level of a slope that rose eastward against the Apennines. The surrounding area was salted here and there with the small dwellings of the local peasants. The roof of his house was low and conventionally flat. It was cheaper that way, he remembered. It also added to the impression that the house had grown out of the ground.

There was no sound as he sat lost in contemplation except for the occasional snuffling of his mount, which interrupted the persistent song of a lark somewhere in the middistance. Like most Romans, Silva held a reverence for the land. The earth, reeking of its richness after a heavy rain the night before, seemed to embrace him through odor alone. Welcome home, soldier . . . temporarily.

A peasant rode past on a mule and saluted Silva with the stump of an upraised finger. He was a stranger to Silva, but here away from the city, people exchanged some kind of greeting whether they knew each other or not. They don't care whether I've won a battle or lost one, he thought. For the locals, everywhere beyond the confines of this little slope was too far away to be of much interest. So it might have been for Flavius Silva.

He kicked his reluctant horse toward the house. How different his homecoming from what he had envisioned! There were no tribunes flanking him and no escort of stalwart legionaries riding behind.

As the features of the house became individually apparent, he appraised them one by one. There were first the vines, which had been well established long before he bought the land. They looked healthy as far as he knew, which he realized now more than ever before, was not very much. He smiled when he remembered that his original plan had been to buy a few cows, sheep, and goats and allow them to graze through the vines when they were not actually producing. Experts had finally convinced him that giving animals a free run of the vineyard would certainly mean the end of it. I know so little, he thought. I know only how to organize a mob for killing and then lead them to the slaughter.

He stopped at the edge of his land, dismounted, and walked slowly up the hill, absorbing more details. Because of the lateness of the day the laborers and craftsmen had gone, and the contractor himself must have left early—so he would have time to count his money, Silva thought sourly. It was a good thing to arrive so unexpectedly. He could at least see where so much of his fortune had gone without someone trying to convince him that it had been well spent.

Silva said to Cicero, "How do you like the place, old friend? Behold a cozy little cottage with the price of a palace. The owner has been absent. Let this be a lesson if you ever decide to build a tree house."

Silva thought of his local bankers, the firm of Maximus and Vibo. They were charging him eight percent on the money he had borrowed to build the house. That was considerably above the average six percent, but as they pointed out, Silva was a soldier and might be killed. Then where would the firm of Maximus and Vibo be?

The house looked to be almost completely built now, and for the past seven years, Maximus and Vibo had been paid their interest. Was it any wonder that the word for "banker" and "Syrian," in Gaul, were the same?

Silva tied his horse to a thick vine and mounted the steps in the terrace, which extended from the west side of the house. The steps, he noted, were cut from marble as specified, and there was a tile mosaic representing a vineyard on the terrace that was not finished. Silva's instant reaction was to track down the artist and demand completion; then he remembered that it would not make the slightest difference in his future.

He had entered upon the house from the western view side and so reversed the usual approach to any Roman dwelling. He moved into the peristyle, which was smaller than he had envisioned from the plan. Where grass and flowers should have been by now, there was only an assortment of broken stones, bits of plaster, and mounds of earth. The fountain in the center was yet to be completed.

His hand strayed to Cicero, and he said, "Damned lonely place, isn't it?"

The design of the house was unique to Roman fashion because the peristyle was not a separate area but ran down both sides. The western end had two sleeping chambers placed on each side; the one on Silva's left was to be his own. He entered it and was surprised to see the bed frame he had ordered. If the house had been in Rome he knew that the frame would have been stolen long ago.

There was a mural on the wall of his bedchamber that he disliked instantly. Ten thousand sesterces for *that?* An abomination! The artist, Colpurnius Fobatus, had not even had the grace to sign it. He must have been drunk, or maybe he was ashamed of it.

Silva retreated so rapidly from the bedchamber that Cicero nearly lost balance on his shoulder and emitted a shriek of protest. The sound echoed through the peristyle, and the sense of vacancy it created nearly caused Silva to forsake further exploration. "Shut up!" he said as Cicero continued shrieking.

When the parrot had quieted, Silva strolled slowly along the columns of the peristyle. They were supposed to have been cut from Etruscan marble, but as far as Silva could see, they looked like just any other marble. Why did he fail to appreciate their special beauty? Had the carvers thrown pearls to swine? "I don't know marble," he said to Cicero. "I don't know anything except soldiering."

Silva looked into the next room, which he had intended would be his library. It contained a long, low table of cypress. Someone had thrown a cloth over the highly polished surface to protect it. Well done. A nice piece of furniture if a trifle elegant for a retired soldier.

He stepped into the atrium and crossed to the toilet. More marble. The seat looked satisfactory, but there was no light in the place. He should speak to Mamillianus, the architect, and have him design a proper window. Latticework? But now, what difference would it make? One could not dismantle the whole house and take it to Lusitania on mule-back.

Here in the toilet there were still some exposed lead pipes, which were placed within the walls throughout the house and would provide warmth in the wintertime. The water circulating through the pipes was heated by a wood fire just inside the atrium; the resulting pressure differential would keep the water in motion. Many Roman houses had installed the system, which supposedly was worth the considerable cost. Silva remembered he was not much interested in such an installation when he was sweating in the desert heat of Masada.

He went to the front door, which faced on the village street. A heavy bronze lock secured the door, but there was no key. He muttered to Cicero, "All thieves are advised to go round to the back of the house, which is wide open. And the view is better."

He searched for a key and soon decided it must be in the pocket of the contractor's tunic. He reversed his steps and rejoined his horse in the vineyard. He mounted and rode the short distance to a busy inn situated below the Temple Fortuna Primigenia. Once in his room he ordered a dish of water for Cicero and a bottle of the house wine for himself. Wine from the Praeneste region was famous; if he was not going to grow the grapes for it himself, he could at least taste it.

The view from his window was stunning in the very last rays of the sun. There below, less than half a mile away, was the house he had dreamed about for so long. At last I have come home, he thought . . . but there is nothing here. My world is empty without Domitillia.

Several children were playing tag in the street below Silva's window. Across the street near an open food stand three youths were playing at knucklebones. It was that twilight time when Romans were the most relaxed and given over entirely to their pleasures.

Watching the youths and drinking the wine, which he found disappointing, Silva thought of Reuben, who would come tomorrow if all went as planned. Now it would be mandatory to revise his plans for Reuben as well as his own. It had been his intention to Romanize him as much as possible, then send him off to Athens to absorb some philosophy. Perhaps half a year or more there, then he would continue eastward to Rhodes for his rhetoric, and on the way home spend enough time in Alexandria to acquire at least a basic knowledge of medicine. Ultimately, he would be ready to face the Roman world with certain advantages, and he could specialize in what appealed to him. Was it fair to haul him off to Lusitania?

Brooding on Reuben transported him all too easily back to Masada. Poor Gallus, the brilliant engineer who designed the ramp. Silva winced. He could still see the arrow protruding from his neck. Images of Paternus and Severas, who often guarded the entrance to his tent, flicked across his mind; and of Epos his Numidian, who did his best to make his tent a home. It was difficult to admit that except for his youth the only home he had ever known had been a tent. What had happened to his old desert comrades? Young Attius and Liberalis could be accounted for; they were presently exploring the joys of Rome. Marcus Fronto, that troublesome decurion of the first cohort? Drummed out of the Tenth and set loose in the desert. No one knew if he survived. And what about old Plinius, whose length of service in the Tenth was much longer than any other legionary? He was discharged despite his objections; the Tenth was the only home he knew and he wanted to die in the ranks. The gods knew that he had enough chances. Plinius' service came to an end with his *Missio Honesta vel Justa* entitling him to certain benefits. He was awarded a small plot of land near Tarentum, which fortunately coincided with his desires.

Silva left the window and poured himself another cup of wine. It had been so long since he had drunk anything except vinegar water that he found the first cup was already affecting him. It was almost dark in the room and Cicero, who had very deliberately defecated on the floor when he first arrived, seemed to be dozing while perched on a shelf to the left of the window. Silva raised his glass to him. "Wake up, nuisance! Answer some questions! What can I do about Domitillia? Ask her to spend the rest of her life in a tent? And Reuben? I gave my right hand to his future. Did that mean as a street boy? What have I done, birdbrain? Give me a solution."

That night, for the first time in more than five years, Silva fell into a drunken slumber. While the sun was still behind the Apennines the next morning, Silva massaged his aching head, vowed never to drink another drop of wine, and set about his preparations. He bought four sound horses and two mules for a third of the price he would have paid in Rome. He was careful to explain to whoever was interested that his destination was Tarentum; he was taking his sister and a nephew to see her grandfather before he dies. A legacy was involved, of course, and thus the mission would be completely understood by anyone on the entire Peninsula. Old Plinius would do for the grandfather, and it would please the rascal to be involved in such a project. Unfortunately, he would never know about it because Silva intended that they would depart, turn around, then proceed in the opposite direction. To that end he bought a crudely drawn map that showed the Roman roadworks both north and south. He longed for the much greater detail available on military maps, but none was to be had in Praeneste.

There were other more important problems. They would need a tent for the long journey to Lusitania. He bought one from a peasant who used it for lambing. They would need cooking utensils. What for? Domitillia *cooking?* It suddenly occurred to him that she would summon a slave to make a cup of hot water. There would be no slaves. Flavius Silva, late of the army, would do the honors—grain whole and raw, or made into cakes—legionary style. They would need flasks to hold the vinegar water to wash the grain down. The specter of Domitillia drinking vinegar water amused him temporarily.

Silva bought knives in case they augmented their meals with some kind of game, but soon regretted it. Who was going to do the hunting and the killing when they would be fleeing for their lives? He bought goat cheese and a few vegetables in the public market and regretted his haste. The vegetables would be rotten before their little expedition set off. Ummidus Fabatus, the Tenth's resourceful supply officer, where are you now? Generals don't know how to do these things.

Silva was taken aback by the errors he was making. While he had been careful to buy an extra horse in case one went lame, he had not been able to buy more than two saddles. Reuben would have to ride bareback.

As the day proceeded and his funds became alarmingly short, Silva had countless misgivings. Always confident in battle, always quick and resolute in the face of military challenges, he had now to reassure himself constantly that he was doing things right. "I'm falling to pieces," he grunted to Cicero. "We are outnumbered and being outflanked."

The odds for victory were poor, he finally admitted. He had a tunic, a pair of sandals, the stuff he had bought for their escape, and three hundred and ten sesterces remaining. This was the real world where military men should never venture, he concluded. He hoped Domitillia would understand his limitations and call up her boundless reserve of good humor to ease their escape.

TWENTY

PREPARATIONS FOR A triumphal funeral had begun on word of Vespasian's death and had now reached a feverish pitch. All shops, businesses, and courts of law were closed. Although Titus had tried to prepare himself for the shock of his father's death, he was deeply saddened. Even his proclamation as the new Emperor failed to stir him. Instead, he found relief and a strange exhilaration in overseeing the details of the coming funeral ceremony. To those in charge he was adamant.

"It must be a celebration of his greatness, which will be related by the great-grandchildren of the Empire to their great-grandchildren. We will mourn according to the Law of the Twelve Tables, but we will also forge our own traditions. We must celebrate his union with the gods. You will go now to your various assignments and see that they are achieved at whatever the cost.

"We have four days remaining and I want what was to have been the original solemnity of a mere triumph multiplied to reflect our joy in the ultimate glory of the man. I want a hundred kettle-drummers and a hundred camel-drummers in the parade. I want five hundred fifers . . . and a hundred or so bagpipers. I want two hundred finger-drummers spanking their instruments as if driving out snakes . . . I want acrobats, each at least a hundred paces throughout the procession, because I want to keep the public's attention. I want every elephant the state owns . . . I believe there were twenty-three at

321

last count . . . and I want them properly adorned with tapestries and their riders dressed in joyful reds. I want music . . . lots of it, interspersed throughout the parade. I want some Jews and at least a few Christianii, properly haltered and led with ropes, just to remind them and our own people of how they came to be here. They need not be in chains and will be released after the ceremony . . . nor are they to be abused unless necessary.

"I understand my sister's wagon is ready and I'll inspect it this afternoon. My brother will lead the procession, mounted on a horse, my sister with her husband will be in the middle, and I'll bring up the rear. Those of you in charge of security will now consult with the *frumentarii* on any problems they foresee. I want every Praetorian in full armor . . . everyone spit-and-polish and shining.

"Because there's not enough room for the anticipated crowds, we will build the funeral pyre in the Campus Martius instead of the Forum. It must be completed by tomorrow, and I want a guard of honor stationed there starting tomorrow morning. There must be four hundred of them on duty until a day after the flames subside. I want each man to assume the parade rest posture during his time on post; spears will be held to the ground point down and the standards the same."

Titus nodded to his newly appointed minister of protocol, Aurelius Grypus, a man of patrician family who had served with him in Judea. "Aurelius . . . be careful that the dignitaries march in some order instead of stumbling along like a crowd of refugees. They should march two by two whether they like it or not. They should be sequenced as far as possible according to their rank and honors, with the finest bringing up the last. There will be some out-of-joint noses in that group. I leave it to you to soothe ruffled feelings and keep resentment at a minimum." Titus smiled. "Perhaps a long swallow of the finest Falernum or an Albanum for each dignitary may ease any distress."

"I doubt it, Sire," Grypus said amid polite laughter from the other aides. "But I'll do my utmost to avoid offense."

"You will reserve one place in the procession just ahead of me for General Flavius Silva, legate of Judea. He is just returned and is suffering somewhat from the usual fevers of the place. It's possible he may not be able to attend."

"Understood, Sire."

On the following day Titus met with the Senate and made a deliberate show of attending upon them in their own territory, rather than inviting them to the palace. He was determined to heal the wounds that his father's inevitable differences with the senators had caused. He was careful to keep his deportment modest. For this important occasion, called an Edictus, all the senators wore togas with the broad purple stripe. After the routine sacrifice had been made to Jupiter and the auguries had been found favorable, Titus was promptly appointed consul. Since the death of the Republic and the rise of the Empire, the office had been increasingly honorary, and the Emperors had rarely bothered with officiating during senatorial sessions. Titus did not promise any better, but he wanted the senators to believe that he valued their existence. Let them argue and pass decrees on religion, the distribution of public funds for pleasure, appointments of ambassadors and praetors to the provinces, inquiries into public crimes, taxes, and the gods only knew what assortment of details. But the Emperor should have more important things on his mind. As long as he had the army behind him and the senators knew he had it, he could change anything that might displease him.

He vowed not to even hint of the restlessness he saw in his brother. There was a boil that must soon burst.

"My noble friends," he began in his most modest tone, "we gather now at a critical hour in the life of our Empire. A few days hence we will officially mourn the death of my father . . . beloved Papa to members of the Flavian family. It is my proposal that we will also celebrate, and for this I seek your approval and participation. Vespasian brought many of you to these honored seats. I assume you are grateful for such trust and high station, and will continue to protect and treasure your duties as I do mine. Those senators who were here before my father should also regret his passing, because in the nine years that he led our country we achieved victories and prosperity beyond our imaginations. He was always ready to consult with you and take such wisdom as you cared to share. I pray for the same opportunities and your tolerance.

"My noble friends . . . there were disagreements with Vespasian the soldier, and disagreements with Vespasian the Emperor. But with very few exceptions I like to think such opposing views were to the ultimate benefit of the Empire. Certainly the Pax Romana is of benefit to every human being on earth. With the help of our armies it is my intention to maintain it."

Titus then reviewed Vespasian's entire career and enumerated his accomplishments one by one. When he had finished, he made formal announcement that four days hence at the third hour, their presence was requested in the Campus Martius, where they would attend upon the advice of the funeral master. Full senatorial robes would be worn plus such decorations as they had been awarded. The funeral procession would be a triumph and would be greatly enhanced by their presence. It would follow along the Via Lata, pass through the center of the city and Forum, then swing down to the Circus Flaminius and follow the Tiber until it returned to the Campus Martius. An appropriate sacrifice to the gods would be made of fifty prime bulls, and the cremation fire would be ignited. For the balance of the day and for the ensuing two days, games, chariot races, and gladiatorial contests were scheduled at every public gathering place. Thus, as Vespasian joined the gods the Roman citizen would have every opportunity to speed him on his way with gratitude and rejoicing.

"And so, noble friends," he concluded, "I beg you to trust the son as you did the father. May the world know that this august body and the throne stand as one."

Titus bowed his head, and while the uproar of applause was still echoing throughout the Curia, he followed his twelve lictors out of the building to greet a populace nearly gone wild with approval and anticipation. The public demonstration was so enthusiastic that Titus was obliged to halt several times in spite of the strenuous efforts of his lictors to clear the way. It was the first truly hot day of the year, and the mass of pushing, shoving, laughing, and yelling humanity seemed to suck the very limited air of the Forum dry. The mob raised clouds of dust despite the recent rains; some suffocated in the press and squabble and were trodden upon or carried away.

Yet their delirious, "Hail Caesar! . . . Hail Titus Vespasianus!" punctuating their screaming was at first sweet music to Titus' ears. He could not restrain himself from smiling and waving. His sense that he was off to a good and popular beginning was very satisfying. I must take the joys now, he reminded himself, because too soon I will hear laments from various sections of the Empire and there will be more than enough enemies to ruin my sleep.

After Titus left the crowd behind and started up the Palatine Hill, he suddenly experienced a new sense of loneliness. Yes, he was the supreme master of the Empire, but where was the Flavian family? Domitian had refused to attend the special session of the Senate and had declined to make any contribution whatsoever to his father's triumphal funeral. He had grudgingly agreed that he would appear at the head of the parade, but had demanded a white horse of the most distinguished ancestry or he would not ride. Titus had tried to find a horse to fit his wishes before he realized that it was his own splendid Arabian Domitian was after. Very well, if that was what little brother wanted, he would have it.

Domitian's sullen mood had persisted even after they arrived at Reate. When they first approached their father's body, Titus said he regretted that he was too late to press his mouth to Vespasian's and draw his last breath so his soul would enter him. Domitian scoffed at the tradition as nonsense and speculated on the sanity of a man who would kiss a corpse.

Titus had managed to contain his anger. He tenderly closed their father's eyes and mouth, and he longed for Domitillia to mourn with him. Later, when he watched the *pollinctures* bathe his father in warm water and perfume him, they asked if he would put a coin in Vespasian's mouth for Charon. None could be found; not so much as a sesterce was in the house. Finally, one of the Praetorians offered a Greek drachma, which he kept as a souvenir, and Titus placed it on his father's tongue despite Domitian's insistence that the local farmers should be asked to provide a Roman coin.

"No," Titus said. "Papa would approve of the drachma because the treasury will not lose a sesterce just to give him a ferry ride across the Styx."

After his little procession had passed through the Forum and came to the arch that his father had erected in honor of his Judean victories, Titus dismissed his lictors. Many craftsmen were still working on the arch; it amused him to see them redouble their efforts on his approach and then, as if mesmerized, almost cease working when he paused to watch them. A sculptor swung down from the scaffolding that supported several of his fellows against the side of the arch. He approached Titus, cap in hand.

The sculptor was powdered with stone granules from his chiseling, but there was no denying the cockiness of his stride as he halted before the man he must know could make or ruin him forever. A pair of saucy eyes peered from the white mask of his face as he regarded his Emperor critically. His comrades, still on the scaffold, were jabbering in hushed tones, amazed at his temerity.

"Sire," the sculptor said without so much as a nod of his head. "I am Lupus Servilianus, master sculptor."

"So I see." Titus found his bold attitude amusing. "And I'm Flavius Titus, your new Emperor. Greetings."

Servilianus cocked his head and did not appear to be the slightest impressed. "I don't think I did you very well." He glanced back at the arch momentarily. "In fact, your neck is too long."

"Here . . . or there?" Titus asked, nodding at the arch.

"There. But then I've never had a good look at you. And then you have more hair. I thought you were almost bald, like your brother."

Titus glanced at his aides who had surrounded him protectively when the lictors had departed. He knew they were fuming inside, yearning to tell this cheeky fellow to watch his tongue.

"I do Jews better than I do Romans," Lupus Servilianus said. "When your father first put me on the job I told him that despair is easier to carve than satisfaction."

"It must be a challenge to portray either one."

Servilianus seemed not to hear his Emperor. He was lost in his study of the frieze on which he had been working. "I told your father that, but he wasn't listening. I've almost made a botch of it."

"There are times when an Emperor has other things on his mind," Titus said, still amused. The man was incredible, he thought. He could have been talking to the local basket weaver. He asked, "How long have you been working on this, Servilianus?"

"Six years."

"And you're still finding fault?"

"Of course. Nothing that I ever create is perfect."

"When do you think you'll be finished?"

"Never. Because it will never be perfect."

Titus glanced at his aides, hoping to find that they were sharing in his enjoyment of the moment. He saw only disapproval. Of course, he thought, I am no longer allowed to chat with a marvelous man like this sculptor. He's a freedman at best and there can be no mutual understanding allowed. If the Emperor were to send for this honest fellow and ask him to come to the Palatine for an ordinary talk and nothing more, the daggers of jealousy would soon be drawn and the association would not be allowed to flourish. And so Flavius Titus Vespasianus would not have acquired a new friend.

Titus reached out and touched Servilianus on his dusty shoulder. "I like your work," he said simply. "I'll grow a longer neck."

As Titus turned away he saw that the sculptor was still so totally absorbed in staring up at his work he seemed unaware of his Emperor's departure. A shame. Just a little distance away in the Forum the crowd had hailed him joyously. Now this man, an artist to his dusty toes, had not thought it necessary to even say farewell. There were some things about being Emperor that Titus did not like.

His sudden sense of isolation caused him to order his horse and an escort of Praetorians. He rode at a brisk trot to the house of Marcus Arrecinus Clemens. He had deliberately not troubled to warn him of his forthcoming arrival.

Clemens was terror-stricken when a breathless slave informed him that the Emperor was waiting in the atrium. He had been breaking his fast very decorously in an attempt to lose some flesh—a small portion of boiled tree fungi with a spicy fish sauce—and now he wondered if somehow his rebellious association with Domitian had been discovered. Rolling his eyes and wobbling his head more than usual, he made haste to the atrium, bowed deeply, and opened his arms wide to his Emperor.

"Your Majesty!" he panted anxiously. "Your presence has graced our house forever! Had we but known—"

"Don't fret about it, Marcus. I'm pleased to see you looking so well since, of course, we're expecting you to ride with Domitillia in the funeral."

"Of course, Your Majesty. All is in readiness. Allow me to take this opportunity to offer my condolences."

"Thank you. Now I'd like to see my sister. You'll understand that I'd like to see her alone."

"Of course, Your Majesty! I understand perfectly. My wife has been devastated."

Clemens rolled his eyes, spun around, and waddled off at high speed. The skirts of his tunic fluttered about his fat rump like the tail of a bird.

Titus remembered he had never much liked the man. But, dear gods, he was rich!

During the few moments that Titus was alone he examined the atrium, which he was reminded would put many rooms in the palace to shame. The mosaics on the floor were masterpieces, the colums around the oval perimeter were of a marble that he had never seen before, each one so polished that it reflected his image. Thus he observed twelve Tituses moving near the pillars, and he attempted to make a face for each one. Soon, they all remained identical and he tired of the game. Between the columns there were statues and statuettes of bronze or obsidian, and the head of a Greek woman that appeared to be of solid gold. Titus attempted to lift it and could not—either it was truly of gold, he decided, or it was screwed to its pedestal. There was one statue of black marble, obviously an Egyptian woman, that he found strangely erotic and haunting. He stood staring at it, his feet wide apart, his arms akimbo, utterly captivated until he became aware that a youth stood near him.

"It's beautiful, is it not?" Reuben said.

"Yes . . . she is," Titus said softly. Then, as if returning from far away, he asked, "Who are you?"

"Reuben, son of Eleazar ben Yair."

"Ah, yes. You're the Jew boy."

"I've come to take you to Domitillia."

"I will remind you to employ the address . . . Sire."

"Follow me." Reuben turned away without the slightest change of expression. Titus thought that he would have the boy whipped until he said Sire a hundred times, then changed his mind. It was Domitillia who should be whipped for harboring such a rude rascal.

Domitillia arose when her brother approached her in the peristyle and said with careful coldness, "Your Majesty." She bowed her head ever so slightly.

"Get rid of him," Titus said, nodding at Reuben. "And I suggest you teach him some manners."

Domitillia waved her hand to dismiss Reuben, but he hesitated. "Do I have to say Sire to him?" he asked.

"Yes. He is the Emperor."

"I would rather say Sire to Flavius Silva. He's more of a man." Reuben turned on his heel and walked away.

Titus thought suddenly that it would take less patience to endure the insults of a whole nation. "Does he know," he asked acidly, "that I could have him crucified for that kind of behavior?"

"I'm sure he does."

"What makes him behave that way?"

"The Jews are a tough people. You should know. He was challenging you. He doesn't understand that he's conquered."

"That's something I intend to bring home to both Romans and his people during the funeral. That's one of the matters I've come to discuss."

"I find it difficult to speak of Papa with you now."

"Why? The loss of Papa is painful for both of us."

"And for Domitian."

"He doesn't give a damn."

"He does," she said, "he just won't show it. When will you ever learn that he's different from you?"

Two of Marcus Clemens' pet storks began a noisy squabble in the aviary just off the peristyle. As the shrill racket continued, Domitillia allowed her ever-radiant eyes to slide around in the direction of the aviary and remain fixed. It was as if she had forgotten Titus' overbearing presence.

Now Titus saw, as he had before, that his sister was the absolute mistress of removing herself beyond the bounds of any conversation that triggered discomfort or boredom, and he was determined to bring her back. He waited until the storks subsided and then said, "I did not come here to discuss our peculiar brother. I came hoping to share our sympathies in private and to inquire after your situation."

"By now I thought you'd have sent me packing . . . off to

some remote island." She did not trouble to turn her head toward him. "What are you waiting for?"

"I'm waiting for some sense to come to your head. I'm not inhuman, you know."

"Really? I've not had the opportunity to congratulate you upon your official elevation. Papa's dearest wish is now fulfilled."

"I want you to ride with Marcus in the funeral. At his side, happily—just as I had planned for the triumph—"

"Papa is dead. There is no need for me to be there now." Her voice was husky, flat, and scarred with weariness.

"You would deny him that respect?"

"Papa is now immortal or should be. He doesn't need me traipsing along behind his carcass, pretending to be the true and good wife of a man I loathe. Papa was always simple and direct, and I'm his daughter. He hated hypocrisy and I will not mock his beliefs."

Titus shook his head vigorously. Reasoning with his sister, he thought, was like catching snowflakes to make a ball. The first caught melted in his hand before the job could be finished. And reasoning with a woman in love was not even a realistic possibility. Still, he hoped, there must be some way to reach through to his sister.

"Dear little Domitillia," he began, "can't you understand that it's important that the Flavian family be properly represented at this critical time? Papa also believed very strongly in his obligations, and now that he is gone he would say it is our duty to the Roman people to reassure them. If they see a fractured family riddled with dissension, the rumor-mongers will be inventing the worst kind of news, and the plotters and schemers of every variety will descend on the divided throne and pick at it like buzzards. But if they see a strong and united family in command, then most people will be content. It's as simple as that. We cannot rule well from a house divided."

"By the gods!" she said vigorously. "Are you haranguing a Legion or addressing your sister? You're asking me to throw away the man I love and spend the rest of my life with a loamy potato? Crucify me! Burn me! I don't care. But I damn well *refuse!*"

A long silence fell between them. Titus walked to the edge of the peristyle and stared up at the sky. When he spoke again he kept his back to her. A wistful tone came to his voice as if he had somehow managed to return to his youth, when he had been the older brother of the Flavian children and had tried to protect and guide them. "I came here," he began in monotone, "because you and I have suffered a terrible loss and there is no one else in the world I can share it with . . . except you. I learned this morning, after I came out of the Senate, how lonely this job can be . . . and I cannot see any prospect of that changing. I'm like a man standing alone in the middle of a thunderstorm. He hears the thunder and knows the lightning is going to strike somewhere, but he hopes it won't hit him. There is no one he can turn to and say, 'Please hold a shield over my head,' no one to hold his hand, no one to even pick him up if lightning bowls him over. I need you . . . and I need Flavius Silva. He is exactly the man I wanted to rally not only his Legion, but the whole army to my rule. Flavius is the key. He is respected by his fellow soldiers, and if Domitian continues to give me trouble, Flavius' influence with the military is absolutely necessary. I'll go so far as to say I may not last very long without him."

Titus paused and massaged the back of his neck to relieve his taut muscles. "I promised a sculptor today that I would grow a longer neck."

"I wouldn't," Domitillia snapped. Then she added with a half smile, "If things are as bad as you say they are, then there'll only be more room for the headsman's ax. Why don't you stop feeling sorry for yourself?"

"Thank you, dear sister, for your kindness and warm understanding."

"I am simply returning the same you've given me."

Titus turned away from the sky and faced his sister. "Have you seen Flavius as I directed?"

"Yes."

"And with what result? Did you tell him that your affair must cease?"

"I was impressed when I realized that you are deliberately throwing away one of the finest and most loyal soldiers you'll ever have. The man has given most of his life to Rome—"

"I'm *not* throwing him away! I *need* him! I told him he would have full honors . . . he would ride in the funeral close to my side . . . he will be given whatever title he wants. Soon

I'll want him to bring certain Legions home to the Peninsula where they'll be handy . . . just in case. I can't place a man in a job like that who is distracted by an affair with my sister —married or unmarried."

"So your solution to that problem is to send one of us away."

"I've no other choice."

Domitillia stood and looked at her brother in silence for a moment. She remained perfectly still except for her eyes, which explored Titus as carefully as she might a new mosaic. At last she said, "Goodbye, Titus . . ." and turned away. She did not look back.

Soon after Emperor Titus Vespasianus made his melancholy departure from the house of Marcus Clemens, the master himself called for his litter and made a hasty exit. He urged his four bearers, the most tireless and powerful in Rome, to their utmost speed. If they slowed even moderately while trying to make passage through the worm-hole streets of the city, jampacked with people at this hour, he cried out threats from behind the swinging curtains that protected him from the public eye. It was a long way to Domitian's house and the shortest route lay straight through the worst part of the city. Here the stinking, incredibly noisy streets wound through the lower abdomen of Rome like rectal tubing and smelled the same. Here dead bodies were often left lying for days before anyone got around to burning them. Garbage and personal slops were tossed out the windows regardless of who might be passing below. The fights of every variety were of such common occurrence there was rarely any hue and cry. It was thought to be deliberate suicide to walk these streets at night without heavily armed guards. During the daylight hours the press of bodies in the inner streets became almost solid, and no wheeled traffic was allowed.

Marcus Arrecinus Clemens was now attired in a fresh tunic because the surprise visit of the Emperor to his household had so unnerved him that he had dripped sweat from every crease in his plump body. His nerves were still twanging and he was beginning to question the wisdom of backing Domitian in his ambitions. Now he found the shaking of the litter a welcome counterpoint to the almost uncontrollable wobble of his head.

The synchronous motions somewhat soothed the inner terror that had feasted upon him ever since he began thinking about such an unforeseen development. How much did Titus know? There had to be some very important reason why he had chosen to visit his house so suddenly and casually—almost as if he were a neighbor dropping by to share a problem concerning their water supply. The death of Vespasian was the most plausible reason, of course, but there must be something else. Something was amiss, something that might well constitute a threat to himself.

Clemens pushed and twisted at his button nose as if it might pick up some signal that would indicate the way he should turn, or who to beware of; but so far there had been no definite indications. Even so, he thought, it was imperative that he explore this matter with Domitian and with that fellow Scribonia if he was available. He had sent a fast foot messenger ahead in hopes they would be awaiting his arrival. Money was power, but there was unseen hazard marching in his direction. He told himself that he could smell it.

Flavius Silva counted this day as being one of the most pleasant and rewarding of his life. Centurion Piso had arrived in Praeneste bringing Reuben, and the reunion of all three of them became surprisingly warm. Piso said that he had given his attachment to the Tenth Legion considerable thought, and if Silva approved, he would like to be reassigned.

Silva said he would be delighted to see Piso back on muster and added, "At the moment I'm in a bit of hot water myself, but I have hopes things will be straightened out shortly. Meanwhile, I'll send off a letter bearing my seal that will accomplish the necessary paperwork. By the time it all goes to Judea and back, the cause of your court martial will have been forgotten."

Soon afterward, prepared to return to Rome with the two horses he had borrowed from Domitillia, Piso spoke to Silva openly while his strong face barely concealed his emotions. "I'm proud to have served under you, General. I wish you great fortune wherever you may be." He added very carefully, "The same blessings upon whoever may share your life."

Even Reuben joined in the ambience of the moment and brought himself to thank Piso for his attentions. He explained, not unkindly, that it was impossible for him to forgive any Roman who had been at Masada, including the General, but he supposed God would take his vengeance in due time.

Silva laughed. "Do I gather that you're condemning us to Pluto's underworld?"

"You have condemned yourselves. Pluto and the Greek god Hades are the same. We Jews have our own ideas about what happens to bad people."

"Who told you so much?"

"The rabbis in Alexandria."

They all touched hands gently before Piso departed. After he had disappeared behind a cut in the road, Silva rested his hand on Reuben's shoulder. He did not resist. "There goes a very brave man," Silva said quietly.

"He's a repentant murderer," Reuben said, but Silva noticed the venom was gone from his tone.

"Do you still think the same about me?"

"I don't think you're sorry about anything you've ever done. That's why you're a general."

"You're very wrong . . . Son. There are times when I regret having done many things. Now come with me. I'll show you where you almost lived."

Silva had not intended to show Reuben the house, but he could not seem to keep away from it himself. Perhaps, he reasoned, if Reuben understood that his own life was in disorder and that every Roman had problems, his hostility might gradually disappear.

Almost at once Silva discovered his theory had merit. After the luxury of Domitillia's house, the place in Praeneste looked almost humble and its unfinished state contributed to the air of overall dejection. When they came upon the contractor, he was taking his ease at the end of the peristyle. Here the view down the slope was the very best and nicely complemented the local cheese and wine for which the contractor had developed a great fondness.

Silva approached the contractor from behind. "I'm sorry to so rudely disturb you . . ."

The contractor turned, saw Silva, and gasped for air. He set his wine and cheese down on a cracked square of marble and arose very reluctantly. "Well, well, *well!*" he grunted. "I thought you were in Judea."

"So I see. Is this your usual mealtime? Midafternoon? Where are your workers?"

"They're not working today."

"Why? It doesn't look like anyone has done any actual work here in some time."

"The plasterers and the masons are on strike. So are the coppersmiths, the cement workers, and the carpenters. You see there is much to be done."

"I do indeed. But they're being paid?"

"Only at half rate. Good craftsmen are hard to find."

"Paid out of your purse?"

"Yes."

"Isn't that ultimately out of mine? It all goes on the bill?"

"True. "

"Why are they on strike? What did I ever do to them except pay and pay?"

"Oh, it's not because of you, Sire. Working conditions for those guilds are not satisfactory in Rome, and they're showing their sympathy for the craftsmen there."

"But this isn't Rome. It's more than twenty miles to Rome."

"I'm aware of that, General. What will be, will be." The contractor managed a weak smile and spread his hands palms upward.

After Silva had made it very clear to the contractor that he was discharged and should absent himself from the premises forever, he added, "You and all your kind have become so greedy you've forgotten how to work. Just keep that attitude and you'll see the whole Roman economy collapse. Then there will be no money to pay the legionaries who don't know about quitting time. And then the Legions will disperse and some of them will come home to find people like you sitting on your ass and saying what will be, will be. And behind the Legions will come the barbarians from all directions, and you'll all find yourselves working to the song of a whip instead of the sesterce. Now get out of here before I say something nasty."

A new admiration warmed Reuben's black eyes when he said, "I remember my father yelling down at you from Masada and you yelling back at him. I remember he said you had a way with words."

Silva eased his arm around Reuben and said, "Let's sit down and look at the view. It doesn't cost anything."

The glow of the late afternoon sun, Silva thought, matched the warmth that grew between them during the next few hours. They sat looking down at the distant countryside until the mists of evening floated in from the direction of the sea. At first they spoke hesitantly, a few words at a time. They spoke of the Jews and the Romans, of Masada and Judea, of Egypt and Britain and Gaul, and even of Germany, where Silva had not been for a long time. They spoke of Domitillia and Piso, of Titus and Vespasian, and of what they hoped to obtain from their own lives. Their exchanges were man to man, and Silva was ever more impressed with Reuben's keen intelligence and unique maturity.

They were laughing at Silva's story of his sea voyage with Cicero when darkness came. Silva knew a sense of satisfaction he had never experienced in his life. He hardly dared believe that at last he had won a son.

From the darkness he said cautiously, "Would you consider someday, perhaps if a stranger asked your name . . . would you consider answering . . . 'Reuben Silva'?"

"No."

Silva's spirits darkened with the twilight. He had presumed too much and the long silence told him he had been too hasty.

At last, Reuben cleared his throat as if to make an important declaration: "We might try Reuben ben Yair Silva."

The following evening Silva sent Reuben to his tiny room over the stables of the inn. There had been many frustrations during the day and he was grateful for Reuben's continued desire to help. Changing a whole life-style on limited funds, he had discovered, was difficult. He had never realized how much help a military man received. "A general without a staff is like a donkey without ears and legs," he told Reuben.

Returning to his own room, he stood at the window and yawned at the stars for a time. Then he said good night to Cicero and lay down on the simple bunk.

Silva slept soundly until he knew he must be dreaming, and yet instinct told him that he was no longer alone. He was sure he heard a voice say softly, "Greetings." He dismissed the notion that he had heard anything, rolled over on his side, and wished vaguely that Reuben could share the same room with him. Everything about this little inn was vague, perhaps because the heavy silence of Praeneste at night made his sleep all the deeper.

A vague . . . perfume? How soothing . . . these dreams. He was floating on a cushion of delicate scents. No soldier had ever slept better.

"Greetings, my love."

A whisper, echoing. Soft fingers on his face, then passing across his lips. Dream into nightmare? Was someone trying to kill him?

He twisted suddenly, then raised himself on his elbows and blinked at the darkness. Someone was sitting on the edge of the bed.

He reached out desperately to shove the person away when he heard her voice again. "You sleep like a child," she said.

Domitillia!

He pulled the dark figure to him and found her mouth. They rocked slightly in possession of each other, saying nothing until they were momentarily satisfied. "Tell me this dream will last," he said.

"It will. Touch me." She took his hand and brought it to her lips. "I had to be with you."

"How did you find me?"

"Piso said where, and a fine horse said, go, woman."

He heard the mischief in her voice and knew she was smiling.

"Where's your lamp?" she asked. "I'll light it."

"No. Leave it be. I can see you without light."

"How can you do that? Why did I waste time beautifying myself?"

"I see you all the time in my thoughts. I only lack the flesh." He brought her head down to him and kissed her again.

"General Silver Tongue," she said when he released her.

She removed her cloak and said, "This cot is only big enough for one."

"We are one."

"Then move over. I'm coming in."

The coolness of her flesh excited him. So smooth . . . like soft marble might be, he thought.

They lay tightly against each other until he said, "I'm not sure I like you bouncing around on a horse . . . in your condition."

"Poof. It will do him good. One should learn to ride at an early age."

"How do you know it's a him?"

"My astrologer. Besides, I wouldn't dare produce anything but a future emperor."

Silva was about to say that he had never had such a realistic dream when he felt her caress him. He forgot everything else and thrust himself against her.

"This bed squeaks," she said, still laughing softly. "Very distracting when I'm feeling so naughty."

"Think of it as singing, not squeaking."

"I'm in bed with the wrong man . . . a poet instead of a soldier."

"We're all the same in the dark," he said.

"That's what they say about women."

He began to kiss her breasts. She squirmed in pleasure. The bed squeaked, and she chuckled softly.

"Be quiet," he said. "You'll wake Cicero."

"A squeaky bed and a squawky bird. I can't win."

"You just have." He rolled over on top of her and for a long time there was only the sound of the bed.

Later, when they lay closely in the darkness, he asked, "Do you have any idea what you're getting into? We have a lot of problems coming our way."

"When things are too rough for others, they'll be just right for us."

"It's a long way to Lusitania and things never go quite as planned."

"How long will it take?"

"At least a month. We can take a military road as far as Genua and the Via Aurelia as far as Antibes. But those roads are patrolled. A city lady and a young Jew and a man with a limp who obviously isn't a farmer or tradesman will be very conspicuous."

"I can't keep up with you. Now you're old General Gloom."

"I just want to warn you. I have trouble seeing you grubbing for food in some filthy peasant's barn or squatting in the woods for relief . . . if there are any woods. There may be no decent place to bathe for weeks . . . and I'm afraid we're going to be very short of money."

"Are you beating a retreat, General? I won't let you off my hook."

"If it wouldn't wake up the whole inn, I'd give you a spanking for saying that."

She laughed and bit him lightly on the shoulder. "The honeymoon is over. We've gone from desire to default. Papa warned me about soldiers, but I didn't listen."

Somewhere in the street below they heard a cock crow. "Now," she said, "I must go before it's light. Go back to your dreams and remember this one was real."

She slipped out of the bed before he could restrain her. After a brief search in the dark for her clothes, she bent down to kiss him fervently. "I'll be in the parade. I owe that to Papa. But as soon as it's over I'll come to you here. Never doubt that you are my breath of life."

"Wait. I'll go down with you."

"No. It will be better if I go alone. My groom has watered and fed my horse, and this disgracefully adulterous one must slither away before it's light enough to be recognized."

TWENTY-ONE

JULIUS SCRIBONIA LIKED to think that these meetings represented the triumvirate of the future. He had engineered this meeting out of his own sense of urgency, a wondrous situation when he looked back only a short time and thought how far separated he was from the royal family, not to mention the richest man in the Empire. Now, although he was careful to be properly deferential toward Domitian, he considered himself the equal of Marcus Arrecinus Clemens. "We are at that moment in history when we should start making it," he said solemnly. "All of the factors are in the right place and, except for the triumphal funeral, the timing is perfect. Even the ceremony may be an advantage, since everyone in Rome will be preoccupied, and we can do what we must do without too much interference. I must point out that there may never again be such a favorable time and we should not let it pass unused."

Scribonia was pleased to find both Domitian and Marcus Clemens quite sober. More perfect timing, he thought.

"I don't like Silva staying at a government house," Domitian said. "He's too close to my brother. We've got to stop fooling ourselves. Silva may be just another general, but he has at least two Legions sworn to him, and very quickly he could have more. The result could be disastrous for us."

Scribonia smiled in a way that he hoped was only slightly patronizing and toyed with the eight rings on his fingers. "Exactly," he said. "Silva is an exceedingly dangerous man. He absolutely must be eliminated from the scene. And incidentally, he is no longer at the government house."

Scribonia saw Domitian blush and thought they might be in for a fit of temper. She was almost disappointed to see Domitian pull one foot up to his lap and massage it vigorously.

"What's the matter with your foot?" Marcus Clemens asked.

"Cramps. My legs, too. Night and day. They're driving me out of my mind." He glanced at Scribonia, who was astonished to detect a twinkle in his eyes. "Too much of your damned liquid maybe?"

"I disclaim both credit and blame, Your Grace." Were these clowns ever going to concentrate on the main issue, he wondered. If they would just give him a free hand they could fiddle away the next week, and at the end of it he would present them with the Empire. He said, "One of my contacts has been talking with the parade master of the funeral. He was told by one of Titus' aides to reserve a place for Silva just in front of Titus. That indicates to me that Silva will soon be invested with some high office, and that would be very unfavorable for us. A combination of Silva and Titus," he added with heavy emphasis on both names, "would make it virtually impossible for us or anyone else to bring about a change in the government."

"What do you think we should do?" Domitian asked. Scribonia saw that he was irritated, whether because of his teeth, his feet, or the subject of discussion she could not be sure.

"We must be realistic. My informants have advised me that Silva is no longer at the government house, but at Praeneste. I don't know why he departed, but his absence leaves the Jew, Josephus, there alone. I can guarantee he'll send an urgent request for Titus to come to him. That's all we need. Titus will never return to the palace, and he will be found with the Jew who will, of course, be taken care of by our people. They will only know what they see. It's really a very simple and not even an expensive design."

"And then what?" Domitian asked dubiously.

"Once the preliminary details are accomplished, it will be my honor to escort you to the Senate, where they will proclaim you Emperor. They will have no choice." Scribonia glanced at Marcus Clemens and sensed that he was resentful.

He hastened to make repairs. "Marcus, of course, will precede both of us into the Senate. . . . In fact, it would be appropriate if you will make a brief eulogy on your late brother-in-law and describe, as you may think providential, how close the brothers were in their desire to cooperate with the senators. You might even include some remarks on how fortunate we Romans are to have a leader like Domitian so ready and able to take over. You might care to explain how difficult a change might be under any other circumstances . . . readjustment of a totally different political philosophy and all that. Finally, you could put a taste of fear in their mouths by reminding them of the calamities of civil war should they delay in approving the proper line of succession. All the rest will take care of itself."

"What about Silva?" Marcus Clemens asked, and it was obvious that his pique had passed. "What is he going to be doing all this time?"

Scribonia smiled and caressed his rings. "For answer to that very astute query, we must first ask ourselves certain questions. Silva is preparing for some kind of journey . . . apparently not a military venture. Someone is going with him. Who? Something has gone wrong. Why is he departing in such a simple fashion if he is actually going to ride in that parade? If he is hiding something, what is it?"

Scribonia allowed his questions to float quietly down to the polished marble floor. He watched Domitian's eyes carefully and was rewarded with what he took to be an acknowledgment of their secret information. "For all we know," Domitian said, "Silva may just be engaged in a frivolity . . . perhaps only some woman is involved, and he is being discreet?"

Scribonia was momentarily aghast. Was Domitian about to reveal his sister's infidelity? Out of playful cruelty was he about to ruin the triumvirate? Marcus Clemens' enthusiasm was weak enough now without creating any possible antagonism in him.

Scribonia was almost instantly relieved. Domitian's lips formed only the words "my sister," but no sound came from them. Scribonia nodded to indicate that he understood the inference and glanced at Marcus Clemens. He appeared to be unaware of their silent exchange.

Domitian stuck his thumb in his mouth and massaged a

lower tooth. He seemed lost in thought as he alternately removed his thumb, studied it, then sent it back to work on his tooth. When he spoke again, his thumb garbled his words. "I agree we should not sit back and just await developments."

"If I may suggest then, Sire, we should begin by confining General Silva."

"And how would you propose to do that?" Marcus Clemens asked.

Scribonia turned to Domitian. "As a member of the royal household, you may make such demands on the Praetorians as you please. It's their sworn duty to protect you. You've only to suppose there exists a threat to your life, and the Praetorians are bound to act. If you will authorize me, I'll make the necessary arrangements."

Domitian grunted. He squirmed in his chair and fiddled with the embroidery along the edges of his tunic. "Very well. Proceed with absolute secrecy. Bring him back to the city and arrange for the necessary accommodations."

"When do we strike?" Marcus Clemens asked.

"I've had word from Africa," Scribonia said. "The Twenty-second Legion, commanded by Petronius Niges, is definitely ours for only two million sesterces."

Domitian smiled. "On the delivery of six million we can have the First Alaudae and the Twentieth Valeria in Germany. They will march on the day it arrives."

"But let us be patient," Scribonia urged. "My diversion of the Praetorians is not yet fully developed. Let's wait until after the funeral."

They rode at a brisk trot with occasional breaks into a canter all the way to Rome. Silva reviewed the strange events of the day and tried to understand why Titus should have such a change of resolve. The decurion of the Praetorians had been noncommittal. He had found Silva in the inn and after saluting said, "Sire, you are to come with us."

"Why? What's this all about?" Silva had asked.

"I don't know, Sire. I'm simply on imperial business."

"How did you know I was here?"

"I was told, Sire."

"Who told you?"

"My centurion, Sire."

Obviously the man knew little, if anything.

"I'd appreciate it if you didn't make it difficult," the decurion said, while he eyed his detachment of twenty.

Silva went to his room, picked up Cicero, and placed him on his shoulder. He told Cicero to wake up, they were moving out. The Praetorian said it was a nice bird.

"There will be a boy, too," Silva said. "He'll have to come along."

"No, Sire, I'm sorry."

"Are you giving me an order?" Silva enjoyed putting a bite in his voice. It had been a long time.

"I'm not authorized to bring anyone but you."

"Well, I'll damn well authorize it!" Silva was aware that his temper was rising. This shovel-faced Praetorian was going to do exactly as he had been ordered and nothing more.

"We brought only one extra horse, Sire."

"If the boy doesn't go, I don't go."

The muscles in the decurion's face twisted the skin of his face until it looked like kelp. His bagged eyes became forlorn. "Please, Sire," he said quietly, "I don't want any trouble."

"Well, you've just launched a monumental trouble!" Silva heard his voice rise. "The boy can ride behind me." He cut his protest short. Suddenly, he realized that this was an arrest. Titus had sent for him and either he was about to be forgiven or condemned. Reuben was probably better off out of the way. "Very well, decurion," he said acidly, "have it your way. But I must speak to the boy before we leave."

"Don't be long, Sire."

"What difference does it make?" Silva asked as he swaggered out to the stables of the inn and climbed the steps to Reuben's cubicle. These silly peacock Praetorians would see how a legionary general kept his dignity regardless of the circumstances.

He found Reuben pursuing what had become his favorite hobby. He was making a sketch of what looked like the mountain of Masada. Silva thought he displayed very definite talent and had encouraged his efforts at every opportunity. "Very well done," he said, "but I must disturb you. Something is happening, Son. I'm not sure what. Here's money to pay the bill and for the public coach to Rome. Go to the house of Domitillia. Tell her our plans must be postponed. Tell her I'm perfectly all right and not in any danger. I'll get a message to her as soon as this matter is settled."

"What is the trouble?"

"No trouble, I think, just something to do with Vespasian's funeral."

"I want to go with you."

"Better not. Just follow orders."

Reuben took his hand, gripped it firmly, then released it. Silva could not bear to look into his eyes because he knew what they would be saying.

It was nearly sundown when they passed through the Porta Praenestina. There was an unseasonal chill in the air, and despite the hard riding, Silva envied the Praetorians the cloaks they wore over their armor. The warmest place on his body was where Cicero squatted on his shoulder. He became increasingly uneasy when they passed the Campus Martius, then the Caput Africae, and instead of continuing along the Clivus Scauri toward the Palatine Hill as he supposed they would, they turned away from it and finally halted before an unfamiliar building on the Vicus Cyclopis. There they all dismounted, and when Silva's feet touched the ground his horse was taken from him. He was asked to follow the decurion. Two Praetorians strode along at his side and two more, he noticed, followed along behind.

They entered the building through an archway. Silva detected an odor that was familiar but refused identity, a pungent musk and tart smell mixed with the scent of urine and excretion. The toilets, he thought, must never be cleaned, or was it simply the obvious age of the building? He followed the decurion along a hallway, then turned down a flight of worn steps into semidarkness. "What is this place?" Silva asked.

His question was ignored.

They emerged into a courtyard where a single, naked infant sat on the carcass of a dead mule. The child was screaming and blubbering in the gray light. Silva noticed he was a male and that his skin was covered with dirt and red pustules. I am having a real nightmare this time, he thought. Where was the mother? He saw her then, a bundle of rags, squatting in the corner of the yard and defecating.

They passed from the courtyard through another arch, descended more steps to a lower level, and entered upon a crumbling peristyle that might once have graced a fine house. Here the area was in ruins with sagging columns and a litter of broken cornices, friezes, capitols, pipes, and tiles scattered along the way. The onetime peristyle terminated at a high stone wall, which embraced a wide double door. Two Praetorians stood guard on a parapet above it, and Silva discovered the source of the odor that had been so hauntingly familiar to him. A number of dead bodies, most quite naked, were stacked just beside the double door. Silva was not sure, but he thought he heard a low rumble of many human voices beyond the high wall. He was sure Titus had not been of a mind to do him honor by sending him to such a place. Perhaps, he thought, he is just demonstrating what might happen if I fail to follow instructions.

The decurion passed the double door and the corpses without so much as a glance. He continued along the wall until he came to another stairway leading to a curved path down to another level. Here it was nearly dark, for there was only a narrow slot between the wall and the building. There was a cave cut in the solid rock beneath the building and a deep moat between the end of the stairs and the floor of the cave. It was some distance from one side of the moat to the other, more than any man or beast could jump without a long run.

The Praetorians brought a heavy plank from the wall and laid it across the moat. The decurion indicated that Silva should cross it. He complied, holding himself as straight as if he were going for a morning stroll. The moment his feet were firmly on the floor of the cave the plank was pulled away.

"Thank you for your patience, Sire," the decurion said.

Silva looked about him. It was obvious that the only entrance or exit of this place required crossing the moat. There was no water that he could see, nor any sign of food. There was a worn wooden bench and nothing more. Nothing, Silva thought, and I have suddenly become nothing.

The decurion and his men started away. Silva called out to them. "I'm hungry!"

"Eat that chicken on your shoulder!" one of the Praetorians called out to him. The decurion hit the man so smartly across the mouth that blood came to his lips.

"I demand something to eat!" Silva ordered.

The decurion and his men turned and soon disappeared beyond the steps.

Silva examined his surroundings more carefully and concluded almost at once that escape was impossible. He ventured to the edge of the moat and looked down into a black void. Both sides of the chasm were sheer. The moat made the cave far more secure than a locked door.

He sat down on the bench and stroked Cicero for a time. He watched the last of the twilight fail and listened to the human sounds beyond the high wall. It was becoming a continuous babble of wailings, cries, shouts, moans, gibberish, and very occasional laughter.

And Flavius Silva Nonius Bassus, an ordinary man who had somehow become a Roman general, wondered if he had suddenly gone mad.

TWENTY-TWO

WHILE A HOST of craftsmen were working on images and representations of the gods Hercules, Minerva, Bacchus, Jupiter, Mars, and Venus, others were engaged in fashioning satyrs and maenads intended to give the triumphal funeral a lighter side. Heavily armed Praetorians were collecting the spoils of war from the imperial vaults; silver scabbards, gold sword belts, gold embroidered saddlecloths, and a massive assembly of military weapons were transported to the Campus Martius in preparation for its display.

Wagons were deployed throughout the countryside near Rome for the gathering of flowers; the estimated requirement for lining the streets with floral offerings was estimated at fifty thousand pounds.

Those who had known Vespasian personally said that he would have been horrified to know that a half million sesterces were set aside in the imperial treasury for distribution by the major dignitaries in the parade. Typical and sinister-looking engines of war, four large catapults, and two of the smaller *scorpiones* and *ballistae,* plus two *carroballistae* mounted on mobile carriages, with eleven men assigned to simulate the action of each machine in battle, were being prepared. Also brought to the Campus Martius and set down beside the other weapons were six *onagers*, the heavy catapults known affectionately as the "wild ass." Such engines were capable of throwing stones weighing more than fifty pounds as far as five hundred yards. A regular crew of five rehearsed its simulated operation. Also joining the arsenal were iron pointed wall borers, various crowbars and hooks for tearing away masonry, and an enormous battering ram complete with a protective shed, which most parade officials agreed would never pass through the narrowest streets of the planned route. They had other worries. It was found that there was a shortage of the incense required for the seventy mobile altars; couriers had been dispatched to basilicas and country temples in hopes of rounding up more.

At various meeting places throughout the city choruses of singers were rehearsing songs composed for the triumph, which now had been slightly altered to fit a funeral. Musicians by the hundreds were practicing new and old tunes under the direction of every music master in Rome. Special corrals had been erected for the oxen that would draw the big parade wagons; now their horns were being gilded and garlands prepared for their heads.

Mimes and actors were busily rehearsing and dancers were contesting with them for suitable space to practice new routines depicting the career and honors of Vespasian. Their inevitable disagreements sometimes became violent. It seemed that almost the entire energies of Rome were devoted to some kind of preparation for the ceremony. The ambassadors and their aides from Parthia, Mesopotamia, Armenia, Syria, Cappadocia, Bithynia, Egypt, Cyrenaica, Numidia, Dacia, Macedonia, Spain, Baetica, Mauretania, and Lusitania were trying on new robes for the occasion, assuring themselves that their depilatory needs were properly attended and the hair of their heads arranged according to their native fashions.

After a miserable night Flavius Silva tried to comfort Cicero, who seemed to recognize that things had gone badly. His customary squawking had been replaced by a soft catlike mewing, and he cocked his head and closed his eyes as if pouting. Silva knew the bird must be both thirsty and hungry —as indeed we both are, he thought. He stroked Cicero and whispered soothing confidences to him as if what he wanted to say must remain unheard by the countless people who were making such an uproar beyond the high wall.

Silva kept watching the narrow patch of sky that separated his prison from the high wall. Although he could not see the sun, he judged from the shadow on the wall that it must have risen. Now he saw a vaguely familiar figure descending the steps beyond the moat. He was wearing a white tunic strapped with a red belt, and Silva noticed that he minced delicately down the stairs as if he feared to damage the stone. When Silva saw that his fingers were covered with rings, he knew he was staring at Julius Scribonia. He jumped to his feet.

Scribonia halted on the opposite side of the moat, folded his arms across his chest, and smiled. "Greetings . . . General."

Silva waited, suppressing the urge to attempt to leap across the moat and seize Scribonia by the throat. Obviously, he was still asleep and dreaming, for Julius Scribonia was long since dead and his display of finger rings would now be visible only to the fish in the Mediterranean. "May I suppose, General, that you're rather surprised to see me?"

Silva kept his silence. He was not going to catch himself talking to a ghost in his dreams.

"It's been quite a spell since that night on the beach, hasn't it, General? Such a soft and lovely night . . . with Domitillia in your arms . . . and murder in your heart. Have you forgotten what we do with murderers and other criminals in Rome, dear General? We use them in the games."

Scribonia glanced up at the high wall behind him. "Noisy place, isn't it? But then all those people are going to provide good sport for us. There are several days of games scheduled after Vespasian's funeral . . . or did you know that, dear General? And you? Your role should provide a most amusing spectacle. We'll see if your bullyboy way will work with certain animals . . ."

Silva rubbed at his good eye. This was incredible. He was having illusions, and yet there was Cicero looking across the moat at the taunting figure who paced slowly back and forth. His rhythm was casual, as if time was unimportant for him, and he carried one bejeweled hand on his hip.

"Dear me," Scribonia was saying. "What a pity you're so isolated here. A handsome man, an expert lover, shall we say, and a glamorous soldier given to seducing other men's wives for his amusement will be much missed, I should think. What a loss it will be for the carnal delight of our Roman ladies. I'm thinking of one in particular who occupies a very high place. Let us not even whisper her name, but she must soon resort to masturbation. I invite you to envision that voluptuous individual leaning back and toying with her clitoris, her labia minora, and her labia majora. What a delicious piece of ass she must have been for you! And now will be for the next venturesome soldier."

Scribonia paused and stood listening to the raucous sounds from beyond the high wall. His dark eyes glistened as if wet with tears of joy. "Tsk, tsk," he said, smiling, "you *do* have the most noisy neighbors. I hope you'll have no trouble sleeping tonight. I myself would have arranged for more comfortable accommodations, but you're such a slippery fellow. Tell me, what *were* you going to do with those four horses? I myself don't quite see you behind a plow, yet I cannot believe you would be stupid enough to attempt an overland escape. But then perhaps you are?"

Silva could no longer contain himself. His voice became as hard as the metal of his sword had once been: "Next time, you won't get away from me."

"But my dear man! You don't seem to understand! There won't be a next time. Unless you learn to fly across the moat. Tomorrow is the funeral and the next day the games commence. I shall be obliging and see to it that you're fitted somewhere into the first day. Would you prefer to die in the morning or in the afternoon? You deserve some choice, since no one will know that the bloody wreckage of the man they have watched expire was the great and renowned General Silva. You'll enter the arena in the sequence after the gladiators, I suppose, and no one will know you from the rest of the criminals and troublemakers who have been collected for the celebration. If anyone should recognize you, I fear it will be too late. I myself intend to enjoy your struggle to the utmost. Please be brave."

"I want to talk with the Emperor."

"Do you now? Oh, I'm sure Titus will come rushing here just to hear what you have to say. Alas, he doesn't know where you are. *No* one knows where you are . . . except me. You are, shall we say, incognito? You are nameless, a cipher. You will enter the arena nameless and what is left of you will be carried out nameless. If anyone should ever ask me what happened to you, I'll say that I haven't the faintest notion. I will suppose that you have gone back to Judea. You and your messy bird. Now before I leave, would you like to tell me about those horses? I've always been the victim of an insatiable curiosity, and in return for satisfying that, I might see that you are thrown a crust of bread and perhaps even a few drops of water."

"I bought the horses because their anuses reminded me of you."

Scribonia laughed. "Dear, dear! What a dreadful thing to say. Now you've hurt my feelings. The offer of bread and water is rescinded. Farewell, General Silva. Except when you're taken to the arena, this will be the last time you'll see another human being."

Scribonia waggled his jeweled fingers at Silva, turned on his heel, and still smiling, ascended the steps.

Silva stood for a time staring down at the moat and listening to the sounds beyond the wall. He shook his head in dismay. How in a matter of two months could he have fallen so far from grace? Reprimands, yes . . . perhaps he deserved something of the kind. But *ad bestia?* Was Scribonia bluffing, just enjoying a few twists before real authority in the person of an emissary from Titus arrived to apologize? Shades of Pomponius Falco, that degenerate who had come to his camp at Masada and tried to disrupt his whole campaign in the Emperor's name.

Suddenly, Silva shifted his attention to the narrow strip of sky, now a brilliant cobalt blue. He shook his fists at the sky as if he had found an audience there, and he shouted with all the power of his lungs: "Hear me, whoever you are who runs this rotten place! Come immediately . . . on the double! There's been a mistake! I am General Flavius Silva, commander of the Tenth Legion and legate of Judea! Come and you'll be rewarded! I give my right hand to that!"

Silva's words bounced off the high wall, echoed along its length, then reechoed at the back of the cave and down into the moat. He realized at last that no one was listening, nor could they have heard him if they were. His straight back sagged and he covered his eyes with his hands. The same despair that had overwhelmed him when he left Masada took hold of him. He knew he was not afraid to die. He simply wanted to die with honor.

He turned back to the bench and sat down. He caressed Cicero's back with slow, even gestures. After a time he emitted a dry chuckle. What was it Epictetus had written? "What is born must perish . . . for I am part of the whole as the hour is part of the day. I must come on as the hour . . . and like the hour pass away . . ."

On this glorious day, when the Roman sun smiled down upon the city and just enough breeze drifted in from the Tyrrhenian Sea to perfect the temperature, Domitillia did her best to retain her sense of humor while she packed. Instinctively, she had begun as if she were bound on an imperial mission requiring gowns and sandals, and jewelry to match. When all about her chambers was a flurry of preparations, she realized the confusion had infected her own thinking. Flavius had said to bring no more than she could carry in her two hands, and laughing at her jumbled thoughts, which were so unlike her, she selected presents for each of her slaves.

"Here Julia, . . . this red gown for you. It will look smashing on you! Fortuna, . . . this necklace for you! Made to match your lovely skin. Lidea, . . . try this little silk piece to complement your figure . . . and Drusilla, here's just the thing for you! Paula, . . . somewhere in this mess there's a pair of earrings to match those green eyes."

As more and more of Domitillia's possessions were distributed, the shyness left the girls completely and their voices rose in continuous lilting screams of surprise and delight. Domitillia concluded that she had never had such a fulfilling hour in her life, and she wondered why she had not thought to do this annually.

Such was the noise and movement all about her that she failed to notice her husband was standing at the entrance to her chambers. Now he sauntered toward her, his head wobbling slightly, his chins tucked in as tightly against his neck as he could manage, and his attitude pugnacious. He dismissed the slave girls with a wave of his hand and they scattered, running away in a cloud of whispers and carrying their prizes through their special doorway.

When they had gone, Marcus Arrecinus Clemens faced his wife and cleared his throat. "What's this all about?" he asked coldly.

"We were having a party. It's a shame you had to spoil it."

Clemens rubbed the perspiration from his forehead with the

sleeve of a tunic. He surveyed the room, and the corners of his petulant mouth twisted downward. "You've been packing," he said flatly. "When you're planning a trip it would be more considerate if you informed your husband. Where are you going?"

"I'm not sure." Domitillia had never seen such a strange and angry expression in her husband's eyes. She was sure she saw something more than disapproval.

"Is the Jew boy going with you?"

"He just arrived. I haven't had a chance to talk to him yet."

"I thought we were rid of him and now he's back . . . without troubling for my permission."

Domitillia made a deliberate attempt to put her new and strangely persistent fears aside. She sat down on the bed, trying to compose herself, and for distraction began toying with an empty jewel box. "Since it's obvious you are displeased with me, I don't care to discuss this any further. I must request that you leave my chambers."

"Not until we have things sorted out." Clemens' head began to wobble erratically and his protruding eyes became wider than ever. He clasped his hands behind his back and spread his feet wide as if poised for an earthquake.

"Marcus," she said, "if you are about to deliver one of your ultimatums, do so and get it over with. Then leave me in peace."

"Who does the Jew boy belong to?"

"No one . . . as yet."

"All right then. Who *will* he belong to? Our other uninvited guest is an officer in the Tenth Legion . . . Flavius Silva's Legion. Is this a coincidence? Just what is he doing here?"

"Resting."

"Resting? A Legion officer? Or waiting, perhaps. Get rid of him today."

"Why?" Domitillia had never seen her husband so resolute. He was posed before her like a sullen bull, and she sensed that something more than Reuben and Piso was disturbing him.

"Because great events are in the making and I don't want any spies in my house."

"Spies? You make more sense when you're drunk than when you're sober. But very well. My lord and master has spoken."

"Pack your sarcasm in your bags and take it with you."

Suddenly, Domitillia knew she must learn more. This was no ordinary Marcus Clemens who challenged her now. Something was inspiring him to efforts beyond his usual flaccid self. There was something very formidable about him. She found it almost frightening.

"Marcus? Are you involved in something you should not be?"

"That's my business."

"Your business is imports and banking. You've never been so tense before. Could you possibly be involved with that man Scribonia?"

"That is also my business."

Domitillia hesitated. She was guessing, but she thought she saw her answer in his eyes. "If I'm gone for long, what will you do?"

"Cheer."

"Thank you. That's all I needed to know."

As soon as she could dress and regain her poise, Domitillia took Reuben to her brickworks. On the way he told her how the Praetorians had come for the General and how he had said that she should not worry about him. Her spirits sank. What kind of tricks was Titus playing now?

"The General told me to find Centurion Piso and stay with him."

"Good. That's where we're going."

At the brickworks all activities had ceased in anticipation of the grand event to be celebrated on the morrow. There was no sign of any human about and even the furnaces were cold. She led Reuben quickly through the complex and entered a tunnel in the hillside where long ago the original owner had brought out clay. It was unused now since the supply of good clay had long since been exhausted.

They walked rapidly through the tunnel until the light from an aperture in the roof penetrated the gloom. She turned down a steep flight of steps and they entered upon a large vaulted room carved out of the sandstone. Some two dozen people, men and women and a few children, were gathered around a cluster of burning candles. They were listening to Centurion Piso and were enrapt at what he was saying. "I'll give you the word of Paul who suffered for him in a place very near where you are now . . ."

"They're Christianii," Domitillia whispered. "I allow them to meet here weekly because they have no other place to go."

Reuben recoiled instinctively. "Are you one of them?" he asked in a whisper.

"No. But what they believe is interesting. I like to help them."

Piso saw them and arose at once. He came toward them quickly. Domitillia explained that Reuben must be kept out of sight and that Silva was in some kind of trouble. "I'll go now to see my brother, Titus, and return tonight," she said. "Since your Christus was a Jew, I assume you won't mind giving shelter to one?"

"Be assured of his welcome, Your Grace." Piso put his big hand on Reuben's shoulder. "We've declared an armistice. He's forsaken his feistiness."

"I wouldn't depend on it." Domitillia smiled.

Domitillia was in such haste that she went directly to the Capitoline Hill. She was too impatient to wait for her litter and was reluctant to return to her house, where she might encounter her husband again.

She hurried through the relatively empty streets on foot, her gown dancing with her determined efforts. Her haste was such that some who saw her thought she must be a madwoman and gave her no more than a cursory glance. A pack of cocky youths taunted her as she passed and made clicking noises with their teeth and fingers, calling out claims of their sexual prowess. She ignored them. An ancient beggar, squatting against a building like a foundation stone, cried pitifully on her approach and cursed her roundly as she continued on her way.

When Domitillia arrived at the palace she swept by the Praetorian guards as if they did not exist. When three of Titus' bureaucratic minions tried to bar her way to his audience chamber, she tossed her head contemptuously and told them to go back to their scribblings. At the door to the chamber a perplexed Praetorian decided to obey her order. "Move your enormous carcass and open that door this instant! I'm in a hurry!"

She passed the open door and found Titus talking to three men. He was saying, "When the funeral is over I want you on your way immediately. You will go by the fastest transport available to Tyre and Sidon, and wherever else in Syria you deem it necessary to discover why those people can do so much with so little . . . and if I may say so, make fools of us. Why can they make dyes and silk and glass and sell it to us at outrageous prices? What's wrong with our Roman industry that every day it shows further deterioration both in quantity and quality? Go to Damascus if necessary. And be back here within sixty days, ready to give me a full report on why those people who are supposed to have been conquered the last time they had the heart for fighting are now running our economy!"

One of his visitors, Lucillus Bassus, said, "I wouldn't go so far as to say that, Sire. Admittedly, our balance of trade with Syria is not encouraging but that will change—"

"Will it? Not unless we get off our asses and go back to work. I want to know why Antioch has a system for lighting their streets at night, when our citizens don't dare leave their homes without an escort of thugs. You can walk four and a half miles in Antioch without exposing yourself either to the sun or rain or murderers. The streets are paved with granite. The homes have good water and plenty of it. What's wrong with us? You find out . . ."

Titus looked away from his audience and saw his sister standing in the doorway. He arose slowly and the others stood immediately.

"You know my sister," Titus said. The three men bowed together. "I apologize for her intrusion. It's quite unexpected."

"No," Domitillia said, "it is I who must apologize. But it is absolutely necessary that I see you now . . . Your Majesty."

"If you'll forgive us?" Titus said to the delegates, who backed hastily toward the door. Lucillus Bassus said that their business had indeed been concluded and that they understood their instructions perfectly.

When they had gone and the door was closed after them, Titus said that he hoped Domitillia had come to him as the bearer of the news he wanted to hear. No other excuse would be suitable for such a rude intrusion. If she was not bringing the news that an abortion had been accomplished, he would instruct the Praetorians to take her away.

"I've discovered that an Emperor has no time for trivial matters," he said coldly. "Thus far, your lack of cooperation and support during a most difficult transition has not been exactly inspiring."

"I am not here because of triviality."

"Good. Then sit down."

"I prefer to stand." My brother, Domitillia thought, could easily become a tyrant if he was not so soft inside.

"Why are you panting?" Titus asked.

"Because I'm mad and scared and worried about your sanity. And I've been hurrying and every hour may be precious. My dear husband, the man you value so highly, or say you do, is mixed up with a man called Scribonia and our Domitian."

Titus ran his fingers through his curly hair and shook his head in disbelief. "Sounds like they're lonely. How do you come by this information?"

"Mostly intuition."

"Fine! That's a reliable foundation. I'm a busy man, Sister. Has your husband suddenly learned about you and Silva?"

"No."

Titus rose from behind the long marble table, which Domitillia remembered had so long served their father. It suited Titus admirably now, she thought, or was it that he suited it? They were both distinguished by a natural grandeur and solidity that matched the Empire perfectly. Titus sighed.

"Damn it, woman, did it ever occur to you just to behave like you should? Thousands of Roman women can screw their heads off with all kinds of lovers, but they're not princesses of the Empire. All things pass in a few years, including lovers. Why destroy a marriage that's convenient and very advantageous financially? Would you kick a hole in the bottom of a boat to see if it will sink? I fail to understand why you can't look a few years down the road and see the regrets you will have accumulated while you try to make do on a soldier's pension. You're a popular Roman matron. You have countless friends, a fine house, and all the slaves you need. You're a patroness of artists, you run your own brickworks, you might be sent on more imperial missions in the future . . ."

Titus spread his hands in entreaty. "Why in the name of all the gods do you have to be so stubborn? Why do you have to betray your family and your nation just for a single soldier?"

"As I've told you before, I love him."

"Isn't that wonderful! And for him you'd risk not only your freedom, but your whole life?"

"Yes . . . but I've come to compromise." She advanced toward her brother and reached for his hand. "I will ride in the parade with Marcus. In addition, I'll spend one year in his house appearing to outsiders as his true wife and . . . I will have an abortion. All of this if you give me your right hand that at the end of one year you will release me from all obligations."

Titus smacked his hands together. "Fine!" He raised his right hand and made a fist.

"Not so fast. You must free Flavius and restore him to full honors."

"Easy. I'll get word to Praeneste immediately."

Domitillia hesitated. She made no attempt to conceal her irritation. "How can I trust you when you lie so?"

"I don't understand."

"Flavius is not in Praeneste and you know it. Where have you locked him up?"

"I haven't locked him up anywhere. He's under personal arrest and obviously he wanted to go to Praeneste. That's permissible as long as I know where he is."

"Then, why did you send the Praetorians for him?"

"I didn't! What are you talking about?"

She told him then what she had heard from Reuben. She said that there was no use compromising with a man, Emperor or not, who would so deliberately lie to his sister. "I don't know why you are so proud of the Flavii. We're a rotten family. Papa has barely had his last breath and you proclaim yourself Emperor before the Senate or anyone else has a chance to say no! Then you lie to your sister. As if that isn't enough, I wouldn't be surprised if your own brother is planning to toss you off the throne as soon as he can. What kind of a Roman family is that? We're better suited to hauling garbage. Now, why have you thrown your lifelong friend into prison?"

"I haven't. He's in Praeneste. I suppose he's staying in his new house."

"You lie. The Praetorians came and took him away from the inn."

Titus frowned. He clapped his hands twice and an aide opened the big door. Titus told him to bring the Praetorian duty officer to him on the double. "I don't know what you're talking about, but I suppose we should get to the bottom of it. Sit down and have a glass of wine or a snack. I intend to prove that the present head of the Flavii tribe is not so bad as you seem to think."

The commander of the Praetorians presently on duty was a tall and handsome tribune who arrived almost at once and saluted smartly. "Tertullus," Titus said, "have I given you any orders whatsoever within the last two days . . . especially concerning the bringing of any individual from Praeneste?"

"No, Sire."

"To your knowledge, have I given such an order to anyone else?"

"No, Sire."

"Then I will now give you an order and I expect immediate compliance. You will communicate with your headquarters and find out who ordered Praetorians to perform such a duty. I want the times and the names of the Praetorians involved, what was done with the individual, and where he is now. You will execute my order instantly!"

The tribune saluted and departed without hesitation.

"I hope," Titus said, looking Domitillia straight in the eyes, "that I've not sent him galloping off on a mere rumor. I find it both discouraging and touching that you will believe a Jewish boy before you will take the word of your own brother."

"Reuben has given me no cause to doubt his word."

Thunderstorms rumbled all through the afternoon and the darkness of the cave was relieved only by the frequent flashes of lightning. It rained heavily. During one shower Silva saw a man slowly descending the steps on the opposite side of the moat. He was a blond man, muscular and stocky; Silva was certain he must be a German. He hoped that he was a jailer or someone who would bring him food, but when he called out to him the man simply stared in his direction, wiped the rain from his face, and shook his head as if he had not understood.

The man looked about him carefully, then tilted his head to look at the lightning flashing across the sky. He shook his long wet hair out of his eyes and stood transfixed for a moment.

Then he sighed heavily, turned about without paying the slightest attention to Silva or Cicero, and slowly ascended the steps. Soon he had vanished in the same silence he had come.

"I wonder," Silva said as he stroked Cicero, "I wonder who that could have been?" He could not remember when he had known such a moment of loneliness. Hoping to save his reason as the darkness folded over him, he thought more about the man. He must not have been a prisoner or he would not have been so casual. He was not a jailer, for he wore none of their paraphernalia; a dirty wet tunic and a pair of much-worn sandals were his only trappings.

Suddenly, Silva decided that he might be Charon or his representative. "But wait," he whispered to Cicero. "He came and looked, but he made no invitation. He just came and looked and went away because he decided the time was not yet come. Suppose he was only letting me know that he was near and when the right moment came he would act?"

Silva listened to the babble on the other side of the high wall for a time and continued to stroke Cicero, who made occasional squeaks of unhappiness. "Don't you see that it really makes sense . . . the only thing that does make sense in this madhouse? That man was Charon and the moat is the River Styx. If the right time had come, he would have put down the plank and offered transportation to the other side. But he knew the time has not come, Cicero, and that is . . . very encouraging."

Silva lifted Cicero off his knee and placed him on the bench. He walked to the very edge of the moat and leaned as far out as he dared. Now he could see the end of the steps and the upper landing where it turned away from the high wall and extended into the old building above him. There was no sign of anyone in the gloom.

Was he losing his reason? He had seen that man as clearly as he now saw the high wall; he was not a transparent ghost, but a solid individual of possibly German origin. Hunger, he remembered, played strange tricks on the mind. Of course! That was it! Simple hunger had caused him to see things that were only illusions.

The first star appeared in the gap between the high wall and the lip of his cave. Silva found strange comfort in it. He turned back to Cicero and said through his parched lips, "Of course, my friend, that man was only part of a mirage."

Julius Scribonia was pleased with his arrangements. He had made a second call upon Joseph ben Matthias at the government house and found that the Jew had apparently done some heavy thinking. For he agreed that he had possibly been neglectful of Domitian in his writings and would consider it beneficial to spend some time with him to better record his deeds.

Alas, Scribonia thought. It was an audience that would never take place. By this time tomorrow night the Jew would be stretched across the body of Titus Flavius Vespasianus . . . both quite dead.

"It's quite important that you record the enormous contrasts between the two brothers. Hot metal is more easily shaped than cold. Therefore, I suggest you send off an urgent request to see Titus here . . . tomorrow night."

"But he'll be very busy with preparations for the next day."

"All the better. You'll see him at the height of his powers."

"What if he can't come?"

"He will. The invitation from you will be irresistible. History demands your observations of two men on the eve of such an occasion."

Scribonia took a piece of paper from the stack of Josephus' writing table. "Put your signature on the bottom. I'll compose an invitation that will persuade our glorious Emperor to give you more than a little of his time."

Josephus recoiled. "I don't like this."

"Come now! Why not? You're only serving history. I'll promise Domitian will come as well. Imagine! What a rare opportunity for you . . . the two brothers in the same room together and your facile pen to record their words for posterity. If you delay any longer I may cancel the opportunity."

Josephus took up his stylus and made the quick flourishes of his signature.

TWENTY-THREE

THE FOLLOWING EVENING Domitian decided that something must be done to balance the solemnity of the morrow and to assuage the atmosphere of depression that surrounded him. His eyesight was increasingly troublesome and his aching tooth had been pulled and left him bleeding goblets of blood for the better part of the day. The sponge soaked in the juice of angora root had reduced the pain of extraction to a tolerable level, but the anesthetic effect had made him dizzy and, much to his surprise, feeling lecherous. "What we both need," he said to Marcus Clemens, who had come crying to him with his domestic woes, "what we both really need is a forgetful fuck. Very important category, Marcus. Show me the man who can remember his troubles when he has a girl or a pretty boy to toy with him, and I'll show you a man who deserves to be castrated."

Domitian summoned Julius Scribonia and told him to provide all the ingredients he considered appropriate for a "refreshment of the spirit": a brace of boys and girls less than twenty years old and a full amphora of his aphrodisiacal wine. "Include a few musicians if you can kidnap any from the funeral rehearsal, and also a few mimes." He winced when he tried to smile and ran his tongue speculatively around his lips. "We may need some rest between bouts," he grunted, and slapped Marcus Clemens hard on the shoulder. "Our fat bull here is wounded and we must restore his sense of values."

Scribonia congratulated himself on his foresight. Not only

had he written an inspired message above Josephus' signature, but he had learned from a palace informant that Titus planned to visit the government house and the Jew at least briefly. It was also appropriate that Domitian would be in the mood for relaxation. He was far removed from the government house and heavily preoccupied with his playful friends, so there would be no way to suspect him of having a hand in his brother's passing. Perhaps, Scribonia thought with a sense of self-admiration for his inventiveness, it might be logical to postpone Vespasian's grand funeral and combine it with that of Titus?

By now Scribonia had assembled the list of participants for any sort of sexual activity Domitian might fancy. He had also laid aside three amphorae of what he now thought of as "the Gaullic disease," and he was ready to watch and reflect upon the stimulating effect it had on his master. Alas, even if the power of the liquid was genuine, it was not for him, he thought. The Spanish boy was still missing and had such a stranglehold on his heart that he could not bring himself to take a true interest in any other. The misbegotten of the world like himself, he thought, are the ones who take their loves seriously because they know that they are not likely to find another. Once the naturally deprived have discovered a love, their very bones are endowed with dedication to their lover's happiness. No substitute for the Spanish boy would be acceptable to him until after a long interval of sexual mourning.

Within an hour Scribonia had all the elements in place, and Domitian's house rang with music, shrill cries of delight, and the soft running pad of bare feet. Scribonia found that he was immensely satisfied with his ability to provide such simple joys in so short a time. Both Domitian and Marcus Clemens were now quite drunk and had shed the sundry inhibitions that had so troubled them. Both had long since kicked off their sandals and, being naked except for short tunics, disported themselves by chasing their guests along the peristyle and out into the formal gardens where the objects of their clumsy pursuit sometimes allowed themselves to be captured.

The merriment was a strange contrast, he thought, to the affairs soon to occur in the government house. Even now the four humanoids who had sold their services for a mere fifty sesterces were awaiting the arrival of a man whose name and status would be unknown to them. Their orders were clear. Kill the visitor and then the Jew. Place them together and leave evidence of a struggle.

Scribonia was enjoying the spectacle with the eyes of a connoisseur, regretting only that he was not inspired to join the fun, when he turned to see an officer of the Praetorians standing just behind him. "Julius Scribonia?"

"I am he."

"The Emperor wishes to see you."

While the final preparations for Vespasian's triumphal funeral continued through most of the night, Flavius Silva did his best to sleep on the narrow wooden bench. At least it offered partial protection against the squadrons of nocturnal roaches, which now carpeted the floor of the cavern. A wind had come up, but instead of bringing refreshment it swished around the back areas of the cavern and drove out a powerful odor of excrement left by previous tenants.

Silva tried every old warrior's nostrum he could remember to ease the fierce activity of his thoughts, but there seemed to be no escaping the realization that by the day after tomorrow he would no longer exist. It was strange, he thought; now all of the hazards he had faced in battles seemed to have been the experiences of another man. In combat there was no time to dwell on the certainty of death. Here there was not much else to do and the contemplation brought on a sort of floating sensation. Was this nature's way of making the prospect tolerable? In battle the realistic acceptance of death was essential to a true soldier, yet there was always the conviction that escape from any serious harm was very possible. Wars, he thought, would never be fought if the element of chance was removed. The legionary in the ranks knew he had a chance to survive, as did his centurion and his general; his comrades might fall, but he would be spared.

Trying desperately to sleep, Silva attempted to estimate how many men he had seen die during his campaigns. Five thousand? Ten? And he had walked around or climbed over the bodies of half as many. It was the eyes that had impressed him with their look of surprise, as if their owners had been tricked. The lips were still, but the eyes talked, perhaps more eloquently than they ever had when their proprietor was alive.

The passing of most soldiers went unnoticed except for a statistical insertion in the military records. But on the morrow Vespasian, who had also known the close breath of death, would be celebrated. He would be gone with the honors so important to military men because soldiering was the only job in which death was an accepted function. For a Roman of good family and an officer in the army to die in disgrace was unthinkable. As a consequence, many Roman officers who had fallen into disgrace had chosen to fall on their swords, thereby mitigating whatever had brought them to shame. And thus a tradition had long been established. Whether it was a battle lost, funds stolen, or a superior insulted, the soldier who took his own life was absolved of the wrong and his memory was honored.

"Aye!" Silva groaned in the darkness. There was no sword at hand nor would there be. But Scribonia was going to be disappointed. There would be no *ad bestia* for Flavius Silva.

There was the moat. Just before darkness he had bent down to make a careful inspection of the moat. It appeared to narrow at some distance down, but he could not see the bottom. There was no question that if he threw himself into that chasm his acceptance of death would be of his own choice. He would be vindicated. Farewell, General Flavius Silva, Commander of the Tenth Frentensis, Legate of Judea. There would be ample time when they came to fetch him during those few moments when they were descending the steps before they reached the level of the cavern. He must be alert when dawn came. There would be time to step to the edge of the moat and deliberately take the final step into eternity before their very eyes.

Silva managed a smile as he found himself hoping that Julius Scribonia himself would be a witness to his demise.

It was nearly midnight and Titus had reluctantly decided to forgo the pleasure he always found in reminiscing with Joseph ben Matthias. He was exhausted with the countless duties of the Empire, some so new to him that he found his decision making irksome. The forthcoming funeral had brought several knotty problems into the clear, and some sort of mandate had to be issued on each. There was the matter of religious display at the funeral, which he thought should reflect the belief of the

Flavian house and the Emperor, however dubious and violated that belief might be. And there must be a token compromise with the new religions now popular among the Roman public. The Vestal Virgins, of course, were still held in great honor, and the Emperor stood as the head priest of the official government religion. Yet the old styles of worshiping a pantheon of Roman gods was shredding, as if some unknown wind had been tearing at the fabric that had served for so many centuries. The priests of the Luperci still held their ceremonial dancing on fiesta days, and the Arval Brethren still uttered their prayers in a Latin so ancient that few citizens understood more than an occasional word; but the majority of Romans had turned away from such esoteric performances. Astrology was now extremely popular and determined the day-to-day life of many Romans, as well as some senatorial decisions.

Indeed, Titus thought, as he reviewed what should be included in the triumphal parade, the old gods have become a Roman joke, and even the poor have lost faith in their powers. New religions brought home by Roman soldiers and by merchants and traders who came to the center of the Empire were ever more prominent. Even before his father's reign any attempt to stifle the imports was thought not to be worth the trouble.

The erosion of traditional Roman worship was furthered by popular interest in Isis, the Egyptian goddess of fertility, motherhood, and trade—a combination, Titus thought cynically, that just about covered everything. Originally, the worship of Isis under the direction of her bald-headed priests was forbidden, but Caligula had succumbed to her exotic powers and had built a great temple in the Field of Mars honoring the divinity.

The invasion of sundry religions had now become a flood, and Titus decided to omit most of them from the parade. Why, he reasoned, should he include the worship of Pythagoras, that vegetable eater who had preached reincarnation? Or of the Syrian goddess Atargatis, known as *dea Syria* to the eccentric bundle of Romans who had adopted her. The same must hold for Aziz, a god of the sun, or another sun god from Parthia called Mithras, brought back by legionaries who had been away so long they no longer heard the gods of their homeland. And there was *Yahweh,* the deity of the Christians, who was easily removable from the triumphal parade, since the god of that sect was invisible.

After consulting with his staff, Titus concluded that it was better to let the Roman gods bid farewell to a great Roman citizen, a man who would have been the last to endorse a fracture in the stolid marble of Roman religion.

Immediately after Titus had dismissed his staff and admonished them to take to their beds because he wanted the best of their energies in the morning, Julius Scribonia was brought before him. He stood uncertainly in the doorway, flanked by a pair of Praetorians. Titus noticed at once the collection of jewelry adorning his fingers. Scribonia bowed low, keeping his face aimed overlong at the marble floor. Titus found his obsequious manner annoying and his unctuous voice more so.

"Your Majesty. I am overwhelmed with the honor you have chosen to lay upon this humble citizen."

The bastard is reminding me that he's a Roman citizen, Titus thought, and therefore entitled to a full trial for whatever mischief he's been up to.

"I've seen you before," Titus said flatly. He remembered the man now. He had been among Domitillia's party when she went off to Judea. There had been a crowd of dignitaries as there always was when any of the imperial family embarked, and even Vespasian had journeyed to Ostia to see his daughter off. Somewhere in the crowd, Titus recalled, he had seen that same powdered face and had wondered if he might be one of Domitillia's hairdressers or fashion designers. Yet now, if his information was correct, the man had been a minor functionary with the *frumentarii* for several years.

"I suppose you'd like to know why I've summoned you," Titus said. He waved the guards away and slumped down in his chair. By all the gods, he was tired! He yawned and scratched at his left forearm where a mild case of eczema had appeared. The damn Greek doctors had given him a salve that had so far been ineffective.

"If I may remark, Your Majesty, I'm quite mystified that you should call upon me at this most crucial time. Please accept my deep sympathies for the loss of your father. The Empire is most fortunate that his glory has been passed on to such a deserving and able son."

"The words tinkle prettily on your lips, Citizen Scribonia. Is that the kind of bullshit you feed my brother?"

"Your Majesty expresses himself in a most interesting fashion. Your lessons in rhetoric when you went to Greece as a young man were not wasted. I am in awe."

"You are also my brother's pot licker and you're also in trouble."

Scribonia hesitated, then played nervously with the rings on his fingers. "Trouble, Your Majesty? I realize that the Emperor is the father and mother of all Romans, and I would be the last to cause you even the slightest distress. My devotion—"

"Shut your loose mouth!" Titus rose quickly from his chair. "Who authorized you to use Praetorians?"

Scribonia's eyes said that he was hardly aware of their existence. "Praetorians, Your Majesty? I'm afraid I don't understand . . ."

"I have been informed that you called for twenty Praetorians in my brother's name. Am I to believe they took off on their own volition?"

Scribonia hesitated, then smiled. He bowed his head slightly. "Your Majesty. It is with the utmost reluctance that I must tell you that treason is involved."

"Flavius Silva a traitor? I find that hard to believe." Titus decided to go along with the man, at least for a time. It was amusing to watch him squirming. "And what was my old friend Silva planning to do?"

"I knew he was your friend, Your Majesty, and I certainly had no desire to disillusion you."

"You've made an accusation. Would you care to back it up?"

"Only if I'm guaranteed immunity, Your Majesty. Unpleasant news is sometimes more difficult to deliver than to receive."

"Are you trying to bargain with me?"

"Oh no! Selfishly, I was just thinking of my future."

"I'm thinking of your future. You have attached yourself to my brother. What has he to do with all this?"

"Absolutely nothing! But out of loyalty to you he agreed it wise to bring Silva in for interrogation."

Scribonia seemed pleased with himself, and Titus thought

he had seldom met such a devious man. "What was Silva planning to do?"

"He came here via Africa and did his best while en route to stir up the Legions against you. Given his liberty, he would soon persuade the whole army you are their adversary."

"Who told you this? Where did you find such information?"

Scribonia remained silent. Titus approached him slowly, then very suddenly kicked him in the groin. Scribonia grunted and sank to his knees moaning.

"Answer me!" Titus commanded. "Now that it seems you actually have a pair of balls, stop your sniveling and answer me!"

Scribonia clutched at his abdomen and groaned heavily. While his head was still down, Titus brought his knee up sharply into his face and the blow sent Scribonia sprawling. "If you don't give tongue immediately, I'll have it cut out of your head!"

Scribonia tried to mouth a reply, but his words were unintelligible. Titus saw with satisfaction that his nose was bleeding as he squirmed to his feet. "You're very lucky, Julius Scribonia. For reasons of my own, I'm determined to keep this between us. Ordinarily, I would have called in the guards to reason with you. They are inclined to be much rougher than I."

"Your Majesty," Scribonia whined. It seemed all he was capable of enunciating.

"Since only a member of the imperial family can call upon the Praetorians, I want to know how and why you persuaded my brother to authorize such an expedition."

"Silva . . . is an enemy . . ." Scribonia mumbled. He wiped at his nose with the back of his hand and stared horrified at the blood on his rings.

"An enemy of whom?"

"Of Your Majesty . . . and your brother."

"Nonsense. He hardly knows my brother and he's served me faithfully for years. I want to know who put such ideas in your silly head?"

Scribonia sighed forlornly. He was gradually recapturing his breath. "Your Majesty underestimates Flavius Silva. Like other ambitious generals in the past, he would become Emperor. But first he must eliminate your brother . . ." Fear had replaced the confusion in Scribonia's eyes. He seemed to have lost his poise entirely as he reached out for some defense. ". . . and then he must come to you. He has already begun." Despite his desperation, Scribonia managed to inject a hint of mystery in his voice.

"What do you mean by that?"

"I would fear for my life if I told you."

"You're asking for another kick in the balls." Titus wondered if he should simply snap his fingers for the guards and have this cunning idiot beaten until he answered questions directly, or should he play him like a fish and perhaps learn more. "Why should you fear for your life over anything you might tell me?"

"Because it's extremely personal . . . to you."

"Out with it, then. I'll decide whether you'll live or not, but if you give me one more evasive answer, my decision is made."

"Your . . . sister, Sire. Flavius Silva has seduced her. She is one more step toward the throne for your faithful general."

Titus was momentarily stunned. How did this wretch find out about Domitillia? If he knew, who else knew?

Titus recovered quickly. How far had this thing gone? "On what do you base that ridiculous accusation?" he asked as if he was not really interested in Scribonia's response.

"I saw it with my own eyes, Sire. On the beach in Judea."

"I think you're lying." He was probably not lying, Titus cautioned himself. About the beach . . . perhaps, but as for their copulating, he knew much more than he should. "I suppose you've told this fable to Domitian?" Of course he had, Titus decided, and he might have passed on the same story to Marcus Clemens.

Titus scratched at his forearm while his weary mind tried to adjust the fact he had just learned with what he already knew. Visions of his lost Berenice flashed through his thoughts and caused him to concede that Domitillia had come to him and offered an acceptable compromise because she was sincere in her love for Flavius Silva. There were no other reasons for her to do so. But Domitian . . . ? Were Domitian and Marcus

Clemens urged on by this bejeweled scoundrel who knew far too much?

"Where is Flavius Silva now?" Titus demanded.

"In view of the situation, Your Majesty, I made arrangements for his safekeeping."

Titus slapped Scribonia across the mouth. "I asked you *where!*"

"In the prison on the Vicus Cyclopis."

Titus snapped his fingers, the doors opened immediately, and two Praetorians stepped inside. "Take this man to the Cyclopis," he said carelessly. "See to it that he replaces General Flavius Silva . . . body for body. Bring the General back here and give him a room until morning."

The Praetorians seized Scribonia and lifted him off his feet. He kicked and pleaded, "But Your Majesty! I have a right to a full hearing . . . as a citizen . . ."

"Your right is mine. Your trial will be posthumous and I plan to attend."

When Titus learned that Silva had been brought to the palace, he roused himself from his weariness and resolved to see him. Despite this foolishness with Domitillia, he was still a loyal friend and at least deserved some apology.

He found Silva in a small room with a commanding view of the Forum. He was stretched out on the narrow bed and was snoring softly. An oil lamp was still burning above the bed and Silva's sandals were neatly aligned beneath it. Titus studied the man's face for a moment. The sublime slumber of the true soldier, he thought. Once the guard was down and the battle done, no human except an infant slept in such profound peace. Flavius Silva was the lucky one; his mind was not troubled unceasingly with plans and intrigues and barricades of lies, which made judgment difficult. He reached down and shook him gently. "Come to life, old friend. Your Emperor would speak with you."

And also like a born soldier, Titus thought, Silva awakened instantly. It was as if his guard had never really been down.

Silva rolled off his bed and immediately stood at attention. "Sire!" he said.

"Relax. Sit down. I regret disturbing you."

Silva said that he was honored and thanked Titus for his liberation. "And I regret the way I must smell," he said. "The Cyclopis has an odor that could be said to be incomparable."

"You can bathe in the morning, which is almost here." Titus looked at the lamp for a moment, and the flame illuminated the near exhaustion in his eyes. "I must apologize for the rather rough treatment you've found here at home. What happened? Do you prefer the Cyclopis to the comforts of the government house?"

"I thought you put me there."

"Old friend, listen to me carefully. This job has already changed me. Now I understand how very valuable a friend is because I've discovered that an Emperor has so few he can trust."

"I've let you down," Silva said. He soothed his bad eye with his fingertips and added, "But Domitillia is no ordinary woman."

"I'm very aware of that . . . and I envy you. Because my Berenice is the daughter of a Jewish king, she had no choice but exile. I've lost her . . . perhaps forever. So I understand your problem."

Titus placed his fists on his hips and stared at the lamp. He rocked slightly back and forth on his feet. His eyes were so nearly closed he seemed to have fallen asleep standing. "Do you think you could wait for a year?"

"What do you mean by that, Sire?"

"Because within that time I would not be surprised if Marcus Clemens proved himself a traitor."

Silva remembered what Domitillia had told him in Judea and his pulse quickened.

Titus continued, as if he were alone in the room. He knew only that he needed real sleep, the kind he had just witnessed in Flavius Silva, for ever since Papa had died he had been besieged with proposals, schemes, and problems beyond measure, most of them previously unknown to him. There seemed to have been no time to do anything right . . . "What I'm trying to say, old friend, is that Clemens is up to something and I don't know what. He has so much money, I have to take him seriously, and he sees too much of my brother to make me comfortable. Unfortunately, he is married to my sister, and he has already bought dozens of senators. So I can't just haul him off somewhere for interrogation. Confidentially, the Flavian hold on the throne is extremely tenuous just now, and I dare not repeat the bloody pattern of previous new emperors. I am like a blind man walking a tightrope and must feel my way. If trouble in the Flavian family is even suspected, every aspirant from Britain to Mesopotamia will be on us like hyenas. I need a year to settle things down. I need time to let Marcus Clemens give me enough evidence to accuse him before the Senate. Then, if you wish, I could approve a divorce for Domitillia. Since her marriage is one in name only, it will not be so bad for you . . . or for her. She has agreed to wait and I ask the same of you."

Silva spoke without hesitation. "Certainly, Sire. My life is yours."

They stared at each other for a moment in silence. Then, suddenly, the stiffness between them crumbled and they embraced passionately.

"Only a stupid king would start out hurting his friends," Titus muttered, and he thought that he must be very near to tears. "But I can make repairs. Now, there's one more thorn in our friendship. While I sympathize with your desire to honor Papa, I believe your presence in the parade would be inappropriate and awkward. Papa was an old-fashioned traditionalist and he would never allow himself to approve of your recent conduct. You can watch the parade from here . . . the best view to be had in Rome. Immediately after the parade has passed, you will return to your command *pro tem*. Your aides, Attius and Liberalis, will be waiting for you at the Basilica Julia and will be supplied with all necessary gear for the journey. I will not see you again this year, nor will Domitillia. Is that agreed?"

"Yes, Sire! But the Jewish boy I'm adopting . . . I was obliged to leave him in Praeneste."

"Do you want him to go with you?"

"It would be better for his education if he could stay here with Domitillia."

"I'll arrange it."

They embraced and hugged each other for an instant, then

Titus broke away and started for the entry. Silva called after him, "Can I write her a note?"

"Compose it now and hand it to one of my aides. I'll deliver it myself."

"Be careful!"

Titus turned long enough to smile and said, "The same for you. Remember, you'll soon be a real father."

THE TRIUMPH

TWENTY-FOUR

THE COMPLEX CEREMONIES commemorating both the triumphs and the death of the Emperor Caesar Vespasian Augustus, Pontifex Maximus, holder of the tribunical power for six years, emperor thirteen times, father of his country, consul seven times, and censor, began upon the Field of Mars at the second hour after dawn. The designator, or *dominus funeris*, had already been hours on the scene, organizing the sequence of the units, changing one for another according to various troubles with gear or personnel, arguing and cajoling, and soothing the feelings of those who thought whatever was should be otherwise.

The designator was following the dictates of the Emperor Titus because he knew that when the pageant was over he would more likely be remembered for things that went wrong than for those that proceeded without fault. Thus, the Solonic law that limited the number of flute players in a funeral to ten was ignored; some two hundred had been gathered and assigned to various divisions of the parade. At least half of them were hopeless amateurs of so little talent that the designator assigned them to positions close to the bagpipers where their tootling would hardly be heard. There was also the Law of the Twelve Tables, which forbade female mourners from tearing out their hair during the ceremonies, and the designator dispatched his assistants among the estimated five thousand women who apparently considered Vespasian a personal loss with the message that such ancient and barbaric demonstra-

376

tions of grief would not be tolerated by parade marshals. The female mourners could cry out in an attempt to bring back the soul of Vespasian and might so express their sorrow as often as the urge struck them. Titus conformed to the common Roman belief that the souls of the unburied wandered for a hundred years along the banks of the River Styx before they were allowed to cross, and while there was no danger of such delay for his father, the repetition of his name in any reverent form might speed the resolution of the gods in his behalf.

Now, as the sun brought renewed vigor to the people of Rome and its light danced across the helmets of the Praetorians assembled about the great burial couch with its gold and purple coverlet, one hundred trumpeters heralded the excitement soon to follow. The elephants waiting in their assigned positions on the Field of Mars had not been usefully employed for some time and were already proving fractious. They responded to the blaring of the trumpets with a great and primeval bellowing of their own. As their excitement mounted, the drivers beat fiercely upon their heads to prevent a stampede, but two bull elephants broke away and, charging through the throngs of spectators, killed three of them; twenty others were injured before the elephants were subdued.

The designator was only momentarily distracted, because more than a hundred thousand people had gathered before the parade had even begun and his responsibility did not include the wet-nursing of spectators. Half a million were expected to view at least part of the ceremonies and, as always was the case with Roman crowds, total control was impossible.

While the sharp notes of the trumpets echoed across the field and the buildings of the adjacent city, those senators first assigned to march beside the wagon bearing the burial couch drifted into place with an air of independence, as if demonstrating that theirs was a separate company and they were not obligated to observe special reverence for the royal family.

All was noise and shouting and apparent confusion. The two hundred pipers at the head of the column could not restrain themselves from exploratory and independent rehearsals of their shrill music. Waiting next in line were the trumpeters, followed by the mourning women, and then the better flute players. Next were the actors and buffoons, who were actively rehearsing their roles. Their faces were entirely concealed behind a variety of masks, or else they had applied cosmetics with such skill that they resembled well-known figures of Roman legend. The designator hoped Titus would not take too close a look at them, since many were already drunk.

Resounding cheers echoed and reechoed across the field and down the course of the Tiber when a column of Praetorians was observed approaching from the Palatine and the Emperor Titus was seen in their midst. In contrast to the helmeted Praetorians in their glittering armor, he was clothed in a black robe and wore no ornament of any kind. Behind him, also mounted on a spirited white horse and identically attired, was Domitian, and behind the two brothers rode Domitillia in a wagon with her husband at her side. She was wearing a white robe in accordance with the custom for the Emperor's daughter.

The cheering and applause rose and spread even to the outermost regions of the city where the proceedings could not possibly be seen. Yet the sound was infectious; every Roman knew that Titus would be the best of emperors as his father had been before him. Vespasian's name resounded and rebounded through the streets covering the distance between the Field of Mars and the Forum with the speed and force of huge ocean swells.

Once Titus and his imperial relatives had taken their proper positions, the designator waved his wand at the orchestra, which immediately preceded the burial couch and wagon. Instantly, the wild and exotic music of Rome called upon all to heed its sensuous overtones. For the Romans had borrowed from the Greeks, from Asia Minor, Syria, and Egypt, and had combined the eastern minor tones and rhythms with their own. Fresh with the new day and special inspiration, a hundred drummers, tuba players, pipers, and cymbalists rendered a ferocious rhapsody of savage power. All of the participants in the parade, as well as the multitudes who stood waiting to view it, and even the imperial party, were impassioned by the music and reminded that they were witnesses to a great historical event.

When the cohort of mounted Praetorians appeared on schedule and began clearing the Via Lata so the procession could enter the city itself, the designator was reasonably satisfied that all the elements of the procession were in order.

He moved rapidly on his horse, back and forth across the field, assuring himself that the wagons with the spoils of war—a jumble of silver scabbards, gold sword belts, gold-embroidered saddlecloths, tin plates, spears, standards, shields, and helmets—plus Vespasian's many awards, were properly guarded, and that the single cohort of Syrian auxiliaries who happened to be available for the occasion kept their spears head-to-ground. He saw to it that the lictors preceding Titus carried their fasces inverted, and that the Jews acting in the role of captives seemed properly chained and sufficiently subdued to discourage trouble.

The designator was so devoted to his work that he nearly passed the Emperor without pausing, but after responding to his salute Titus waved him on with a smile; the designator was relieved that he had not offended. How much better, he thought, was this display than the breast-beating hysteria and cheek-tearing indulged in by more traditional Romans despite the prohibitions of the Law of the Twelve Tables. Yes, Titus was a great man with his eye on the future instead of the past, and his specifications for this event clearly indicated his desire to accept new ideas. No wonder the public adored Titus! Who else would include such eye-catchers as a hippopotamus and separate cages of lions, tigers, and eagles in his father's funeral—all to remind Romans that the most elaborate and bloody spectacles would follow the final ceremonies.

Although Silva could not see the formations in the Field of Mars from his window, he could look directly down upon the Forum, and he knew he would be able to view the parade as it emerged from behind the Capitoline Hill and entered the Via Sacra.

Silva saw that Cicero was becoming increasingly nervous as the pulsating rumble of distant drums began. He went to the window and saw in the distance how people had crowded into every available space to watch the parade. Screaming children darted everywhere through the streets and there were three, four, and even five people in every window. The balconies were perilously overloaded and the sides of the streets were packed solid with people. Every possible point of vantage had been taken in the Forum, with many people having found their way to the rooftops. The equestrian statue of Julius Caesar in the center of the Forum was almost totally obscured by the bodies of clinging children whose numbers seemed to multiply even as Silva watched them. Bonfires were being built everywhere space could be found, and many spectators were breaking their morning fast over the heat. The smoke from the fires rose straight up in the still air and formed a forest of dark columns all along the route.

Silva wondered if he could bear watching Domitillia riding beside her husband. They were a long time to come as yet, he thought. After the Syrian cavalry came the gladiators—about two hundred, Silva estimated. They cleared away the few stragglers who refused to leave the streets and those more bold who thought to defend their advantageous perches. The gladiators, fresh from their school, were merciless when resisted and soon had the way cleared.

Just behind the advancing gladiators were the torchbearers and trumpeters, both still so full of vigor they set a lively pace to the march of the column. Silva was willing to wager that those in the rear would be obliged to move at a trot if they intended to keep in the main body of the parade.

Next came the engines of war hauled by mules, six large catapults, ten bolt throwers, and a gigantic ram with its goat head newly painted. They were followed by a navy float, the reproduction of a ship manned by a hundred sailors.

A large contingent of drummers followed the float, and after them came a mixture of pipers and priests numbering about three hundred. Next came satyrs and maenads making sport of the spectators as well as of the parade displays; and then, as if intended to remind the public that this was not a show but a solemn occasion, came many of the Roman gods. Their faces were concealed behind masks of Hercules, Minerva, Bacchus, Jupiter, Ceres, Juno, Mercury, and those two gods so revered by military men, Mars and Venus.

The sweet odors from the incense burners floated up the Palatine Hill along with the clatter of wagon wheels against the paving stones. When the drummers paused momentarily in their pounding, the tinkling of countless finger bells could be heard.

Now, the first members of the royal family appeared, preceded by a dozen lictors. Silva thought the expression on Domitian's face was more sour than sad, perhaps because he was having trouble with his horse. The steed was a prancer and Domitian was a mediocre horseman who fought the reins and used their support rather than the weight of his body to keep his seat. From time to time he would reach into his saddlebag and toss a handful of coins to the spectators, who instantly went into a wild scramble for possession. Silva concluded there was not the slightest hint of style in the way Domitian made his distribution. He threw the coins at the people as if to hurt them, and not a hint of a smile creased his lips. Even so, there were shouts of approval when he passed and, Silva noted, a great deal of caterwauling for more coins.

Watching Domitian caused Silva to think of Scribonia and the look of terror in his eyes when he had been shoved across the moat by the Praetorians. He kept insisting they had no right to confine him anywhere, much less beyond the moat, and he swore he would see them in the highest court, where their perfidy would be punished by a thousand lashes of the bastinado. He must have known from the moment he crossed the moat what his future would be. Looking back as he mounted the steps toward freedom, Silva had seen that Scribonia was weeping.

Ten Vestal Virgins followed close behind Domitian; Silva wondered why the usual twelve were not appearing. Then came a herd of oxen to be sacrificed with an attending herd of priests who went to great trouble, Silva thought, to avoid stepping into their droppings.

There was even more confusion of sounds when the parade passed through the uncompleted Arch of Titus and turned southward at the unfinished Coliseum. The column turned again at the Circus Maximus to head back along the bank of the Tiber toward the Field of Mars. Lacking wind to transport sound, the drumming, fifing, shouting, and trumpeting were now all in counterpoint, and Silva found that in spite of his lack of participation the combined sounds caused his flesh to tingle. A chill swept through him as he thought that never again would he ever see such pomp and splendor. He remained spellbound as a contingent of singers came down from the Capitoline chanting songs written especially for the occasion. They sang praises of Vespasian, of his good works, of his courage, and of his resolve. As they marched and sang they strewed flowers along the paving stones.

There followed a long train of freedmen carrying vials of perfume and spreading it upon those spectators within reach.

Next, as if in deliberate contrast, came a large party of flutists and kettle-drummers who alternated their raucous percussions with the quavering mystical notes of a band of pipers. They were followed by a company of acrobats and dancers who endeavored to suggest in pantomime the tragic loss of Vespasian and the gain of the Empire in Titus.

A host of Egyptians came by, yelling at the brilliant morning in words Silva could not understand, but presumed were in praise of Vespasian. Their constant chants were accompanied by the persistent chinging of a hundred tambourines and the outrageous shouts of dervishes apparently gone berserk in their grief. Silva's heart began to pound almost as if obedient to the foreign beat of the drums when he next saw a large company of dignitaries, proud and austere of carriage. He knew they were the ambassadors of Spain and Lusitania, Numidia, Cyrenaica, Syria, Mesopotamia, Armenia, Dacia and Bithynia, Dalmatia, Illyricum, Gaul, Cyprus, Asia, and Egypt, together with their most favored relatives and attendants. Each wore the most formal robes and accoutrements native to their lands, and Silva sensed that for the first time in his life he was looking at the whole Empire displayed before him. Only Britain and Germany were missing, because they were not yet considered totally subject to Rome. Their absence reminded him that unsung legionaries, whose continued vigils on the frontiers made such a grand celebration possible, were also not represented. It was the law that no armed units except Praetorians were allowed to enter the city.

Then he saw her in the distance, riding in a lavishly decorated wagon with her husband, and he forgot all else.

While inhaling the mixture of smoke from the torches, incense, and perfume, he stared in agony at Domitillia's slow approach. She stood as if she were alone in the chariot, her lovely face more serene than he had ever seen it.

She did not wave to the crowd; indeed, he thought, she seemed oblivious of their presence despite their calling and cheering of her name.

Silva caught his breath and assured himself that he was looking at the most beautiful woman he had ever seen. He had to force back the urge to call out to her. Once she looked up, and for a moment he thought that she had discovered him in the window; but her gaze continued past the Palatine until she was staring at the open sky. Silva watched her as the wagon disappeared beyond the Arch of Titus. He was delighted to see that she had not spoken as much as a word to Marcus Clemens. "I will wait," he called after her as if she could hear him. "I'll wait forever. There is no true life for me without you near. Listen to me, little princess! Hear me try to tell you that for Flavius Silva you are his very breath!"

After Domitillia's wagon had gone, Silva experienced a shocking letdown; all the verve he had accumulated since his talk with Titus had left him. Silva reached for Cicero, who squatted on the window ledge, and smoothed his feathers as if the gesture might ease his own distress. "Teach me patience, you undergrown chicken."

A large group of standard-bearers came soon after, and then all of the senators who could walk preceded the great wagon bearing Vespasian's final couch. From his high vantage Silva could see the corpse clothed in a purple gown embroidered with gold. Vespasian wore a crown of laurel and a branch of it was clutched in his right hand. His left hand held an ivory scepter topped with a golden eagle. From his neck hung a golden bell that Silva knew was customarily filled with a magic preservative against evil. Silva saw that his face had been painted a vermilion in keeping with a statue of Jupiter on festival days.

The wagon bearing the couch was very grand, gilded everywhere and adorned with ivory. It was drawn by four huge horses and surrounded by marching senators, legati, and especially honored tribunes. A handful of notable citizens wearing immaculate white followed immediately behind the wagon. They formed a square about the single slave who carried a golden crown and who never during the rest of his life would be so honored. Moments before the fires of cremation were lit it would be his duty to place the crown on Vespasian's head and whisper into his ear, "Remember, thou art a man. . . ."

Fourteen wagons filled with spoils came next with two maniples of Praetorians marching beside them. Then appeared the Jews in light chains, also guarded by Praetorians. Some of the Jews pretended humility as they had been ordered to do if they expected immediate release after the ceremonies, but others of a more recalcitrant nature taunted the crowd and even their guards with repeated accusations of hypocrisy. To Silva's surprise no one seemed particularly interested in their actions, and he was reminded that yesterday's war was readily forgotten. It had been Joseph ben Matthias who had told him that nearly all of the Jews brought back as captives after the fall of Jerusalem had, during the intervening years, either been killed, died, or assimilated. Titus, therefore, had been obliged to commandeer a great number of native-born Jews to reenact the roles of their unfortunate predecessors.

Silva was relieved when another group of lictors appeared, their fasces wreathed in laurel and held inverted. Behind them, seated easily upon a white horse, rode the Emperor Titus. He was smiling and waving at the crowds, a magnificent figure despite his black robe. Occasionally, he would reach into his saddlebag and toss coins toward the adoring faces of the people, but his largesse was obviously not necessary to ensure his popularity. The crowds cheered wildly at the very sight of him and continued cheering regardless of whether he threw coins or not. Silva found himself wishing that Titus would rule throughout the rest of his own lifetime, for it appeared that Rome might even surpass itself under such a popular administration. Why, he wondered momentarily, should Titus be so concerned about his ability to retain the throne? Then he remembered that emperors were not maintained by an adoring public, but by the army and the Senate.

The roar of the people's approval nearly obliterated even the beating of the drums, and as it drifted up the Palatine, Silva was compelled to join in the mass approbations. Alone in this room, high above the city, with only Cicero to hear him, he was astounded to discover himself standing at the window, shouting at the top of his lungs. "Hail Titus! . . . Hail Titus . . . Hail Caesar Titus Vespasianus!"

Silva's overwhelming sense of excitement became distracted by a movement on the grass-covered parapet directly below the window. He watched in dismay as a Roman archer emerged silently from the floor below and casually inserted an arrow in his longbow. He raised the bow, settled his feet, and bent his knees slightly. He took his time and waited until his entire concentration was on the tip of his arrow.

Silva's momentary impression was that he must be dreaming, or was he watching some kind of pantomime intended to demonstrate the marvelous skill of the Syrian archers who were deployed in nearly every campaign?

He very suddenly realized that the archer was aiming at the parade and was leading his quarry . . . waiting for the exact moment when his arrow would fly true to his target. His position was ideal. A downward shot would keep the arrow's trajectory in almost a straight line. Even a clumsy Syrian archer would be sure to hit his target.

Yet this man seemed to be dissatisfied. Something was in his line of sight that Silva could not appreciate. The archer moved one pace to his left, which placed him almost directly below Silva's window. He drew his arm back again and bent his bow. He waited—poised to let fly.

In that instant Silva realized that his target must be Titus.

Silva's reaction was immediate. Almost without thinking, he stepped up on the windowsill and leaped outward. He arched through the air and came down on the archer with his arms extended. The man crumpled beneath him.

Moments later Silva regained consciousness. He rose to his knees with difficulty and looked down on the parade. It was proceeding as before, and Titus rode on unaware amid his flowing red banners.

Silva glanced at the prostrate archer. His head was askew, turned nearly full around toward his back. Obviously, his neck was broken, and he was not breathing. The arrow he had intended to shoot was still in the bow.

As Silva staggered to his feet, a pair of Praetorians ran toward him, their swords drawn. They halted in confusion when they saw the archer was dead, and they glanced incredulously at the open window far above.

"It seems I spoiled his aim," Silva said quietly. "Look around to make sure he was alone."

He turned and limped painfully away. This sort of gymnastics, he thought, was not meant for a man with a bad leg. Assassination attempts had been routine problems for nearly all Roman Emperors. But this one had the curious merit of careful planning. Silva wondered how much Marcus Clemens or Julius Scribonia might have had to do with the archer's deadly purpose.

THE TRIUMPH
* * *

The procession had made the circuit of the city and returned to the Field of Mars just after the sun had passed the zenith. The designator was pleased to note that everything was almost on schedule. Here a great funeral pyre had been erected and steps constructed to reach the top. As the various elements of the parade returned to the field and dispersed, the wagon bearing Vespasian's couch was brought alongside the pyre. Nearby, ditches had been dug and the fires had already been lit for the roasting of five hundred oxen to be sacrificed. The priests, the butchers, and the cooks were sweating over their work before the end of the column arrived.

Ten husky slaves moved Vespasian's couch from the wagon to a position atop the pyre. The priests made their final preparations, anointing the feet of the corpse with sheep oil to ease his walk through the Elysian Fields, and laying out the traditional supply of beans, lettuce, bread, and eggs against the possibility of his hunger. Finally, they covered Vespasian's face with a veil, because Titus was now the Pontifex Maximus and as such must not be allowed to see the face of the corpse when the spirit departed. All but two of the priests descended from the bier scattering incense, myrrh, and cassia to please the spirit in the afterlife.

The funeral pyre was built of wood soaked in pitch in order to burn easily and it was styled in the form of an altar with four equal sides. As the parade broke up, those military officers who had served with Vespasian were asked to surround the pyre. They were issued old swords and were instructed to circle the pyre three times from right to left, striking their weapons against one another's as they marched. Then, at the proper moment, Titus would throw his father's helmet and sword into the fire, and they would perform the same act with their own swords. To have been chosen for this part of the funeral ceremony was the highest of honors, and those now gathered were solemn and most assiduous in carrying out their individual actions.

The lack of wind created a pall of smoke over the Field of Mars, and the odor of the roasting oxen was heavy in the air. It seemed that the entire population of the city surrounded the field, but the noise from their chattering was remarkably subdued in comparison with their number. Some had come solely for the free food and edged as closely as they could to the cooking pits, while others had come to pay their last respects to a man they had admired.

Domitillia left her husband the instant their wagon stopped and departed without a word to him. She thought that at least she was being consistent, since they had not exchanged even the slightest civility during the parade. She went directly to Titus, who took her hand and greeted her warmly.

"I think it went well so far," he said. "Here is something that may convince you of my devotion."

He held out the note from Silva.

She took it without interest, unrolled it enough to glance at the signature, and gasped. She turned away. Her hands trembled as she read:

> My Love,
> I must depart without embracing you. But soon, although it will seem like an eternity, I can hold you forever. Trust Titus. He has given his hand that we will be together in a year . . . or less. For you, I would wait until the end of time.
>
> Your . . .

She turned back to Titus and was reaching for his hand when Domitian arrived and pushed her aside. He was perspiring heavily and already smelled of wine. "What have you done with my friend Scribonia?" he demanded of Titus.

The new Emperor smiled easily, then shrugged his shoulders. "I must say you choose strange company. I'm not sure what's happened to him."

"You lie, Brother! You've stolen him for your own use. You're jealous that I should attract such a man. You've stolen everything I have. . . . Why should you stop with Julius Scribonia? I demand to be told what you've done with him!"

Titus took a deep breath and made a visible effort to contain his temper. He spoke slowly. "I command you to lower your voice and attempt one of your rare smiles. We are being watched by a great many people. "

Titus' calm manner seemed to further enrage Domitian. "A pox on the people! Where is my man?"

Domitian's eyes widened unnaturally and he started to

lunge for Titus. His movement was blocked almost instantly by Domitillia, who slipped between them. She raked his neck with her sharp fingernails and he backed away.

"You bitch!" he cried out and wiped at the spittle gathered at the corners of his mouth.

"Shut your mouth!" Domitillia said. "You're drunk! Remember where you are! We're here to honor Papa, not disgrace him!"

Even as she spoke the trumpeters blew a forlorn series of notes—the signal for the three Flavians to mount the steps to the bier. "Come!" Domitillia said fiercely. "Settle your troubles elsewhere."

Titus and a grumbling Domitian followed her, keeping their distance as they climbed slowly up the long series of steps. Once they had gained the summit, the drummers took over and continued their muffled roll until all three stood beside the bier.

There followed a long silence, then Domitillia reached for the small vial of tears, the lachrymatory, which custom said she must place beside her father. Suddenly, she found that the vial was superfluous because her eyes were wet. Now, for the first time, she realized that a man she had loved so very much was no more. She wiped her cheek and gathered a fresh tear to drop on her father, then closed her eyes and murmured to herself, "One year, Papa . . . maybe less than a year, and I will be with my other love. Both you and I shall have ours forever."

While Titus averted his eyes, Domitian removed the veil over his father's face and pulled back his eyelids that he might see in the next world.

Then the slave bent down and whispered his message in Vespasian's ear: "Remember . . . thou art a man."

The two priests who flanked him began chanting, *"Ave . . . ave . . . ave . . . ,"* calling upon the spirits to recognize the importance of the moment.

Titus began his *laudatio,* an oration that he kept to a minimum because he said his father had been a man of few words and would not approve of a lengthy speech. He spoke only of his reverence for the aims of the great Augustus and of his service under the Emperor Nero. He spoke of Greece and Judea and Britain and Egypt, the countries in which his father had served with distinction. He said that the restoration of liberty, the *Libertas Restituta* as it appeared on the coins Vespasian had issued, had been his father's ambition since he took the throne. Likewise, his adoption of the office of censor had enabled him to guide the senators of Rome toward a completely enlightened government.

During all of Titus' short eulogy there remained a heavy silence over the Field of Mars, and his clear voice could be heard distinctly in the farthest ranks of the crowd. As the three Flavians turned away from the bier and started their descent of the pyre, the drummers began a slow beat and all the priests in the field began chanting a forlorn lament. Torchbearers touched their flames to the wood as the imperial family reached the ground, and the fires began crackling almost at once.

More priests led the three Flavians to the votive jar in which Vespasian's ashes would be stored. It was explained to them that afterward they would sprinkle the urn three times with pure water shaken from a branch of laurel, and then they would pronounce the solemn word, *Ilicet* . . . "you may depart."

Thus did Flavius Vespasianus, founder of the Flavian dynasty, pass on to the islands of the blessed.

TWENTY-FIVE

WHILE THE *VISCERATIO*, the distribution of meat, was gratefully accepted by many of Rome's people, it caused agonized reactions in the great Cyclopis prison. The odors from the Field of Mars drifted very slowly to the east and were recognized by the more than two hundred prisoners who would soon be sacrificed to the beasts. Hungry and distraught with their coming fate, they wailed a heavy and enduring chorus of woe.

Waiting impatiently in his cavern, Julius Scribonia thought it curious that the people beyond the great wall who would die by this afternoon, or certainly by tomorrow, were so interested in eating today. Were they compelled to provide more nourishment for the beasts? His own appetite had left him, although he had not the slightest doubt that his release would be only a matter of hours. Domitian, of course, would be at the funeral along with Marcus Clemens; both were therefore unable to do anything at the moment, but surely they would soon find time to effect his release. He knew so much about their plans that they dared not let him out of their keeping for long.

Such was Scribonia's mood of equanimity that he was astonished when a hirsute squad of German jailers came bounding across the moat like so many bears and seized upon him without exchanging a sound. "Take your smelly hands off me!" Scribonia shouted, but they ignored him. "You stinking animals, put me down or I'll have you all burned to cinders!"

THE TRIUMPH

His entreaties and curses were ignored as they carried him across the moat and along the passageway between the cavern and the great wall of the prison. When they came to the heavy doors, they opened them and threw the kicking Scribonia, feet first, into a crowd of prisoners who had gathered to see what all the fuss was about. They pushed and pulled at Scribonia, marveling at the fine material of his tunic and exclaiming at the beauty of his rings. When he tried to rise from the dust, they shoved him back down and demanded to know what a man of his obvious wealth and station had done to deserve *ad bestia*. When he protested that he must be left alone, they laughed, struck at him, and pulled his hair until he became a bloody rag doll whimpering in their midst.

At last they left him groveling in the dirt, taunting him with laughter and ridicule. Why would he be so anxious to preserve himself when he would be dead tomorrow? Everyone in this compound of the Cyclopis was destined to die for the amusement of Romans, and they could see no reason why Scribonia should consider himself an exception. Finally, like children bored with a broken toy, they left him and fell to other diversions.

Scribonia lay in the dirt for some time, barely conscious and croaking to the earth itself of his need for water. Everything except his tunic had been taken from him; his rings and bracelets and bejeweled belt chain had become the sources of vicious argument among the condemned of Rome. He closed his eyes and thought of the beach in Judea where he had managed to escape with his life. Perhaps if he had even a few drops of water . . . ?

He slipped into near delirium as twilight came to the compound. And for a moment he could not believe what his remaining senses told him was true, for a rather delicate hand appeared in the soft light and held a cup of water to his lips. When he had sucked at the cup and raised his eyes, he recognized the Spanish boy. Even in his great distress, he contrived a smile and whispered his gratitude.

Then he said, "You, too, my pretty thing?"

The Spanish boy nodded and much of Julius Scribonia's misery left him.

THE TRIUMPH

* * *

Never had there been such a tremendous effort to entertain the people of Rome. Every amphitheater in the city and many open fields were temporarily transformed into arenas. The Circus Maximus, the Circus Flaminius, the Circus Varianus, and even the uncompleted Coliseum were pressed into service for the games following the triumphal funeral. Four hundred gladiators were scheduled to fight in these arenas, and the cries of *"mitte!"* to spare the life of a downed gladiator who had been especially brave, or of *"jugula!"* as the sword was held to the waiting throat, came from every direction. In some arenas the gladiators were obliged to fight in the nude, the quicker for an impatient crowd to view their victory or defeat. In other places the wearing of armor was permitted, and the *mirmillos* who were heavily armed were matched against the *retiarius* whose only weapons were a net and trident.

Admission to all of the games including the various races in the circuses was free, and the population was often at their wits' end arranging their schedules to assure themselves they would not waste time on lesser events and miss those more exciting. Soon, with the excess of blood pumping from wounds everywhere and the constant cheering or reviling of the fighters, a strange all-powerful hysteria took hold of the people; by nightfall they were insatiable. Even oddments of entertainment failed to stimulate the crowds; they yawned as dwarfs fought each other and were nearly as bored when muscular Germanic females assaulted each other with a ferocity and deadliness unseen in male gladiators.

After the solemnities of the funeral, the games commenced and continued until they were closed for lack of light. Many spectators were dizzy with wine and inclined to imitate the carnage they had just observed, so that pugnacity was everywhere and many left their blood in the streets. Only children were entirely safe as most people scurried for the relative protection of their homes.

Titus made a token appearance at the races in the Circus Maximus, but left almost immediately to attend the affairs of the Empire. He was so fatigued from events of the previous day and night that he retired early and left orders not to be awakened except for a major emergency.

Domitian's resentment of his brother became increasingly

violent throughout the balance of the day. He insisted that more and more wine be brought to him until by nightfall he was incapable of controlling himself. Once Titus had departed, he insulted as many senators as he could find, urinated where and when he pleased, and shouted to whomever would listen that his brother was a liar and a thief. Most Romans tried to ignore him. Finally, a squad of Praetorians dragged him to his home and left him there in a stupor.

Once Marcus Clemens had returned to the familiarity of his own house he sank into a similarly dark mood. He drank enough wine to render himself oblivious of the modest pain of an enema. Later, he took a long bath in which he would have drowned save for the alertness of a slave who hauled him sputtering from the pool. After he had regained his wind, he dined on a meal of thirty small Lusitanian doves, which set so poorly with him that he was obliged to spend a long time in his *vomitorium*. There, between upheavals, he decided that he would withdraw his financial support from Domitian. It was bad business. The man seemed to have suddenly fallen apart since the death of his father and the disappearance of Julius Scribonia. Instead of using his intelligence during these crucial days, he had become lost in oaths of vengeance and joys of invective. Domitian seemed a more likely candidate for the house of the demented rather than as leader of the Empire.

At last he made his way through the great house to Domitillia's chambers. He found the entrance barred and locked, and he decided that he was too tired to care.

The people confined in the Cyclopis prison were scheduled to appear on the following noon in the Amphitheatrum Castrense which, though small, was selected because it had the facilities to confine both humans and beasts until their turn came. Since the *ad bestia* events were relatively rare and so different from the gladiatorial contests, people fought for the relatively few seats of advantage, and every inch of space throughout the arena was packed with spectators. A huge crowd of latecomers was obliged to wait outside the entrances until some spectators, either having seen enough or desirous of viewing other shows, had departed.

Attending the events in the Castrense was Domitian's first choice. He liked the Castrense because it was so small it made easier demands on his distance vision; after so much recent carousing, he was having trouble focusing on anything not nearby. He arrived soon after noon and took his place in the royal enclosure. He was comfortable and appeared to be jolly, for he liked the sense of power his status as judge provided. With a flick of his head or a turn of his thumb, he could give the crowd the life of a prisoner or deny it. Unlike the gladiatorial contests, Domitian did not expect any decisions need be made today. An *ad bestia* program almost always ended with the same results.

The beasts had been confined long before Vespasian's death, and since the official announcement of the program, they had been denied food of any kind. There were altogether twenty tigers in splendid condition except for their flattened bellies, and fourteen lions. Three wild boars with huge tusks were considered by some as the most dangerous antagonists of all because of the swiftness of their charging. A score of leopards whined and paced their cages restlessly in search of food. Poisonous snakes caged in a huge basket were reserved for the middle of the show, since they were to be used for the first time in Rome. No one knew what the snakes would do once a human was tied hand and foot and thrown in their midst; actually, the snakes appeared more inclined to sleep than to attack. That possibility made the game master nervous.

Julius Scribonia, along with some one hundred others in Cyclopis, were marched to the Castrense soon after dawn. If they dragged their feet even momentarily, they were whipped unmercifully by the guards. Even so, several fell by the wayside. The majority of the condemned were criminals who had been found guilty of every variety of crime from murder to petty theft, or rape of a proven good citizen, or incitement against the government. Nearly all were male, but a flock of hags who had been involved in a smuggling scheme made up the tail of the procession. When they fell too far behind they were whipped until they closed the gap, and their cries of anguish often exceeded the wrathful yelling of their escort.

Some captives had been recently confined, while others, apprehended months before, were hardly more than gaunt-eyed skeletons. The director of the Castrense viewed them on arrival with open distaste. He complained that his beasts were in for a sorry feast.

Only one man stood out from the other prisoners; his incongruous appearance as well as his bearing captured every eye. He wore the remnants of what had obviously once been an extremely expensive tunic, and his sandals were also of ostentatious design. Except for his face, which was swollen and discolored, he appeared in good health with flesh on his bones and challenging eyes. He kept his back straight and his chin defiantly in the air, almost as if he were taking a morning stroll. Beside him, walking hand in hand with him, was a dark youth who fixed his eyes straight ahead.

"If you run now, pretty thing, you might get away," Scribonia said.

"No. You're not afraid. Neither am I."

"Very foolish of you. They should not do this to you just for thieving."

As they entered the Castrense, the director saw the Spanish boy and tore him away from Scribonia. "He doesn't belong with you!"

"Quite right," Scribonia said haughtily. "Take him home with you. You must admit he's too pretty to die."

"Is he diseased?"

"Of course. With any luck it will spread to you."

The director smashed his fist into Scribonia's jaw and nearly knocked him down, but Scribonia caught himself and turned quickly to spit in his face. He was immediately shoved on by a guard. The director had his hands full trying to hold onto the Spanish boy.

Domitian stood up and waved his hand to start the events, but there was no response to his signal. The arena remained empty and the roar of the crowd's approval soon turned to eruptions of anger and complaint. Domitian himself was displeased and demanded to know the cause of the delay. While he waited for a reply, he experimented using just one eye and then alternately the other, trying to discover which would provide him with the best view of the arena. He found any combination less than satisfying. His visual inadequacy contributed to his growing irritation, and he vowed he would have the director thrown in with the beasts unless something happened soon. At last he was told that the director had been temporarily disabled. One of the prisoners, a Spanish boy, had bitten him, leaving him with such a severe wound that he had trouble assembling his program. The youth had escaped during the resulting confusion.

Domitian blushed and insisted that the first event start, regardless of the director's health. Soon afterward the crowd let out a frenzied roar and then fell almost silent as a middle-aged man entered the arena. He was filthy, his hair matted, and his eyes were glazed with fear. He stared unseeing at the crowd. As he took a few halting steps forward, an enormous boar was released from a trapdoor on the opposite side of the arena.

Although the boar had huge tusks, he seemed to be lethargic. Like the man the boar took a few steps forward, halted, and glanced up at the crowd. He shook his head as if trying to get his bearings, then sniffed at the ground.

Soon the silence of the crowd was broken by raucous shouts of encouragement. "Look straight ahead, pig!" . . . "He's right in front of you!" . . . "The damn pig is blind!"

Domitian drummed his fingers on the arm of his chair. Despite his impatience he managed a chuckle. "That monster would do better on my table."

As time passed the boar seemed to lose all interest in the proceedings. The crowd threw epithets at him. One particularly strident voice kept repeating, "You're a rabbit! Come on! We don't have all day, rabbit!"

The crowd seemed to ignore the man who stood dumb, as if uninterested in his situation. Someone in the crowd threw an orange peel at him which brought on a cascade of peelings from all sides of the oval. Then the man moved and, as if suddenly alerted to danger, the boar lowered his head and stared across the arena. They had seen each other at last. The silence suddenly became so heavy that cheering from the nearby Circus Varianus could be heard.

The boar swept his head back and forth, surveying the ground before him. Finally he lowered his head and charged. The urgent yelling of the crowd obliterated the staccato beat of the boar's hooves against the crowd.

The man tried to dodge to one side. The boar swerved and caught him full on, his curved tusks sinking into the man's groin. The pandemonium of noise was so overwhelming that the man's screams went unheard. The boar shoved him back against the barricade and tossed him into the air. When the man lay kicking and still screaming in the dust, the boar charged again. Blood spurted from the man's side and the boar's tusks brought up a length of intestine.

There was obviously no need for a decision in this event, so Domitian sat back to watch the boar lunge repeatedly at the bloody bundle. Soon what had been a man was limp and silent. Domitian regretted that his eyesight did not permit him to see what was left of the man's face. He drummed his fingers while a spearman approached the boar from behind and dispatched it with a single thrust.

Event after event followed with barely tolerable delays. The lions were especially vicious and the crowd roared approval as the beasts chased the frantic prisoners from one end of the oval to the other. The sun was hot now and the smell of blood made the beasts ever more voracious. A few prisoners tried to fight back, but their bare hands were poor defense against the animal strength of their attackers. The lions presented a problem, because once their quarry was beneath their paws, they tended to settle down quietly until their appetites were satisfied. Archers were called in to kill them as soon as their attacks lost excitement.

Julius Scribonia forced himself to watch the events in the arena. He reasoned that if he could tolerate being witness to the bloody destruction of others, he might more easily accept his own. He had attended only two *ad bestia* events in his lifetime, but from a quite different position. Now he was disappointed by what he considered a total lack of human fortitude in the individuals surrounding him. When his companions were taken from the holding pen and shoved violently into the sunlit arena, some sank to their knees while others threw themselves down and clawed at the sand. Some ran in circles, crying out their terror and beseeching the people in the amphitheater to save them. When the mauling began, they screamed outrageously and continued until they had no breath remaining.

Scribonia was determined to show a quite different attitude. By all the gods, if this was to be his end, then the world would remember Julius Scribonia as an extraordinary man.

Perhaps, he thought, this might be one of Domitian's sadistic tricks; he would be held until the very last, and if his behavior had been satisfying, he would be confirmed as Domitian's first minister. Perhaps the great man considered this as just a different way to call attention to himself. He would show himself as the savior of the helpless. Yet it was Titus, not Domitian, who had condemned him here. Why had Domitian failed to intervene if, indeed, he knew what had happened? Was he in one of his furies because the Syrian archer had failed to find his target?

By standing on the tips of his toes, Scribonia could see Domitian's figure lounging in the shade of the royal box. Certainly he would make some signal to save his invaluable aide.

The dying would be easy, Scribonia tried to persuade himself; only this uncertainty was difficult.

Suddenly, two burly Gauls seized him. They propelled him expertly toward the arena as he did his utmost to arrive with at least a hint of dignity. This was impossible, however, for the Gauls kicked him so forcefully into the sunlight that he fell down, and his recovery was anything but graceful. As he regained his feet and deliberately flicked the sand from the remnants of his tunic, he was conscious mainly of the deafening noise, which was all-pervading and seemed to weigh of itself. The sound so confused him that he had trouble identifying it as originating in the thousands of faces he saw turned down at him. He saw the spectators gesturing at him, their fists pounding the sunlit air, their mouths open, their bodies swaying and arms waving—all in unified movement like the surface of a circular ocean. He was impressed with his own rejection of fear. Here, he tried to persuade himself, was his own triumph. Unlike Vespasian, who could not have known the extent of his funeral, this must be the supreme moment in the life of Julius Scribonia. Very well, he would not disappoint the crowd.

He took a breath and smiled up at the spectators. He blew kisses in every direction and was rewarded with several rounds of enthusiastic applause.

He looked up at Domitian, who was barely visible in the shadows of his awning. He extended his arms to him and called his name, but his voice was overwhelmed by the roar of the crowd. Surely, even if Domitian could not hear him, he must be aware of the crowd's approval, and he would call off this uncomfortable charade before it was too late.

Yet Domitian gave no sign of recognition. There was no

special movement in the shade of the awning, and Scribonia could find no way to ascertain Domitian's mood.

A gate on the opposite side of the arena swung wide and two spotted leopards vaulted onto the sand. They stood transfixed, snarling at the crowd for a moment. Then he saw that they were aware of him.

Once again, he looked up at Domitian. There was still no movement of any note in the royal box. I must do *something*, Scribonia thought—anything to invite rescue. And yes, I must prove the honor of Julius Scribonia.

The sound of the crowd reverberated through the arena like thunder. The noise was far more powerful than during any of the preceding events, he thought. Event? The end of so much talent was merely an event? This raucous, foul, and spitting scum were enjoying an orgasm through the death of a man far superior to themselves. This simply could not be!

He would prove it now, this instant. He thought that Domitian was only waiting for the last moment. So Julius Scribonia advanced step by step toward the leopards—slowly, lest he overexcite them.

Far above the sand, Domitian opened his eyes and squinted at the brilliant arena. During the midafternoon he had become satiated with the continuing series of spectacles and had dozed off. Now, still drowsy, he managed to focus his gaze on one end of the arena and saw two animals he took to be leopards. "Frightful beasts," he muttered. His comment was intended to assure those about him that he could see the arena as well as any of them, when, in fact, the combination of his nap and the brilliant sun had further obscured his vision.

He saw a man advancing toward the leopards, and again he squinted, trying to see him better. There was something vaguely familiar about him. His walk was that of a strutting peacock, and even at this critical moment his arrogant air seemed undiminished. He looked up at the crowd and bowed as if he were accepting some kind of a reward.

Domitian thought that the sun must have temporarily blinded him. He closed and reopened his eyes.

"That fellow reminds me of our friend Scribonia," Domitian muttered to an aide. He was vaguely amused at his discovery. Scribonia? Impossible!

Domitian leaned as far forward as he could, trying to verify his impression. To his astonishment he saw the man approach the leopards within a yard, stand calmly for a moment, and then advance and kick one of the beasts in the mouth.

A mighty roar of approval rose from the crowd. The man disappeared almost instantly beneath a furious explosion of tawny spotted skin.

At last the crowd became subdued and called angrily to Domitian that such a man deserved to live. Yet true to his dual self, Domitian wanted no displays of discontent on this day. As his favorite aide, Julius Scribonia, was so fond of saying, "Timing is everything." And the time for arousing the public in his own behalf, he decided, was not now.

Domitian found himself blushing alarmingly. He complained of a disorder in his bowels, stood up, and left the Castrense.

While en route to his house, Domitian regretted not having acted more promptly in behalf of the man who resembled Julius Scribonia. But then he forgave himself. Scribonia was like a jackal; he had never much liked him, anyway.

A man like that, overly ambitious for his master, was usually thinking of replacing him.

During the same afternoon, Domitillia was overjoyed to learn that Centurion Piso waited upon her in the cavern below her brickworks. Drusilla, the slave girl, brought word that the works were deserted. Rome had come to a halt. Almost the entire population, it seemed, had taken advantage of the various games.

She flicked a drop of perfume behind her ear out of habit rather than intention, and left her chambers immediately. She found Piso alone and praying silently in the cavern she now thought of as his own. "You're on your knees to your invisible god?"

"Yes. I pray for you and for General Silva . . . and for all the poor of Rome."

"Why?"

Piso laughed softly. "Perhaps because I'm going back to the Legion and I want to leave a good impression behind me."

"I shall miss you. Sometimes I almost understand you."

"Thank you, God." Still amused, Piso rolled his eyes upward. "The day of your miracles is not yet done."

"There you go, talking to a ghost again. . . . Now, please do the same for me. When you see your general, find a moment to speak confidentially. Tell him . . . there is no question whatever. Regardless of circumstances, we will meet soon and spend the rest of our lives together."

Piso hesitated, then said thoughtfully, "I understand."

By dusk General Flavius Silva was well on the road to Brundisium. His little party was riding fine horses from the Emperor's stables. They were well provisioned with tents and food for those reaches of the long journey ahead where little was available. Attius and Liberalis rode at Silva's side as they had done in Africa, but they sensed that their master was in a far different mood than he had been then. Now he always stared straight ahead, yet it was as if his eyes were dead and saw nothing. They were puzzled because they were accustomed to Silva's particular enthusiasms—his verbal appreciation of color on a mountain in the distance, the perspective down a long valley, the smoke of a cottage, or a star at twilight.

When the sun stood on the horizon, Silva broke his reverie, pulled up his mount, and announced that they would camp for the night. As the legionaries set up the tents and built a fire, he walked away from the others and stood on a small hill nearby. He stood until the daylight was gone, looking back toward Rome, and he remained as motionless as if he had been set in stone.

The twilight had faded almost entirely when Silva saw something moving along the road and heard the hollow clatter of hooves striking the rhythm of a gallop. Soon he saw the horse and rider. He watched his approach with interest because he seemed to be in such haste. Then, suddenly, Silva recognized the horse as the big bay he had bought at Praeneste. And the rider? He knew a terrible moment of uncertainty, and then there was no question in his mind.

He raised his right hand high and called out to the rider with unrestrained joy: "Reuben! Reuben! We are here!"

Then he ran toward the road as fast as his bad leg would permit.

AUTHOR'S NOTE

Many of the people involved in this story are based on real historical characters and many of their activities are factual. Yet despite the popular impression, Roman history is frequently capricious and rife with contradictions. For dramatic reasons I have taken a few minor liberties in the passages of time and in the relationship between one character and another.

Thanks to a number of renowned experts and my own efforts toward diligent research, I pray that most facts are correct. I apologize for any errors that might be worth disputing, but the happenings of more than 1,900 years ago are inevitably subject to the mind and suppositions of the modern beholder.

Among many others, I am most grateful to these individuals for their special assistance: The Comtessa Fedle Caproni and her husband, Pietro Armani, who assembled Roman experts many times in their house for the sole purpose of furthering my education; my thanks to Dr. Carl Nylander of the Swedish Institute in Rome and to the historians at the Roman Museum of Antiquities and the German Archeological Institute.

My research would have been far more difficult without the frequent aid of Letitia Bucci Casari of Rome, Professor Fasolo on Praeneste, and Festo Geiovanelli in the Museum of Roman Civilization at Eur. My thanks again to Professors Palloturio, Santini, and Sergio Roatta, archeologists, and Engineer Santo Mario for his knowledge of the catacombs beneath what was once Domitillia's land.

My further appreciation to Professor Marie Ricciardi of the Ostia Museum for her welcome to that ancient port.